AWAKE IN THE DARK

SISTER SEEKERS BOOK 9

BY
A.S. ETASKI

Published by Corpus Nexus Press
ISBN: 978-1-949552-19-5

etaski.com
etaski.com/sister-seekers
miurag.etaski.com
www.patreon.com/etaski
www.goodreads.com/etaski
www.bookbub.com/authors/a-s-etaski
www.facebook.com/asetaski
mastodon.online/@etaski

Cover Design by Eris Adderly
Book layout by DocKangey

Dedicated to RainbowNight & the reimagined "Sandman"

The comics showed me how to write this epic the first time. The show adaptation proved I can make the story whole writing it a second.

To all of us who seek purpose and healing in our dreams.

Dedicated to RainbowNight & the reimagined "Sandman"

The comics showed me how to write this epic the first time. The show adaptation proved I can make the story whole writing it a second.

To all of us who seek purpose and healing in our dreams.

CHAPTER 1

PRIESTESS LELINAHDARA - THE PALACE OF SIVARAUS

TARRA REACHED THE TWELFTH FLOOR OF THE PALACE USING THE SPIRAL STAIRS and her own two feet.

It's been a while.

Panting, the Confessor Lelinahdara regretted her lack of even a sip of water. She also cursed the stubborn grip of her recent paranoia against stepping into the common jump circles within the stairwell. After all, who *might* be marking her passage?

Except for one deceased Conceiver, how is it different from before?

Tarra had continually asked herself these questions ever since Wilsira died. The Sanctuary had become a mess of tattered habits. Priestesses and acolytes alike snatched at every morsel of influence like they would starve.

Her own habitual vigilance had been made worse when she discovered the private jump circles. Once used only by the Conceiver, they allowed the Headmaster and that goddess-damned Elder to move in or out of the Sanctuary without her awareness.

How dare they try to leave me out of this?

She, the Confessor, had been the one to reveal Wilsira's treason. *She* had been the one to show the Queen the hidden, undeniable demonic taint in the Consorts' blood, despite centuries of the Conceiver's reassurances. Gleaning magical strength from the Abyss without turning the Davrin into Sathoet was impossible to maintain forever.

And I proved it.

As a reward, the Confessor had been assigned to work *with* Elder D'Shea and Headmaster Phaelous to untangle Wilsira's tangled mess of bloodlines. They were to discover if anything could be salvaged while the Matron Houses screamed and wrung their hands.

Meanwhile, Tarra was certain Varessa and Phaelous were not sharing all insights on their mutual progress. Never a surprise and not much of a betrayal, but the Priestess dared not lose track of their furtive doings on that account.

They could cut me out of any new discovery. Claim the honors and power for themselves.

The Sisterhood could certainly use the lift after their recent losses, and Phaelous hardly had cause to protest if the Mother of his son rose in influence over Sivaraus.

Or what little a brooding, Houseless sorceress can gain after the Valshraess claimed her only child. Where is Shyntre, anyway? I haven't heard gossip of him around the Palace for a while.

The Priestess brushed her hands together before sliding the smooth door open, putting D'Shea's volatile bua from her mind in anticipation of dealing with several others, including her own.

The walls and floor of the twelfth level were dominated by painted shades of white and grey interwoven with dark, appropriate shadows. The tapestries and banners covering large segments of the stone were abstract but unsettling, reds and oranges slashing through them, suggesting violence if not depicting it.

If someone wasn't supposed to be here, they might have some difficulty looking away from one of these hanging works of art.

The entire floor was home to one kind of resident: the Sathoet, who were sealed in a chamber behind an iron door located at the end of the hypnotic passageway. The half-blood sons of the Priestesses were not always contained here, but most were summoned only to participate in a ritual or a punishment.

Every Priestess-Mother Tarra had ever known, excepting two, needed time away from their grotesque and rowdy offspring.

Otherwise we'd never get any planning done.

Wilsira had been infamous for always keeping her Sathoet nearby, a gleefully cruel extension of herself. The others said Kerse had been there from the moment of his birth through his first fifty turns, helping to launch her vicious, three-century rule of the Sanctuary.

Every Priestess had wondered at some point whether *this* was the secret of her bold inspirations and cunning intrigue; each of them had either considered or attempted to mimic her methods. Power-hungry slits who had gone all the way with their demonic sons never reached an envious end, always losing more than they wanted to give. If anything, Wilsira had used every one of them to her advantage, subjugating her competitors further through their sons.

Meanwhile, for two centuries, Tarra could never muster the desire to coddle her own bua like Wilsira, no matter her ambitions.

There must be another way.

A good thing, too. Even the Conceiver had ultimately fallen due to her half-blood son. Tarra relished how Kerse's death had brought Wilsira low, weak, and vulnerable. She hadn't missed her chance to cut the last threads of the Conceiver's influence with her own hand.

A pity I never had the chance to thank Sirana for doing her part.

The novice's fate seemed eerily similar to the other Priestess who had kept her Sathoet beside her since his birth.

Irrwaer and Vesram were here one cycle, gone the next. And General Rausery with them.

The acolyte had begun as a healer's apprentice; her attitude had been the opposite of the Conceiver: harmless and hardly rising in rank after birthing her Sathoet. Irrwaer had been content working in the infirmary on the fifth floor for centuries.

Her half-blood bua, Vesram, had been unusually cooperative and quiet for a demon's son. Tarra had often been aggravated to witness Irrwaer's Sathoet allowed into sacred spaces where other demonbloods were banished, for no reason other than he didn't make noise and was easy to ignore.

Just like his bland, ever-toiling Mother.

Tarra's nearest age-mate had refused to share her secret for gaining a tolerable son before she disappeared. Now, thanks to her closer contacts with the Queen, the Confessor wondered about the healer-Priestess, knowing where and how Sirana had vanished.

I'd assumed Irrwaer and her bua had been sent to the Drider Pit for unwisely offending someone, and the General's absence was a coincidence.

This time, the pressure on Varessa D'Shea while General Rausery was gone had become too obvious for her to hide. It sparked enough memories of other times it had happened for Tarra to finally recognize a pattern, including a third time the General had been gone with Shyntre.

How often did the Red Sister General leave the Deepearth? Why? One of those times, did Rausery take Irrwaer and Vesram away? Once, there'd been a time Varessa might have traded with her to know.

How the decades reweave the web.

The heavy, familiar musk at the end of the hall drew Tarra back to her present, her body standing before a foreboding, double-wide iron door inscribed with runes and magical carvings.

The Confessor placed her palm upon the inscription in the panel, murmuring her private entrance spell. The command was unique to each Priestess, though the results were the same: pushing all the demonbloods toward the rear of the chamber but alerting her son of her arrival.

The right-hand door slid open just wide enough for Tarra to squeeze sideways into the dark space. Once her heel passed the threshold, however, the door resealed itself.

High upon the walls, the blue, heatless lanterns remained steadfast yet failed to drive the creeping shadows far enough to confirm whether this place had corners. A pale, drifting mist always seemed present, yet its function was less a hint of the temperature or presence of water and more like the incense which kept some ritual participants cooperative.

Hisses and throaty chuckles rolled forward from the rear of the chamber before bodies moved forward once again. Some crawled upon the floor; some clung to the walls or crept along the ceiling.

Tarra heard the Sathoet sniffing for her, detecting or sampling her aura through unique senses. From necessity, she had learned how to turn her magical impression such that it seemed too sour or too strong to all but one demonblood in this room.

"Motherrr," Dyar crooned in welcome, his yellow eyes glowing in the dark.

Her son was the closest half-blood approaching her upon the floor: broad-shouldered and muscular, using all four limbs to walk and remain beneath her. His nose was pushed up like a bat despite the long muzzle full of sharp teeth, his white mane lightening in the shallow light to trace his spine the whole way down his back. He'd lost his loincloth somewhere; Tarra would have to find him another.

"Come," the Priestess commanded, motioning for him to follow her to the exit. She never stayed long enough to tempt the others, knowing what had happened to some Red Sisters left in the center of this chamber.

Another difference between Wilsira and the rest of us.

Tarra knew from Dyar's own lips that every Sathoet on the twelfth floor had enjoyed a taste of the Conceiver's aura at some point or another. His own Mother shuddered, recalling the contorted, blissful look on the bua's deformed face.

Disgusting.

As always, Dyar obeyed his Priestess and stayed quiet while leaving the chamber. As soon as the door separated them from his brothers, however, the Sathoet's snuffling grew louder as he sought new scents beyond his confinement.

"You'll have to wait at least until we get off this floor," Tarra said.

The Sathoet dipped his chin to her, his long, dark arms reaching in front of them, hands and bare feet padding along the floor as he hunched to keep his head barely below her shoulders.

"Whhhere, Mother?" he whispered.

"The dungeon," she replied stiffly. "We shall be walking the whole way down. If no one sees you before we get there, I shall give you a reward."

Dyar rumbled in his throat, his mood lifted by curiosity and anticipation as the lines of his form began to blur around the edges.

"Lelinahdara. We welcome Braqth's Hand."

The Guardsvrin of the Gate sounded tenser than last time. She waited to be signaled before dispelling the ward and opening the metal gate.

Hmm. Can you sense my son, Delga?

The older cait had cornered an enviable position among the other wardens. Her modest magical skill had placed her farthest from the filth, perched atop a smooth-walled tunnel with a long, well-lit ramp leading down and curving around.

When Tarra stepped through, she crowded the Guardsvrin on the "wrong" side, forcing Delga to release her hold on the gate and step against the wall to avoid jostling the Priestess. This granted Dyar the space to enter the dungeon first, padding past her, silent and unseen.

"Any new deaths since last I was here, Delga?" asked Tarra, adjusting her gloves and double-checking no hem dragged upon the dirty ground.

Her assumption that the Gate Guardsvrin would recall the last time was intentional, a test. As the one to witness everyone who went in and out of her gate, they said her memory was impeccable.

"Two," the elder cait answered and provided their names.

Tarra didn't know them; she nodded with satisfaction. "Good."

The Confessor descended the smooth, bending path, Dyar padding along behind her on his hands and feet. He made the effort to keep his claws from clicking the stone, and she was aware of his constant sniffing of scents. His eagerness to explore outside the Sathoet chamber overwhelmed even these noxious sources.

Then again, his blood enjoys the scents of prey who can't escape.

She still hadn't decided on his reward if they left the dungeons without him being seen, but the truth was she didn't anticipate he would maintain his self-control every moment. Particularly when she tested her subject's own calm in his presence.

10

Perhaps roaming outside for part of the cycle is reward enough.

At the bottom of the ramp was a balcony used and guarded by wardens. Below was a large, open circle with a drain grate in the center, where groups of prisoners chained together could be overseen from above. Sometimes this was where they resolved disputes but more often carried out sentenced punishments for entertainment.

The Cloister doesn't differ much from this, does it? Tarra smirked in the cool, heatless light. *Perhaps the Prime designed them both at the same time?*

She *could* take the rough, steep stairs carved along the wall down into the well-lit pit. She could take the rawest, widest hallway into filth. Doors would be on either side of her the whole way down; she'd hear and glean curiosities from the prisoners present. With her escort, she was safe enough.

Instead, Lelinahdara let herself into the third door on the balcony, startling the wardens dozing in their barracks and passing without pause. They did not question her as she took the hidden stairs to the winding hall of the left-wing, her invisible son sneaking behind her.

This might be one choice difference between the Cloister and the Palace dungeon: every cell had two ways in or out. Tarra had never gone deep enough into the Prime's barracks to know if that was true in the Red Sisters, but here, underneath the Palace, the door which opened was a prisoner's first hint as to the fate of their next few moments.

With dungeon doors lining the wall on her right side, the runed slabs alternated in their ease of access. Some were solid, hinge-less stone with a food-and-waste exchange slot built at ground level. Others bore some other way to peer into the cell or interact with the prisoner closer to eye level, be it on the door itself or off to one side.

The cell selected for each prisoner depended on the condemner's preference or whim, for she usually knew the frequency of visits to the unfortunate after they were dragged away. Davrin were held for some purpose benefiting Sivaraus, and few were totally forgotten or left to rot when they had other uses.

At the least, they would be given to Auranka in her Drider Pit. Dead or alive, she would take them as children or food.

Not all prisoners in this convoluted vault were Davrin Elves, and some didn't require eye contact before they were dealt with. That, or the meeting of gazes was not only unpleasant but ill-advised.

Would the Ornilleth still be here had the Conceiver not insisted on keeping it outside of the city's limits?

Tarra pursed her lips, wondering why she wasn't hearing about that from those above her. Surely, they were concerned about retaliation if the mind flayer had reached its conclave with that enslaved Red Sister. Perhaps it had never made it, and somehow the Queen knew?

Alas, not my focus. The Sisterhood must clean up that mess. I am to unravel the Consort lineages and provide an alternative to strengthening our magic. If I succeed, I rise above all those cunts who've so enjoyed kicking down at me ever since I arrived.

Dyar snuffled audibly while Tarra held her breath passing by one cell. The exchange slot was open, and a bucket pushed outside. The door she sought lay another ten or so down; she'd recognize the runes when she saw them, as she'd been here twice before.

Without my son. We'll see if Curgia says anything different this time.

Tarra glanced at the empty space beside her, noting the delicate shifts of dust beneath his feet and hands.

Hmm. Besides the screaming.

The cell she aimed for had no physical window, but deep runes covered a panel to the right of the door. Tarra placed her bare hand upon the blank space in the middle, read them as written, and was granted a look through the stone at the prisoner unaware she was being watched.

Curgia Itlaunaduv, the Second Daughter of the Tenth House, shifted and grunted uncomfortably on her thinly padded cot positioned between both her doors against the wall. She had a water pitcher and some uneaten food on a small table, a stalwart, heatless candle nearby, and one of the luxurious waste collection seats that didn't require sliding a bucket through the bottom of the door.

The Noble neared her birthing, having been taken during the mass execution of the Consorts and their offspring half a turn ago. Her condition afforded her more food, cleanliness, and comforts compared to many kept down here. She still complained, of course.

This would probably be the last time Tarra could visit Curgia before the Valsharess would decide what was to be done with her and her infant.

"*Ichthrensha*," she murmured with her hand upon the runes, and the door slid open to a gasp of alarm inside. "Follow me."

Dyar quickly squeezed into the cell, wrapped in camouflaging light but sniffing the air with a slurp of drool that gave him away. Nonetheless, Curgia missed the telling sign as her eyes fixed upon the Priestess and the door closing behind her.

"C-Confessor?" she croaked, rubbing her eyes with a fist as she struggled to sit up.

Tarra smiled at the bloated mata. "Curgia, my sweet. How has your Reverie been? Peaceful, I hope."

"Uhm. Y-yes, Confessor. I am … better."

The wary flickering of the Noble's eyes was promising.

"You seem more cognizant," Tarra said. "Are the visions fading as you grow close? Have you seen your child's face?"

Curgia jolted like she touched something red-hot, gritting her teeth and managing to sit up with her bare feet on the floor. "Ah … yes, Priestess. I've seen … a cait."

Tarra felt amused by her own surprise. *Sometimes I think we bear only sons within these walls.* "Truly? Excellent, Second Daughter. Well done."

"Will I go home, then?" Curgia asked cautiously, weaving a bit.

"You will, most likely. The Valsharess hasn't decided on your child, however."

"Wh-what? What could She … want with her?"

The Confessor smirked. "Now, now, sweet. We're aware the Consort who sired that child was once a healer for the Sanctuary. All healers and their offspring must stay and be trained on the fifth floor of the Sanctuary. I told you this."

"No, but …" Curgia squinted at her. "Uh. Was? Was a healer? Did something happen to Enoquis? I … I never felt anything … after …"

Tarra frowned. "After what, Curgia?"

"After I dreamed … that you were wrong." The Noble swallowed, looking nauseated. "He's … not dead. The Sisterhood missed him. I know it."

"I highly doubt this," Tarra said snidely. "None of the Consorts escaped."

Tears shimmered in her red eyes. "But he's not dead! I have dreamt it!"

I don't have time for this.

"But what about your *other* sire?" the Confessor began.

The Noble froze then looked away. "Other ... sire?"

"Yes. The other sire. He's dead, for certain. Him and your tainted blood."

Curgia stared at the wall, her eyes widening at some memory. "I ... I've never ... No. This is my first."

"Your second," Tarra replied tartly.

"My first! I earned it!"

"Indeed, you did. I doubt either of your sisters would have had the spine to meet a Priestess in her own quarters. May we try once more to prompt your memory?" Tarra waved her hand. "Show yourself."

Curgia's eyes grew huge when a Sathoet appeared in her cell. Hearing the low, sinister chuckle, she began to scream, making Tarra wince. Several ear-bending moments passed before her words made any sense.

"No, no, stay — *no*, s-stay away! You can't, you can't t-touch m-m ... ! Not now, not again, never, Conceiver, never, please!"

Dyar perked up, tilting his head to listen. He hissed, testing both Davrin females by taking a step closer to the prison cot. Curgia wailed, pressing her back to the stone, scraping her bare heels against the edge.

Tarra commanded, "Stop."

Her Sathoet obeyed, staring at the pregnant Noble, his white mane beginning to rise along his spine as Tarra whispered underneath Curgia's continued sobbing. Dyar glanced at his mother, eager for another command, shuddering as he felt her tug demandingly at his aura.

"*Ilthfu'qata*," Tarra hissed, pulling magical threads into her words, weaving her spell across her mind and the Noble's while pushing her son out of it. She needed his strength, not his active participation.

Yet, Dyar moaned to feel what she took from him, his mane standing fully on end. He squatted down to the floor, reaching to fondle himself through his loincloth, and Tarra nearly lost her focus as her fluidly weaving fingers tensed into claws.

Stop! Don't touch it!

The half-blood bua whined, but his Mother ignored him as she finished her incantation. Curgia's cheeks were soaked when her weeping stopped abruptly, her dark red eyes staring at the single light source in her cell until she looked like Bathila down in Wilsira's Forming Pit. When Tarra was certain — and relieved — that her spell had stabilized with the desired effect, only then did she admonish her ugly, presuming bua.

This isn't fertility magic, Dyar. Your mother's reach goes far beyond what Wilsira taught you. That's why she's dead, and I live.

The Sathoet growled.

Was that resentment? How dare he?

Silence. Another sound, and you've earned no reward at all.

The broad-shouldered brute stayed in his squat, lowering his white-bristled chin, yellow eyes peering at the floor or perhaps at his forlorn erection pressing out from his barely hidden groin. Tarra shook her head and refused to look closer, regretting, not for the first time, her acceptance of the Conceiver's offer to train her wild bua to obey her.

Goddess-damned Conceiver ... I should have known when Irrwaer refused her offer with Vesram that Wilsira would only confuse him.

Yet it would have been easy for Irrwaer to refuse. Dyar's behavior had been atrocious compared to Vesram. Destructive, loud, manic, responding to nothing but his own name. No matter how much Tarra whipped and threatened him with worse if he didn't start listening to her, he enjoyed defecating and tossing that odious filth at the servants.

The gossip spoken about her during that time burned her ears. *Detestable.*

Now, at least, Dyar sat dutifully on the floor, waiting on her.

Like Kerse. Like Vesram.

Would it last now that the Conceiver was dead? Tarra quelled the chill which tried to rise at the thought.

Enough of that.

"Curgia," the Confessor commanded, her voice causing Dyar's back to arch briefly. "Can you hear me?"

The pregnant Noble breathed in slowly, her eyes draining tears as she stared at the light. She nodded affirmatively.

"Speak. Whom do you hear?"

"Priestess."

"Which Priestess? My title."

Curgia choked on a sob. "C-Conceiver."

Tarra smirked dryly. *Galling but necessary.* "Tell me about your first child. Name the sire."

"Uh ... Enoquis."

"No! Kerse."

The Noble recoiled, drawing up an arm as if to fend off a strike that did not happen.

"It was Kerse, wasn't it?"

The Noble trembled. "Y-your son, Conceiver ... forced me ..."

"Oh? Did I lose sight of him at the worship ball, and you teased him?"

"N-no ..."

"That's what you claimed."

"Y-you were there! You *approved.*" Curgia shuddered, eyes flicking to Dyar sulking on the ground. Her voice dropped to a disbelieving whisper. "You ... watched us." She shuddered, recoiling. "You watched *him!*"

Here we are, cait. I was right.

Tarra smiled despite her revulsion at the image painted in her mind. "But the Valsharess would not approve of such a birth. Surely you knew it could not last, that the Conceiver would end it somehow. What were you to do for me that would prevent the Court from knowing what happened?"

"I-I don't remember."

"Unacceptable. The Conceiver always gets what she wants. What was it? What did I get?"

Curgia swallowed. "You wanted her name."

"Her name?"

"Yes ... Another cait. Lost her ..." The Noble forced her distant gaze in the direction of the Priestess, seeming to focus on the shadows around her. "D-did you hear it? Did you take her name?"

The Confessor pursed her lips. That was a good question. What would Wilsira have done with that name if she had? "Perhaps. Was that the same eve you lost her?"

Curgia spoke urgently. "Something was wrong, I was in such agony! And Enoquis ... healed me before I followed her into the Abyss."

Juliran's son again? The Confessor refrained from rolling her eyes, smile fading as the topic slid into that obsessive rambling from the besotted Noble.

"He cleansed the scars, giving me *his* daughter instead of that beast!" The Noble's eyes glittered. "She's pure and beautiful. I've seen her! H-He offers much over any Sathoet! That Consort is your most blessed son, Conceiver, you *must* protect him!"

Would that I could. Now I'm curious.

Had the Consort really done all that? Tarra found it hard to believe from what she remembered of Juliran's child. Like all Consorts, the healer bua had gone by so many names: Sil, Vithran, Enoquis. Young Sil had stood out among so many only because he'd been present on the fifth floor when Elder D'Shea had birthed Shyntre.

Curgia must be hallucinating, imagining a grander event than what had happened. She would not relent on her insistence that the healer was alive. In fact, the greater detail the Noble spilled as she babbled on about the eve she'd miscarried Kerse's spawn, the more suspicious Tarra became.

"Tell me more. Remember all you can after I took her name and the cramping started."

"Y-yes, I remember now. A R-Red Sister and a wizard with gold in his eyes carried me bleeding to Enoquis."

Shyntre had been there? *Interesting.*

"What do you recall of this Red Sister escorting the Conceiver at your House?"

Curgia blinked repeatedly, staring between the floor and Dyar. "Sh-she had eyes like sapphires, and she had been watching me for quad-spans. Telling me to be patient and wait for you to contact me."

Blue eyes. Heh. Only one Red Sister this could be.

Sirana had clearly been acting on orders. It could not be coincidence that Elder D'Shea's favored novice and her troublesome wizard son had been traveling with Wilsira and Kerse to torment the Second Daughter of House Itlaun when, later, those same two Davrin would help to kill the Sathoet, bringing down his Mother at last.

Hm. Sirana and Enoquis are gone, but Shyntre lives at the Palace now.

Perhaps the Valsharess would allow the Confessor to speak with him about what happened at House Itlaun.

I have good reason to ask.

D'Shea's fiery bua might help make sense out of Curgia's claims or even the Conceiver's notes and runes down in the Forming Pit. After all, what could Wilsira have wanted with the Abyssal name of her Sathoet's reluctantly carried offspring if such children would never have taken their first breath?

The simplest answer seemed to be a sacrifice to Braqth for greater power. But how? What did she discover about her son beyond his confirmed fertility in siring children?

Tarra was yanked from her thoughts when Dyar growled at Curgia for glaring at him. His eyes flicked to her swollen belly as he flexed his hands. The Noble's face collapsed near to despair as she clutched her middle and balled up protectively.

"No!" she squeaked.

Sigh.

"He shall not harm the child," Tarra reassured her, her voice hard as stone for her son. "She belongs to the Valsharess, and he knows it."

Dyar chuffed through his nose, and Curgia dragged her blanket up to fist the hem beneath her chin.

"I want to go home, P-Priestess."

"Not until we've seen to your safe birthing, Itlaunaduv."

Tired of grinding stone with this interrogation, Tarra needed a break. Maybe get rid of her son if he would be a distraction. She gestured to him, turning toward the cell's outer door. "I shall return later."

"Conceiver, could you … ?"

Tarra paused. "Hm?"

"Could you bring Enoquis with you? H-he'd make sure the birthing is safe. For ... the Valsharess."

The Priestess sighed. *Blame the Prime and her pack of deformed rutters for making that impossible.*

Nonetheless, other information about poor Sil's time outside the Sanctuary might help with Wilsira's tangle of runes and bloodlines.

If Varessa won't speak straight enough, perhaps her son will.

And if neither of them would, there was always a prompt from the Valsharess through Phaelous.

Dyar started whining again after they left Curgia's cell, his aura lapping intrusively at hers, disrupting every other thought as it began.

"What?" she bit off impatiently.

"Back to chamberrr?" he asked morosely.

"Yes. I have many things to attend to and can't have you at my heels."

"Rrreward?"

"No. You don't deserve one."

He snarled. "You sssaid if none sssaw going down!"

She rounded on him. "Don't talk back to me! And you should not have threatened Curgia's baby."

"Never did! I hate, but I obey, Motherrr!"

"Quiet!"

Dyar's aura flared as he growled loudly enough to cause shuffling in some of the nearest cells. His yellow eyes stared at her, and Tarra felt something strange. Something ... intangible. Slip a little.

Try to open her up.

No!

The Confessor seized her son's mane, gripping it lightly. "Stay! Don't you move!"

His lip curled. "Never left, Motherrr. You did."

Tarra saw the youth her bua had once been in his face, the wavering visage of a massive tantrum which would end with his shit smeared on the walls. Dismay swept through her to imagine regressing to those times without Wilsira.

"You want your reward?"

"I obey! You sssaid! I hungerrr!"

Hunger?

Reluctantly, Tarra glanced down where his hand flapped around his groin. He didn't touch it, but his erection hadn't passed, hadn't gone flaccid. It strained, hot and hard, the glans having grown a massive wet spot over the passing mark. The Confessor looked away from it.

"Will you return to the chamber without further tantrums if we ... sate this?"

Dyar's appetite shone in his eyes. "Yesss, Motherrr. Yes!"

He reached for her sandal, caressing her ankle. Tarra recoiled.

"No! No, I meant ..." She caught her panic in her throat, forcing it down. "I meant I'll ... find you a cait."

Her Sathoet glowered for an instant, sucking in some excessive saliva before he bowed. "Like Kerrrse ... ?"

"Um. What?"

"Like Currrgia. Watch us. Approve."

Tarra's face screwed up. "You're pushing it, Dyar. Do you want to spill in a cait before you return or not?"

His nose wrinkled in a pout as his shoulders slumped. "Want cait."

"Fine."

Tarra led them briskly through the hall and up the stairs to the warden's balcony and barracks. She found one of the dozing caits alone, neither waiting for her or standing at attention after they had slipped by the first time.

She knew a Priestess of Braqth was down here. She should have been ready.

The Priestess ignored the brief memory of having told the wardens to look the other way when she came down here, motioning her Sathoet Son to go inside. He smiled, so she granted him a light, encouraging pat on the shoulder before she gave him a little push.

The cait inside awoke as Tarra shut the door, setting both a lock and silence ward on it so she didn't have to see or listen to the inevitable distraction from how Wilsira had warped her son.

I'll figure this out after I've earned my new place with the Valsharess. He'll learn to worship his Mother properly.

Not ask to fuck her every time he was let out of his room.

Chapter 2

Elder D'Shea - The Sisterhood Cloister, Sivaraus

Varessa had arrived in her quarters quite recently, finishing a vigorous scrub-down when Rausery identified herself outside her stone door. She was alone. The Sorceress exhaled.

Not even time for a meal, it seems.

The Elder General proved her wrong by stepping through with a gently steaming platter.

As the door closed with D'Shea's silent command, she sniffed the air. "What's that?"

Her peer smirked. "Food. Made it myself in the mess."

"No, I mean, what's that smell? It's odd."

"Huh, well." Rausery sniffed at the tray of mixed and mashed brown fodder. "The dried mushrooms I collected on the Surface. I was saving them. They chew and taste like brined meat."

Curious despite herself, D'Shea finished wrapping her body and feet in warmth as Rausery tugged a utility table from the wall, putting it closer to the center of the room. She placed the platter on it. Next, the General claimed the spare chair for herself, leaving D'Shea to choose her own seat.

The Sorceress selected her favorite from her desk, never missing a chance to enjoy the comfortable padding for her bottom. She didn't ask if Rausery had brought her own spoon, she knew she had, and neither of them needed plates. However, first she retrieved a sealed bottle of a spiced tonic and two small, metal cups.

Once D'Shea sat down, Rausery took the first large scoopful, as was customary between them, claiming bits from all around the edge and the middle, consuming it while her peer watched. D'Shea would wait as long as she liked before joining in or choosing not to eat at all.

The latter was unlikely, given the timing and her empty belly, but Rausery had stopped questioning her about this particular ritual centuries ago.

"I don't blame you," a younger General had once said. "You lived centuries at Court where you didn't know what they put in your food. I always got my own, one way or another."

Indeed. How many times had she come awake in a place she didn't remember having gone to after sitting to eat?

Not every meal. Not even most of them. But often enough to never know.

D'Shea couldn't wait to get out of the Palace. Although, in all her efforts, she hadn't known this would require the Prime doing what she did best.

Not unlike when the Consorts lost their usefulness, when many paid the price.

Aware how she'd gripped the arm of her chair, D'Shea reached for the bottle to break the melted wax and twist the rim clear. Pouring each cup halfway and placing one closer to the General, the Sorceress sipped on her tonic while her peer watched. A balanced trade.

Rausery nodded to acknowledge the cup but ignored the drink for now, taking another savory mouthful secured from three different edges than before. D'Shea would have to lift her spoon soon or the meal would be half gone before she tasted it.

"Wanted to talk about the Consort and the Sanctuary," the Elder General said then.

D'Shea arched an eyebrow. "Why? I have him under our control."

"Our control?"

Goddess, that dry smirk was familiar.

"The Sisterhood." She sipped again, the mild burn on her tongue and aromatic lift into her nose a welcome focus. "As opposed to the Sanctuary, or Auranka."

"Yeah, I figured. I hope the Valsharess at least knows where he is?"

"She does. She approved."

"Good. Wasn't sure from our last time at the Palace, because the Prime sure as fuck hasn't asked yet."

"Because the Valsharess knows she'd be too tempted to take some Sisters to go find him and beat him bloody after the pregnancy tests."

Rausery grimaced. "So, you've been told to keep mum?"

"Correct." The Sorceress offered her own wry expression. "Speaking of the last audience at the Palace, I would like to talk about my Lead in the deep tunnels while you're here."

"Heh." Rausery scooted out another blob of the hearty-smelling paste and scraped up another bite. "Not much there. Jaunda spilled what she had to the Valsharess behind the curtain, leaving me with not much but practical travel tasks."

"Such as?"

"Such as updating the map of where she's been. She's staying away from the Elder Mind conclave, at least."

"Hm. Well. Even that was more than I've been able to parse for myself while you've been gone. May I see that map?"

Rausery shrugged. "Sure. If you give me more about that healer."

"Like what?"

"Did you know Sirana carried by him when she left?"

D'Shea exhaled. "I did."

Her peer frowned. "And the Prime?"

"She does not.."

"The Queen?"

A slight smile. "Yes."

Rausery narrowed her eyes. "Big intelligence gap."

"It pleased the Valsharess for me not to say. What more would I need to keep that for Her?"

"But you did the same with Corpora Thena."

"Not exactly the same. The Prime demanded the fallout but was too slow following up." D'Shea shrugged. "When standing before Her, I had no choice but to tell Her."

Rausery smirked. "So you used Thena with the Queen before the Prime could, for some benefit I'm not seeing?"

Varessa smiled, holding her peer's gaze.

The General casually pointed a finger. "That's what I want to talk about. What's going on with that bua staying with the only Matron you'd trust with him?"

The Elder Sorceress exhaled, accepting the confirmation that the General indeed knew where Auslan was. *But does she know about Shyntre? I took my bua there after Rausery's return ...*

"Before we get too far from Jaunda," she deflected, "have you *any* idea how close she might be to her goal?"

Rausery frowned with a hint of annoyance as the subject swung around to her. "You mean, when she'll get to stay in Sivaraus?"

"No, not when she will stay. How close she might be to her goal."

Her peer made a face. "I don't know her goal, Varessa. If it's not to spy on the flayer nest that took Reishel, I don't know what she's doing for the Queen."

D'Shea blew softly through her nose. "I can tell you she's looking for a den."

White eyebrows lifted high. "Oh? How do you know?"

"I was there when she was compelled." The Sorceress pursed her lips but forced herself to lift her spoon and aim for the cooling platter. The General had taken a third of the meal but had paused to wait for her. "Once the Valsharess tied off the spell and released her, Jaunda said, 'I will search for his den.'"

"Huh. Weirdly loose compulsion to mutter that aloud right after."

D'Shea pushed a lump of curled mushroom into the mash before picking up her first spoonful. Her hand balanced the bite without lifting toward her mouth. "I've seen such compulsions before. A test to make sure she *can* say what is necessary to others she meets later."

"Yeah?"

"Have you never had a compulsion on you?"

"I wouldn't say that." Rausery smirked, glancing down at the platter then her spoon. The pause drew out as if she waited for D'Shea to finally partake of her dinner. Once the Sorceress fed herself, the General spoke.

"Whose den is she looking for?"

"I am not sure." The Sorceress ate, carefully chewing and tasting her food. *Wow. That does taste like salted meat.*

Rausery grinned at her expression and resumed eating. "You must have an idea. I can't imagine you abiding by Deep Traders knowing more about Jaunda's goal than you do."

One corner of her mouth twitched as D'Shea took another bite. "Mm. True enough. Unfortunately, the ideas I have are from archives. I certainly don't have the Deep Trader contacts you have."

Rausery licked some drying matter from her spoon. She shrugged. "Tell me about the archives, then."

"So casual, Elder. That's not a good idea right now." D'Shea cleared her throat and sipped her drink. "Do you mean to tell me you haven't made *one* motion toward keeping an eye on Jaunda out in the wilderness since you got back?"

The General set down her spoon before putting both elbows on the table, folding her gloved hands over muscular forearms. Her calm gaze was one of the most difficult to read in the Cloister due to its simplicity.

"I'm hearing what you're saying, Elder Sorceress," she said, "and rest assured I have some ideas for getting Jaunda some effective back-up."

D'Shea breathed out.

"But if you're not saying anything about archives right now, then I want to talk about the Consort. Like I first said."

I have more to look into with Phaelous.

"About what, exactly?" D'Shea prompted. "You know *where* he is, and who is his guardian. You know Corpora Thena is paying for her stupidity leading the others to harass him in solitary. You know about Sirana, and it's largely because of her that he's still alive. The Queen wants a healer of his quality, not to mention all confirmed pureblood children he sires. He must be kept safe and available should the Elder Mind retaliate."

When *the Elder Mind retaliates.*

The General smiled, finishing up her portion of the meal while leaving slightly less than half for her. She finally picked up the spiced tonic to sip it, grimacing slightly. "So She wants Sirana's infant but let her go to the Surface?"

"She has mentioned … Visions."

"Ah." Rausery flicked that topic to the side. "Mm, so Matron Thalluen just keeps him safe? And we keep the Red Sisters away from him."

"That is enough, yes."

"Then what did I hear about you moving Shyntre there, too?"

D'Shea stared at her, her mouth tightening.

Rausery tilted her head. "What? I have eyes in the market, D'Shea, same as you. You both rode out of the Palace a while ago, but they lost track of you. I put it together, that's all. You know I can't help you guard the damned healer if I don't have any glimpse of your web design. So, what's going on there?"

The Sorceress considered how loosely woven this part of her plans had truly been. She thought about the promises she'd made to the Valsharess to get her son out of the Palace and with someone whose life depended on him.

More improvisation than I prefer, but She surprised me.

"The Queen," D'Shea began, "wants the Sisterhood ready for the next conflict with the Ornilleth, correct?"

"Yep."

"Part of that objective is this Consort-healer —"

"You already said."

"No. I didn't say what She told me, yet."

Rausery closed her lips and motioned for her to continue.

"She said Auslan could save Red Sisters and fighters attacked by mind flayers *if* his magic can be weaned off of his Priestess conditioning."

Her peer frowned in thought, sipping from her cup again, which reminded D'Shea to take another bite of food though her appetite waned from the turn of subject.

"What conditioning?" Rausery asked.

"His healing is entangled with his service. He cannot do one without the other or he becomes ill."

27

The light of understanding appeared in the General's face. "Ah. The reason Sirana caught and Curgia Itlaunaduv is still in the dungeon after the purge?"

"Correct. And Corpora Thena, as well. I imagine after three cycles in that cell, he was trying to heal the damage they caused him. He wasn't made to withstand what we do." D'Shea suppressed a shudder, scraping up the last of the food into a neat pile. "As soon as I sort a few things out with Lelinahdara, Thena must be removed from the Cloister for the duration of her pregnancy."

Rausery made a face. "Yeah, I know. Bad time to be losing the leading head on that group. Suna's gonna have fits getting reassigned."

"On that, briefly," the Sorceress added, "I would like to claim Panagan for direct tutoring. It's time she discovers her potential."

"Agreed," the General said without pushback. "She's yours. Put her through your paces. We'll need whatever she can do."

"Thank you."

A pity she can't meet Gaelan's level quickly enough.

"And thanks for telling me about that Ornilleth value in that bua. I had no idea."

"Neither had I," she replied with regret. "We could have saved Reishel and the others."

"Yeah." Rausery rubbed her mouth in thought before looking up. "Does that mean his healing has been protecting Jaunda that way? Or at least wiping out the cobwebs each time?"

D'Shea blinked, but then admonished herself for the surprise. "I believe so. She passed the Valsharess's last interview, didn't she?"

"That she did." Rausery smiled in a way that prompted suspicion. "So ..."

D'Shea sighed. "Yes?"

"I take it Jaunda's not pregnant from being healed by him."

"She is not. Fortunately."

"So the weaning is working?" Rausery stared at her. "Or is it not, and that's why you need Shyntre at House Thalluen?"

Goddess, you're stubborn, General.

D'Shea smirked. "Essentially correct, yes."

"Something else, too, huh? Alright." The General looked pleased enough. "Let me know when you need time to check on them. I'll help cover for you and stay dumb with the Prime on what you're doing."

The Sorceress felt mollified. "That would be welcome."

"Done. I always respected your son, you know. Different perspective, a will like iron. He's a lot like you and taken well to some of the toughest training we have. If you've got him on a task with the healer to save more Sisters from getting mind-flayed or abducted, I'd want to see it done."

D'Shea's mouth had gone slack while she spoke. She lifted her chin. "Uh. Thank you. And I can still see that map?"

"Yeah. Next thing, if you want."

Tempting, but she resisted the impulse to end their sit-down this moment. "Is there anything I can do for you?"

There was. She could see it.

"You're regularly going into the Sanctuary, right?" Rausery asked. "To work with the Headmaster and Confessor?"

D'Shea wrinkled her nose. "Unfortunately."

"Have you been to the Consort floor since the purge?"

"Not for a while. Why?"

Rausery shrugged. "Did you look underneath any beds?"

"What?"

"They slept on raised beds, right? Not pallets like us."

"Why would you ask? Is something there?"

The General smiled. "There was during Qivni's time, as I've heard it."

Qivni. Of course.

D'Shea finished up her food before she forgot in her contemplation, then she poured another half-cup of tonic. Leaning into her padded chair, she sighed and sipped. "I will check for you."

Rausery shrugged. "Not really for me. Information might be too old anyway."

Not necessarily, and it could be for you.

D'Shea watched her peer, noting the gold at her temples, the fine lines of her face, her eyes still sharp and bright. The last secret conversation signed with Phaelous flashed before her eyes.

Wilsira was very interested in Rausery's line, Varessa, as the Matriarch of the surrogates bearing the pure sons of the Priestesses.

What line? Rausery only had Tahna, who should have been a Red Sister like her Mother but was made to serve in the Sanctuary.

Rausery also had half-siblings or cousins she didn't name in her time under the Prime. But Tahna must have known who a few of them were, and they might have known each other. I've found notes of Wilsira tracking specific Davrin among the commoners and noting them as relatives to Rausery. I assume the Conceiver must have extracted them from Rausery's Daughter.

The ... healer. Whom we are researching?

Probable. Not confirmed, but probable, given the timing.

Auslan was probably Tahna's son.

And, if so, D'Shea had tasked Rohenvi with guarding Rausery's grandson.

Should I tell her? Or does she suspect?

As the silence lengthened, Rausery looked up from her own considerations. "What is it, Varessa?"

Her voice was so steady, her tone straightforward.

She can anticipate enough in Sivaraus to play the game, to move the pieces with confidence, but never has a mask on doing it.

D'Shea lifted one shoulder. "Do you recognize the name Bathila?"

The General paused to think and shook her head. "Nope. Who's Bathila?"

"She is the last surrogate Wilsira had been using to birth the Consorts."

"What?"

"She's alive and pregnant in the Sanctuary, for the moment."

"Wait." The General shook her head again. "You found one unborn Consort left from Wilsira's brood?"

D'Shea nodded. "Unborn and kept, per the Valshuress, until we confirm the lineage and any taint within. I believe we are close to finding out."

"Hmph." Rausery looked to one side for a moment. "The 'last' surrogate. Meaning there have been other matas squeezing pretty buas out for the Conceiver all this time?"

The Sorceress kept her breath and gaze steady, her face calm. "Yes. Quite a lot of others over the centuries. Most of them commoners."

"*Pfeh*," the General chuffed and set down her cup, watching the table as she grumbled. "Yeah. Not surprised. We know the spider-suckers are too scratched up inside to do it themselves. Fucking Priestesses."

The Sorceress smirked, nodding agreement, and finished her second cup. Abruptly, Rausery pushed her chair back, moving it off to the side as if she had heard enough. She picked up the dirtied platter to take with her while D'Shea sat calmly in her seat.

"I'll let you know what I find out about Jaunda in the deep tunnels," she said frankly before letting herself out.

The Elder Sorceress sat alone, watching her secure door for a time after it had shut. If the General *hadn't* suspected a specific fate of her Daughter during her time in the Sanctuary, well, she did now.

But she never knew about Auslan.

Or others the Sisterhood killed. Rausery herself had taken some of those strokes.

Phaelous had told her all this was too early in their search to bring to the Valsharess, and thus too early to suggest it to the Elder General. Yet, for once, D'Shea hesitated to guess her peer's response should that confirmation come to them all in time.

Like me, she keeps the influence best suited to her.

As disconcerting as these working theories were, the question remained, why Rausery's bloodline? Why did Wilsira use Tahna and her common-blood cousins to create 'pureblood' Consorts? Why Bathila, held in the Forming Pit by the Queen's Grace?

All told, the Conceiver might have preferred to use House D'Shea for such a project, if it still existed.

She wouldn't be the first.

Phaelous had found Beliza D'Shea's lineage in the archives, suggesting this ancestor to be a key branch in the bloodline of many Priestesses who had risen in the Sanctuary.

Including Wilsira.

In addition, the Valsharess had recently and outright *claimed* Varessa's own son in front of her, just as She had claimed Phaelous and the handful of Headmaster Ja'Prohns before him.

She may be too old or 'scratched up inside' to manage bearing a son of Her own. She continues needing one for some reason.

D'Shea closed her eyes as they started to burn. She shuddered on a sob. It took several tries, several breaths and gulping down a painful fear to bring herself under control.

No matter what She did to him, he is still my blood. My son.

Shyntre was more content with Rausery's likely grandson than anywhere else in Sivaraus, and D'Shea couldn't imagine a better companion for her angry and lonely bua.

Chapter 3

Shyntre - House Thalluen, Sivaraus

"Huh," Shyntre breathed, carefully turning another page of the weak-spined journal.

Auslan turned his head toward the small desk, wrapped in blankets on the bed and resting. "Hmm?"

The wizard shrugged. "The Deep Trade routes seem more populated than in the tunnels leading to the Surface."

The healer turned onto his side, facing him though pulling the blankets up to his chin. "Oh?"

"Yeah." Shyntre tapped his fingers. "As if the Great Cavern is the 'top' of a crest or an anthill, with all the tunnels spreading down and out."

"Anthill?"

He smiled ruefully. "Ground insects on the Surface. They're everywhere. They behave like tiny Ornilleth, all their eggs around one elder laying them, and the others building, finding food, and working for defense of that one. I always thought their 'hills' in the dirt echoed the Deepearth tunnels."

The former Consort blinked at him. "Strange."

"Not really. A lot of life echoes itself. Up or down."

"Oh. And most life down here is ... underneath Sivaraus?"

"Correct. Except for the Tragar stronghold, I think."

Auslan paused. "How far down does it go? The Deepearth."

"I don't know. But these notes suggest places that have never seen a Davrin, or at least not often. However, they all seem to know Ornilleth as a threat. The Yutogul, especially."

The healer made a face. "Yoo-toh ... ?"

"Gul," he finished. "Yutogul."

"Yutogul. And what are those?"

"I haven't met one, but they sound to me like the only other race down here that uses elemental magic. Water. They like water, live in it."

"They can swim?"

"Swim and breathe like a fish. But they can also breathe air if needed. I think they would die if they got too far from a lake or river, though."

The healer's scarlet eyes shone in wonder, making Shyntre smile again. "What else is underneath us? Larger things a trader might run into."

"Hm. Smaller and larger drakes."

"Like the riding lizards?"

"Where we got them, I think. Some have wings, though, and are too small to ride."

"Ah yes, I've heard of those."

"You have?"

"Yes. Mostly Matrons complaining about them as poor pets, though I never saw one."

Shyntre chuckled. "They're smarter than Pyte and Uroan, that's for certain."

He turned several pages, reading the helpful journal, as new images painted in his mind from the astonishing precision of the description. The room fell quiet as the wizard gradually became reabsorbed in the words.

"So," Auslan broke into his concentration. "I presume Matron Thalluen has read this? She has an idea what's out there?"

"Huh?" Shyntre blinked. "Oh. Yes, she said as much."

The healer's bare arms lay outside the blankets as his fingers worried at the hem. "And she has no care that you might share this with the Valsharess."

"All of this is already in the Tower libraries," Shyntre admitted. "What's different about this one is that I could create a map with certain landmarks."

"That's what I mean. Would the Queen want to know who wrote it? Or scribed it?"

"No, not really. The Headmaster might, but I don't have to tell him."

"Hm. Why does Matron Thalluen have it?"

Shyntre shrugged. "A lot of her wealth comes from the good water wells. She'd have an interest in water sources outside Sivaraus, I think. Most Matrons tap into the Deep Traders and run little excursions farther down."

"Like … like the Red Sisters and you going up?" His brother wetted his lips when Shyntre looked over. "Were you looking for something? Can you say?"

The wizard paused at the force of collision between his memory and his present: the stark sunlight, cold wind, and spicy needles on the trees and mountains against the scratching, smothering darkness of Sivaraus.

Almost half my lifetime ago.

Sirana would have been an infant in Rohenvi's care. As much as it meant to him, Shyntre had the sense he couldn't remember everything from that trip. He did not even have certainty about the purpose.

"I really wanted to go," the young wizard murmured, turning back one page after realizing he hadn't grasped everything on it. "Rausery made it happen, but I paid for it."

I spent more time in the Cloister 'training' than you spent in solitary, brother, and it was worse.

Not Rausery's idea. Always the Prime with that shit.

Auslan did not follow that unspoken thread. "How old were you?"

"One-hundred fifteen."

The former Consort might not be able to read, but he could count far beyond his fingers. "Fifty turns after Irrwaer vanished from the Sanctuary?"

Shyntre frowned. "Who?"

The healer sat up, bracing himself on his palms. He was bare from the waist up; Shyntre tried not to get distracted.

"Irrwaer. The healer-acolyte to my Mother? She was going to be the

Priestess managing the fifth-floor infirmaries after Priestess Juliran."

The wizard made a face and shrugged. "I haven't paid attention to Sanctuary politics in decades."

"Unless the Conceiver forced you to."

Shyntre grunted. "Yeah. In her sadistic, manipulated 'crises.'"

His brother exhaled patiently. "Irrwaer took care of us for a time. She took care of *you* as an infant. I was there."

The wizard raised an eyebrow. "Sure, but why expect I'm going to remember that?"

"I thought perhaps you had met her again, later, after ..."

The healer trailed off.

Shyntre's stomach tensed. "After what?"

"After the ... th-the Valsharess claimed you?"

The tears which sprang up caught him unaware; angrily, he blinked them away. "Mm. No. I didn't. And she'd hardly be the first Priestess to vanish."

"I know, but I overheard the Conceiver talking about her. Five decades after she disappeared."

"What? How?" Shyntre regretted the brusqueness in his tone as his brother's eyes glistened with unshed tears.

Auslan swallowed. "My Mother died under ... strange circumstances. Somehow, the Conceiver claimed ownership of me after her. I did not understand her claim."

Argh.

"I remember," the wizard muttered. "I'm sorry. That was a rockhead thing to say."

His brother took another deep breath, choosing his next words. "If Priestess Irrwaer had lived to succeed Juliran, I would have gone to her." The Consort took a moment to normalize his voice when it began to break. "Two healers, like me, gone in half a century, both of whom were intended to head the infirmary. No apparent response from the Valsharess despite that their magic is much greater than buas."

Shyntre wanted to cut in with a snide remark but let Auslan continue.

"After them, the fifth floor went to Lelinahdara —"

"A Confessor?" He squinted in suspicion.

"She is hardly there, from what I've heard. It is mostly acolytes handling the injured and sick until one of them makes Priestess. Yet, I didn't even stay with the Priestess heading that floor. I went to the Conceiver, and something she said made me think Irrwaer and her Sathoet went up to the Surface ahead of you. And the Valsharess had something to do with it."

This time, Shyntre refrained from blurting out the first cautious denial which leapt into his head. "Ahead of me, huh? Was she, um, looking for something?"

The healer's gaze held steady. "Well. Something built? Is anything ... ?"

Shyntre let go of Rohenvi's journal pages and wiped his hands on his robes. "There's a tower. Sort of like the Wizard's Tower."

"Ah-hah. Is that where you went?"

A tiny ball of pain burst within his throat, and the tears returned.

"Shyntre?"

He shook his head, refusing to confirm. To confess.

Almost. I tried. I got so close. A dream ...

A dream had suggested that if he reached that tower on the Surface, he would be rescued. If he had found that place, he would not have returned to the Palace.

And if I had, Ta'suil would be down here alone. Or dead.

Shyntre looked away and schooled his voice harshly. "No. I didn't go there. But I've heard Rausery mention it. She saw it later, I know. Different trip."

"I see."

The wizard watched his brother's face as he weighed whether to continue. He made the choice easier for him.

"What are you thinking, Ta'suil?"

The healer sighed, relaxing a little. "Well ... The Valsharess. General Rausery. The Conceiver. You. All know something about the Surface, and Irrwaer vanished there. Which is curious because she helped Elder D'Shea with your birth —"

"What? She did?"

Auslan held his eyes up with growing difficulty. "And she cared for you until you were taken away from her. Later, she was sent upward. Now, Sirana was sent away to the Surface as well, and I essentially belong to *your* Mother. I-I've come in a circle to where it began for me."

Shyntre rubbed his face, saying nothing.

"Do you not ... do you not *see* any of this web starting when Elder D'Shea gave birth to you in the Sanctuary and left you there?"

Goddess dammit.

Shyntre drummed his fingers. "I do, and I hate it. I also don't know what happened to Irrwaer. I didn't go with Rausery to look for her if that's what you were asking."

"That seems strange, given how soon after you left."

"Yeah, well, every matron in this city is strange. From the top down."

Glancing at the bed, Shyntre saw Auslan worrying his blanket and thought on the present problem: the reason Elder D'Shea had peeled him away from the Palace to begin with.

Which I haven't told him yet. Shyntre checked ahead a couple of pages, eyes drawn to some sketches of mushrooms and their annotated descriptions. He sighed. *Will I pretend as if he knows the reason why I'm here? Push it right up to the moment my Mother steps in the door?*

"Hey, a question on Irrwaer," he began.

Auslan straightened up. "Yes?"

"Was she like you? I mean, did she need sensual connection to heal and stay well?"

His brother blinked in shock, blurting a short laugh before pasting his hand across his mouth.

"What?" Shyntre's mouth quirked despite himself. "Why laugh?"

"Oh, um." The former Consort cleared his throat. "Because Irrwaer avoided sex wherever she could."

Shyntre lifted his head and turned in his chair. "So, she could heal without sex."

"Yes." Auslan shrugged. "She might have undergone the same training I did later, but I understood she ... felt no desire to pursue it."

"Hmph. I would have, too, in her place." The wizard flexed an ankle which had grown stiff. "What about any other healers you knew? They're all locked up in the Sanctuary, right?"

"Ah, well …" The Consort looked away and didn't answer at first. "I knew only Irrwaer and Mother as healers. If there were others, I wasn't introduced."

The following pause tightened awkwardly.

Shyntre frowned. "Wait. Who trained you to heal?"

A pulse surged in Auslan's throat. He looked down. "Irrwaer did not want to train any Consorts, be they healers or not. The only Priestess available to teach me was my Mother, Juliran."

The wizard's stomach turned with illness and rage, despite knowing no bua got out of the Sanctuary without having lain with a Priestess. She was too-often a mother-figure.

That all rolled down from Wilsira and Kerse with their games. What was it like before them?

The Headmaster's son grasped for words. "But … Irrwaer *could* have taught you without sex?"

"That's not what they wanted from me."

Of course not.

Shyntre growled, "And your Mother wouldn't let you practice with anyone else? Was she *that* jealous?"

"Yes," Auslan answered both questions, twisting the blanket in his lap. "Very. Even if the Conceiver or the Valsharess Herself ordered Priestess Juliran to make certain my magic was *not* tethered to my function, my Mother wouldn't have given me to another's bed."

Shyntre shook his head. "But you said Irrwaer cared for both of us."

"Indeed. She did."

"So Juliran trusted her with vulnerable buas. Did something happen?"

"Yes. I grew up." Extraordinarily, Auslan watched him without blinking. "Irrwaer had her own son to care for by then anyway, and again, she did not *want* me that way even if Mother had been willing to consider it."

Shyntre grunted irritably, gripping the edge of the desk. *Crippling his talent never had to be an issue at all. Fucking Priestesses warp everything and everyone they touch.*

He caught Auslan staring at him. "What?"

"I wish you could remember her."

"Who, Priestess Irrwaer?"

"Yes."

"Why do you want that?"

"Because ..." His brother's eyes trailed the wall. "I dreamed about her, and I thought you did, too?"

"What do you mean?"

The Consort steadied his breath.

Uh-oh.

"When we ... discovered each other?" The beautiful but pensive face watched him. "I dreamed of Irrwaer that eve, but I thought it was *you* 'seeing' her on the Surface. I only followed you there. And now that you are *here*, I ... I am *certain* we dreamed about Sirana the same way. I do not know why, but we've both seen caits with strong bonds to us who have left us."

" ... I see."

"Do you not believe me? Sirana was real. Couldn't Irrwaer have been? Could we not have bonds with caits who meant us no harm?"

I didn't believe that before. But for half a turn, She's been wanting to make the dreams happen somehow. She believes I can, otherwise why make it a command in exchange for Matron Thalluen's well-being?

Shyntre swallowed. "No, no, Ta'suil, I believe you."

When he looked up, Auslan's face had warmed visibly, his fists clutching the blanket closer over his groin. The Consort's lips and eyes answered with a pure desire, simpler than his.

"I am glad. Might we ... Might we rediscover old grounds, my first?"

Heat swept through his chest like molten lava.

My first.

He never told Juliran.

Never told anyone.

"While we can," Auslan finished.

40

Shyntre couldn't look away. How easy *not* to say why he was here, not even to *try* and complete his tasks until the Elder Sorceress came to check on them. Why should he make it easier for *any* female, be she cait, Matron, Elder, or Queen?

While we can. We're dreaming of Sirana already. That's something.

"When we 'discovered' each other," the wizard echoed, a sly, involuntary smile growing on his lips as he recalled that time inside the Sanctuary. "Still worth it."

I just don't know how it ends.

Auslan's grin was brilliant, the pull to him on the bed revived. Shyntre closed Rohenvi's journal with care, setting it aside, and stood up to loosen and drop his wizard's robes. Auslan admired him, shared his excitement, but also looked perturbed when the wizard nearly left his clothing on the floor.

Sigh. Alright.

Shyntre picked up his garments, shook them out, and folded them neatly on the supply table. The healer's shoulders relaxed, and he shifted to make room, offering the warm spot as he got into the bed. The small peek of white fur beneath the blanket confirmed he was nude.

"Come here," the wizard whispered, reaching as he slid beneath the covers, smooth sheets drawn across his answering arousal.

The buas had settled down and embraced front-to-front, both erect. Auslan guided him in the slower kisses he wanted, sustaining their lips touching until their bellies were mutually sticky. Shyntre inhaled the mixed, moist scent deeply, eyes closed, and returned in his mind to that eve in the Sanctuary.

We never did mount each other like the Red Sisters do …

Nonetheless, the exploration had been intense. Something beyond description had happened between them. More than once. That time had not been young, fumbling sex.

Innocently, for either a moment or an eternity, his hurting aura had untangled itself under the healer's gentle touch. Unseen strands within a sonorous current had been lovingly groomed, soothed, and threaded into a familiar pattern with a new foundation. Strengthened by an uncorrupted heart, he'd been rewoven stronger than before into a brighter being.

Into two of us.

An experience of joy in which, for once, he wasn't also in pain.

For the first time since I could remember.

That early feeling returned as if it had been waiting for them.

We have been waiting.

For centuries.

"Hahh-*huh!*" Auslan exclaimed, tilting his head as Shyntre's palm caressed and coaxed his erection to its limit.

The wizard shifted closer still, holding him tightly, biting his neck as he exposed it. "Yes. Cum on me, Ta'suil …"

"Ah-are you certain … ?"

"Come on."

He sped up his rhythm, watching the ecstatic moment of panic before bliss overwhelmed his brother.

"*Augh! Ohh, Shhhyn …* uh!"

The first hot splash struck his gut beneath the blankets, followed by several more. "Oh, yeah … ."

Better *he* was stained than the just-dried sheets.

Still scalding hot.

Ta'suil panted as the tension left him abruptly, a light sweat upon his brow as he blinked up at him. "Ohh … Thank you."

Shyntre grinned and kissed him. Then, together, their eyes flicked toward the secret passage in the corner.

"And you?" the Consort asked. "How do you prefer … ?"

Fast recovery. But we can't exactly go all cycle, can we?

Nowhere in Sivaraus were they *that* safe.

"Hm. Your mouth?"

His lover's smile slanted awkwardly. "Oh, um. Do you … want me to 'clean my mess?' "

Oops.

Shyntre shook his head, making sure he showed teeth in his smile. "No, not at all. I can wipe off, first? I didn't … I didn't *plan* this, obviously."

Ta'suil believed him. He had thought about it this time, but the shadows of the Cloister remained too large for him.

"Yes, please," he whispered.

"I'll be back." Shyntre tossed the cover aside, holding his damp middle with one hand as he stood up. He looked over his shoulder and winked. "And spotless."

The Consort chuckled, and the wizard regained his feet to wipe down quickly.

Please let Sirana's mother not walk in right now.

His ears perked for the faintest scratch at either door, and the wizard used the cool water and a damp cloth to scrub semen off his belly before wiping it with a dry one. His erection hardly had time to flag in the comparative chill before he neatly draped each cloth to dry and slipped into bed, lying on his side and facing his heart's brother.

The moment he did, Auslan ducked under the covers with an eagerness that sent the wizard's heart into his throat. His toes curled when the hot, wet mouth engulfed his cock; his eyes slid shut as a soft hand cradled his sack.

"Fffuuu …"

Shyntre reached for long, silky hair without thinking; in response, the soft hand left his balls and wrapped around his hip, cradling his lower back as the passionate service continued. The song was back, and yearned-for magic flowed between them as his aura relaxed. And he gave what was needed for them both.

Oh my Goddess …

He couldn't think but could feel. And he *felt* …

Complete.

As all his muscles tightened, Shyntre kept his groan soft as his companion's hands when he came. His prick nudged Auslan's throat before releasing its load between generous lips. Auslan didn't spill a drop, swallowing first and licking him clean. When his efforts grew too thorough, Shyntre hissed a soft request to ease off, and the Consort surfaced at once, placing his head on the pillow.

A sparkling, scarlet gaze and warm, contented smile helped Shyntre relax He breathed out slowly, nodding, his eyelids drooping as he yawned.

"Mm. Nice."

Auslan chuckled, reaching to stroke his cheek. "I am grateful you are here, even if you haven't yet said the real reason."

Shit.

He cracked an eye. "I've said. I was brought here to make sure you became healthy."

"So I am. Thank you, again, I am grateful. I was so lonely." Auslan glanced at the secret door. "But ... what else? What do they want?"

Shyntre pointed languidly. "You waited till *now* to prod?"

"You are always at your calmest. What does the Elder Sorceress want?"

"Hmph." The wizard drifted in his afterglow, one side of his mouth forming a dry smirk. "Oh ... she wants me to 'train' you to heal without needing sex. So you'd have a function outside the bedchamber, with which she can play advocate with the Queen."

"Oh." Auslan pulled the blanket over his bare shoulder and beneath his chin. "I don't ... know if I can. I became ill when I tried."

"I know. I'm still thinking. If my Mother comes for a report, I'll tell her I needed you well, first, before we could do anything."

The Consort swallowed. "And she ... would advocate for me? As in ..."

"As in, clemency from the fate of the other Consorts, because you're a healer they can use for others besides Matrons and their Daughters."

"Oh ..." Auslan's focus fractured, flicking around the room as his thoughts turned inward. "Mm. Like ... Red Sisters?"

Shyntre rolled his eyes. "Probably." Then his sign conversation with Matron Rohenvi struck him over the head. He got up on his elbow. "Oh. Yeah, you healed Jaunda, right?"

Auslan looked embarrassed. "Yes, but it ... drained me."

"Because you didn't fuck afterward." The wizard rubbed his chin, knowing well how his brother's talents affected others. "I'm surprised she didn't just ... well, press you down."

"She would have. Matron Rohenvi would not allow it."

"That's interesting."

And a relief to hear the corroboration matched what he'd learned from

Sirana's mother.

Shyntre watched his bedmate's face grow hot, his expression one that wasn't sure how to feel about this. It made sense; Auslan would have to be familiar with Jaunda's aura by now to heal her repeatedly. He wouldn't be able to help becoming aroused.

Not after what Juliran insisted he learn under her.

How to begin untangling decades of experience like that?

"Maybe the next time the Lead comes for your healing," Shyntre suggested, "I could … watch? To help keep you safe, and maybe 'see' or sense something which might help."

His brother's eyes brightened. "Ah … so, you would ask the Elder Sorceress for permission to stay until Jaunda returns?"

Shyntre grinned. "We can take the shot, right?"

"Hm." The Consort's face warmed further. "Right."

The moment was cut short when a familiar scratch sounded behind the wall leading to the hidden door, and both buas scrambled out of bed to don some clothes.

Chapter 4

Jaunda - The Deepearth wilderness

You return, city traveler? Welcome!

Jaunda's eyes followed the easy glide of webbed, amphibious fingers, amazed how well she understood the smaller, hospitable biped.

Yutogul were not an outwardly elegant race to engage in the wilderness, with their big, dark eyes, wide mouths full of tiny, hidden teeth, and mottled, damp skin. Often hunched and bow-legged, they rose silently out of ponds, lakes, and streams, or clung to wet rocks behind waterfalls and in damp caves.

Still the only things out here glad to see me.

They seemed to know all the nooks, shortcuts, and whispers of their area, and she had never glimpsed weapons in their hands despite knowing their favorite trades involved metal tools.

I have a strong chisel and obsidian dagger, the Red Sister signed, sure by now that others hid around them. *Never rust in water. Trade for food, mediator?*

Jaunda watched the clear membrane slide over the surface of those large eyes, keeping them moist. She hesitated to call it a "blink" since the Yutogul never lost sight of her.

But I think that's a smile.

The creature gestured with clear enthusiasm. *Yes, we have food and more. Come rest. Watch with us.★

★I can't stay. Just the food.★ She paused. ★Unless you learned something new since last time?★

The Yutogul tilted their gaze. ★About the Sleeper or the Menace?★

★The Sleeper.★

Is it ever anything else?

★Could have. Related to the Menace.★

Jaunda rolled her eyes. ★You wish?★

Webbed fingers acknowledged the possibility. ★Not known to be irrelevant.★

★But useless as a lead.★

The mediator shrugged. ★Still new from last meeting.★

True.

The Valsharess *was* concerned about the mind flayers grabbing Reishel, even if Jaunda's compulsion didn't address it directly. How often did D'Shea gather threads like this, continually combing through them, swapping and threading them through Sivaraus even if something would tug on them for a century?

Jaunda couldn't keep track of that, and in a lot of cases, her Elder Sorceress didn't want her to. The Lead didn't chase or collect threads; she let them tangle and unravel on their own as long as she could keep her feet out of the loops or give them a swift cut when they threatened the whole.

Unfortunately, her Queen had made that old way impossible this time.

I've got to do something different or I'm never staying home.

With a silent sigh, Jaunda asked, ★What do you want if I stay?★

The mediator perked up, motioning toward the Red Sister's gloved hand hiding the ring which warned if Ornilleth were nearby. The Lead was convinced this negotiator was a mage of some sort to have known about it from the start, yet their water clan had not tried to steal it.

★Watch and guard for us,★ the Yutogul signed. ★Will be good time.★

Right.

The Red Sister cocked a grin. ★What's 'good' about it?★

★Spawn pool,★ the mediator answered with a light pursing of thick lips. ★Time for band clasping.★

Jaunda opened her mouth on a question but then closed it.

Was that a flirt, or were they just looking forward to it?

Spawn pool?

Yes. Clasping mates. Clusters are best for bonds and progeny, but the Menace can sense us. It uses bonding to ambush. You sense the flayers first, Queen guard. Watch us, warn us. We will trade new knowledge and a span of food even if no danger.

Jaunda stared at the mediator, her ears pricking at greater splashes around the bend which *could* be many gathering to cuddle in a smaller pool.

Time to make more of themselves, huh?

A span's worth of food was generous for a dagger and chisel, even if their information wasn't of much use.

Shows how important the timing is to them, at least.

The job was also a familiar one, too, thanks to all the orgies with the Noble crops in the Sanctuary over the decades.

How long does it take to ... spawn?

The Yutogul massaged one shoulder and the side of their neck, thinking. *Less than one cycle.*

Jaunda blinked. *That's a long time clasping.*

Why we ask for capable guard, Davrin. We give half food now, the rest and your new knowledge after.

The Queen's messenger waited to see if she felt sick at all.

Deal, she signed.

As the frolicking tightened down in the calm, hidden pool, Jaunda took a walk around the connected perimeter, keeping her senses open as she cleared the next five open spaces. Her ring was cool and quiet, and the only intrusive thought to enter her mind was the possibility of attaching her Feldeu when she took up her watch.

So far, so good.

The Yutogul had their escape route right beneath their paddling feet, while Jaunda had been introduced to hers by the mediator: a high outlook usually used by the drakes, a burrow crossing into a segment of labyrinth unattached to the main routes where larger groups could travel at speed.

Is tight, but you will fit, the mediator signed.

The Red Sister smirked with a silent nod. *I usually do.*

Satisfied to start her watch, Jaunda packed her half-span of food, made sure she could dart out in an instant, and made her simple nest in the drake outcrop above the orgy.

They sure make the water cloudy.

Although the Yutogul were water-breathers for as long as they needed to be, this "band clasping" thing seemed to need a lot more air, somehow adding the sense that this particular pool might be as important as the act. Why would they cram over thirty of them together otherwise? Leaving no room to swim but enough to rub shoulders, embracing in pairs, triads, or more.

Heh. Fun.

A group coupling like this among Davrin in Sivaraus would be pretty loud. Lots of grunting, slapping, panting, and crying. But then, they had the strong walls and magic to afford the luxury of unfettered noise.

Here, Jaunda listened carefully to the way the swimmers' breathing changed amid slightly louder splashing. The aquatic band could gasp and pant like any creature filling their chests to keep up with the sex, but they oddly never got in sync among themselves like it would have with her kind.

Over the next several marks, the Lead decided the changes in temperature were the useful measures of their progress and arousal.

Warmer. Thicker.

None of this called to her specifically, of course, she was the wrong kind and not interested in breeding anyway. But neither was it repulsive or the least bit fetid. If the Lead hadn't been guarding them, watching the entire thing, she might have dismissed the warmer vapors and wafting scents as a warm spring encouraging a brief bloom of fragrant, glowing moss and waterweed. Not a whiff of decay.

And thinking of moss, that was the other fun thing: the Yutogul glowed in the dark. Their mottled skin revealed green and blue spots Jaunda never knew they had.

A good time. Heh.

About halfway through her watch with the pool resembling uroan milk, Jaunda shifted to relieve sore spots against the stone. Growing bored though not agitated, she tugged off her gloves and pulled out her Feldeu, tracing its familiar shape and texture with her fingers, noting abrasion from normal use and travel.

Around three and a half centuries since I got my piece, and I still don't know what it's made of.

If she'd been on her regular rounds at the Cloister, Jaunda would be collecting the tools from her subordinates to drop off to the Headmaster for their usual maintenance.

Still holding up.

Moving her belt up and out of the way so she could get her leathers down to midthigh, Jaunda licked the base bulb clean of dust as she tested her slit with bare fingers. Plenty of glide from her idle observance.

She spread her thighs, cold stone with little grit pressing into her naked ass. With the wide knob wedged between her netherlips, Jaunda paused, leaning to the right to peer at the writhing pool of Yutogul. She wasn't sure if pricks of any size squeezed into holes beneath the surface, and she certainly couldn't tell which was which in that case, but the Davrin recognized a universal bliss of finger and lip touching well enough.

Even if the sensitive spots are surprising.

Jaunda pushed hard, gasping quietly at the abrupt fill and strain in her cunt. Well-worked muscles clamped down tight in welcome, the bulb damned difficult to remove even before she muttered the command word.

How well her Sisters knew that part, too. The Lead always gave the new recruits one chance to tug her Feldeu out before she used it on them. None in the last century had succeeded. Jael had come close.

Sirana hadn't really tried because that altar magic had that tight grip on her cunt. *Blue Eyes peaked from pretty much everything I did to her. Made my head spin.*

Jaunda's slit always responded to the prelude of wielding a cock, moistening, and swelling like a greedy mouth ready to gobble it down. Red Sisters never forgot how to take a cock if they wanted to keep giving it; the Prime made sure of that. But, for one reason or another, Jaunda's last lesson had been so long ago that this transition between taking and owning her Feldeu, the spreading itself, was ever fleeting.

She barely recalled what she was *supposed* to feel as a cait in Sivaraus anymore. The bodies, the roles, and expectations ... All of it kind of blended together by now, and she felt too old to be called a cait, anyway.

As the breeding clasp continued below her, the Red Sister lounged in the safe outcrop, idly stroking her renewed erection with one hand, teasing the live, sensitive head with two fingers to feel the tingle. She didn't lose focus on her ring, quite visible while she touched herself, nor did she try to mute any of her senses.

She kept at it. *Might as well relax while I can.*

Most Sisters needed someone to bend over sooner or later, to relieve the aggression and frustration which built up while wearing the magical cock. While every cait who'd ever tried the Feldeu found it infinitely preferable to those numb, humiliating bobber-belts, their own climax wasn't guaranteed. One had to *work* to get over that edge, why a fair number of the younger ones moved beyond vicious if they rutted too long.

Jaunda knew she was one of the few who'd figured out how to coax a quiet peak alone with just her hands. As a result, she could wear the enchanted appendage for longer periods of time without turning fuck-stupid. She didn't tend to brag about it, though.

Don't need extra attention from the Prime.

The Yutogul splashed more, a little louder. One of them finally hissed and huffed in a way Jaunda could recognize.

Ah. Did it feel as good as it sounded?

Her hips lifted; buttocks clenched without thinking. Her palm clasped her pole, applying firm friction. She made less noise than those she guarded, her ears and nose taking in hints that the frolicking clusters might be near a gratifying end.

Ohhh, yeah. Me, too.

Her cock quivered, her head lolled, hair falling into her face. Annoyed, she brushed damp locks from her forehead, eyes fixed on the near ceiling as the first rush uncoiled gradually between her legs. It flowed like that milky water, sweeping with accelerating speed through her gut, her pole, her chest and whole body, finally filling her head with striking pleasure.

She grunted. Muscles flexed. Body rocking gently in place until the coasting ended, her glossy glans pointed straight up. She felt the faintest caress of cool air around that tip.

Goddess ...

Heart beating in her ears, Jaunda sniffed the air, looked around for anything she had missed in those brief, eternal moments. Then, not the first time, she *really* thought someone was watching her.

Her eyes swept every quiver of Radiants on every surface, her ring merely as warm as her Feldeu.

Hum. Didn't fuck up, I guess.

Lucky this time, especially given this was the first chance she'd had to get off since the last time Auslan had healed her at House Thalluen.

Jaunda sat up, tucking her Feldeu against her belly and into her leathers without removing it for now. With pants and belt in place and minimal mess to tend to, she straightened and resumed her guard of the small, frothing pool.

The Yutogul seemed set to continue for a while longer, but a few of them had finally withdrawn, their bundles breaking up and drifting toward the fringe. She saw an oddly relatable, sleepy exhaustion on their faces before six heads dipped below the water and did not resurface.

Huh.

Jaunda peered around for the mediator, spotting them clasped with three others. *Guess that's the only one that matters to me.*

And if they all disappeared, one by one, and retracted their deal on the rest of the food and that tease of information?

Eh. I still have the chisel and dagger.

Plus, she'd tugged out some much-needed release she hadn't been able to get since the Valsharess's sentence. She came out ahead, by her view. Meanwhile, the Yutogul got their new crop of babies without "the Menace" spoiling their fun.

No one could complain if it ended that way.

It all balances out eventually.

The mediator, impressively, retained the strength to climb up to the outcrop, hauling a water-resistant bundle which had been stashed out of sight.

★Thanks,★ Jaunda signed, accepting it and taking a brief look inside.

Satisfied, she handed out the two tools promised, which the Yutogul eagerly claimed without another sign, watching as the Red Sister rebalanced her pack, adjusted her hood, and stepped toward the ledge to climb down.

★Wait,★ the mediator moved to block her. ★The new trade.★

Jaunda sighed. ★Fine. What have you heard?★

Nictitating eyelids swept over that deep gaze before they motioned toward the drake-burrow emergency escape. ★If you go that way, you pass nests. The drakes see from above as we do from below.★

★Yeah?★ The Lead smirked. ★If they do, they don't say.★

★You must watch them. They share much without talk.★

★I don't have time for that.★

★What good to rush from tunnel to tunnel?★

Jaunda shrugged. ★Sooner or later, one will have what I'm looking for.★

★But you tire, Davrin. And you are smart. Smarter than this.★

Not my doing. What do you care, anyway? Not like you'll risk guiding me away from your waters.

The Red Sister tapped fingers on her pack straps, eyes scanning the moist, quiet cave. The pool was empty, and the water looked filthy now but would clear up in the next cycle or two. The mediator rubbed the loose flesh beneath their jaw, as if pondering what else to say to persuade her to go the way of the drakes.

Go ahead. Just don't lie.

What does that way have to do with the Menace, anyway? she prompted, expecting to see a delayed recollection in ever suggesting that.

Instead, the Yutogul's concern renewed, seizing on it. *Recent thralls disturbing their nests. Unusual movement. And … possibly … * A vague hand wave. *Some of your own?*

Deep Traders, you mean?

A group possibly the least helpful to her in the entire Deepearth.

Not certain, the mediator replied.

You wouldn't be.

Jaunda shrugged. *Unusual thrall movement hunting the drakes in a remote passageway, and maybe some Davrin groups that way. Do I understand you?*

Yes, Queen's guard.

Not at all what she was searching for, and more dangerous in every respect. *Add some Tragar on top of the pile, how 'bout?*

But might not want drakes, her guide finally admitted. *No capture, just clearing nests. Could be the markings in a circle among the drakes.*

The Lead's attention jerked back. *What markings? Like, runes?*

The Yutogul bobbed its head. *Been there generations, quiet until the Menace prodded it. Now, it hums.*

Hums. A fuckin' rune circle way out here?

You could have mentioned that at the beginning, Jaunda signed dryly. *I'll squeeze in and explore that way.*

The mediator lifted their chin, looking poised before dipping their torso in thanks. *May the scent become what you seek, Davrin. Return through when you must.*

Good thing I like tight places.

Jaunda kept telling herself this around every bend, despite a few spots in that burrow where her breath hitched.

No way I would have gone this way earlier, no matter the spell.

Small bones, broken and gnawed, scraped along the rock beneath her body. She spotted scratches in the rock along with old, dry scales and coarse white hairs stuck in the creases. Occasional strips of rotting cloth stolen from caravans, and patches of soft, cooling moss used for their nests left a trail for the Red Sister to follow.

As for the rest of the desiccated, crumbling dirt beneath her elbows … Probably drake pellets.

I've crawled in worse.

Three times Jaunda needed to settle down and catch her breath, reflecting whether these contortions would be any easier without the cock pressing against her stomach. The awkward shape, quickened hunger, and heightened awareness of every shift between her legs was the cost for those short bursts of strength or speed when she needed them.

Bah. No room to take it off anyway.

Eventually, the burrow opened into an old riverbed with plenty of room to stretch — once she waited and cleared it, of course. The Lead rested on her belly, chin propped on one fist, turgid cock settled into a comfortable depression as she slowed her breath into silence. Sensing the darkness around her, she never shifted a pebble. Her ring demanded none of her attention.

Nothing nearby. Some rustling far down to the right …

Was that a squawk? She listened again.

Yes.

Yes, it was.

Fucking drakes.

The mediator hadn't lied about a detail so far, and the thought circled back to Jaunda that if Ornilleth *had* approached the Yutogul breeding frenzy, and if Jaunda *had* needed to dive out of there at once, she'd have been headed in the direction promised when they made a deal, even if she'd left half her food.

The swimmers always made it easy to work with them, even when no caravans were nearby.

Why is it like this? Does the Valsharess have some deal with them I don't know about?

Her Royal Highness hadn't mentioned anything like that, at least not while Jaunda had had her head on straight. The Lead Sister had taken the general advice which had been circling among the Deep Traders for centuries.

The Yutogul don't like to lie if they don't have to and usually offer the easiest deal to meet. If you can find 'em. No use threatening them or trying to trick them to show, though. It's never worth the time lost, they make sure of it.

They never attacked first, supposedly. The same couldn't be said for the drakes.

Or anything else in the Deepearth, for that matter.

Once her breath had settled and the way was clear, Jaunda crawled out into the dry riverbed.

Gotta keep going. Find the circle.

If it proved what she thought it might be, she might find a head-start on searching new parts of the deep for the den of the Black Dragon.

Assuming She isn't dreaming that part.

Jaunda entered the drake territory after deciding to remove, clean, and stash her Feldeu, lest she get too tense or irritated by the noise and do something stupid.

Nonetheless, the Yutogul's claim of having to watch the drakes to get their meaning seemed overstated. Most made it clear they protected their nest and food, maybe some little squirts, too, plus their own winged ass. Some spat mucous at her, others hurled air as barks or snarls.

The drakes numbered in scores, living in nests high above a narrow canyon. The convoluted path switched endlessly back and forth, rising and dropping for most of the cycle. Near the end of it, Jaunda smelled the slow-flowing water and hovering vapor of a deep stream or river.

That whole time, no drake was eager to come off the higher cliffs and ceilings to dive at her, not while she stayed away from the walls and made herself easy to see. Telling, given the known danger of a drake swarm if their nests had more empty bellies than usual.

Jaunda figured the mediator was right about recent thralls harassing them, however. These drakes were hiding rather than harassing her. A pity, that. If the little beasts couldn't say if Ornilleth thralls had been around, then Jaunda couldn't ask them about a rune circle or what the last visitor had looked like.

The Red Sister passed numerous ledges where a magic circle *could* have been but, for now, she cleared the ground-level nooks large enough to poke her head in. None of them had drake nests — too easy to attack and corner one — and what few creatures would use them as burrows so close to the drakes were too small to be a threat.

A few caves contained some old trinkets, bits of rotting cloth and leather, and dull pieces of pitted tools. The scaly thieves had been in the area for a while. She pondered ways of bribing the drakes, maybe with the Yutogul food, to let her climb up and take a peek on their ledges without getting her nose bitten off.

Might work, but I need to clear the canyon first.

It was a long stretch.

Shortly before the deep water and dead-end came into view, something Jaunda had taken for a stone on her left disappeared out of her periphery. She paused, noting the way the Radiants subtly lost warmth. A sign consistent with a body having sat there for a while yet failed to show a trail leading where the heat source had gone.

Hm. That's new.

The fled creature wasn't anywhere near her size. She could assume another sneaking drake kept watch.

Stories say they can vanish in a breath and escape any cage.

Within moments, Jaunda's compulsion urged her to return the way she came without much of a rest, making careful notes on the ledges she'd missed before. Again, the nesters hid, hissed, and snarled if she drifted too close to the walls but declined to attack her as a group. They didn't even seem too curious about what she carried.

You all gotta smell the fish. What the fuck happened to make you hermits?

The Red Sister traveled up the canyon a second time, reaching the point where she'd first come out of the burrow and taking a second cycle of supplies to do it. By then, her back and leg muscles burned.

Back where I started, and a quarter of my food gone. Great.

So pointless. Why force a wandering mission with random sickness and vague feelings? All of it attached to a Davrin who *wasn't* a mage! She could have walked by the rune circle *twice* and she'd have had no clue she missed it. She felt drab the whole time, like she was failing some test whose end was just out of reach.

Doesn't matter. Turn around.

The Lead started to walk away but stopped on her left boot, turning her ear toward the burrow.

Something scratched the stone, farther back.

Unpanicked. Deliberate crawling.

Had something followed her from the Yutogul pool?

Huh.

At least the Queen's spell allowed self-defense.

The Red Sister set up a stakeout to wait with eyes on the burrow. *Shouldn't take long.*

Gradually, the tiny scratch which had attracted her attention drew closer but didn't get much louder. Definitely a body like hers, shifting and shuffling in a belly-crawl as she had through that passage. What she assumed was the head appeared, a dark-wrapped blob without much definition.

Could be Pyte, Ketro, Tragar, anything except the drakes or fish-people themselves ...

When the rest of the body slid out and scaled down the stone to solid ground, it became obvious.

Davrin. Fuck me.

Jaunda blinked as a second one followed the first. *Goddess damn it. How many followed me? Did the negotiator give me away?*

She waited, read their body language and their hands as easily as if she'd been standing next to them.

Just the two.

They were dressed to conceal their hair, ears, features, and tools, their profiles low enough to squeeze into small places with minimal chance of getting snagged or stuck.

They made it through there faster than I did.

She admired their movement as, with little effort, they slipped into a crease of rock and crouched down. They must have hidden near her a few times, but she'd missed them, because their hands gave away that they were following her.

For how long?

The Lead's body warmed as a smirk lifted one corner of her mouth.

Let's find out, sweetmeats.

Chapter 5

The Lead Sister waited out her concealed stalkers with her own hood covering her hair. This interval was not without a lingering regret that she hadn't pissed in a while.

Time passed in silence, and finally her targets emerged and began to track her. She waited for them to pass, allowing them to move deeper into the drake canyon, until her Dark Sight lost track of their outlines. She still heard their careful footfalls.

Worn, soft boots like mine.

One of them — the shorter one without a cloak — had a longer blade across her back which Jaunda had missed as they crawled out. The weapon was expertly padded and strapped to resist shifting from the torso or clinking with metal. The grip didn't readily appear to her sight, either: both matted against light reflection and its outline somehow broken up and muted to Dark Sight.

Clever. Who made that?

She'd tossed the idea they might be Red Sisters, having discarded earlier that they could be from the Queen's Army.

Any in the Fringe camp that good get recruited into the Sisterhood fast.

Most likely, these were elite House Guard from a higher Matron.

Cute.

The Lead could incapacitate them, requiring her to either interrogate or dispatch them. The time she'd take on the task would probably be interrupted by dwindling food or the Queen's invisible push.

Could I fuck them first?

Such impulses had consequences; she knew from centuries as a Sister. More surprising was the meddling memory of the healer-Consort's touch and Rohveni's complete denial to indulge herself with him, which had been followed by the geas preventing so much as a short break from her mission to ram a willing Sister.

Been alone with my own hand for quad-spans out here.

Still, a pleasure hunt would make a lot of noise and might set off the drakes somehow, never mind drawing what else might be living within earshot. That hadn't mattered with the Surfacers and the pale Elf; the Red Sister had confirmed the tunnels near the exit barren of anything large enough to be a threat.

Not so underneath Sivaraus. Creatures large enough to be a problem thrived down here. She'd follow them as far as they'll go. Maybe negotiate, find out why they were here and who they work for.

Probably the only smart move.

Their response would determine what happened after that.

Jaunda didn't let the pair get too far ahead in case the drakes sounded off twice in their annoyed scuffling as the Davrin invaded their nesting grounds. The winged reptiles did not attack, however, and the couple in front of her were wary but not inexperienced in tracking through wild areas. They betrayed no fear of the creatures above them.

Hmm.

Soon enough, Jaunda had reached the point where either the drakes would give the Lead away or the unknown trackers might realize her trail doubled back and would meet her face-to-face.

The Red Sister would let it play out.

Almost a mark later as Jaunda approached another bend, she slowed to listen and smell the air before she eased around. *Closer.* They'd slowed down, and she saw why.

The black-clad Davrin with the sword had spotted something which made her turn around and creep in Jaunda's direction. The other cait had hidden as back-up.

Not bad.

The tracker wore a mask over her lower face, most expression obscured when she spotted Jaunda and froze a split-instant before shifting a foot and lifting her hands.

She knew how to fight.

Jaunda grinned, raising one hand to sign, ★Where you from?★

The masked Davrin weighed the response, moving one hand in a neutral tone without threat. ★Low Gate.★

Heh.

★Me, too.★ The Lead tilted her head. ★Who's your top?★

Jaunda wasn't sure if the eye movement — the only part of the face she could see — was confusion or panic. Visible eyebrows might have helped.

The Davrin moved back. ★Who is yours?★

The Lead gleaned neither a flicker nor tell which might've given away her partner. Jaunda pretended like she wasn't there and smirked. ★The Elder Prime.★

As if that wasn't obvious from her uniform, even without the color. The tracker wasn't surprised, either. Probably a delay tactic to get a few nerves under control as Jaunda waited for an answer.

After a pause, she signed, ★You gonna surprise me or not?★

The other's gaze held steady after a blink. Jaunda took a step forward; her stalker took a step back. A few drakes above their heads hissed and gurgled in their throats. The Red Sister never took her eyes away, though her ears waited for any other warning. Meanwhile, her target hesitated to respond.

Is she struggling with what answer to give?

They couldn't be out here on their own, could they?

Jaunda nearly tipped her hand from impatience to suggest they already knew who she was, that they could name their target in the deep tunnels. She imagined D'Shea here doing the questioning, however, and waited, keeping her hands still to offer nothing more.

Finally, the tracker signed, ★Mission within a mission, Red Sister.★

Jaunda scoffed, rolling her eyes, but froze when something shifted above again. This time, the tracker's eyes flicked upward.

Fine.

★Don't look like any Sister of mine,★ Jaunda signed as she took two more steps forward. ★None of us use a sword like that. Will you draw it or not? Show me.★

The tracker backed up, watching her hands without preparing a reply. At the end of her question, the Lead flicked a pellet she'd been palming toward her target's feet. The black-clad figure spotted the motion, summoning an extraordinary spring to her step before flipping backward. Outstretched hands touched the stone twice before the nubile body swept upright and regained her feet.

If it had been a real web or powder pellet, she would have escaped its reach.

Now I know why this one doesn't wear a cloak.

Jaunda grinned as the drakes emitted warning hisses and snarls in their nests at the disturbance. She signed, ★Still not drawing that sword?★

Empty hands signed, ★Sister, not Army or House Guard — !★

She read no more, rushing the shorter Davrin and colliding with a hard shove that should have taken her off her feet. The tracker rolled with the momentum and within a gasp was on the balls of her feet again.

Sire-fucker.

The Lead took a swing at her head to keep her moving farther from her partner, risking the chance to rush the dexterous stalker a second time. Instead of pushing, her strong hands gripped dark cloth too tightly for her target to jump away. A drake squawked loudly as they struggled for a flick.

"No, stop!" the watcher cried out.

Definitely a cait.

"Keep back," Jaunda growled as she swung the tracker along with her, the shorter one's boots clearing the ground.

They settled into a nearby crevice that would shield them from any pitched weapon, and Jaunda slammed her captive against the stone to knock the air out of her. It didn't work well enough thanks to that sword crossing her back. The rough, uncomfortable grunt was satisfying even before she snatched hold of her throat with one hand, squeezing hard enough to stop breath.

"Let him go!"

Jaunda paused, staring at wide, alarmed eyes as air wheezed through open lips hidden by cloth. She reached to grab the Davrin's crotch, and he flinched in her grip, dangling like a landed fish.

Has all the soft parts a bua should. Fuck me.

"Let him go, Red Sister," the other cait demanded, betraying her anger as she hovered outside the crevice. "Or I promise you'll regret it."

"That a threat?" Jaunda rumbled.

"A warning. He will be missed, even if injured and taken out of the fight."

The . . . fight?

Against the wall with his feet on the stone, the masked bua stared in silence, concentrating solely on breathing. There were a few things he could have done to attempt an escape if he was trained in any way beyond backflips, but he offered no "warnings" of his own.

Meanwhile, the drakes quieted their snarls. A few wings flapped and scaled bodies slithered closer, curious about the scuffle.

"Why are you following me?" Jaunda asked him directly.

He didn't strain to speak; he didn't have to. Lifting one hand from the grip on her bracers, the bua signed, *Mission within mission. Test within test.*

"By whose order?"

His eyes crinkled at the corners. The bua should have pissed himself or at least been quaking, avoiding eye contact, but he wasn't. All she had was a speeding pulse beneath her thumb.

May I retrieve something, Lead? he asked. *To show you. No trick.*

Jaunda arched an eyebrow, refraining from looking toward the cait outside the crevice but knowing she didn't have infinite time before the angry protector might try something. Her scent was becoming sour.

64

Fine. Show me.

The masked bua nodded slightly and reached slowly for something attached to his belt behind him. It took time and concentration to detach it, and Jaunda loosened her fist, giving him more air to work with. He took it gratefully, the rapid blink of his eyes suggesting he'd been growing lightheaded.

The armed tracker pulled out a damaged piece of armor. *A bracer.*

It looked familiar.

"So?" she asked.

"Look with light," the cait grumbled.

Sigh.

Jaunda released the bua and took firm hold of the bracer, reaching for a low glowstone with her other hand. Her body blocked his escape unless he wanted to fight his way out of the crevice or encourage the cait to jump her.

Yeah, try.

Smirking, the Lead whispered for the lowest glow of her stone. The bright red leather became instantly identifiable.

Red Sister armor.

Not just that. Abrasions suggested both normal wear and some recent conflict. There was a weird, dried substance staining most of it, and a faint but memorable scent that Jaunda had breathed in before.

The Ornilleth prison.

The Sisterhood had recovered all Sirana's gear from the site. The only way these two could have gotten a piece was through the Sisterhood. *Not possible.* In any case, Sirana's armor hadn't been smeared with this mind flayer slime.

The explanation for this chilled Jaunda's gut. *Reishel.*

"Alright, bua," she admitted. "You have my attention."

He exhaled softly but, before he could sign more, the cait spoke, clipping her tone shy of a demand.

"Then let him out so we can talk."

"Watch it, cait, unless you have no clue who you've been following." Jaunda twisted her neck and winked, tucking the scrap of Reishel's gear on her belt. "If you don't, continue to push me. It'll be fun."

The bua waved politely for her attention and signed more calmly than his partner. *I am Vik. She is Halena. We are here to help, Lead Sister.*

Alright, that was a good start.

Jaunda grunted softly, noting some movement on the canyons' walls which were making Halena nervous. "Again, by who's order? Not the Queen."

Vik shook his head once, his eyes ticking to the side.

Fuckin' bold.

Jaunda doused her glowstone, slipped it into its pouch, and lifted her hands for her next question. *Help me how? You know why I'm wasting time out here?*

A jolt of pain stabbed her in the gut, and she curled her lip.

Vik's eyes seemed wary. *No, we do not.*

Then how you going to help?

*We've … been sent — *

Who sent you?

*By our Third — *

Who the fuck is that?

* — to find the Rin'oveaus.*

Jaunda gritted her teeth, forcing her aggravated hands to pause. *The who?*

Deep mercenaries, Vik signed. *They frequently guard and guide the Deep traders. They know the labyrinth down here. They can find anything.* The bua motioned to Reishel's armor piece. *They found that. Traded it to us recently.*

Us? Traded it where?

"*Psst, psst!*" Halena hissed, drawing Jaunda's attention to a drake which had its head partly wedged into the peak of the rock crevice. She held a rock, preparing to throw it.

"Wait —" Vik said.

Too late.

The dark reptile darted away from the stone and scuttled out of view but within moments prepared its response, releasing the loudest, ear-spiking shriek Jaunda had heard in a while.

"*Eeeeeeyaauup-yaup-yaup!*"

"*Augh, fuck!!*"

Her hands snapped to her ears above anything else, and Vik and Halena staggered while the cry bounced and reverberated around them. The canyon grew much louder as drakes emerged to defend their nesting grounds.

Aw, shit.

"Can't sense magic, can you?" the Red Sister growled, pushing Vik out of the tiny crevice with a one-handed shove.

"Huh?" he stuttered.

Halena reached to pull him closer to her and a greater distance from the Lead. One drake swept low over their heads in an attempt to dust their brains.

"The Yutogul said there was a magic circle in here! I'm looking for that!"

Jaunda tossed a handful of sneezing powder at three drakes preparing to dive off a boulder. They retreated before getting a deep sniff, though they began to cough. One utterly vanished.

"Magic circle?"

"Can't go back, but the far end stops at water," she snarled, keeping watch around them, noticing the swelling flaps of skin as a few new drakes sucked in air, preparing to blow her dust back at them.

The little fuckers *were* smart!

"This way!"

A trio of drakes puffed the Red Sister's powder into a cloud which Jaunda avoided but the other two were caught briefly. The canyon filled with alarmed squawking and flapping wings.

"Come on!"

"*Kaff! Kaff! Kaff!*"

"And answer me!" she bellowed over her shoulder. "Are you mages?"

"N-no!" Vik choked as Halena shook her head desperately.

Great.

Three mundane Davrin looking for a rune circle.

Some help.

Jaunda and her stalkers ducked three more air attacks, her ears baffled by odd bursts of air and amplified hisses. Quickly, she realized that if the nesting beasts had *wanted* to collide and drop onto them to bite their flesh, they could have.

They just want us out.

So did she.

"Nothing lethal unless they draw blood first!" she barked.

"What?" Halena yelped, nearly tripping when Vik stabilized her.

"No weapons! No more rocks unless you want your bones picked clean."

The bua jerked his head in a nod. "Understood, Lead."

At least he's smart enough.

But how to get the fuck out of this place? The cycle-long canyon was a dead end both ways for sprinting Davrin, and they wouldn't stumble over the rune circle at this pace.

Vik never reached for his sword and Halena, it turned out, had a crossbow strapped under her cloak. Jaunda saved her web pellets simply because she didn't have enough to ensnare them all, and she certainly wasn't going to pitch all her daggers at them.

For another mark, the drakes harried them in groups of three or four, falling back to rest on the upper ledges before surging forward on the wing to keep them moving. Jaunda and her two spies figured out the pattern and took opportunities to slow down and catch their breath when they could.

Finally, the Red Sister spotted a glint of yellow in the depths of darkness.

A familiar glint.

As they ran closer, she realized the glint was a tiny pair of eyes in retreat; probably another drake scurrying up the wall to a ledge. It paused to look down, eyes glowing. The outline was missing a pair of wings.

What the fuck?

They'd entered a part of the canyon Jaunda remembered because it had seemed like a gap in the drake nests. Plenty of noise behind them, some alarm rising ahead, but not a lot where they were.

Jaunda stopped; Halena collided against her.

"Watch it," she grumbled, squinting up at the shelf.

Neither spy chose to speak or sign.

"Can you see that?" she asked as the creature slithered into deep shadow.

Vik whispered with caution. "See what, Lead?"

She could detect no scratching or snuffling up there, and the harrying drakes had dropped back, at last stopping their squawks, choosing not to pursue them farther.

"A cave up there. To the left, about two-third up."

They looked; Halena murmured, "Maybe."

"I'm gonna check."

"Lead —" Vik began.

"Come with if you have a 'test within a test.' Or don't."

They stayed close with no interest to go their own way.

Fine.

Maybe some hodge-podge of mercenaries willing to trade with Darvin could offer another lead after the Yutogul.

Assuming this rune circle turns out to be bunk.

Jaunda reached the spot underneath the cave and started climbing, seeking firm holds before pulling herself higher.

"Stay there," she ordered. "I'll check if it's occupied."

The pair obeyed without speaking aloud, and she couldn't see any sign they might have shared. That didn't matter, though, as she had to be cautious peeking over the ledge once she reached it. She did smell ... *something* that belonged in the wilderness, but not drake shit, nesting scraps, or gnawed bones.

The Lead paused, listening, hearing nothing inside. The beast might have vanished like a few of them seemed to or held still at the rear. Maybe waiting to ambush.

Jaunda exhaled slowly through her nose, prepared a web pellet, and showed her head to the cave.

Nothing launched out to try to bite it off.

In fact, the longer she waited, the more sure she was that the cave was empty.

Alright.

The Red Sister climbed with care onto the ledge, prepared to snare anything that came at her. Soon, she regained her feet, reaching for her glowstone with her other hand. Sniffing the dusty air, she summoned the dimmest bit of pale light by which to see the floor.

Motherfucker.

Runes carved into stone. Clean-edged, unbroken, and familiar.

Jaunda smirked, clearing the rest of the cave before leaning out where the other two could see her. She signed for them to join her before ducking back to the circle. Using a cloth, she dusted some of the grit away to create greater contrast in the glow light.

"The Yutogul said this was here," she murmured, turning her head. "Have any idea where it leads?"

"Uh. No, Lead. We didn't know it was here."

Still odd that the bua was doing all the talking. In fact, now that Vik wasn't cornered with Jaunda separating the two, Halena was much calmer. She might be humbled for causing that skirmish with the drakes.

Jaunda finished her dusting and stood up, turning around. "So you followed me with a suggestion to … what? Return the way we came to find the Rin'oveaus?"

The spies shook their heads, and Vik said, "The water at the end leads out. There are a few air pockets to get to the next system."

Ah. Yeah, that would have been the thing to try without knowing about this ring.

Jaunda gestured. "Wanna go this way?"

Halena bit her lip. "What if we can't jump back?"

"*Pfeh.* What if we reach Sivaraus? That'd be worse." The Red Sister chuckled, dousing the glowstone's light by slipping it into its pouch. "In your scenario, we'll ask about the Rin'oveaus where we are, and start walking back. Or swimming, who knows? Either way, I'll be going this way."

"You know how to use it, Lead?" Vik asked.

"Of course."

"But you can't read the runes? Maybe they give a hint where it leads."

"Nope." She grinned, hands on her hips. "Just that Davrin mages made them."

For their mission, that had to be good enough.

Certainly is for mine.

The three of them stood in the circle, reacclimating to complete darkness. The pair watched as Jaunda closed her eyes and concentrated on the piece of imbued gold buried beneath her skin above her left breast. For a moment, she thought her newer ring warmed in response.

Her eyes flew open.

What is it? the two asked together.

Nothing.

The feeling was gone as soon as it came.

"Give me a tick," Jaunda muttered, refocusing on the familiar trigger for jump circles. It should work.

Eventually, the insertion responded again, sending a spike of magic through her heart. Clenching her fists, she saw the runes behind her eyelids when they lit up in yellow and red.

Jump.

The runes obeyed.

The three Davrin vanished within the jump circle, its predetermined distance folding in on itself, sending the Elves of Sivaraus elsewhere in the Deepearth.

CHAPTER 6

SOME SMELLS WERE UNFAMILIAR BUT MOST RECOGNIZABLE. THEY STOOD SOME-where without light, bare stone beneath their boots, and if there were water, it lay too far to hear the drips or trickling current.

Good for the circle or it might be covered in lichen and slippery moss or slimy shit.

Jaunda held still, testing her new companions' patience as she gave her senses time to pick up all they could. A single-entry crevice appeared before her eyes, like the one they'd left behind but without the squawking drakes and distant water. The protected space was just large enough for the three of them to lie down in Reverie outside the circle if they wanted.

Her ears picked up an odd breeze but no sentient voices, bootsteps, or crawlers. A few startled skitters emptied their hidden crevice but nothing too large. She detected the soft buzz of flying insects, maybe some jumpers, which meant good things for finding food and water.

Wait here, the Red Sister signed, stepping slowly enough out of the circle to avoid the noise which might give them away.

Cautiously, she poked her head out, appraising the single tunnel out-side and below them. They would have to climb down roughly as far as they'd climbed at the canyon. Her nose and the skin of her cheeks recognized a passage with clean, open air moving in its own current.

72

Not caved in, not disrupted by water or magma, yet not frequently traveled. Either undiscovered or too remote off the trade routes.

Why, then, would someone build that first circle in the middle of a drake canyon to come here? Had something been here? How old was it, anyway, and who used it most?

It still worked for me. Weird to think about now. Jaunda twisted her neck, peering each way. *So, which way?*

They looked the same, unremarkable. One way was as good as the other, at least until they found something. Jaunda turned around, pausing to notice Vik and Halena had stepped out of the circle, but she hadn't heard them.

Hm. Pretty good.

The bua studied the walls, first by Dark Sight and then by touch. Halena watched his back, less curious about what he was doing and more concerned with Jaunda.

The Lead met the other cait's eyes and grinned, signing, ★Safe for a glowstone. No drakes guarding this passage.★

The masked female blinked in surprise but tapped Vik's shoulder and repeated the same sign. He brought out one of his own stones to inspect the walls. The rock shone.

The exposed veins of raw silver and gold were subtle, in strips thin enough not to jump out to their Dark Sight. The metal decorated the crevice, draping delicately above and around the rune circle carved in the floor. Jaunda didn't have an eye for spotting raw gems, but she would wager this place would have some. Oddly, upon close inspection, not one silver or gold vein showed *within* the worn floor itself.

The Tragar would love to find this place.

Vik scratched at some of the metal with his gloved finger as if trying to pry off a piece. Not easy, as it turned out, and he gave up in favor of looking around.

Jaunda could wait and see if he found something else interesting. She kept her ear at the edge of the shelter while Halena kept eyes on her. How were these two supposed to help her again?

And who fucking sent them?

Although she'd stroked to a good peak not long ago, the gradual takeover of Davrin warmth and scents in this new location threatened to distract her. Halena glowering at her didn't help; challenges like that were a turn-on for the Lead, especially as she wondered idly about their partnership.

Do they fuck each other on rest breaks?

And was that protective jealousy the Lead saw in the cait's narrowed eyes? Or was this a bodyguard taking her task seriously?

Relax, Hal. Side-by-side, I'd choose your ass over his.

Unless Vik offered first, of course. Jaunda wouldn't refuse, especially with slim pickings out here. He might enjoy it. She'd regularly met Noble bua in Sivaraus as curious as they were terrified when she stood in the same room.

The Houses all knew the gossip about her "torture weapon," and the Lead had obliged several half-erect Nobles who, according to her Elder, hadn't done anything wrong. Jaunda always found some small transgression, giving them what they hinted for on their safe, soft bed. She always made sure their bodies would remember their "punishment" for several cycles afterward in case the spurt stains on their sheets didn't remind them often enough.

Keep the rep of the Sisterhood going.

*Hehh … mmrrmm … *

Jaunda blinked and craned her neck, pointing her ear at varied angles to catch the air current in the open tunnel below. She couldn't see as much thanks to Vik's light, but that shouldn't affect her ears. Yet, she wasn't sure if that rumbling murmur had come from farther out in either direction or was a trick of the draft.

Odd.

Jaunda reined in the direction of her thoughts then, paying closer attention to their surroundings. These two weren't from among the Noble stock, anyway, but supposedly came from the same place she had.

Davrin in Low Gate got no benefit from *I'm-curious-but-I-shouldn't* games, so they didn't play them. A trade only. Even then, risks would be involved.

Same thing here. If I want to fuck either of them, it's by trade or by force.
★Good to know.★

The Lead's heart surged, heat bursting through her chest and spreading out. She straightened up and peered around, sniffing and tasting the air in case something intentionally messed with her ears.

Vik turned around before Halena could tap his shoulder. ★What is it, Lead?★

Jaunda grimaced as she hesitated at first. ★Did you hear a whisper just now?★

Predictably, she read their concern.

★Ornilleth?★

Fuck, I hope not.

★No. But you *didn't* hear anything?★

They shook their heads once.

Great. Have I dulled my edge already?

Jaunda frowned. ★What about any yellow eyes in the tunnels?★

★What about it?★ Halena asked with a mix of unease and irritation.

★Heard about anything like that? Or seen it?★

Vik shook his head. ★No, not really. Stories of yellow eyes come from Sivaraus.★

The Sathoet. Yeah. Jaunda exhaled silently, ear trained to the tunnel. *But yellow eyes led us here.*

That small, wingless drake had climbed up and disappeared. *A yellow-eyed drake.* All the other drakes she'd seen had black or red eyes.

She would need to check this out; she couldn't refuse.

Then maybe get so far from Sivaraus, I'll never make it back. Goddess damn it.

The Red Sister wrinkled her nose, shook out the lingering sense of dread, and signed to Vik, ★So, any thoughts on this cave?★

The masked bua shrugged. ★I am not a miner, but the veins of ore seem odd to me. It's hard to explain why.★

★Try.★

When he just looked at her, Jaunda prompted, ★Anything to do with why the floor or rune circle doesn't have ore?★

He motioned an affirmative. ★It is as if the metal was molten and seeped into the smallest cracks from above like dripping water but stopped before it reached the floor.*

Fuckin' weird. Jaunda looked behind her again. *Sooo, stay here and wait a while or go exploring?*

Her flayer detection ring was quiet, and this place *somewhat* looked like a den of the sort she sought. She didn't feel sick thinking of staying or going, but her heart thumped harder than she liked.

Could she be much closer to her goal than she thought? Had the Yutogul known? Surely, they hadn't been the ones to build the rune circle. Only Davrin could have, right?

Argh. I'm not built for this kind of scheming.

I want to check out the tunnel, Jaunda signed. *Both ways. I'll come here for Reverie. You can stay.*

The bua lifted his chin. *Let us come with you, Lead.*

I travel faster alone.

Fast is only worthwhile if you know the destination.

The Lead paused. *Point.* Then she smirked. *And if we find what I'm looking for before we find the mercenaries?*

You're not looking for mind flayers, right? Halena asked.

Nope, looking to avoid them.

Then we will come, Vik replied with confidence.

Jaunda grinned at him, adjusting her pack for the first time since they arrived. *Fine. Douse the light. We'll climb down when Dark Sight kicks in.*

Having no better ideas between them, the traveling Davrin took the relatively flat path to the left. At first, Vik was curious if the ore veins had spread out from that one cave, but they agreed using light wasn't wise on the first walk through.

Maybe on the way back.

In the meantime, the tunnel's twists weren't too steep nor the turns sharp. After two marks, Jaunda thought they could be getting closer to water based on the various growths which appeared on the stones. The creepers and crawlers within them were familiar enough to feel connected to the deep routes but the collective scents smelled different enough to know they were spans' worth of walking out from Sivaraus.

Just no idea how far, after that jump.

They could probably go back the same way, though.

Hopefully the drakes won't be waiting for us.

Jaunda stopped when she heard a soft, low rumble. Almost like ... *A laugh?*

Vik and Halena paused to stare at her like they hadn't picked it up.

At the same time, the Valsharess's ring pulsed with concerning heat again, identical to the moment before they used the jump circle. She inspected the ground around their feet, her tagalongs doing the same with even less insight.

We're nowhere near the circle. And now the feeling's gone ...

On the edge of her hearing, the quiet rumble sounded again, making her think of falling water. *A river, maybe?*

If no one *had* made that laugh and the noise was a rolling body of water bouncing around, then she had a nickname in mind for this new system.

I'm gonna call it the Tittering Shafts.

★Ha! Disparaging to some of those with *a shaft but not bad.★*

Jaunda slowed, rubbing her eyes against the blurry sensation in her head. The voice was low and murmuring. Was that her talking to herself?

Fuck. Been out here alone too long.

★Not to worry. You're not alone anymore. Look, you've brought friends.★

Her heart pounded in her ears now, loud enough for the two spies to hear, which set them on edge at once.

Vik tapped her arm to draw her eyes. ★Lead? What do you sense?★

Halena's face pinched with concern as she looked ahead. ★Should we turn back?★

*★Oh, please don't. You are **so** close.★*

Shit.

Jaunda swallowed nausea but couldn't tell if the Queen was being a cunt or this was a natural desire to puke from abject fear. She raised one hand. *I think ... I found what I was looking for. You might want to leave.*

They won't.

We can't, Lead, Vik answered. *We were sent to find the Rin'oveaus first, but then we were sent after you.*

Why?

Because like you, we're running out of time to come through with something Sivaraus can use to defend itself. We know the conclave is growing restless.

Bright bua. You should listen to him.

Fuck.

Alright, she signed, beckoning them to follow to the end and wherever the winding tunnel would lead.

Jaunda focused her breath against the tension as she led the way, managing to slow her heart and avoid explicit thoughts about not making it out of ... whatever trouble was coming. The nausea had receded, and the male voice was quiet for now. Her geas was satisfied with her actions.

I think.

The Red Sister was aware she was required to wager everything on the hope that they *hadn't* jumped in right next to the conclave without knowing and that this *wasn't* the Elder Mind playing tricks to lure them in.

At least Vik and Halena didn't seem to be acting any different, and her ring was cool and quiet.

Still ...

Was this how Reishel had felt there at the end? Had it been like this, calm and reassuring, with a sense of knowing where to go? Had the urge to struggle and survive vanished?

Hmm. Often it is. Not always. It depends on the mind.

The Lead made a face in the dark, noting as the voice in her head sounded bigger somehow, but more ... male.

Not reassuring, whoever you are.

You know who I am. You're managing your nerves quite well for a mundane.

Jaunda smirked. *You'd like me to think so.*

Oh no, it's all you, Red Sister. I haven't taken anything from you but a bit of privacy.

Why, you bored?

Heh. You could say that. I'm delighted you've tried so hard to find me.

The calluses on her feet would attest to the effort so far. When her legs carried her around the last bend, her nose filled with water vapor. She could hear a distant waterfall in a new landscape straight ahead.

Rising from a deep chasm. A canyon.

Very good. Come meet me at the edge, Red Sister. I look forward to seeing you.

Jaunda stopped, and Vik nearly ran into her. He caught his squeak in his throat before it escaped, and Halena drew him away with a hand on his shoulder.

Who sent you? the Lead asked yet again. *If you are capable of saying, say it now.*

Why? Halena demanded. *What's wrong?*

The Lead was convinced they hadn't heard so much as a whisper of him. Her hand wavered. *Because I'm not ... capable.*

... of saying why we are here.

Patience, Sister.

Vik looked to be taking her seriously but shrugged his shoulders. *We can't leave without you, Lead. We can't use the circle. We don't know where we are. It could take half a turn to reach the city.*

But we still can't tell you, Halena insisted. *We'd put a lot of common Davrin in danger. Maybe even Matrons.*

Jaunda scowled. *And you think just standing here being cryptic won't get forced out of me by the Valsharess? Then they'll be hunting for you.*

They were shocked. Alarmed about the direct link with the Queen.

Not good.

No, it's not.

Do you not report to the Elder Sorceress? Vik signed, swallowed.

Isn't that breaking the chain of command?

Smart bua.

Jaunda's heart continued pounding, and she ground her teeth. *If you know about a restless conclave, you must know about what happened with the Sisterhood to spur that.*

Not … really, Lead, the masked bua admitted.

Fuck.

We're not told everything on our missions outside Sivaraus for a reason, Halena said. *Same as you. If someone catches and interrogates us.*

Fair enough.

The deep, male voice chuckled under the drone of the falls.

Finally, Vik looked ahead with concern. *Who is up there?*

My objective, Jaunda signed. *And I know as much as you do, apparently. I can't guarantee a goddess-damned thing for your safety or freedom, but it would help to know who pushed you into the shit river with me *before* we move on to the chasm up ahead.*

That it would.

Vik and Halena exchanged looks; their eyes fused for several moments as they argued without words. The cait showed alarm at the consequences of compromising their contacts. The bua had accepted they were fucked if Jaunda reported directly to the Valsharess about this. They struggled in silence to decide, both heartbeats audible alongside hers.

The Elder General, Vik signed before he could second-guess.

Jaunda stared down at him.

But not … directly, he clarified. *We're not under the Sisterhood.*

Obviously, but still …

Rausery's behind this?

Interesting. I am glad to see she's still trying new things.

Fuckin' goddess.

Mmrrm. We'll see.

Jaunda pursed her lips, watching her two spies. Or maybe they were real back-up in some way she didn't grasp. They accepted the objective without knowing the full scope and credited Elder Rausery.

Not like Red Sisters don't do the same.

Assuming they were telling the truth.

They are, but they're protecting someone.

Jaunda refrained from rolling her eyes. *You wanna tell me what's going on, mind-sneak?*

Absolutely not. Such information is never for free.

Didn't she know it?

What is the matter, Lead? Vik asked after waving his hand at her. *You keep acting like you're listening to someone.*

She hesitated with her hand lifted then motioned with her jaw toward the end of the tunnel. Then she said aloud, "I am. Mostly sure it's not a mind flayer, though."

Vik looked wary and, finally, Halena gave in, folding her arms and exhaling as she looked at her bua companion. She whispered under her breath, "We're fucked."

Jaunda heard another chuckle in her head.

But we'll stick with you, Vik added, not yet ready to use his voice on this side of the jump circle.

Her end-goal hummed in higher pitch, with glee. The Lead shook her head and started walking toward him.

This will be fun.

At least tell me, am I walking toward your den?

You are, Queen's messenger.

She picked up her pace to a jog, letting the others overcome their surprise and hurry to catch up.

Chapter 7

A SHORT, STONE LEDGE SPREAD OUT BEYOND THE END OF THE TUNNEL. As Jaunda approached it, her senses confirmed a massive chasm with both a ceiling too high and a bottom too low to see either one with Dark Sight.

The waterfall is to the left. Still a long way off.

Correct. If I were you, I'd not seek it out unless I had a specific purpose to do so.

The Lead paused at the right-side limit of cover, craning her neck to peer up at the wall above before exposing herself on the ledge. *Why not?*

She received the impression of a sharp, hungry grin hovering in the darkness.

The very worst you can imagine is not far from there. They would love to discover you.

The worst I can imagine are the Ornilleth. Or you.

Then you have an under-worked imagination.

The Red Sister detected nothing clinging to the walls above or to the sides but remained in place as Vik and Halena slipped in beside her with backs to the rock and waited.

Gradually, Jaunda's sight made out another ledge on the far side of the chasm and another tunnel roughly level to where she stood. As if there might have once been a stone bridge.

Will you step out where I can see you?

Can't you already?

Not with my waking eyes.

This chasm isn't your den, is it?

No.

Your hunting grounds?

He chuckled. *The whole of the Deepearth are my hunting grounds if you would be concerned about that.*

She drew in air through her nose and smelled nothing.

Where are you?

On the ledge. I've been waiting for a while.

Jaunda heard someone around the corner and to the right, sniffing the air. Was he sitting? Or lying down? Was he really there?

I know your scents much better now. I can track you if necessary.

Good bluff. I can't smell you.

He exhaled. "I know you are there."

Vik's and Halena's bodies jolted in place beside her.

"Come on out, won't you?"

The quiet, polite voice speaking in their native tongue, much different than the humored, bass rumble in Jaunda's head. They realized an instant after her how near the source was.

Who is that? Vik signed.

He and Halena looked confused, as they should be. This physical voice sounded normal, though the accent was a little odd.

Jaunda took a steady breath and stepped out. Her hands clear and empty but her body ready, she turned to face the figure sitting on the ground. The stranger's back was pressed to the wall, knees drawn up to rest his arms. Even without light, she could tell his skin was smooth and dark, his hair stark white and cut short.

He lifted his face to Jaunda and smiled with normal teeth. Not a bestial fang to be seen.

Goddess, why did he look … *Familiar?*

Do I? Why is that?

"Your eyes," she said aloud.

"Oh?" he replied, extending his limbs to stand up.

As the apparent Davrin straightened out, Jaunda noted he wore a drab, common outfit which drew no sensual attention to his form. He was shorter than her but was obviously athletic compared to many buas, kind of like Vik.

The exceedingly short hair was unusual, though. Jaunda usually preferred hers cropped close like that — low fuss and staying out of her eyes — but she'd been so busy since the Ornilleth escaped that it had grown out long enough to be aggravating.

The truly striking trait, however, was his eyes, because the Lead was *certain* she'd seen that shape aplenty.

All over the Fringe plantations.

The nameless bua smirked. "May I ask for a face who has these eyes?"

Jaunda didn't have to dig through her memory. She saw the novice's fiery expressions flash through her mind's eye. A match.

Jael.

He hummed, a brief glint appearing in his left eye as he nodded, satisfied. Finally, he leaned his lithe body to look toward the tunnel. "Are your shadows coming out soon?"

"I'll, um, introduce you. What's your name?"

His Aurenthin's gaze darted to her. "What is yours?"

"Jaunda."

"Jaunda." He tilted his head. "No title? No House? No Queen's Writ?"

She shrugged. "Can't trade that for a fart out here. I've always been Jaunda."

"*Heh!* Hmm." He paused to think as if weighing something on a nod. "I've always been Lethrix." His tongue poked out briefly before disappearing behind his lips, his eyes fixed on her, unblinking. "A pleasure. Jaunda."

The sibilant quality of his pleasantries threatened to send a shiver up her spine. The Lead bowed her head and took one step back, pulling in a steady breath before motioning for her "shadows" to emerge onto the ledge. "Lethrix. This is Vik and Halena."

The bua looked up, down, and all around the chasm as he came out first, his cait shielding him as she arched a bewildered, suspicious eyebrow at the other bua.

Once Vik was satisfied there were no other Davrin on the walls, he looked at Jaunda. "Is … this who you were looking for? The only one?"

Lethrix cocked a grin at her, waiting expectantly.

"Yeah, I think so," she answered honestly.

"You *think*?" Halena muttered under her breath.

Vik nudged her with his elbow, keeping his eyes on the other two. "Are you, perchance, one of the Rin'oveaus, Lethrix?"

The other bua chortled, folding his arms. "No, Vik. But I've heard of them. Everyone in this area has. Sometimes they pass through here."

"Could you help us find them?"

Lethrix's Aurenthin face scrunched up as he tapped his chin in thought. "Maybe. That depends on if you have a trade that could supersede their last request for secrecy."

"I see."

By his hesitance, Jaunda guessed Vik wasn't equipped with a juicy bribe any more than she was.

"But I do *not* see," Lethrix continued, motioning around his face. "I would like to. Remove your masks if you wish to talk further."

Halena squeezed Vik's arm harshly. "No! We compromised too many telling her. We must hide our faces."

Lethrix rolled his eyes but shrugged. "So, we cannot bargain. Very well. You may leave any time you wish."

Although Jaunda heard no threat in his tone, an inexplicable shock of warning surged through her gut. She signed sternly for the couple to stay. "Don't leave."

Vik's body suggested he was unsettled by something as well. "We won't. And … who is this that you would travel so far to find him?"

Jaunda looked back, waiting expectantly.

"What?" Lethrix asked. "Can you not answer?"

She ground her teeth, answering Vik the best she could. "I was looking for his den. But I found *him* first."

"My den?" Lethrix echoed, sounding and appearing displeased.

"Yeah." Jaunda gathered her resolve to look him in the face. "And I still mean to."

"Odd. Your Valsharess doesn't usually leave treats on my doorstep." He narrowed his eyes, showing teeth that would be threatening if they were sharp. "Do you … *want* something there?"

Jaunda saw the gold in his eyes despite the lack of light. She swallowed. "I … n-need to find it. That's all."

"Had I been there, would I not be enough for her?"

"I-I don't know."

Lethrix backed up and briefly paced, clearly irritated at first but then curious. Maybe amused.

I am each of those, Jaunda. Your message is wrapped in silk delicate enough to kill you if I simply tear it open. I shall have to think of another way.

Her fists clenched. *Great.*

He paused in his steps closer to the three Davrin and lifted bare, Elven hands to inspect them with a crooked grin. "Well. *These* can't see the task complete."

Lethrix changed as he spoke, talons erupting from his fingers, his voice dropping from a Davrin bua down into the range Jaunda had heard in her head. He dropped to his hands and feet and grew swiftly, enlarged to a size that crowded the trio of Dark Elves closer on the ledge.

"Hey!" Halena cried in alarm.

Jaunda surged to catch them as they stumbled too close to the edge. Vik clutched Halena, who took the Lead's forearm as she braced herself backward. All three slid down or collapsed to their knees as serpentine coils blocked any retreat. They could neither sprint to the tunnel nor tight-walk it along the thin trail leading toward the waterfall.

She stared at the ledge where claws on four bestial feet dug into the rock. Above, a lengthy neck arched and twisted to peer at them. Jaunda met his eyes and froze in place, for once unaware of her racing heart.

The fuckin' gold eyes from my dreams.

Lethrix chuckled, an unsettling echo bouncing around as his lips peeled back to expose jaws and teeth capable of snapping her into three pieces with a single bite. A long, forked tongue slipped out and whipped the air near her head, just missing her.

"Watch it!" she barked, her boot slipping on grit terrifyingly close to a lethal fall. "You're too close, let us by!"

"Almost done," he rumbled.

His shoulders rolled, first sprouting one new talon on each side, followed by wrapped layers of leathery skin. These expanded into the massive wings which had been missing from her glimpse of the tiny drake earlier. They stretched out, taking up the last shred of the space.

Before she could warn him again, the Dragon's wings shoved the Red Sister and her shadows off the cliff. The Davrin Elves fell down the chasm toward the river, each too shocked to scream.

Jaunda faced the unseen ceiling with nothing at her back or beneath her feet. She dropped through emptiness with nothing slowing her down. She watched Lethrix grip the ledge, his wings out full as if he prepared to soar as she could not. Her thoughts ran full on into ludicrous.

Where could he even fly down here?

That monster was too large for any tunnel or cavern in the Deepearth. *Except maybe the Great Cavern.*

When the Dragon leaped from the ledge, she lost sight of him as her heart seized in her chest and something intangible ripped through her.

Failed. Goddess ... hurts.

She clenched her teeth, squeezing her eyes shut, waiting to make impact with the rock and water at the bottom.

May her head go dark just as quickly.

A roaring whoosh swept in to batter her ears, and she anticipated the tumbling river rapids engulfing around her.

Then, inextricably, her body slowed down ...

She hit something, but not hard enough to knock her wind out.

⋆Grab hold.⋆

Her hands obeyed, strength filling her grip as the pain in her chest surged, forcing out a deep groan of agony. She found the rough ridges on his spine and oriented herself flat and facedown along them. She held on, her thighs squeezed against massive, warm muscle covered in scales.

Goddess … !

The magical torment inside her set her to quaking, and Lethrix growled as if he could feel it.

We'll find my den, Jaunda. Don't pass out. You shall make it.

The torture eased as she fought to breathe through the swift rise toward the ceiling. Her heart was beating fast but steady, and she managed to suck in cool air as it rippled over wetness on her cheeks.

Jaunda couldn't open her eyes until she felt a firm landing and heard the crunch of pebbles and grit beneath the Dragon's feet. She filled her lungs several times as Lethrix looked over his shoulder quite easily. His shining eyes appraised her clinging to his back between his wings. The Lead didn't have full control over tremors yet but fixed eyes on him with a snarl.

"What about the other two?"

He blinked once, his large body shifting backward on his haunches, spinal column tensing to hold up his core as he lifted two front legs, or arms … *or whatever.*

Jaunda focused on the bodies of Vik and Halena lying in his palms like two snatched rats. They were limp, unconscious, and presumably alive.

"They're unhurt," he rumbled, inspecting his live catches and giving them a sniff. "What? Do you feel concern for them, Red Sister?"

"I hardly know them," she muttered. "But I'd have questions if you chose to save me but not them from your own stumble."

Lethrix showed his teeth, his tail hovering over the chasm. "That wasn't a stumble."

"What, you knocked us off on purpose?"

"I did."

"Why the fuck … ?" Jaunda stopped herself and growled, shaking her head when it began to ache.

I don't care to know right now.

Very well. You've had quite a shock.

Lethrix chuckled deeply at her look and placed her two shadows on the ground in front of him. Jaunda peered farther out around them, noting the Dragon had landed on a different ledge across the chasm from where they'd been. She could see where they'd fallen.

Swiveling her head the other way, she easily spotted a nearby tunnel leading farther away from the jump circle.

Not that we could easily reach it on our own.

Jaunda felt a twinge in her gut. She couldn't go back anyway.

We'll find my den.

His thought touched her like fresh air in her lungs. *You better mean that.*

"Heh. Would you mind sliding off and helping your companions onto my back?"

She blinked. "Huh?"

Lethrix arched one scaly eye-ridge. "I must shrink a little more to squeeze into this tunnel with three Baenar on my back."

"Three what? Bay-nar?"

"Exactly. It would be easier to judge our collective size with all passengers in place. I presume you will do a better job positioning them than me."

She gripped his scales. "Are ya gonna knock me or them off the ledge for chortles?"

He swung his lightly bristled chin. "No. I received my answers. No purpose to repeating the question."

Right ...

"And if I put them up here with me, we'll find your den?"

He grinned. "Correct. Or you will die."

Thanks.

You're welcome.

Her feet tingled inside her boots as Jaunda swung a leg over to slide off the largest riding lizard she'd ever ridden. She kneeled beside Halena first as the closest and checked her pulse, keeping her nose open for blood while quickly evaluating her. Then she moved to Vik. Both seemed alright.

Jaunda lifted the bua to a sitting position first, pulling his arm and torso across her shoulders before lifting him off the ground. Lethrix hummed as if he was pleased to watch the Lead carry and align the first Davrin belly-down along his spine.

"Watch the bua's eggs," the Dragon suggested. "I know it's easy to forget when you don't have them."

Jaunda huffed, reaching between Vik's thighs to make sure they weren't squished against the scales. "He's fine."

Lethrix laughed softly as she left to retrieve Halena next, who wasn't much heavier than Vik. Soon enough, Jaunda had the cait draped partly over the bua riding in front, turning Halena's head so her cheek pressed to his back rather than the sword sheath.

Neither of them woke up during the jostling; they barely groaned in complaint. It seemed weird.

"Excellent," Lethrix praised in her native tongue. "Now you. Then I will adjust my size."

Jaunda gripped the spinal ridges again and, from a standing jump, hauled herself up to get her legs on either side of the Dragon. She shuffled forward to make sure she could reach either Vik or Halena if they started to slip but remained upright herself.

Lethrix fell silent as she waited for his next remark that never came. Instead, bit by bit, she realized he became … smaller. The quadruped Dragon shrank in a way that would have been easy to miss if she wasn't on edge. Hard scales slid subtly along her leathers between her legs, and she had to shift as the ridges rolled across her crotch.

Whoa.

Good, I hope?

She cocked an eyebrow. *Not bad. Usually need a bit more.*

He showed a hint of fang. **Me, too.**

The black Dragon paused as if waiting for a reply; the Red Sister just narrowed her eyes. This slightly smaller version shrugged, stretched, and yawned like he was adjusting to his new skin.

Whoa!

Jaunda shifted herself and the two unconscious Davrin once again to adapt to the new size.

Perfect.

Better be.

With a sweep of his tail which seemed playful, Lethrix ducked his head and walked on four legs into the new tunnel, raising his wings to shield them on either side like a tent.

This won't take long, messenger. We'll satisfy your quibbling geas and then we'll reach an agreement.

An agreement?

He didn't answer this time, so Jaunda held on, making sure her heart and breath continued while preventing Vik and Halena from tumbling off the Deep Dragon's back.

She still had no idea what she was supposed to do when she finally "found" his den.

RIDING LETHRIX DIDN'T FEEL LIKE THE SADDLED SWAY OF THE LIZARDS IN SIVA-raus, bending their spines side-to-side with bellies closer to the ground. His spine remained remarkably level, his gait smooth, tail held high and lightly tapping the stone on alternating sides behind them.

Occasionally, his wings dragged against an outcrop or stalactite, assuming the legendary beast didn't just push it out of his way.

His neck proved immensely flexible as he curved it up and back to smile at her upside-down, flicking his tongue.

The third time, Jaunda asked why.

"Haven't you done the same, Lead Sister?"

Have I … ?

If he meant standing in the same room with potential novices and grinning …

"Yeah, I suppose. Testing their nerves for possible recruitment." Jaunda smirked. "Can't be the same reason, right?"

He hummed. "Not exactly, no, but not far off. Of course, there's the *other* reason, too."

The other reason.

Sirana was the last one Jaunda had teased with her unsettling smiles, which she couldn't really help anyway.

Especially that one time, after the Sanctuary orgy, when the Lead had made sure she could bathe herself without drowning. The intoxicated Noble had fallen over but still obeyed, displaying her well-used netherhole before getting in the tub.

"Mmm," Lethrix hummed. "Striking blue eyes, and delicious despite how tired she looked. The revelry must have been intense."

Jaunda grumbled. "You *sure* you're not a mind flayer?"

"Any mage can do what I'm doing when you keep your thoughts at the fore of your mind, which you do more often when you're alone for long periods."

"Oh, you know that, huh? How long *have* you been watching me stumble around?"

He ignored that but continued.

"If I *were* to act like the Ornilleth — or a servant of Braqth, for that matter — you'd be getting off my back this moment to duck underneath and vigorously stroke my cock with those quality leather gloves, *and* you'd have no say in the matter. If I felt annoyed, you'd bear the awareness of performing it. For certain, you could not *choose* willful enjoyment despite being pushed to the wall, hmm?"

The Dragon paused while that sank in.

Although a shiver ran up her spine at his description, Jaunda chuffed wryly. "You call all this flirting?"

"Not exactly, but I know you understand."

She heard the grin in his voice, curling one nostril as she entertained the parallels he'd pointed out. Yes, in an odd way, she did understand. It didn't scare her.

"That 'agreement' you mentioned. You want sex?"

His long, black neck curved his head upside down to peer at her. His jaw missed a healthy scrape along the ceiling, and his spread of ivory horns pointed at the ground.

"I have been Asleep since before you were born, Red Sister," he said, "and I just Woke. Unless you have a better offer inside that sac of spider-silk blocking part of your mind, I would enjoy learning about that magical item strapped to the small of your back."

Jaunda blinked at him. "My Feldeu?"

"That's right."

She thought about how he could easily change shape, so it would work. But something felt off. "You want me to fuck you with it?"

"Perhaps later," he cooed, his vertical pupils sliding up to Vik and Halena between his wings. "It depends on how adventurous the play gets and who is involved."

He wanted to play? Or rather, he *would* play in some fashion or other.

Jaunda glanced down at Rausery's spies. "Would you let them go if they *didn't* want to play?"

He showed rows of teeth before his tongue dipped out into view. "Of courssse."

Jaunda wasn't sure whether to believe him with that hiss and expression.

Lethrix blinked gold eyes which shone in the dark. "Does that mean *you* will stay? Do you *want* to play, Jaunda? Has too much time passed without that delectable release for you, as well?"

She tapped a few scales, flushed with a sensation she didn't quite know how to interpret. "We can discuss it. Like you said."

"Excellent." The Dragon bent his head into a natural orientation. "Soon, then. We're almost there."

Finally, Vik turned his head with a soft moan, and Halena followed soon after. They were waking up, about to discover they weren't dead.

Jaunda watched Halena reach for the bua's hand first, her hand fumbling until she found his arm and followed it down. The bua squeezed her. Vik's eyes were open now, and their hearts started to pound, first his and then the cait's.

Their bodies warmed, and neither panicked in those first few flicks.

At that moment, the Lead admitted to herself she was as curious as her legendary target what challenge was soon to happen between them.

Indeed, Lethrix chuckled. *Always better than discovering these things* *alone, isn't it?*[*]

CHAPTER 8

THE CLOSER THEY DREW TO WHERE LETHRIX CARRIED THEM, THE LESS JAUNDA could control her breath and body, and she didn't know why. When their serpentine mount emerged from one tunnel into a chasm alarmingly similar to where they'd first met, the Red Sister gasped louder despite her efforts, her body shuddering.

"Are you injured?" Halena whispered over her shoulder, her tone at once irritated and frightened.

The Lead shook her head, gripping the nearest thing for balance as her head swam. "Nuh-uh …"

"S-stop that!" the cait hissed back, swatting at Jaunda's hand clutching the crease between her hips and thigh.

The Red Sister clapped her palm on the shadow's shoulder instead, and Halena growled. She still sounded scared.

"Hold still, Haly," Vik murmured to his partner, audibly swallowing as Lethrix began their crossing over the chasm.

The Dragon used a narrow, stone bridge which had not existed above the dark plunge before. When she looked down, Jaunda froze.

I don't understand. Did we double back somehow? Where did the bridge come from?

⋆Good questions.⋆

Jaunda took a deeper breath and closed her eyes against the sight. Though she shook, the Lead focused on her other senses. The only *other* difference seemed to be the lack of running water. No river rapids or waterfall rumbled in the distance.

Suddenly, Lethrix stopped dead-center where the bridge was slimmest. Not enough space for the Davrin to jump off unless they wanted to plummet down the chasm.

"Oh, Goddess, keep going," Halena whispered. "Don't stop!"

"Hold that thought," the Dragon replied, ever amused, and curving his neck around to spy them from one golden eye. "You seem overwhelmed by something, Red Sister."

"Y-yeah," she forced through her teeth, unnerved by the rising, inexplicable sensation as her eyes opened. She tried not to look down. "But not ... pain."

"What does it feel like?"

As if ...

"Like what?"

As if she were about to step out of the Deepearth and into real sunlight.

"That, but ... stronger."

"Interesting."

Her eyelid twitched. "Is it you?"

His eye glimmered in the dark. "No, it's not me. Perhaps it's the opposite of what you felt being knocked from the ledge. Not 'failure', but ... ?"

Jaunda blinked. *Victory?*

Close. I'd call it success.

His implication took longer to sink in than it should have.

Slowly, Jaunda peered around the massive space and deep, black hole above which the black Dragon balanced on a tiny stretch of stone.

This can't be ...

She caught and crushed her doubt like an insect when that sense of *freedom* returned.

She could take a full breath.

"Is this your den?"

Lethrix showed teeth, tilting his head. "Do any of you care to dismount?"

"You mean here?" Vik peeped, glancing over the side.

"Yes."

"No!" Halena gasped, shuffling forward to hold her bua firmly in place on the Dragon's back.

"Very well. What about you, Lead?"

Jaunda narrowed her focus on the suspicious curve of his lips beneath an unblinking gaze. She swung her leg over and into the open air, watching every tick of his expression as she did.

"Lead, *wait!*" Vik cried as she slipped down his flank.

The Red Sister's boots landed on solid ground beside the dark, serpentine body, and still she refused to look down. Her feet touched then nudged some debris out of the way. Two pieces clinked together like coins.

She held still, one hand on Lethrix's flank, as his neck lowered his head to her eye level. His smirk turned into a full, startling grin.

Congratulations, Jaunda. Welcome.

We're here?

We are.

The sense of lifting achievement broke like a dam. With one last shudder, Jaunda felt the geas slide off like iron grease, the weight vanishing from her mind.

I'm free.

Her chest filled and released.

… Now what?

"Lead?"

Catching herself staring into an odd, twinkling void, Jaunda blinked, looking away from Lethrix to the pair straddling him. Their mouths agape. She smiled at their expressions.

"Am I walking on air?"

"You … were," Halena admitted, dragging her eyes away to scan the rest of the chasm.

The ceiling was shrinking gradually, like Lethrix a bit ago, and subtly enough to startle them to notice. Metallic, glimmering sparks teased their peripheries, keeping them looking all around them, but every time they swiveled their heads, drab rock drew closer.

Meanwhile, the emptiness beneath the Red Sister's feet had filled in with rough but level stone. As soon as all three Davrin confirmed this, the Dragon rocked his hind end first away and then forward with a snap, flinging Vik and Halena off his back and plummeting toward Jaunda.

"Shit!"

She could break the fall only for one. She chose Halena as Vik's body signaled that he knew how to fall into a roll. The cait had as much gear as she did, and the two collapsed under the awkward weight with a grunt.

"*Oof!*"

"*Argh!* Alright, alright, let me go!"

Jaunda couldn't help chortling at the way the younger shadow writhed like a pincerworm to get out of her hands.

"Uh, Hal?"

The Davrin females looked toward Vik, who had remained in his crouch and stared up, wide-eyed, as Lethrix hummed with what sounded like a stretch.

"Ahhh. That's better."

As Halena rolled away and scrambled beside Vik, the Red Sister reappraised their host. Standing erect, Lethrix's rough, taloned feet and thick legs had shrunk proportionately to mimic the sentient races. His torso reminded her of an exceptionally athletic bua in the Queen's Army, but his clawed hands, thick arms, and broad shoulders seemed strong enough to break someone's neck.

The Dragon had kept his wings, the golden eyes were the same, and his long, serpent's tail coiled languidly against the ground, the lively tip flicking side-to-side.

Three shapes so far. Is this the real one?

Not even close, Red Sister.

Lethrix's smirking face echoed theirs in form, though he still had a muzzle, if less pronounced than before. His lips stretched generously over his predator's teeth, forming a playful bunch to his cheeks. The hairless, reptilian head lacked obvious ears but bore plenty of decoration with a crown of white horns arching backward, each separated by smaller lines of hard, black ridges.

Well?

Well, what?

★Will this work for you?★

Jaunda scanned the muscular form covered in glossy, black scales. Her face scrunched as her eyes lingered around his groin, where she'd expected to see a prick and scrotum, but didn't see a cait's cunt, either. Either the genitals were missing entirely, or they were … hidden?

Wait, *was* he male or had she missed something weird about her mark?

"Disappointed?"

Jaunda blinked at the depth of his voice and climbed to her feet with a shrug. "Um. Just confused."

"Really? I thought *you* would have been harder to surprise with what one bore inside their leggings."

She smirked. "Well, you're not wearing any."

He chuffed, and the Red Sister grinned, reaching behind her to touch her Feldeu. *Still there.*

"Besides," she said, "it's usually Davrin for me, not Dragons. You know, they're either one or the other."

Lethrix arched an eye ridge. "Hm. I suppose you never met any others as adults, have you? Even living centuries. They're too vulnerable in Braqth's cities."

Others? … No, wait.

Jaunda squinted. "Cities? You mean *the* City."

Lethrix's fangs poked out, stark as his eyes, and Vik and Halena shifted their weight in a way that caught the Lead's attention.

She turned. "What?"

"Uhm," Vik began, glancing at Halena as she grimaced but didn't try to stop him this time. "The Rin'oveaus mercenaries we're looking for?"

"Yeah?"

"They are Davrin. And … they're not from Sivaraus."

Jaunda frowned. "You're jesting."

"No, Lead. As far as we know, they avoid the Queen's city and have never been there."

Lethrix purred. "How interesting. Who discovered this, Vik?"

The bua hesitated, barely daring to flick his eyes up before the blackness of the cavern changed suddenly, retreating in the wake of an unseen source of gentle, golden light. The spy pair jumped in surprise and turned back-to-back.

"Don't worry," the Dragon said, his tail relaxing. "The only potential threat is me."

"Right," Halena whispered dryly, taking a needed breath.

Jaunda spied some dark blobs beyond the light's edge, but nothing in the closed space moved or made a sound except them. Within the gentle glow, the floor was clear of either treasure or debris, dotted with stalagmites and a few flat slabs of granite. She didn't see an exit.

Now what?

"Wait, how do we get out?" the cait asked the Dragon, keeping her eyes moving around the cavern.

"You bargain with me."

"You mean we're trapped?"

"Quite trapped. Unless you bargain."

"What? We never knew that!"

Anger bled into her tone as humor bubbled in his.

"Do you not have any gold to pay as tribute?"

"We didn't know we needed it!"

Even though Halena had turned in Lethrix's direction, the cait's eyes couldn't settle on his face. Her focus kept sliding away.

"Oh, dear. Hm. I take it your leaders never gave you another exit strategy?"

"Goddess *damn* it, Vik, what are we going to do?"

Jaunda motioned for her attention. "He's playing, Hal. Been asleep for a while. Think well-rested Dragon looking for company."

Lethrix tilted his head back and laughed, his tail slipping forward to tag and wind around her leg. Jaunda leaped away just in time to avoid getting pulled off balance. "Whoa, hold on."

The Dragon leaned toward her, and Jaunda lifted her hands when his mouth was in range to bite her face. He paused, tongue flicking out teasingly, eyes glowing with mirth.

"One may play with one who commands all the magic in a scenario, or one may bargain with them." Vertical pupils ticked toward her shadows. "I wager you have greater practice in such situations."

"True enough." Jaunda stayed ready to catch a lavender tongue if needed. "Why would you care to bring it up?"

"I prefer experience where possible, and something distinctive brought to the table. The truly privileged or naïve are quite boring." Lethrix straightened up to give her breathing room but stood over a head taller. "Your Queen knows this, but it seems your General's network does not."

Jaunda glanced sidelong at the huddling couple. Vik and Halena had had no idea what they were getting into following her. Not privileged but were they naïve?

Not really. They only must get over the shock.

I tried to tell them, even through the spell.

I don't doubt their determination, Lead. Their means and endurance is tempered with less information.

Hey, I didn't know frik about this, either.

You knew you searched for a Dragon, and neither of them has training like you do. Your Valsharess did not send you at random.

Jaunda cocked an eyebrow, frowning at him. "You said you'd let them go if they didn't want to play with you."

"If that is in our Bargain, of course, I shall." One gold eye glinted as he glanced at them. "Or … they could gain what they seek and more by joining us in negotiations."

"What the … ?" Halena tensed up. "What are you two talking about? What do you want?"

"What do *you* want?" the Dragon countered.

"He could help us find the Rin'oveaus," Vik murmured.

"That I could, bright bua. Or anything else in the Deepearth, for that matter."

Anything? Even Reishel?

The tip of Lethrix's tail lifted inquisitively toward the ceiling. *Who?*

Jaunda grimaced. *Random thought. And knock it off. I'm not bargaining like this.*

Hm. Probably wise.

"I'll be direct, then," Lethrix said aloud, the claws of his left hand reaching to lightly drag along his abdomen, his tail flicking faster for a moment. "I want to rut with as many as will join me, for as long as you're able to endure. In exchange, I shall give you something you need or desire. The precise boundaries of this exchange shall be our Bargain."

The cavern fell dead silent, all movement pausing until Jaunda lifted a finger.

Lethrix smiled eagerly. "Yes, Jaunda?"

"How do you 'rut?'"

"The same as you."

"You have to put something on?"

"More that body and mind must be properly attuned."

The golden eyed legend caressed himself as he spoke, producing an erection for them in a few moments.

Oh, fuck.

Halena cried out in alarm while Jaunda managed to keep her mouth closed, unlike Vik, as they stared. A deep red phallus fast emerged from a groin slit lined with small, fine, purple scales. In the deeper shadows, she'd have missed the opening.

"Ahh, that's better."

His cock was thick and immensely different in shape from her relatively smooth, black Feldeu. He had a fat glans with a narrow, swooping tip, several bumps and ridges along the shaft on the way down to the base, which hinted at a round knob that hadn't slipped free of the straining slit yet.

"Shit … !" whispered the bua forcing himself to look away. He tried to meet Lethrix's eyes, but Jaunda noted he stopped at chest-level. "Uh, maybe I'm not suitable for you to negotiate with?"

"Vik!" Halena bumped his shoulder as Lethrix laughed jovially.

"You're equally welcome to Bargain with me, Vik," the Dragon said with an enormous, toothy smile. "I seek pleasure, not breeding, and you have plenty of attractive options in that regard."

"Uh …" His face was swept with intense heat.

"Yeah, about that," Jaunda interjected. "First condition would be nobody catches anything."

Lethrix dipped his chin. "Agreed. No one will leave my den at risk of becoming pregnant or hosting illness."

Too easy.

He grinned wider. "Next?"

"Next." The Lead glanced at his heavy meat club. "Nobody is injured by you. No blood drawn, no crippling, mutilation, or choking to unconsciousness. No forcing us to bend in ways we aren't formed to bend."

Vik and Halena turned their faces to her in dual horror.

"My, my," the Dragon crooned. "You have witnessed some interesting situations. Hrm. Agreed." He winked at the other two Davrin. "I've broken my fast, and my belly hunger is gone, but have the *other* appetite to sate with my *guests*."

His cock bobbed between his legs, and two heartbeats grew audible.

"A-are we the first to bargain with you like this?" Vik asked.

"Good question. No, you are not."

The bua swallowed.

"Fine," Jaunda said, fighting a smirk, putting her back to her shadows and facing him and his prick. "Then also agree no one takes your phallus, claw, talon —" She leaned to glance behind him. " — or tail, if they are large or sharp enough to cause damage which takes cycles or more to heal."

"Interesting. So a bit of discomfort isn't out of the question?"

She shrugged. "Some like it harder. Or bigger."

"Heh. True."

"And we know you can shift smaller and get rid of the pointy ends, so you can also grow larger if asked."

"Ooo." His eyes shone. "I like flexibility."

"Fine. Just agree to keep your shape compatible with ours and keep it back from torture."

A low, eager rumble filled the cavern. His tail slithered along smooth stone as Lethrix caught her gaze and held it. *And you would know torture by sex if you took it in the ass, wouldn't you?*

Jaunda stared back, keeping her mind quiet for once. "Well?"

"Mmm. Agreed. Anything else?"

"Well, there's what we want in exchange."

"We'll get to that. You began with limits and preferences." He breathed in, his chest expanding as his face relaxed. "I have a few of those if your list is complete?"

"W-wait." Vik took a step forward with his hand up, though Halena caught his shoulder to keep him behind Jaunda. "You said you wanted to rut 'as long as we can endure.' How long are you suggesting?"

The scaly, bipedal beast turned to him. "I'm glad you asked. My recent best is every cycle for a turn."

The cavern fell silent as Lethrix tried not to laugh.

"No fucking way," Halena growled.

The Dragon looked at her though she didn't look up. "Is that a challenge?"

"No, it's not," Jaunda interjected. "I can grasp it. If you can sleep for five centuries, sure, you can fuck for a turn."

The corners of his eyes creased. "I knew you'd be open."

"But the Valsharess warned my Elders that the Elder Mind could become a problem for Sivaraus."

"Oh, did she?"

"Yeah, and my tagalongs are looking for a moving group of fighters, maybe to help with that, before reporting to *their* elders. We don't have that long to play with you."

"Mmm. Understood. How about a mere span?"

"Well —"

"I don't see any food or water here," Halena broke in, crossing her arms tensely, looking sidelong into the dark.

Jaunda motioned to her. "She's got a point."

Lethrix chuckled, stroking his chin with one crooked finger. "Does that mean you will play, Halena?"

"I never said that." She glanced at her bua companion then managed to raise her eyes to the Dragon's chest. "I don't want us to die of thirst waiting to be let out."

"Very well." The large male dipped his head. "For however long you remain in my den, you shall be provided adequate food, water, and time for Elven Reverie."

"*And* you won't stalk us after letting us out. You'll let us go."

The tip of his tail snapped like a whip. "Put in enough effort, and I assure you I shall be too tired to step on your heels."

"Not me," she retorted brazenly, fisting her hands to stop the light quiver.

"Ah, perhaps the only natural response." Lethrix glanced at Jaunda and Vik. "Anything else from you two, or is it my turn?"

Vik said nothing, his scarlet eyes wide but likewise not looking the Dragon in the face. Meanwhile, Jaunda shifted her stance inside her mind: the Sanctuary instead of the Cloister, facing off with a Priestess instead of the Prime. By that view, the Dragon's smile hinted at what she'd be foolish to ignore.

"You mentioned bargaining with magic."

His horned head tilted her way. "Ah, you didn't forget. I am listening."

The Lead lifted a finger. "First, nothing like what I just got rid of."

"No geas?"

"If that's what it was." Jaunda glanced toward Rausery's informers before returning focus to the Black Dragon. "No compulsions. Not on any of us. Don't force us to act like something we're not, ever."

Vik moved closer to Halena when Lethrix's eyes visibly glowed. "Ohh, what an interesting way to say that."

"Why?" Jaunda demanded, narrowing her focus on his face. "What did I say wrong?"

He distracted her by fondling his erection. "Nothing at all, Red Sister. It's just right. So, I agree to use magic to alter my shape as needed for better ... compatibility."

Jaunda nodded. "Yeah."

"But I *refrain* from using magic to compel you into acts with which you do not agree or would prefer not to do."

"Right. Before, during, or after."

"*Heh.* Sounds reasonable. Anything else?"

She rolled that over. "Yeah, another thing."

He sighed softly. "Yes?"

"You won't steal or alter a single piece of possessions we brought here, and we leave with each one. Nothing missing. Especially my Feldeu, my implant, and the gold ring on my right hand."

"Well, curse your web for covering all that." Lethrix grinned. "I'm willing to agree to this on one condition."

Jaunda frowned. "What?"

"I may study them instead."

"And what does 'study them' mean?"

"It means I may handle them and 'taste' them long enough to detect anything unwelcome in my den before returning them to you." He winked. "With the exception of inspecting the implant. *That* can wait until you're naked."

Her body flushed hot despite herself. His cock grew turgid as if in response.

Fuck.

Sssoon.

Jaunda had been doing well keeping her eyes on him until then, but Vik and Halena looked everywhere else, overwhelmed enough to lose track of "negotiations."

Why did this seem easier for her? Why could she meet his eyes but they couldn't? Moreover, why was the idea of fucking *the* Black Dragon after finding him a given conclusion?

We were each alone and looking for opportunity, weren't we?

Jaunda cocked an eyebrow as gold eyes bore into her. *You haven't been 'nudging' me toward that goal, have you?*

Fangs appeared. **Not by any method you haven't used yourself. The magic-laden thread of this leads to your Queen in Sivaraus. If I may say, she made an intriguing choice in you.**

Now he was complimenting her. *Great.*

"Well?"

She blinked. "Well, what?"

"Do I study any magic you brought with you, agreeing to leave it in your possession without altering it?"

"Huh? Oh, yeah. Sounds reasonable."

"Excellent." His tail grew lively. "We've discussed sustenance, shelter, well-being, a guarantee of autonomy, and retaining your possessions, correct?"

"Yeah."

"Then it's my turn to set some boundaries and preferences, and you shall tell me what you want in exchange."

Vik and Halena seemed to snap out of wherever they were.

"Alright," Jaunda replied. "Go."

Lethrix bowed his head. "To begin, you will stay in my den for at least a span. Trust that should I sense something urgent regarding the Elder Mind, I may lift you out and set you free before then. In exchange for this courtesy, you'll neither seek nor remove anything which you did not bring in. Not even a pebble."

Jaunda folded her arms. "Fine. About the same as my initiation into the Sisterhood."

"Heh! I enjoy the parallel." His eyes widened briefly, unnerving the shadows as he addressed them. "These conditions apply to you two as well, unless either of you wishes to leave and wait outside?"

Halena took Vik's shoulders and turned him toward her; they began signing. The messages were fast, brusque, and missing nuance in favor of shorthand, but Jaunda got the gist.

★Go now. Sister can stay.★

Vik jerked his chin. ★Sent to find her. Can't go back.★

★Wait outside.★

★Not enough food or know area — ★

★Look for Rin'oveaus.★

★Could be beyond a span or fail. This is a certain path — ★

★You believe him?!★

"Think of it like a wish granted," Lethrix interjected, making Halena jump in place. "A Bargain once made is seen complete. What we agree to, Davrin, you shall receive."

"In exchange for pleasure?" Vik asked. "And only that."

"Yesss." The Dragon peered between the pair, lingering on Halena. "I could even offer up to the first half-cycle to decide if you will participate and ask for a boon or wait in a corner until we're finished." He grinned. "You'll be fed, of course, and quite safe."

Vik took Halena's wrist, meeting her eyes before leaning to whisper something in her ear. Jaunda strained to listen; Lethrix fell dead still.

I know what I want to ask for. You wait. Take time to think.

Halena shook her head, glaring sternly at her companion. "Do *not*."

"What are you, his matron?" Jaunda remarked.

The cait's face snapped her way. "For once, consider this is none of your business, Red Sister."

Fiesty.

Jaunda smirked. "Yeah, but he's a smart bua. Maybe you should listen to him."

Lethrix snorted, his tail reaching for Jaunda's calf in a firm, playful coil to squeeze. This time, she didn't jump. He exhaled softly in her mind.

I can't wait to watch how you use Fadele's phallus.

Jaunda frowned at the same time Halena gave her an obscene gesture. *Fadele?*

Ah. She is your 'Prime,' I believe.

She has a name?

The Black Dragon chortled, squeezing her leg one more time before drawing in his tail. *I see we shall have an ... enlightening span together. You, me ... and him.*

Vik had taken both Halena's gloved hands and pressed them to his forehead, his back bowed toward her. Jaunda hadn't really seen that gesture so blatantly before, but it convinced the protective cait to wait for him as the bua approached the Dragon on his own.

"Alright." Rausery's Shadow took a deep breath, looking between them and motioning with his hand. "Continue."

CHAPTER 9

THE RED SISTER STRIPPED DOWN AS SHE WOULD IN THE CLOISTER, RELAXING TO confidence and a distinct lack of fear as her armor came off.

Jaunda could wonder all span long if she'd asked for enough from this supposed wish-granter in their "Bargain" in exchange for *attempting* to fuck a Dragon stupid. If she did, she'd put greater value on his perspective than hers and even doubt she had the guts to see it through.

Bah. I'd stiffen like Halena. Gotta stay loose, my body and mind.

Vik was doing better, mimicking Jaunda and voluntarily removing everything he owned to keep in one place. But the bua was nervous, perhaps too young to know exactly what he wanted from an encounter like this.

Not uncommon for buas in Sivaraus.

The air in Lethrix's den had become warmer, comfortable enough to stand in the nude for marks, maybe enough to rest in Reverie without their skin pebbling. At the same time, a water spring had begun burbling nearby, flowing from the nearest wall into two modest pools before flushing out again.

None of them knew if the spring had always been there and the Dragon had been masking it with the rest of his suspected hoard, or if the magical beast had literally summoned it out of the ground. Regardless, they'd each tested it, drinking and rinsing the dust and sweat off their hands and faces.

The formation made it easy to keep their washing separate from their consumption. They could even get rid of their waste, and their host waited patiently as Jaunda and Vik cleaned most of their spans' worth of travel filth from their bodies.

With a similar display of magic, all six of the stone slabs spread around the cavern were layered in frayed and woven mats of fiberstalk padding the top and hanging over the sides. No doubt this would reduce the bruising on elbows, knees, hips, and backs, though the appearance of these relatively flat platforms seemed like a Matron's orgy room blended with the Sanctuary altars.

Lethrix chuckled quietly in her head. *When something works, regardless of body fluid drawn.*

Are you going to spy on my thoughts the entire time?

Yes. For as long as you make it so tempting and easy.

Jaunda pursed her mouth, pushing her hair out of her face. Heard and understood.

Vik stood nude, clean, and silent, staring at a point on the floor, but she didn't know whether he and Lethrix shared any magical exchange. Jaunda looked him over while he wasn't focused on her. The spy had enviably short-cut hair and was quite fit, appearing tougher than Shyntre during his stint with the Sisterhood.

Probably not a soft turn in his entire life.

The bua caught her looking, and when she didn't react beyond a small curl at the corners of her mouth, he gave her a look-over. He seemed impressed, and this made her grin.

"How do you like it?" she whispered. "Top? Bottom? From behind?"

His face grew hot as fire, but his pole also hinted at shedding its flaccid state. Maybe he needed a finger up his ass to coax him further.

"Much as I enjoy your teasing his fear, Red Sister, it can become habitual." Lethrix stepped in behind the shorter Davrin and leaned down, hooking one arm across Vik's chest beneath his pits.

"Whoa, wait!" he cried as his feet left the ground, his body pulled against their host and above the swinging, girthy cock.

"I'd like to test something else, first, if I may?"

"Test what?" Jaunda asked, watching as the Dragon supported Vik's ass with his free hand, the base of his long fingers lightly cradling his balls. She imagined the larger male positioning the bua on the tip of his pole and working his netherhole open before pushing Vik down and impaling him upon it.

Without foreplay? Lethrix chuckled. *Quite the lusty brute, aren't you?*

Jaunda smirked. *Aren't you tempted?*

I've done it before, it has its place. But our harmless, cooperative Vik has done nothing to deserve it, wouldn't you agree?

She met Lethrix's eyes and repeated, "What test?"

He grinned, suggesting with two clawed fingers nudging the skin of Vik's inner thighs that the bua perched on his palm should spread his thighs wider. Vik was motivated to obey, his lithe form shivering from tension, toned muscles standing out.

"Show me if you can bring our clever shadow to full arousal *without* using his netherhole."

"Aw, damn."

Jaunda could appreciate that he didn't dictate exactly how she should do that, though the presentation made a few unspoken suggestions.

Think I have a problem with sucking cock?

The Black Dragon's eye glinted. *I hope not. This span might get repetitive otherwise.*

With a soft huff, Jaunda stepped boldly forward between Vik's legs. She paused to enjoy the enormous eyes and disbelief on his face as she dipped her head and gently fed his prick into her mouth. He sucked in his breath.

I forget this part, she thought. *Feldeus on Sisters are always hard.*

Lethrix chuckled. *Then I'll start farther ahead with you.*

Already there. I'll wait till you catch up.

The Dragon purred as her tongue and lips got to work, her mouth pulling, coaxing more blood into the organ. The bua shuddered, swallowing a whimper.

"Guide her, Vik," Lethrix murmured in his ear. "She asked what you liked, didn't she? Don't keep us guessing now that you've agreed to play."

Jaunda massaged the natural phallus with reasonable patience as it gradually swelled in her mouth, regularly sweeping her annoying hair behind her ears. Vik didn't speak in words but stopped withholding moans of pleasure, which indeed guided her in what he enjoyed most.

Meanwhile, Lethrix encouraged her shadow to relax and fall into it. Vik had to slow his mind first, she knew, and let it get quieter.

That, and stop glancing toward Halena.

Hope he can do it.

"How is the Red Sister performing, Vik? I'm curious."

"G-good …"

The bua had reached his full size as he strained in the Dragon's grip, Jaunda slowly pressing her teeth on his shaft, giving it a firm squeeze and hold for several moments.

"Oh, G-Goddess, I mean, it's great! Sorry for any insult —"

"Don't be," Lethrix said. "I think she bites when she's having fun."

Jaunda chortled with her mouth full of cock, scraping hair back again.

Yeah, I guess, but how much more of this?

Just make him squirt. I'll be satisfied.

So soon, huh?

Heh, heh! As a between-meal snack, perhaps.

Again, Lethrix didn't demand *how* she accomplished this. Any superior at Sivaraus would have told Jaunda to swallow, or aim the launch at the bua's face, or whatever else they wanted to control that abrupt but anticipated mess of semen.

Reach the peak. I can do that.

Resigned to ignoring her slipping hair, Jaunda used one hand to assist, sharing part of the shaft with her slick mouth but also reaching with her other hand for his scrotum, which still rested atop warm Dragon fingers.

No cheating, Lethrix reminded her as his palm shielded Vik's pucker from Jaunda's squirming fingers.

She snickered in her mind. *Not gonna. I just want his bridge.*

Oh?

Yeah. Make room.

"Ah!" Vik cried as Jaunda's fingers slipped in between him and the Dragon, competing for the space to stroke the sensitive ridge behind his balls. "Oh, fff … ! Ai-yah!"

"Good call," Lethrix remarked.

Sure was. With everything else she was doing, she was pushing the writhing bua ruthlessly toward climax.

"L-Lead!" Vik gasped through his teeth. "I'm gonna … !"

Knows to warn a cait, too.

*Heh heh heh … *

Jaunda signed acknowledgment but kept her mouth on his pole and hand pressing firm against the ridge of the bua's crotch. She stroked and sucked the smaller spy, determined to bring him to full, uninterrupted pleasure.

Vik inhaled sharply. "*Ohhhh … !* Ah, oh … ! Goddess …"

And his prick spurted semen unseen between the Red Sister's lips.

Ah, yes, there we are … mmm.

She let Vik finish in her mouth, waiting until the tension drained from his muscles before pulling off. Scraping her hair behind her ears again, she turned and spit his emission onto the den floor.

"Thank you for that," Lethrix said dryly.

The Lead smacked her tongue, gathering the saliva to spit a second time. "Well, buas tend to be bitter."

"And caits?" he asked, shifting a languid Vik in his arms to carry and place him upon one of the mat-covered slabs. "I think they can be rather sour. Sometimes salty."

Jaunda squinted at his expression, which he managed to keep straight for a flick. "Are we still talking sex juices?"

Low laughter filled her ears as his smile broke. "We *could* be. But speaking of which …"

Lethrix approached, reaching with two sharp-tipped fingers toward her crotch. Jaunda felt her eyes widen as she stepped back in protest. "Hey, now."

"Hold still or you'll get jabbed."

"You could make that not a concern."

"Oh, but this is so effective."

He closed the distance, and she stopped her retreat and held still. They stared eye-to-eye as the Dragon's smooth, dry fingers eased between muscular thighs and caressed her netherlips.

He didn't penetrate her but found plenty of natural lubricant. His eyelids drooped, and a purr rose in his throat as he gathered some of it before withdrawing his hand.

"Glad you enjoyed the prelude," he whispered.

Never blinking, Jaunda watched him raise his fingers close enough for a disturbingly long, purple tongue to drop out of his mouth and curl around them, licking and tasting her juices.

She smirked. "Too sour?"

"Not even close. Worth savoring, in fact."

He pulled in his tongue and closed his teeth, drawing air gently through them like he savored either the flavor or the scent. His expression reminded her of D'Shea wearing her silken robe and enjoying a bottle of her favorite fermented drink.

His warm and deeply colored prick still protruded from his groin, thick and dipping halfway to the floor. Impossible to miss, yet she hadn't seen him fondle it since lifting Vik into his arms.

"So." She pointed at it. "Are you next?"

Lethrix paused to study her. "Perhaps later. I noticed how distracted you were by your hair."

Jaunda scraped her fingers through it, practically a reflex by now. "It's not usually this long."

"Indeed, long enough to fall in your eyes but not to weave or bind it behind your ears. Why not cut it?"

She made a face. "Finding you here was more important, apparently."

"Curious."

The Dragon looked around his cavern briefly before extending his arm, and a bright, metal tool appeared in his hand.

"What the fuck is that?"

"Shears." He demonstrated the twin, levered blades, opening and then snapping them shut. "I could trim your hair as short as you like. Then we may continue."

Jaunda shook her head in slight disbelief but then shrugged. "Fuck it, sure. Thanks."

"My pleasure. Choose a mat and have a seat."

THE DRAGON TOOK CARE WITH HIS CLAWS, HER EARS, AND THOSE SHARP SNIPPERS. The metallic noise unsettled her, but she held still as he removed irksome locks from her head. He also produced a large, silver platter to use as a mirror.

"Shorter," she said, watching his eyes and teeth glimmer in the reflection. "Especially between temples and nape."

His phallus was out while he worked, lying like a bloated fish on his thigh as he sat on the slab with one leg up. He hadn't touched it for teasing or relief as far as she'd seen.

Enjoying the anticipation?

Lethrix cropped her hair closer to her scalp. *Very much.*

Aren't you aching?

Not as you might presume.

Uh-huh … Where do you want to start? My cunt? It's kind of aching.

She listened to him inhale and slowly let it out.

Demonstrate your Feldeu for me. Show me how it works.

Jaunda flicked her eyes toward her gear without turning her head. Vik and Halena were near it, watching with quiet interest in their respective places. They didn't speak aloud but might have been trading signs during the unexpected break.

Lethrix had inspected anything magical on them while they drank, cleaned, and settled down once the deal was struck. The Queen's flayer-sensing ring had been first. Upon studying it, he had asked the Lead to place it in her pack for the duration.

"*She is aware you are free of your geas, and she has a general idea where you are,*" the Dragon said, placing the ring in her palm. "*If you wear this while I rut you, she and I might get into a battle over its consonance. If that happens, either I keep it with my Hoard, or the piece will be unreliable for its intended purpose after you leave."*

That had convinced the Lead to tuck the ring away for the duration of their Bargain. He'd had no similar concern about her magic cock, but he'd enjoyed fondling and sniffing it.

"Fascinating. First time holding one since its innovation."

"When was it made?"

"About a century after Fadele formed the Sisterhood."

A pregnant pause.

"When was that?"

He'd clearly expected the question, responding in silence. *Maybe later, Red Sister. If you want to trade something else.*

She'd think about it.

To her surprise, Vik's sword possessed enough magic to have prompted Lethrix to ask for it next. After flicking his tongue through the air around the weapon, and after baring the blade to study with an intense gaze, he'd sheathed it, handing it to Vik with one word.

"Useful."

Halena didn't have anything touched by magic, apparently, and that made Jaunda wonder about their relative ranks in whatever group they were part of. She recalled Halena's warning when she'd first caught them.

"He will be missed, even if injured and taken out of the fight."

Now, getting her hair cut by her host, Jaunda remembered the imbued sliver of wizard's gold behind her left breast. The Dragon noticed when she touched the skin above it.

"That, I cannot recommend what to do," he said, brushing clippings from her shoulder then smoothing his hand across her back. His fingers felt rough but incredibly warm. "The gold is entangled with your aura. It will continue to change as you change."

"Continue?"

"It's already different from what it must have been when first inserted. When did you obtain it?"

"When I made Lead. So I could use the jump circles alone and without a mage."

"Ah."

One corner of her mouth tightened. "So, a tiny piece of gold is not enough threat or value to you to tear it out?"

"Not in this case." Lethrix patted her hip and stood up. The shears and platter-mirror vanished before her eyes. "All done. Now, retrieve your Feldeu, Red Sister. I've been patient."

"I'd wonder why," she said as she slid off the platform and headed toward her equipment, "but I think patience is your 'base' manner if you don't wreck everything after a five-century sleep."

"Hmm. That might have as much to do with youth and age."

Jaunda paused, twisting to look at him. "You saying you're not a young Dragon?"

His eyes glimmered. "Exactly."

"Huh."

She continued her task to retrieve her Feldeu, briefly meeting Halena's anxious gaze when Vik spoke up.

"Do you know any young Dragons?"

"Quite a few." Lethrix's tail shushed across the stone, sweeping to one side. His wings expanded slightly, and he smiled as if welcoming the Red Sister. "They *do* tend to 'wreck everything' when they first Wake up. Poor impulse control, I suppose. Not yet mature."

Vik sounded worried. "Are they nearby?"

"No." Lethrix lifted his jaw to the ceiling. "They're quite far away. The Deepearth is mine. They do not share it with me."

Jaunda's bare-footed step slowed. Lethrix's eyes slid down and up her body again, lingering on the false phallus in her hand.

"The Deepearth is …" she began. "You mean *all* the other Dragons are on the Surface?"

"Where else could they go?" He beckoned, the claws on his fingertips drawing her eyes. "Come here, Jaunda. Climb up and above me."

The Lead reached out, bracing her hand on the matted stone, and was about to spring up when she froze and blinked. "Over you? You mean climb up with you. Or on."

The Dragon shook his head with a smirk and shifted fully onto the platform before settling onto his back. Soon he was sprawled across the mats, taking up almost all the space: wings and arms out to the sides, his legs draped off one end, and heavily scaled feet clinging to the side. His bulky prick jutted out, bobbing above the hard-scaled belly.

"Climb up and *above* me," he repeated with a snicker. "Present your favorite issued equipment where I can better see its function."

Ah.

Jaunda lifted herself onto the platform at Lethrix's left flank, moving steadily from her knees to her feet. She caught his tail swiveling in her periphery, suggesting high eagerness as he waited for her to straddle him at his waist, her legs braced wider than any Davrin in her life.

"Too far," he said, beckoning again. "Up here. Closer."

The only space for her feet was on either side of his thick neck.

She breathed out. *Alright.*

Jaunda expected him to trip her up as she stepped over enviably broad shoulders, her balance precarious and his long reach too tempting. Her host kept his arms down, however, hands drooping off the sides.

His forked tongue reached for her instead, escaping several times through his lips. The purple whip was a long way from licking her cunt but beat out anybody else she'd known by a longshot. That sneaky, purple whip might've been able to side-swipe her ankle without tucking his chin.

He looked up at her, rumbling low in his throat. "Show me your cunt first."

Jaunda smirked and widened her stance, rolling her hips forward in an all-too-familiar way. She reached for her netherlips with the first two fingers of her free hand, pressing and spreading the deep purple flesh open to show him the pink.

The Dragon grabbed hold of his cock. "*Mmrrmm.* Very nice."

Jaunda lifted her detached staff, curling her arm. "Thinking to change how we start?"

"Not at all." His arm moved behind her toward his groin. "Such fascinating craftwork bears deliberate inspection *before* tumbling into a mindless rut. *Heh!* Tempting with cornered prey, though, isn't it? Even knowing you enjoy the anticipation as well."

The Lead arched her brow as she pressed the bulbed base of her Feldeu against her slit, lubricating the toy as she slid and twisted it between her labia. "Oh? How do you know that?"

"You told me." He grinned. "Or rather, *showed* me."

Jaunda exhaled, applying pressure to insert the bulb. She felt her cunt stretch, her mouth opened, and Lethrix's wings quivered.

"Spying on me in Reverie, too?" she asked with a grunt, pushing the wide knob past the early resistance in her slit.

"As you drew closer, and lonelier, in your goal. Your dreams are so vivid, Red Sister, you made it hard to look away."

"Hmph."

With a light swivel of her hips, the base of her Feldeu settled, and she clamped it tight inside. Lethrix reached up then, taking hold of the damp bridge at the bottom, and giving it a mischievous tug before she could stop him.

"Hey!"

"Impressive hold. Do you train *those* muscles, too?"

"Of-fucking-course."

The Dragon chuckled with a hum of delight. "I have a 'bulb' you can use to provide them a workout later."

"You what?" Jaunda glanced over her shoulder at his crotch, spotting yet *more* of his cock emerging from his groin cavity ...

Including a hard, round base that would take real force to work in and no doubt get hung up inside the same as the Sisterhood's favorite weapon.

Oh, fuck.

★Indeed, I'm waiting. What happens next?★

She refocused, cradling the Feldeu with both hands to press it close against her. Without explaining, she whispered the command word to trigger the transformation, witnessing Lethrix's pupils expand with interest. Unable to speak as the magic enveloped her, her wide eyes asked a question.

His tail swished playfully.

★Oh, yes, I heard it.★

Jaunda groaned softly as the false phallus fused with her flesh and mirrored the true form, becoming life-like. The Dragon's tongue lashed the air between them as her groin changed, his languid rumble covering the subtle hum of magic and the slick, sucking noises as her lower body altered its shape to accommodate a perpetual erection.

"Splendid."

Lethrix reached for her again, batting her hand aside when she tried to bat his, and took firm hold of her cock. Jaunda swallowed a growl as heat rushed through her. He tugged downward suggestively.

"Closer."

The space to do that required bracing her knees on either side of his head with his mouth close enough to press scaly lips against her. His tongue could wrap around her pole several times. She wasn't against it.

The Lead got down on her knees above him, tucking her feet beneath his shoulders to anchor herself. Hands braced on her thighs, Jaunda overlooked the abrupt ledge of the platform with nothing to hold onto and nothing to stop her from toppling forward.

Nothing except her host, who covered her hands with his and pushed his snout right up against her, taking an audible whiff.

"*Argh* —"

His tongue shot out and licked her from asshole to pubic hair.

"Whoa! What the fu — ?"

Lethrix had left a slimy trail of goo too thick to be simple saliva.

"Shit, what was that — ?"

Her skin warmed, tingling with concerning intensity.

"*Rrrmmm.*" Heated breath puffed against her crotch and his hands slid higher on her legs, gripping her hips to hold her in place. "Wait."

Jaunda stared down as his tongue extended again, wrapping four times around her rigid staff, which briefly alternated black and lavender in color, both hot and fleshy. She groaned as the Dragon withdrew his tongue long and slow, dragging and twirling her first pleasures of their encounter down her entire length.

"Oh, fuck …"

He left behind thick saliva, the same, rising sensitivity working like a crackling spell on her jutting arousal. His tongue lashed again between her legs, making her body jolt as he applied another layer of goo that had her netherhole twitching and the base of her Feldeu tingling up and deep inside her.

"Shit!"

Jaunda's body shook, her last cry sounding panicked to her own ears as early memories of the Sisterhood rushed in, attempting to drown any sense of the present. Her grip tightened on the legendary beast's wrists near her hips, trying to anchor herself.

What is it, Jaunda? What do you remember?

Wearing this … and losing my mind at first …

Fascinating. Isn't that by design? The Red Sisters become … more aggressive with this attached?

She shivered, her nipples hardening to the point she stared vacantly at them. My trials … Trapped in the Cloister, it was fuck or be fucked …

Unsurprising, with Fadele in charge.

Sh-she wouldn't let Rausery take it off me … for over a quad-span.

Having an erection that long doesn't sound healthy. Why must you wear this will-governing cock so long?

As sore as she made me, I made others sorer …

And she liked that about you.

Yeah. 'Wear it until you love it …'

Heh! So, you were a brute. A beast that would have rutted poor Vik dry a few centuries earlier.

Yeah … She licked her lips, trying to wet a drying mouth. Still do sometimes.

Golden eyes narrowed curiously. *But not mindlessly?*

No. Have to decide to.

Why?

I don't want … rage fucking to control me like it does some others. It doesn't have to. Our Elders showed us that.

Fascinating. If I may say, you're doing well, holding yourself on the edge of the blade.

Lethrix used his tongue on her again, sliding that hot, sizzling appendage against every crease, ridge, and wrinkle. The dizzying effects of his drool were renewed, and aching pleasure coursed through her. Jaunda groaned, heart pounding in her ears.

Choose. Which would you rather have right now? A tight hole to plunge that pole into, or another pole stretching you out? Or does it matter?

She shuddered at his voice in her mind but undecided on the offer as raw memories of the Prime lingered. Trying to see through the haze of lust overtaking her head, D'Shea's Left Hand smirked.

I'll take any hole offered, but only give up mine if I'm beaten in a fight. She smirked, holding his eyes. *It's been a while.*

Heh. I believe that.

Her hips moved unconsciously, her back arching to spread her buttocks before she realized the tip of the Dragon's tongue had squirmed deeper into her pucker, depositing more of his *wanna-fuck* spit as he rimmed her.

"Goddess ..." she gasped aloud, shocked how much her netherhole relaxed.

"Well?" he asked, his tongue extended between his teeth. "Your anther?"

"F-fuck you ... know wha'cher doing, and already tol' you."

Only if I'm beaten in a fight.

Lethrix chuckled, withdrawing his tongue from her ass with another shiver-inducing flick along her bridge. He patted her muscle. "Very well. Get on the cavern floor. Take your time."

Crawling off the platform without a fall held her entire focus. Her feet and hands possessed a disconcerting sensitivity which competed with the more familiar magical intoxication of her Feldeu throbbing with need. Everywhere she touched, her skin seemed determined to count every grain of sand in every hold and step.

At the same time, Lethrix sat up with a too-close whoosh of wings, sliding off the mats, and causing her a disorienting rush of noise and sensation.

"What in fff ... !"

Jaunda spun around to see that Lethrix had shifted into the male Davrin with the Aurenthin eyes. The bua was naked this time, with a similar but taller build to Vik, but with a wide, recognizable grin and sporting an erection that was too bumpy to be fully Elven.

"Let us spar, Jaunda," he said. "I enjoy earning my pleasures."

His voice hadn't changed much despite his size. Strange. She might have thought she hallucinated worse than she was. He stood shorter than her, but his stance suggested he knew how to wrestle.

She squinted at him, trying like all the Void to keep her hands off her slimy, tingling cock when he started stroking his. "What's a 'win' t'you?"

"Hmm, I do not know. How does one 'win' in the Cloister?"

"Pinning."

He grinned wider. "You mean … if one is pinned, they're pinned *twice*?"

Her smirk drew lopsided. "'Sactly."

The Dragon-bua purred. "Deal."

"Heh. Deal within a deal?"

"Indeed. A fight ending in pleasure still meets the Bargain."

She was skeptical. "Either way?"

Wide, gold eyes blinked, the pupils slimming down. "Either way."

Suddenly, there was enough space around them to spar, with most of the previous loose stones gone. Jaunda couldn't think clearly enough to tell whether she had a shot at pinning him first.

Well, he is smaller …

And if she did, would she penetrate him first?

Lethrix chuckled. *✶Thanks to me, you're slicked up and prepared for either outcome.✶*

Good point.

She just wished she wasn't this dizzy.

The Davrin's eyes changed then from red to gold as he focused on her. His voice carried tooth-grinding bass.

"Fight me, Jaunda."

With a deep breath in and blowing it out, the Lead engaged, darting in as if she were in the Cloister, ready to take down a Sister.

The stiff-pricked bua bobbed and weaved out of her way at first, studying her. He let her get closer, until he was a breath away from getting

123

caught. Patiently, despite aching groins, they stayed focused on each other, gradually picking up a back-and-forth, trying to feint and trick their way to count coup. Lethrix watched her intently, curious and fascinated at once.

Interesting.

What?

Nothing.

She nearly tripped him once, pursuing him after a stumble and forcing him into a roll. Jaunda launched forward, grabbing hold of an ankle and yanking the bua toward her.

"Hey, no, not me! *Stop!*"

She froze, blinking furiously before recognizing Vik's voice and realizing she was sprawled *on* his platform instead of ducking behind it where Lethrix had vanished.

The hairs stood up on her nape.

Fuck!

She released Vik's ankle and whirled around, strong legs launching her forward to bull into the golden-eyed bua coming at her.

Finally, they ended up on the ground.

Both her holds and counters to break them, fortunately, were honed from centuries of training and playing with her Sisters. Dizzy head or not, she acted and reacted without thinking. She heard their grunts and gasps, her nose filled with the unusual mix of their sweat and the Draconic drool smeared between them.

Her joints hurt in the way they should while wrestling, abrasions appeared on her skin, and pressure points ached if they stayed pressed against a rocky bump too long. They rolled together, threatening their cracks and crevices with their cocks, struggling to gain the top position, to turn and twist their bodies and secure that one position the other couldn't escape.

The fight felt so *real*. Was he … *not* using his magic or strength to his advantage?

"*Raarrgh … argh … ! Grrrr … whoof!*"

"Getting tired?" he huffed.

"No, are you?" she snarled, muscles quivering from the strain.

He purred and licked her bicep as if to distract her.

It didn't work.

She kept on, determined to pin the bua, trying to force him down long enough to push her cock through the ring between his cheeks. She whispered in his ear, the same as she did with her novices, letting the familiar high and aggression rush through clenched teeth even if the effect wasn't the same.

"Gonna do it ... the moment you slip up ... the instant you make a mistake ... you'll feel me ..."

He didn't return the threats; he focused on outlasting her. Not allowing them to rest.

Eventually, Jaunda's body grew too tired to obey her still-burning spirit. Her head pounded; she was too thirsty; her muscles spasmed and jumped as her grip grew weaker and weaker. Even with boosts from the Feldeu and numerous vials from the wizards, no one had found a way to keep up the fight in perpetuity.

"Ah, *shitfuck!*" Jaunda growled after landing stomach down, feeling the heavy weight. She knew she wouldn't be able to flip him off this time.

The hard cock wedged lengthwise between her ass cheeks.

Shit crystals ...

He laughed. **Do you yield?**

She tried one more time to break his hold and failed. *Yeah. Think I'm fucked.*

I know you are.

He sounded eager.

Lethrix pushed himself up and returned to his larger, two-legged Draconic form before picking her up off the ground by her armpits. His tail shushed a lively rhythm against the stone as he headed for the nearest mat-covered platform.

Although Jaunda's vision swam and she wasn't sure she would stay upright if her opponent suddenly let go, the Lead at least recognized when she was expected to bend over.

The flat stone was about the right height, and the padding wasn't bad.

I've had it worse.

I believe you, Baenar.

He squatted down, his tongue swirling around and into her crinkled star, making her yelp. Next, his rough, scaly hand clapped onto one shoulder, both for leverage and to press her upper body down. The other arm hooked beneath her abdomen and lifted her drooping hips higher, making sure she was at the right height.

Ah, shit …

Then he surprised her, taking hold of her sticky cock, stroking it, experimenting with his grip until a surprised moan of pleasure escaped her mouth.

Ah. Yes.

Lastly, the triangular head nestled between her ass cheeks, pressing firmly against her pucker. Her breath shuddered as he speared it with just the tip, teasing her with it, the rest waiting its turn.

Are you ready?

Only her heartbeat answered at first, as her mind rolled methodically through her preparations for sharp and recurring pain.

I can take it.

I know you can.

His hold on her shoulder firmed up, and his other hand caressed her pole as his own began to penetrate. The Dragon didn't pause once he started but also didn't rush in giving her his whole length.

Jaunda's mouth sagged open as her asshole yielded easily, stretching wider and with greater, welcome sensations than what she'd known on the receiving end of the Prime. She rolled her hips and braced herself to take the rest, moaning louder as the Dragon's hand played with the head of her sensitive phallus. He twisted his fingers and palm around it until he made her ass squeeze down on him in reflex.

Lethrix gasped. *Oh, yes … ! Do you feel that?*

Huh..? She blinked, unable to focus on her surroundings. *Which part?*

He laughed in her mind and patiently finished stuffing his prick in as deep as it would go. Then, he started drawing back, her entire pelvis sizzling as he did. Her legs quaked as he thrust back inside, and something delicious soaked her like a warm waterfall all over.

"*Augh, ohhh!*"

"Yesss!"

She didn't know how much of the Dragon's staff she'd somehow make room for, but now she knew what he'd been talking about.

Do you feel that?

... the F-Feldeu ... ?

*Yes! Very nice, oh ... ! Brilliant ... *

Lethrix released her cock to take hold of her hips, fucking her faster and just as deep. His saliva kept her rear passage slick and welcoming to his use. Not only did the stuff keep her nerves alive and responsive despite physical exhaustion, but she felt every pounding stroke whether his hand caressed her cock or not.

Like magical lightning arcing from her loaded ass to the tip of the sword between her legs.

The sensations didn't run a plateau, either, but kept rising, and building on itself as his cock rubbed incessantly against the firm ball of the magical tool lodged in her cunt.

"Ahh, you feel it, Red Sister. Tell me you do."

Jaunda clutched the mat as he found his pace, like sprinting along a fast-crumbling edge to keep just ahead of it. "Goddess fucking ... *Gahhh!*"

She couldn't stop herself once she started growling, wailing, and moaning. Her own voice spilled out, too much to contain while magic swirled through them, centered on her attached phallus. Sensations tethered to that magic thundered constantly inside her, deeper than the cock fucking her.

Like a waterfall hammering a dam.

High pitches and low, an intense song sometimes cut short, accompanied by a soothing drone, long and drawn out. All of it mixed inside her; her heart raced to keep up. She wasn't sure if she waited to cum, if she had already, or currently *was* and it hadn't stopped.

Never felt anything like this.

"Yesss ..."

Hips slapped harder against her skin as her netherhole relaxed even further to gulp him down. His tail snatched one of her legs, coiling and wrapping up to her thigh. A scalding-hot hand reached to support her abdomen with the palm; he shortened his thrusts but didn't slow down.

Jaunda ... I'm close ...

Fuckin' shit.

A Dragon was about to spray his milky gunk up her ass.

When was the last time any bua did that?

Jaunda's eyes bulged when she felt the first squirt on an in-thrust. She *shouldn't* have been able to feel that.

Worse, it *burned.*

"Ah!"

Lethrix leaned forward to grip the mats with both hands, his claws digging in deep as he held his cock firmly inside. Rumbling, impossibly low, filled the cavern as jets of Dragon spunk collected in her guts, further making her head swim and her tongue heavy.

He pushed to get deeper. Just a little, to wring out every drop of pleasure.

Her ass stretched that small bit more.

Something shifted and began to slide. The pressure increased. A wordless blurt escaped as realization burned through the fog.

Oh, Goddess, the knot ... !

It slipped in. Her anus caught and held it tight, clamping down like a trap. The pressure paralyzed everything but her mouth.

"Oh god — oh *fuck*, fuck!"

Lethrix's tail constricted and he stilled abruptly as if in shock. Then, he threw his head up to the ceiling and bellowed.

Jaunda snatched one instant to try to understand before she was pulled down and ripped through the most breathtaking ride of her life. She might say later that the magic of her Feldeu and the Dragon's cock had joined, becoming one, caught in the same whirlpool. An eternal loop.

Whatever the truth, she focused on nothing else for quite some time.

CHAPTER 10

DREAMWALKING

AVEL STOOD IN DESOLATE SANDS, BAREFOOT AND BAFFLED AS TO HOW HE'D GOTten here. Behind him, the Sun was setting, and his shadow stretched out in front of him, reaching toward a hazy spike of rock breaking the open horizon. He wore only a cool, pale wrap around his waist.

"Ilharn?"

He turned around slowly, looking around him.

"Where are you … ?"

Before him, he saw her tawny eyes, her hands covered in blood as she cornered him. Hands covered in his sire's blood.

His heart tightened in his chest as he remembered.

Ilharn is dead. And I was dragged away to that … prison.

Was he out? Had he escaped her somehow?

After so long, how is that possible?

The quiet felt unnatural, even for an empty desert he'd visited so many times. Insects, rodents, and reptiles often reminded him he was never alone, except for this place. Nothing so small as a fly came to beg drinking the tears which threatened to fall.

Suddenly, a rumble too low for his keen ears chased away the silence, its tremors flowing through the sand. Avel could feel it in his feet first, in his teeth a moment later. The distant quake had originated from behind him, to the West and North. He froze in place.

What should I do? Run? Find a place to hide?

Next came a droning swell and a lingering shush which urged him to turn around. He shielded his eyes with one hand as the fading light changed.

A cloud so enormous as to block the Sun and alter the atmosphere gradually took over the twilight. A dim glow, blue and white, strong enough to light up the brightest part of the evening sky.

What is happening?

Then, rolling toward him like an overflowing river, Avel sensed the underlying pain which followed. Voiceless but essential.

A soul.

Suddenly, Avel feared the night falling, for it would leave him alone in the dark with this sensation. Only suffering to occupy his time.

No. Not again.

If I can find it, perhaps I can heal it.

ONE COULD NEVER PRESUME DISTANCE AS A CONSTANT IN THIS PLACE. A FEW steps toward a deliberate focus on the horizon changed one's periphery beyond what reason would suggest.

The change could seem too quick, as if time were missing or steps skipped over. It could also feel like that mirage which continually shifted just out of reach. Rarely could his feet count the dunes with accuracy, as if he merely moved from one waking dream to another.

If there were any consistency to be had in whether he approached his destination in the end, it might have to do with his drive and clarity of purpose. Such as now.

Someone's hurt. Slowly, he breathed it in. *I ... know this pain.*

The night had just begun. Stars strengthened in their pinpoints of light far above, the sands fading from purple to black. Neither Sister Moon had risen yet, and the bua might trip over something unseen if he moved much faster.

Still, palatial walls rose above the dark purple dunes long before he should have felt any fatigue, and a subtle glow emanated from beyond a dark barrier. He stared at the faded light source without blinking, afraid it might vanish if he did.

That's it.

His destination was extravagant and had been built upon a steep-sided crest of solid rock. The outer, protective walls were sheer and extended the incline even higher into the air, one blending into the other as it cast the largest shadow in the desert.

The architecture seemed familiar in several ways, with its high archways and organic curves, offering many places to hide from sight. Multiple spires arose above as strategic watch points, but the outer walls weaved around the fortress like a sand snake. Loose, sliding rock filled each dip inward while the outward curves of the walls seemed to push out against unwanted visitors.

Lastly, he spotted a drawbridge lying down, resting atop a massive, constructed ramp mostly buried in sand. He paused and looked around the lands surrounding the apparent palace but saw no other buildings or roads.

Unless the rest of the city is buried.

As Avel drew closer, the blue-white glow strengthened to his eyes. As details came into focus, he stopped to study the way the light behaved like water and fire melded together without turning to steam. Heat waves rose high before cooling and falling, flowing downward to roll off the fortress in waves.

I've never seen this before …

Have I?

This light affected the rest of the valley, stirring or waking things to create subtle noises behind him where before it'd been silence. Even his footsteps sounded less muffled as the hardness of distinctive slabs of stones replaced the sinking sand beneath his feet.

Fatigue finally arrived as he began the long, steady climb up the stone ramp leading to the drawbridge and the main gate. With so much empty space around this place, he could not help but believe there must have been many more buildings here before.

… Before what?

Avel panted as he stepped onto the worn bridge and approached the open archway. No obstructions appeared to prevent his entering this palace in the desert.

Inside, the blue-white glow centered near the back, the only light source giving him a sense of the shape and scale. A wide, open space spread out before him, paved with fine-cut stone and lined with columns bearing the weight of two upper floors and defensive walkways.

At the other end was a spacious platform with numerous shallow steps leading to its centerpiece: an ornate, open-aired pavilion sheltering a drinking well.

The bua blinked then rubbed his eyes before refocusing.

The light source was a … body.

Somebody. Trying to drink from the well.

The figure was slumped over a courtyard away, enveloped in roiling light which should hurt the eyes. Somehow, Avel knew this wasn't another Davrin. If not an Elf, what was he to do? Could they even speak the same language?

The body slid off the edge of the pale-yellow stone with a low grunt. The sound bursting from the sprawled bulk triggered a memory, and the tension from it seized him.

Human. Male.

Men were unpredictable around Davrin buas without escorts, and they were dangerous on account. Sometimes they enjoyed Avel's dance, laughing and throwing coins; sometimes they glowered at him or studied him like a predator, considering the best moment to attack.

Still other times, the young ones rallied in loud groups, a morass difficult to tell what any one of them thought about him or those like him. Their minds seemed to vanish behind their eyes as if under a collective spell. Avel had taken his Ilharn's advice and never stayed to confront them.

He hasn't seen me. I can leave.

He should leave.

Before something happens.

The bua spun around, sprinting toward the front gate. He made it two strides before skidding to a stop, for once aware of the sensation of hard stone abrading his heel.

Avel stared in disbelief.

The drawbridge was up. The portcullis was down.

How ... ?

He'd heard nothing.

"*Tanoi akea?*" the man rasped as loudly as he could through the pain.

Avel's heart clenched in his chest, but he couldn't tell if that one throb was terror or empathy. Worse, he felt he should *understand* what the man had said.

"*Anak chea?*"

The man reached out with his arms above his head, struggling to pull his radiant body along the stones as his legs bent and scrabbled behind him. He started crawling toward him, away from the well.

"*Anak chea?*" Another rattling breath. "*Tanoi akea?*"

The front gate was still sealed. The bua's eyes teared up as he struggled to slow his breathing. He wet his mouth and swallowed.

"My name is Avel."

The man stopped in his long path as if resting. Or thinking. He should not have been so close but lay midway across the courtyard. The dark hair was as apparent as the light brown skin on his face and hands. The rest of him was covered with foreign clothing which seemed too warm for the Red Desert.

He's been in a fight.

Far too many recent rents and tears in the clothing and leather armor to be anything else. Beyond them should have been scorched flesh, bleeding slashes, and stab wounds to match the damage. Instead, although the wounds were striking, they were only apparent in his aura.

"Avel," the sorcerer whispered. "Do you recognize what I am?"

The man spoke the Davrin language perfectly.

"N-no," he answered, looking to the sides for a possible escape as the man crawled toward him. "I do not."

"Yes, you do … I am a l-life mage. Like you. You can h-heal me."

He can tell?

"To do so," the bua replied slowly, "I would have to touch you."

"So be it," he rasped, growling in pain. "I am Cris-ri-phon. The S-Sorcerer-General to Her Majesty, the Queen."

The Queen?

Not my Queen …

"H-help me." The large body scraped along the stone, bleeding magic from his wounds. "And name your r-reward."

The man's image suddenly flickered like a mirage then stabilized after a blink. Somehow, the Human was close enough for Avel to make out his face. The Davrin backed up in fright, sidestepping to his right.

Goddess …

Reddened burn marks crossed his eyes, nose, and cheeks. They lacked singe marks, as if something caustic had been thrown in his face. Purple and red streaks showed on his neck and disappeared beneath his collar, as if he'd been bitten by something large and venomous. White and blue threads tangled around him, writhing like earthworms before they spread out to fill the cracks in the courtyard, reluctant to break off but unable to return to the whole.

"Wh-what happened to you?" Avel asked over the roaring blood in his own ears.

The sorcerer's fist shook as it clenched shut, and Cris-ri-phon plopped down as if at the end of his endurance. His breathing wasn't close to normal but didn't seem to be failing yet.

"Heal me, and I shall t-tell you."

Avel looked behind him at the sealed gate and across the courtyard at too many passages hidden by the dark. One could be a way out, or they could be locked. Some might contain something worse than this man.

"Will you set me free?" he asked, moving his feet to make sure the sorcerer couldn't lunge for him if he struck like a snake. "If I help you, will you let me leave, alone and unharmed, to go where I wish?"

The blind Human huffed with contempt. "Is that all you w-want?"

Avel felt an ancient sting in his chest. "It is all I've *ever* wanted."

Rasping breath as the sorcerer thought about it. "Of course, I will."

"Can you open the gate? Or tell me which of these archways leads out of the palace?"

"What do you mean?" Cris-ri-phon chuckled to cover his impatience.

"The gate is closed. Did you not close it?"

Again, the sorcerer hesitated before answering. "I d-don't know. This place is … strange. Like a dream. Heal me, and I shall s-solve that riddle for you."

"And let me go."

"Of course, yes."

He's lying. Or hiding something.

"Now, help me, bua. This *hurts* … *!*"

Avel believed him. He knew how this felt.

Still, what have I gotten myself into?

"May I add one additional boon to hold in reserve?" he asked.

The man growled, "You little …"

"You said to name my reward, Sorcerer-General. Can you not grant it?"

Cris-ri-phon exhaled hoarsely like a hot wind. His body quaked. "I c-can. But n-not if *you* fail to heal my aura. I owe *nothing* then."

The Davrin bua swallowed. "I can heal you. I will not fail."

"P-prove it." His scarred brow pressed to the pale stone. "You will have my gratitude. And my Queen's."

Whoever she is. My own would not approve of this.

But how would he leave otherwise? Could he walk away and leave the sorcerer to unravel? To become …

Something worse.

The bua kneeled and stretched out one arm, barely within distance to hover his hand above Cris-ri-phon's closed fist. Their auras crackled in the space separating them, blending white and blue with gold, purple, and red, each pushing and twisting around the rest until—

"*Argh!*" they cried together, drawing their limbs away until the crackling stopped.

Avel clutched his hand to his chest, shaken at the crush of disrupted life, an unending whorl of waves passing through him.

"You're not —" the Davrin began.

"You are —" the Human said.

" — alone."

" — like me."

Avel blinked. "What did you say?"

"You are," the man repeated with a grimace, "like me."

I am not ...

The sorcerer's blistered mouth twisted into a smile. "How many lifetimes, Avel?"

No. I am not ...

"How many?"

"I d-don't know —"

"I believe you."

"What? I didn't mean —"

"I believe you c-can *heal* me," Cris-ri-phon forced out, pushing his hand forward. "Do it. Now. G-grab on and don't let go."

Avel reached out and saw his hand shaking. "Just ... release me afterward."

"Did we not make a deal?"

"Y-yes?"

"Then touch me."

The healer steeled himself, unconsciously slowing his aura down as he tried again to make contact. His dark hand quivered over the Human's broad fist, and what had shocked before merely hummed this time.

Avel breathed out slowly, calming his own patterns further, gradually bringing the injured mage's whirling pain down into the cool oasis with him.

"*Uhm, mmm ...*" Cris-ri-phon murmured, his tone and body implying this was the first relief he'd experienced in some untold amount of time.

"Hold still," the bua whispered, at last closing the gap to press upon fevered skin, pushing outward with his will at the same time.

The sorcerer gasped sharply, but Avel did not lose focus as he carefully threaded his aura's colors through the wrecked muddle of the other. He must bring some pattern of life back, or it would never sustain itself. It would degrade.

And the pain will never stop. He'll become a lost soul.

A dangerous one.

The deeper he went, the surer Avel felt that he was not the first to do this. Cris-ri-phon bore multitudes of stitches and scars throughout his life mage's aura. Beyond each of those marks of pearly white and sky blue lay weak, muted slashes of shaded grey.

Strange.

As the man settled down, his breathing closer to normal, the Davrin reached with his other hand to rest it on the thick forearm.

Chronic turmoil struggled to flee its new, budding pattern, but the healer kept burgeoning pain under control. Coaxing stitch after stitch, he knitted rents and gaps closed, anchoring each one within brighter spots which might hold together long enough to become a self-sustaining loop.

This ... process shouldn't be so familiar.

If he'd done this before for other Davrin, how could the same method work for a Human? That was the mystery. Cris-ri-phon's aura did not feel like a regular man. His aura had been woven to mimic that of an Elf.

Or something else entirely.

"You were not born this way," he whispered, his doubts ill-defined in a vast sea of possibilities.

"Hm?" The sorcerer's blisters had lessened, as had the swelling and bruising around his eyes which remained closed.

"What happened?" Avel murmured back, studying the unique weave as it accelerated toward renewal. "Who did this to you?"

Avel didn't expect an answer. He let the quiet fill the space so he could better listen to the hum of a healthier aura while finding the weak spots.

"Sovereign ..." Cris-ri-phon breathed.

"Hm? What?"

"Sovereign ..." His eyelids fluttered. "Did this ..."

Sovereign? Of what?

"How?" he asked again. "What happened?"

The man breathed deeper, in rhythm, as if he were on the edge of sleep. The glowing cuts and holes were shrinking; soon, they would be part of the pattern.

"I grew old," the Human said. "But I wanted …"

Avel swallowed, waited, and continued to mend.

" … to return to her."

"Return? To our Queen?"

"Innathi … The Sovereign showed me the way …"

Avel frowned, aware by now that the hum had regained its song, clear enough not to falter while the man regained his strength. Cris-ri-phon rested without pain, and the bua removed his hands to straighten up and stretch.

Glad I did not have to get closer to make this work.

He confirmed the gate had not yet opened.

Now what?

Avel listened to his body, light as a dream though it seemed, to reassure himself that he hadn't injured his aura or given too much to the man. He seemed alright, but something was lacking.

The healer's eyes lifted toward the well at the other end.

I am thirsty …

If he must wait until the sorcerer woke up to let him out, then at least he could get a drink.

Avel stood up, brushed off his knees, and walked farther into the empty courtyard. A few times, he glanced at the columns and the many doors and archways behind them, half-expecting to see menacing eyes glowing in the shadows. Watching him.

Calm. Keep walking.

He stepped barefoot onto the stairs leading to the grand pavilion, reflecting that shelter from the stars was less desirable than shelter from the sun. Moreover, he wasn't glowing as the sorcerer had been. Beneath the fine quality structure, he could barely see the nuance of the well in the center as he reached out. His fingers touched the rough stone, rougher than it should have been.

Hit by a sandstorm recently.

Avel peered around the sides, searching for a bucket, then looked inside for a hook or a crank. There was nothing with which to retrieve the water he smelled underneath the blackness.

Damned Abyss.

Deep down, something moaned, and a shape wavered before his eyes. Avel gripped the sides and ducked, hoping he'd not been seen by whatever might be living in this well.

… No splash.

Yet he was certain the well held *water*. He could smell it, and it made his tongue feel thick and gummy.

Silence.

Resting on one knee, Avel glanced over at Cris-ri-phon, who still slept. He studied the strange man's aura, assured it would continue healing on its own.

Yes. He will recover.

But how long should he wait here? Should he try to find his own way or keep trying for that drink?

Another moan drifted up from the well, urging the hairs at his nape to rise.

"*Mmmaaahhhzzz … … dehhhl … *"

He bit his lip, his vision blurring. He pulled himself up to peer into the well again, his ears wide open, clutching to the well as tightly as he did to some ridiculous hope.

After a moment, he asked, "Sire?"

Is it you?

"Ilharn?"

A brief glimmer of gold winked out, too weak to say if it had really been there. Then, cold lightning and green fire swirled together in the darkness, splintering again, mimicking harsh, leafless trees. A grey mist lightened the darkness until he could see shapes. *Faces.*

A grey-faced warrior woman with ritual scars on her face.

A large-boned man-beast with muted green skin and tusks.

A fantastical wasp-girl with black hair and antennae.

They gazed into a pool at the other end. The warrior woman and man-beast smiled; the girl's two feelers twitched, perking up as her odd, black eyes turned pale blue to focus on him. Avel could have sworn he heard the buzzing of insect wings through the water's window.

"Who are you?" he asked.

Then, the three abruptly looked away and toward someone else out of his limited sight. Their heads tilted and mouths moved, but he could not hear their voice, nor was there a sound when they stepped away from the water's edge. The only one tall enough to remain visible was the tusked man.

Then, another Davrin appeared, looking down the well at him. His smile held an intense interest that discomforted Avel.

"You still exist," he murmured with joy and awe.

The healer could hear him as if they stood on opposite sides of a mirror. *Who ... ? Wait.*

He frowned to recall the last time he'd glimpsed this face during another dreamwalk.

When he'd been with a blue-eyed cait in uniform.

He beckoned us, standing at a merchant's stall.

"Toushek?" he asked.

The intense smile softened into pure pleasure as he breathed out, his voice warm as the eve. "*Ahh*, you begin to remember. I knew you would find a way to send for me."

The bua gripped the well harder. "Did I ... send for you?"

"Of course you did. I have met Sirana." Crimson eyes flared with an icy emerald fire beneath shocking white locks of hair. "I've seen her aura."

Sirana.

The name clubbed him over the head.

How could he ... ?

How could I forget?

"Shall I come retrieve you?" Toushek asked, his mannerisms not at all like a merchant, nor in the way he gazed at him. He was far too regal. "Where are you now?"

The younger bua shivered. "Wh-why?"

"Why? Don't you want to be free, Mazdel?"

If Sirana's name had struck his head like someone trying to get his attention, *this* name pierced his chest like a white-hot arrow. He screamed and fell away from the well, landing hard on bare knees. Toushek called through the water.

"Mazdel! Grandson! Say you want me to come!"

"*You* ..." Cris-ri-phon hissed, too close and above him.

Avel jerked his eyes up, hand clutched over his seizing heart. He couldn't take a full breath as he watched the Human touch the rim of the well then wave his hand over it.

No voice rose from the well. Toushek was gone.

The palace courtyard fell dead silent but for the two of them breathing heavily. The damage in clothing and armor remained on the sorcerer's body, but life and magic worked together within it as he stared with furious, steel-grey eyes.

"You lied to me," said the Zauyrian. "You're not 'Avel.' "

The bua shook his head, scooting on his knees to try regaining his feet. "I did not lie. I *am* Avel —"

Cris-ri-phon swung one leg and kicked, knocking him down before he could stand. "When did you get out of your prison, Mazdel? Where did she take you after the war?"

Oh, Goddess ...

"Get away from me," he croaked, backing up on hands and heels as he tried to avoid another kick. "Or ... or I'll call my grandsire."

The Zauyrian chuckled with a sinister bend. "Even *he* might regret treading where he doesn't belong. Your father would see to that."

"M-my sire's dead!" he cried, quaking to recall the Seer breaking into their home the night she came for him. "Sh-she killed him in front of me!"

"I mean your *father!*" the sorcerer snapped back, ending in a roar. "The old bastard who made you what you are! The reason you are here with me!"

"I don't ..."

"Don't you understand? We can't *die!*"

"I don't know who you're talking about!"

Avel scrambled down the steps of the platform, partly crawling or rolling, his elbows soon raw and his heels stinging from raking the stone. Every time he tried to get up, Cris-ri-phon would rush him, kicking or shoving him over to keep him down until they were on flat ground. There, the larger man dropped, trapping him beneath his weight, and captured his wrists in two large, callused hands.

"J-just let me go," he begged. "You agreed, General, please —"

"I could do now what I couldn't before, '*nephew*,'" the man said, his brown face darkening as his eyes turned ghostly grey. "I could get us out of this eternal trap we've found ourselves in."

"N-no, I don't want your help! Not anymore!"

"Stop struggling." Cris-ri-phon pinned Avel's wrists above his head, his hunger intensifying, staring right through him. "I bet I could make quite a deal for you. I could get the relic back."

"You must keep your deal with me!" the Davrin shouted. "Release me and let me leave!"

"Don't be foolish," the sorcerer snarled. "You want to wander the Desert forever? He couldn't resist such an offer. He'll meet us at the border."

"No!" Avel shouted, defiant. "I *won't* go with you!"

Cris-ri-phon laughed, releasing one wrist to draw back his arm, large hand closing into a fist. "You won't even be aware."

"Stop!"

The Zauyrian threw his full strength into that first strike. Pain exploded at his temple and his vision swam, but somehow didn't go black.

"Go to *sleep!*"

Avel's hands began to burn as if he held hot coals in his palms. He threw up one to meet the next attack, and a gout of flame erupted in the scant air between them. Cris-ri-phon threw himself back, flailing as he was engulfed in fire.

"*Aughh!*"

The moment his other wrist was freed, he threw the second blast of flame, rolling to one side in desperation, managing to get free.

"*Mazdeeeeel!*"

He rose, hitting his elbows and knees with no foot or leg kicking him, and finally pushed himself up to regain his feet. Every impulse screamed at him to run.

Where? Where do I go? I must get out!

Before either man or bua could dismiss the magical fire, water exploded from the well. The frothing geyser blew a hole in the roof of the pavilion, bursting high enough to fall like rain upon half the courtyard. The water was shockingly cold on his hot, dry skin, and put out the fire on the Zauyrian.

Avel turned to witness the source of the water overspilling the platform, expecting Toushek or whoever he really was.

No choice but to go with him.

Still a prisoner, just somewhere else.

What would happen to Sirana? What about their child? Would he never see them in his dreams? What would happen if he never woke up again?

Poor Natia …

Avel blinked as a shadow with metallic gold eyes and black-purple scales climbed out of the well. Long, white spines lifted along his spine like a dorsal fin, and his tail lashed behind him, incredibly long and nimble. The shape of the body told Avel to expect sudden sprints and long leaps upon any target the beast chose as prey.

Those predator's eyes focused on him.

Avel looked toward the front gate. *Still closed.*

"YOU!! You followed me?!" Cris-ri-phon roared, more furious with this creature than he'd been with Avel. "Even here! Do we end this now?" He laughed maniacally as he prepared to cast. "You think you'll succeed where others failed, boy?!"

The fang-filled mouth responded. "*Wolius itre.*"

The sorcerer's hands jerked down uncontrollably, nearly setting the spell down at his feet. "Cur — !"

"*Wic-spical!*"

Cris-ri-phon stumbled like he'd been shoved, falling hard and landing on his back.

Goddess ...

Avel had stared in shock too long. Seconds later, the massive creature had slipped up next to him. He screamed, and the beast hissed back, staring into his eyes.

"Get on, Consort."

Avel swallowed. "G-get on?"

"My back. *Hurry*. I will get you out."

The bua was shaking, but the words sank in. "Y-your price?"

Fangs bared as the talking lizard-cat swung his head to watch the sorcerer trying to get up. "No price. *Move*."

He moved. *Goddess, what am I doing?*

Where the neck met shoulders reached chest-level on Avel, so he had to leap up before swinging his leg over. He gripped several long spines and squeezed his thighs against the flanks, unsure of his hold.

"Can we get over the walls?"

"We will try."

"The Seer's son stays with me!" barked the Zauyrian. "We have a bargain!"

"Keep your bargain for when you will honor it, Deathless."

Avel's rescuer took off for one of the columns, climbing it like a tree trunk toward the upper floors and the watch wall. The healer should have fallen off, but words murmured by the hybrid had created a magical lash-down which kept him firmly in place. Once they reached the top, a powerful gust of wind struck him full in the face. As sand scraped at his cheeks like tiny fingers, he realized the stars were gone.

Covered by a sand cloud.

"He's coming!" Cris-ri-phon bellowed from the quiet of the court-yard. "I hope you get swallowed, *To'vah-krav!* You hear me?! Flayed raw and *swallowed!*"

Neither replied as the hybrid leaped off the palace walls and skidded down the steep hillsides to flee the palace and its haunts at last.

Avel clung for his life as the Dragonchild sprinted for both of theirs, aiming across the dunes to stay ahead of the storm.

CHAPTER 11

AVEL CLUNG TO HIS BEST MEANS OF ESCAPE AS THEY WEAVED THROUGH THE troughs of the dunes. Whenever he shut his eyes, it felt like they slipped faster above the sand. The looming storm blotted out most of the sky, but its front wall remained distant enough that the flying grains of sand swirling in the dips had yet to turn his exposed skin into one big rash.

His rescuer seemed to be overheating underneath him, especially his shoulders. He did not sweat, however, as if he'd been struck by sunstroke and lost too much water to feel anything but fevered.

The deep, huffing breaths reminded him of speeding animals much larger in size. The base of his dorsal spines flexed on occasion, the row testing whether to stand up again, but Avel's weight was enough to keep them flat. The bua couldn't tell whether his Draconic mount approached the edge of his endurance but was afraid to ask, especially when they crested their first dune.

The storm had shifted its shape. The clouds had begun rolling parallel alongside them, stretching thinner as if trying to get ahead of the astonishing, black-scaled runner. Parts of the roiling clouds lightened as if the Sister Moons shone behind them, dissolving their light into the maelstrom to help calm it.

The Davrin began to hope they might not be overtaken and lose their way, wherever that was.

"Where do you take me?"

His words were swept from his lips the moment he said them. Either the hybrid was moving too fast to speak, or he hadn't heard the question. Regardless, the awkward silence didn't last.

Once they crested the next dune and began a new descent, Avel saw the oasis, heard the calming of the wind; he smelled green plants and felt the restful touch of rare vapor caressing his dusty skin.

"Oh ..."

Someone else was there getting a drink. Another four-legged beast. Longer legs, hooves instead of claws, an arched, maned neck leading down an incredible back to a banner-like tail.

As the horse craned his neck around to peer at them, Avel stared at the way the sorrel-red hide shimmered with silver in the barest light the night had to offer. The stallion was one of the most beautiful breeds the bua had ever seen. This caused him to panic as his rescuer did not slow in their approach to the water's edge.

"Wait, don't pounce on him ... !" he blurted.

"*Get off!*" the other male growled as the patch of scales between his shoulder blades reached a scorching temperature, too hot for Avel to rest his skin against without risking blisters.

We're going for the water.

Avel threw himself off the charging hybrid on the right side, aided by his sharp turn to the left. He landed with a grunt, rolling close enough to fear the stallion trampling him when it reared up on hind legs, neighing in alarm.

Behind him, a large splash preceded a smattering of droplets decorating his bare back.

"Whoa, whoa, *whoa!*" he cried, rolling the other direction from the massive animal, his skin coated in sand.

The horse dropped his front legs and did not rear again; he lowered his head, ears pricked forward curiously with one dark eye on him and another on the rippling pond.

"Uh, h-hello," Avel muttered, one empty hand up and out toward the stallion as he took a step closer. "Good boy?"

Nostrils flared near his palm, drawing in his scent then blowing out. He whickered softly in response, seeming to have forgotten about the dangerous predator in the water. The horse blinked once at him, standing with a calm and patience which seemed unreal.

Do I ... know you, somehow?

A series of gentle trickles of water caught his ear, and he looked at the pond as the hybrid surfaced and glided toward them, tail weaving through water, white spines stretching up, and gold eyes shining.

Like some unsettling river serpent.

Avel glanced at the stallion, who watched the approach without concern. He tried to relax his shoulders.

"Um, what can you tell me?" he asked. "Why did you come through the well? How ... how did you know I needed help?"

The hunter crawled halfway out of the water, settling down on his belly with forepaws resting on damp sand, his tail idly flicking along the water's surface.

"I didn't," he answered, his speech somewhat impeded by the shape of his mouth and teeth. "Was following others. Led to you."

Metallic eyes fixed on him, vertical pupils expanding as if to take him in.

Avel swallowed, indicating the stallion, who'd taken to nibbling at some sturdy grass growing near the water. "And him?"

His rescuer looked at the horse without apparent temptation to hunt him. "That one does not talk but is safe. He is old."

"Old?" The Davrin Elf peered at the gleaming hide and strong animal in his prime. "How old?"

"Older than me." Draconic eyes narrowed at him. "Perhaps older than you."

"*Pteh*," he chuffed in doubt. "How could a horse live that long?"

The serpentine hunter lifted a brow ridge as the oasis swirled gently to keep his flanks cool. The answer came soon enough.

Not just a horse.

"Never mind," Avel muttered, pushing to sit up. "I'm Avel. Who are you?"

Those shining eyes stared at him for several moments before he said something. "Avel is not all you are."

Not again.

"Oh?" The bua tried to keep the bitterness in check. "What else do you think I am?"

After a pause, the hybrid said, "Have you looked in a reflection?"

"What? No." He looked around, incredulous. "Do *you* see any mirrors in the middle of the Desert?"

The other smirked, glancing at the liquid swirling around him. "I do."

Damnit.

"No," he refused before the runner said more. "It's too dark out."

His rescuer shrugged his shoulders then stood up out of the oasis, rivulets of water draining between his scales and dripping off his belly into the shallows. "I need to leave."

"What?! Not yet, please! Who are you?"

The hybrid shook his head. "Better not to speak it here."

"Wha ... well, at least tell me why you helped me?"

"Simply to deny those who sought to trick you. You owe me nothing for taking my means of escape." Another smirk. "Indeed, it would seem you gained in your bargains."

Avel climbed to his feet, willing his heart to slow. "How did you know I made a bargain with the sorcerer? You said he must keep it ... just before we went over the wall."

A long, lavender tongue extended between dry, scaly lips, forked and flicking the air like a sand snake. "I could taste it between you."

"Taste it? *How?*"

Again, those golden eyes peered at him. "You should look at yourself."

A shiver went down the Davrin's spine. "No, I ..."

I can't.

"As you will. Still, I cannot stay."

The healer stiffened. "Why not?"

"I endanger you, but —"

"But you brought me here. Do I stay?"

The Dragonchild motioned his muzzle toward the calm, grazing stallion. "*But.* He does not. If the free-runner will let you ride, he will take you where you must go without a price."

Avel gazed at the admittedly captivating steed who bore no signs of serving Human or Elf. *A free-runner without a price ...*

"But what if — ?"

His rescuer had returned to the water, swimming toward the center of the oasis as a long, black shadow.

"Hey!"

The runner, now a swimmer, submerged with surprisingly little noise and barely a splash. Avel stared at the concentric rings expanding from the vanishing point and waited for long enough for any land creature to run out of air.

Yet, the Dragonchild did not resurface.

Dung beetles. Where could he even swim?

Arms wrapped around himself, the Davrin turned. The stallion had stopped munching briefly to watch the ripples settle then returned to the grass.

Glad you don't seem concerned.

The bua looked above him, listening as the wind calmed with startling abruptness, and a patch of clear sky and stars showed through moonlit clouds. A belated sense of exhaustion caught him then, and he sat down on the cooling sand with a long sigh. In time, the Red Desert grew as quiet as when he'd last become aware, before following that glow to the pale Desert palace.

I don't normally meet so many others who seem to know who I am. What is different? What's changed?

Toushek's simple statement returned.

"*I've met Sirana.*"

The cait with blue eyes. One of so many.

"*I've seen her aura.*"

But unlike all the others before, Sirana was alive. She willingly carried their bond-child. The longer she lived, however, the more obvious the pregnancy would become to other eyes.

Like Toushek.

The merchant knew Sirana had caught, Avel was sure. Worse, he recognized the sire ... somehow. His forehead dropped onto his forearms, crossed atop his knees. *What have I done?*

Why hadn't the Queen stopped her yet, or recalled the Red Sister? *No one's made it this far in Her games before ...*

He didn't know what would happen next.

Is there anything I can do to help her?

The soft thud of hooves announced the stallion's approach, followed by a deep breath which rattled his nostrils. With the neck down, ears swiveling but lifted, and a gentle shake of his mane, Avel didn't believe he was about to get stepped on. He waited until the horse loomed above him and stopped, whiffling his fine hair.

"Hello, again," he murmured. "Do you have a name? Or any ideas what to do next?"

The stallion burred with another shake of his mane then stood watching him. Avel pursed his lips.

"Thanks," he said.

The Sister Moons had been rising for a while, he realized, when the last clouds finally cleared. When the light touched the horse directly, the silver sheen of his red coat seemed metallic.

"You're quite beautiful," the Davrin said, hugging his knees tighter. "I imagine others try to capture you a lot, don't they? And somehow, you evade them?"

The stallion's ears were pricked forward, listening to him, and in the next quiet moment, he dipped his head and nudged the bua's bare shoulder with his nose. Avel smiled, though it vanished when the stallion's next nudge was harder, using his forehead. He caught himself before he fell over.

"What? What do you want?"

The horse's graceful neck turned toward the oasis.

"I'm not thirsty," he muttered, despite having been so desperate for a drink at the palace well. When the horse nudged him again, he added, "No, thank you."

The stallion did not leave, or nudge again, but stood over him as if keeping watch. Avel wasn't sure if he dozed off or not, but suddenly witnessed sunrise in the Red Desert.

The colors around them intensified, becoming ore-vibrant with the touch of the Sun Brother. The red and pink horizon gave way to a sky fast becoming blue. The sand deepened like rusted weapons while the grasses and shrubs around the pond turned verdant green. Avel watched the silvery Moons gradually fade from the surface of the water, until it reflected the clear sky.

Clear as a mirror.

The stallion's forehead bumped him from behind. Taken off-guard, he fell to one side, quickly bracing himself on an elbow.

"Hey!"

The sorrel burred and clopped by him to the water. He touched his muzzle to the surface, taking a long drink and barely spilling any when he next lifted his head. He peered back with his rump pointed full at the Davrin, swishing his full, black tail.

Exhaling on a sigh and a laugh, Avel got to his feet and brushed off the dried sand. "I'm sure it's refreshing."

The stallion whickered, nodding his head before going for another gulp as if to prod his envy.

Sigh. I thought the hybrid said he didn't talk.

The stallion was, at least, trying to communicate, and this place felt less lonely than it usually did on account.

If I look now, at least I won't be alone.

Avel approached the water to stand next to the sipping horse. The tough grass under his feet felt so real.

But I'm not really here, am I? The hybrid would have come up for air by now if we were awake.

Trembling from a rising fear he could not identify, the bua kneeled on the damp sand left by his rescuer. The stallion stopped drinking to watch him steel himself, preparing to reach with two hands, to wash off the grit before cupping his hands to drink.

He stopped before he could disrupt the calm, glassy surface of the oasis, when his own face had come into view.

Metallic gold eyes, as he'd seen in his rescuer.

No. They're not the same.

Avel lacked the vertical pupils of the Dragonchild; his pupils were round. He had whites in his eyes, if less pronounced, more than the other male had. The only quality they had in common were irises filled with molten gold, forming a piercing gaze out of the water.

It can't be real. I-I don't know you.

His eyes had always been normal red. *Always.*

This was a dream.

"Do my eyes appear like gold?" he asked.

The stallion whickered again, rubbing a soft nose against his ear and hair. Was that yes or no?

"And ... and what is this?" he demanded of his reflection, lifting his hands to look at the palms before touching his face. "What are all these scars? H-how did I ... ?"

I don't know this face.

His reflection blurred behind tears as his throat started to hurt. Again, the horse nuzzled him and stayed close, sharing his calming aura, which was a good thing. Or he'd be wailing to the sky from the ground by now.

"You are like me. We can't die ..."

Now he understood what Cris-ri-phon had meant. Not his skin that was scarred, but his aura, injured and healed so many times, and by means he did not recognize. Not *him* that had done it; he hadn't healed himself. Whoever had done it had left marks.

So many marks.

How many times had he *almost* died, only to be brought back? Why hadn't he unraveled? Why was he here, why had he not left?

Where is my oblivion?

And why was this only clear to him now?

Avel's shoulders shook with silent sobs until the stallion offered him a strong neck to hold and a thick mane to bury his face into it. He held on, weeping into the coarse hair until he had exhausted himself into a still point. A place without intrusive thoughts or haunting voices, where he could await an answer.

An answer to anything at all.

"Will you let me ride, magnificent one?" he whispered. "Take me to where I must go …"

The stallion's tail swished audibly, and he tapped one hoof upon the sand, burring through his long nose. Reluctantly, Avel loosened his arms, and the horse straightened up, turning to a nearby slope. The stallion carefully kneeled into the slanted sand, offering the Davrin Elf an easier way to climb on.

"Thank you."

His breath as unsteady as his legs, Avel approached and climbed onto the second creature who would carry him away from what troubled him to an unknown destination.

May it be a place I might be welcomed and embraced.

Rather than coveted, hurt, then abandoned.

No storm chased the stallion as it had the Dragonchild, although the Brother Sun stayed at their backs for most of the morning. As a powerful though peaceful light overtook the softness of the dawn, Avel fell into simple enjoyment in a swift but easy lope.

The stallion never seemed to tire, and no obstructions appeared which he could not leap over. His long stride carried them over innumerable dunes, through rocky canyons, and across dry riverbeds with such calm that Avel wondered if the "old" horse knew all the safest trails to take. He did not know where they were going.

Just to the West. *Always West.*

The same as when the Davrin had walked on his bare feet, the horse seemed to cover much greater distance than the strides and the length of the shadows suggested they should. The sand changed shades of red, moving from the darkest red to orange and nearly yellow. He sensed that they were approaching a border. Possibly one which led out of the Desert.

He confirmed this when he spotted a blue ribbon of water ahead.

"No, no, wait," he said into the wind. "Don't cross, please. I cannot leave ..."

He didn't know why, but he *couldn't*.

The stallion cycled massive amounts of air through flared nostrils, the lope speeding up into a gallop.

"Wait ... Stop. Let me off."

His mount didn't slow as the wide, shallow river came into plain view.

"Listen to me! Don't, please!"

The stallion whinnied briefly, tossing his head as he finally began to slow down. The charging gallop became that rolling lope before shifting into a jaunty trot with tail held high.

Better.

"Do. Not. Cross," he said, a desperate demand.

His mount called again, watching the other side as they approached the bank. Tossing his head and shaking out his mane, the stallion trotted up and down the river border.

"What are you doing ... ?"

Avel's voice lapsed once he spotted the figure on the opposite bank. Stark white hair kept in a braid, and dark, pointed ears above a red cloak.

Oh ...

She turned around, confirming the rest of her uniform was red, but the blue eyes and sapphire pendant around her neck were each so vibrant next to the river, he fixated on them even at this distance.

She smiled, lifting an arm and waving. "Auslan!"

A feeling both scorching and chilling swept through him.

Oh, Goddess ...

Sirana.

He leaned forward to bring his leg over the stallion's hindquarters, sliding off the side and gently dropping his feet into the firm sand. Without a single clear thought, he approached the river's edge while she did the same. He could see her teeth.

She was smiling.

He checked around him; no one around him but the stallion who had trotted rather far to graze on a patch of grass.

She's smiling at me.

He waved back, his heartbeat muffling her next words.

"So glad I found you! Can you swim?"

His feet froze in place. "I don't ... know?"

"Alright. Stay there."

Avel watched as his dream warrior stripped out of her cloak, boots, and uniform then hid them in the bushes at the base of a frond tree. Naked, she waded fearlessly into the river though kept her splashing to a minimum as the water climbed up her body. In the middle, she needed to swim before her feet found the ground on the other side but kept her eyes on him to help resist the current.

His mouth went dry as she walked out, liquid draining and sparkling like diamonds on her dark skin. She glanced down at the front of his waist-wrap and grinned. She'd spotted the evidence of erection.

"Auslan," she said again, relieved as she closed the distance. "Is Shyntre anywhere?"

A fierce ache seized his chest, stopping his breath a moment. "Uhm ... H-he is."

Her eyes matched the sky as she scanned it. "Really? Where?"

Here.

"He's, um." He swallowed with difficulty. "Protecting us."

Sirana refocused on him, her face so young and bright. "I guess that makes sense. Before I forget, are you still in the Cloister? You didn't answer last time."

Last time ... ?

He breathed in the scent of her skin, watched a drop of water roll slowly onto her purple, erect nipple. In a different environment, his mouth would have watered. "I ... No. I am not in the ... Cloister."

"You're not. Alright." She looked like she didn't know whether to be relieved or not. "Still in Sivaraus? The Palace?"

He nodded, whispering, "I've never left."

Sirana breathed out through her nose, looking him over again. The smile touching her face suggested she couldn't see the scars or eyes he'd seen in the oasis.

"You know I'm coming back, right?"

His heart sped up as he forced his eyes to meet hers. "Are you?"

"Yeah." She smiled. "I found Jael, she's alive. And we found help to get us back."

"You found help." He couldn't help but answer with a small smile of his own. "Are … are you coming now?"

Her chagrin told him the answer before she spoke. "Um, not yet. I'm stuck in a Dwarven hold for the moment."

"You are where?!" he repeated, alarmed, and she lifted her hands in open apology with a laugh.

She *laughed*.

He wanted to wallow in the sound.

"Oh, no, no, sorry," she said, chuckling. "I'm safe. They're nothing like Tragar, and they aren't afraid of me."

He breathed out. "You're safe … but 'stuck?' "

"Yeah." She shrugged. "Long tale."

He made a conscious effort to widen the weak smile on his lips. "Then I shall hold on … *we* shall hold on to hear it."

She smiled with a stunning, new appreciation he'd never seen before, her aura bright enough to compete with the Sun. When her eyes skimmed over him with frank, uncomplicated desire, he didn't feel dirty and afraid.

Not anymore.

"You look thirsty," she teased, shifting her hips, drawing his eye to the sparkling droplets clinging to her snowy patch.

His cock pressed harder against the cloth around his waist.

"I am *dying* of thirst," he replied earnestly.

"Ah, well, then." She moved closed enough for him to reach her skin with his mouth. "Have a drink?"

He bent down and licked the water from her nipples, and she laughed again with raw delight. Nothing in recent memory triggered such a cascade of satiation and rejuvenation, soothing him so deeply that his scars felt awash in cool shade and sweet water.

Goddess, more … !

The life mage took firm hold of her waist, drinking his first true sustenance in centuries from her skin. He collected the river droplets with his tongue and lips while his hands cupped her curves, cradling the moisture until his mouth could catch up. His efforts were so urgent, Sirana continued to laugh and writhe through his banquet.

The Desert needed more of that song.

Once he'd worked his way down from her neck and breasts to her belly, Avel dropped to his knees, lifting up his wrap to expose his ass and erection to the air.

"Ah," Sirana said with a grin in her voice. "You gonna tug it for me, Auslan?"

"Mm-hmm!"

With one hand gripping her ass and the other wrapped around his cock, he briefly pressed his cheek to the firm, hot ball in her gut. He paused, quivering in humble astonishment that she kept it despite how far she must have traveled.

But the Consort could not think about this long. Every time she moved, the scents of her folds mixed with the river in her fur wafted into his face, capturing his focus, making his mouth water. He *needed* to taste her, to drink renewed life from her.

Avel buried his nose in her thatch, wetting his lips, and licking her labia.

"Ooh, yes," she gasped, bracing her heels farther apart. "Aus — !"

He arched his neck and feasted, sucking firm, darting his tongue along her slit, trying to burrow deeper. Her fingers slid into his hair, and he started jerking harder with one hand, creeping his other toward his warrior's crease as she cooed above him.

"Shhhittt, ohhh …"

Her legs started to tremble, and he lashed faster against her hidden nub, trapping it in the center of a hard-swirling tongue. He made certain her sex could not separate from his mouth as her hips tilted and buttocks twitched.

Then, his fingers found her pucker.

We remember … you like this.

She peeped as he nudged his middle finger partway in, her toes curling in the damp sand. He gave her a second finger, and she climbed fast after that, hunching over and spreading her feet to try and stay upright through her climax.

"Yes ... ! *Goddess!*"

She practically rained on his face.

Like she had in the library.

He smiled against her; his skin delightfully drenched.

"Aughhh-god —" she groaned, panting and twitching. Her breath shuddered when she asked, "Did ... did you come?"

He shook his head, pressed against her, his hand pulling his pole.

"Good."

Sirana stepped a pace away and shoved him backward by the shoulders. Grunting as he landed, he looked up, bleary and intoxicated as she grinned down at him. She leered at his straining cock.

"We better hurry before we get interrupted," she said, coming down to straddle his hips, taking his staff in her hand to nestle it in place.

"Ohmy-*Siraugh* — !" was all he managed before she impaled herself on him.

"Oh, yeah!"

She snatched both his hands, threaded her fingers through his, and pressed them down in the sand on either side of his head. Her eyes shone like her pendant as she peered down at him, a huge grin on her face.

"I'm gonna ride you so hard, you'll think you were that horse."

Then she gathered the leverage to prove she wasn't bluffing.

Fffuuu — !

His head felt like it *might* explode from the intense and sustained pleasure as her body took him deep, caressing and stroking him full-length, over and over. He watched her breasts bounce, the pendant he'd given her swinging, and her face grimacing in concentration. He felt her squeeze his hands as her arm muscles flexed and stood out. She held him down and fucked him full as his heels scraped and dug into the sand as he arched his back.

I-I can't last ... !

"Do it," she demanded. "Come in me."

His eyes popped open, his focus locked on the depth of her eyes.

"Cream me," she hissed, grinding and squeezing him, dragging him right to the edge of the cliff. "Every drop in that sack!"

His eyes rolled upward.

"Do it!"

★*"Yes!" he groaned before barking at the sudden release of his cock exploding inside her. "Sirana! Arrgh★ … !"*

"Ohhh, *yeah!*"

His warrior exhaled in relief while he quivered beneath her. He seemed to coast forever, his flexing staff wrapped in her slick heat, his balls chilled by evaporating juices. Once his body finally relaxed, he began to wake.

The last sensation was her lips touching his.

She'd kissed him like she knew his name.

IN THE SMALL, WINDOWLESS ROOM AT HOUSE THALLUEN, SHYNTRE JOLTED UP-right in bed. He had fallen into Reverie naked, and his cock was bla-tantly out, aching, still *twitching* as it finished ejaculating over his abdomen without his palm touching it.

"Fuck!" he cursed.

His brother cried out the same instant, sitting upright a moment later, shivering. A second erection tented the sheet covering his lap, and a splattered wet spot began to grow. Ta'suil's flushed, bewildered expression mirrored his own when they looked at each other.

What in the Abyss …

Shyntre took a deep, uncomfortable breath at how his companion's face seemed to plead with him for answers.

As if I have any?

He turned back the stained bedding to get up. "I guess we better wash the sheets again."

For once, the healer didn't rush to get cleaning. Auslan looked at his lap, biting his lip. Then, once Shyntre had set the heating stone in the newest bucket of water, he whispered.

"Who is Mazdel?"

Shyntre paused, faced away as he swallowed. Amazing that his mouth wasn't dry for once.

The wizard turned toward the bed, folding his arms. "Who is Avel?"

To his credit, Ta'suil truly considered the question, though he couldn't possibly know the whole answer.

"A treasured son," he said, softly, "taken from the Desert. He needs to return … because someone needs *him*."

Auslan might as well have hurled a stone dead-center against his chest. Shyntre flinched and rubbed the spot above his throbbing heart.

"Yeah," he replied, turning to gather cloths to cleanse the sweat from their skin. "Mazdel is the same."

Chapter 12

Lethrix's Den

Jaunda lay face-up upon the mats, legs splayed and without strength. Her bowels had expelled the largest rush of male cream she'd ever collected within her netherhole, but the stuff still seeped out. A milky slide dripped audibly off the platform when the Dragon cradled her cock in his hands.

Ah, shit.

She groaned as Lethrix whispered the command word for her Feldeu, the same which had initiated the attachment. She felt it detach from her mons, vulva, and clit … and from deep inside.

"Ah, good," he said, slowly twisting and tugging the bulb inside her cunt. "Were this a unique item, I'd think it sloppy to use the same word for both donning and removal."

"*Fuck*," she grunted as he pulled steadily, the final stretch seizing her attention.

"But for something replicated by mages and 'issued' to several units, this allows you and your Sisters to assist each other if something goes wrong, yes?"

She jolted as he removed it completely, though he'd been gentler than her superiors in the Cloister. By Braqth's icy tit, she was sore *everywhere*.

"Yeah," she whispered hoarsely, catching her breath on the damp platform. "Basically."

"Mmm," he responded, staring at her empty holes and extremely sticky crotch, his mouth curling up smugly at the corners. "I presume, at the very least, each Feldeu responds to a unique word unto itself?"

"Correct," she answered on an exhale, wetting her mouth. "Wouldn't be pretty if every cock in the room fell off when a novice joined a gang rut, right?"

Lethrix raised his chin and laughed. "Indeed! I've wondered how this project was going. I remember when Fadele first began experimenting, you know. The Sisterhood seemed madly vicious back then under her leadership alone. Less so with Rausery around, am I right?"

The Lead merely nodded. She doubted she could lift either head or arms for longer than a few seconds. Her ass throbbed fiercely enough that she didn't want to move her hips, even if she were sure her feet could handle her weight and the texture of the floor at the same time.

Her nipples were sore and sensitive from his frequent licking, twisting, and tweaking. Her clit was beyond sensitive, numb from the sheer number of climaxes Lethrix had coaxed from her Feldeu while his cock had been trapped in her ass. He'd spurted with each one.

She didn't know how long they'd been locked together, "sharing" the magic through their phalluses, but she'd never experienced anything like that, and he knew it. Neither had he, apparently. Lucky for her, he didn't bother to lie about it.

His fascination and experimentation had blurred time as he'd caressed and licked her everywhere. He could have teased them both, could have guided the rush and sway of all her senses for three cycles straight and she wouldn't have been able to judge.

She only knew the jism which had bloated her abdomen and flooded the mats when he'd eased out had been collected from more than his first, explosive climax.

Now she felt so light, she might be floating on a raft.

How long do I have to get upright? she thought.

Lethrix smiled down at her. The Dragon had caught his breath. *Until your companions are down as well.* He began to turn toward them. *Which will come sooner than the time you gave them. You're beyond generous.*

She made a face. *Don't bother with false praise.*

He paused, tail flicking. *It's not false, Red Sister.*

Right. You floored me, fucked me loose, limp, and stupid at both ends, and you are barely winded.

His cock responded to that, plumping up, bobbing once. *True. But consider the fact that you are holding your own in a conversation afterward.*

So?

He turned away with a chuckle. *You'll see.*

Jaunda turned her head to follow him as Lethrix chose another matted platform within her field of vision, inviting Vik to change his seat. This moved him farther from Halena camped near the spring, which she protested.

"No, wait — !"

"Do you wish to be part of the negotiations, shadow?"

Vik grimaced as Lethrix turned toward the cait, flirtingly wrapping his tail around the bua's calf and gradually slithering higher up his thigh.

Halena scoffed. "What I 'wish' doesn't matter here, does it?"

"To a point, it does, and consider yourself lucky for that. But do not complain about a bargain where you refused a seat and have no say. I find it rude behavior, especially in my own den."

The cait watched the two males in a tense silence starkly contrasting the Lead's languid observance, who couldn't stand yet, anyway. Regardless of what Halena might do, Jaunda would stay where she was.

Vik climbed onto the new platform, his face hot as he obeyed Lethrix's suggestion to turn around and face him with his legs hanging off the side. The Dragon then pressed the spy down onto his back and spread his legs, giving Vik the same oral treatment with his coiling, lavender tongue that he had Jaunda's Feldeu.

The Red Sister felt a lopsided smirk sliding onto her face as Vik's body arched and he cried out in shocked pleasure. Lethrix needed to hold him down firmly to extend his tongue further, achieving an impressive, all-encompassing grip on the bua's genitals.

Damn.

Jaunda could see how Lethrix's tongue wrapped twice around Vik's cock before sliding once around the base of his scrotum, then finally, the tip crawled flat along his ridge before tucking itself against his crinkled pucker.

"Wh-whoaaa!"

Vik thrashed, or tried to in their host's powerful grip, moaning loud enough to be on the verge of a confused ecstasy as his most intimate skin was thickly glossed with Dragon spit. The tip of the Davrin's cock had begun leaking from its tiny slit within moments.

Even with her head so fuzzy, the Lead started to understand what Lethrix meant. Vik could barely form words once he started to tremble, his eyes losing focus one moment after the next. She wasn't sure what was keeping him from spurting right then in Lethrix's face, either, given how turgid his glans looked, poking up from the squeezing coils of a strong, slimy tongue.

When Lethrix finally stopped tormenting him, he rolled the bua over on the platform, pulling his hips off the edge so the Davrin's feet could find purchase on the stone. Lethrix pried his buttocks apart with rough, clawed thumbs.

Vik didn't panic or cry out then but, astonishingly, tilted his hips back, offering the Dragon a better view of his relaxing purple star. Practically an invitation to the deep red, pointed head hovering above, adjusting its aim.

"*Wait!!*"

Lethrix rumbled in his throat, his tail lashing with annoyance as his toy held still. Vik didn't even look over his shoulder at the interruption.

"Halena," growled their host. "You will make up your mind, or you will be silent. I shall see to the latter if you haven't the discipline on your own."

"B-but he's never had the Red Sister's training!"

"Mm-hm. Impressive, isn't she?" He winked at the dazed Lead and chuckled, leaning forward to wedge his leaking glands between Vik's cheeks and push at his netherhole.

Halena moved closer. "Please, don't take him as hard as you did her. He can't handle it."

The Dragon arched an eye ridge at her and replied by pressing the triangular tip his cock in far enough to prove the bua could stretch to accept him as Jaunda had. Muscles in Vik's back flexed but he didn't cry out as his ring snugged around the ridge of the Dragon's glans; he moaned, instead.

Lethrix paused to allow him to adapt to that much, caressing the bua's shoulders and flanks with one warm hand. "Mm. I'll grant he is loosening slower than Jaunda, but he seems to know what to do."

"What do you mean?"

"Watch."

Lethrix pulled the head of his cock out, wetter than it had looked going in. The cait hesitated as the Dragon's tip penetrated again, opening her companion's ass wider, fitting more of the shaft inside. Vik lifted his chin off the mat on a gasp.

Not pain.

"Ah, yes," their host sighed, moving in and out at that shallow depth a few times as he spoke. "The bua bore down to ease rather than resist my entry."

" ... So?"

"Heh."

As Lethrix rocked against the bua, Jaunda watched tiny measures of the bumpy, red prick gain ground, disappearing in Vik's tight hole with every gentle lunge. Her cunt responded, knowing how it felt.

"My saliva doesn't impart that knowledge, Halena," the Dragon said, "though it encourages pleasure and relaxation. Has Vik played this way before?"

Halena fidgeted. "I don't know. Buas often get in trouble if they're ... caught."

"Caught doing what? This?"

The Dragon pulled his whole length out again, used his tongue to slather Vik's hole with lubricant, and sank his prick in again with a sigh. He was just over halfway as Vik relaxed into the newest push. The bua's staff waved stiffly beneath his belly, and Jaunda caught the glitter of stretchy fluid dripping from the tip.

He wasn't doing poorly at all beneath the Dragon.

"Well, Halena? Are you going to tell his Matron and send him to be lashed?"

"No. And we ... don't have a Matron."

"Like Jaunda. How interesting. Tell me. Do you own him?"

Halena clenched her fists. "No."

"Has Vik made a promise to you or someone not to let other males mount him?"

"Not ... that I know, but —"

"But what?"

"It's ... not accepted."

"Not the case here. I quite accept him, and he quite enjoys this."

Lethrix casually worked the bua's ever-welcoming hole while Vik gripped the sides of the mats with both hands and only used his voice to moan with pleasure. Lethrix hadn't spoken directly to him as he had Jaunda, and she could see why. Whenever Vik's eyes opened at all, they were glazed over.

Meanwhile, Halena scowled with agitation.

He's taunting her. She's making it easy.

"He enjoys it only because you drugged him! Or used magic to force him!"

"Heh. Force has nothing to do with this."

Lethrix grunted as he finally worked the widest part of his shaft in, the under-ridge causing Vik to stiffen up instants before his prick twitched and started ejaculating across the stone.

"*Ohhh*, Goddess, yes!" the bua cried.

The orgasm was a long one, sweeping Vik from head to foot, toes curling, fingers gripping. Lethrix held still until he finished, smirking, at the way the bua's inner muscles massaged him through it. The Dragon showed satisfied fang to the cait as he let his second climaxing Davrin of the eve catch his breath.

"Be truthful, Baenar," he said. "Do you resent Vik recognizing that he has the agency to use his body this way with me without your permission?"

Halena blinked. "What?"

"Do you want to control who he experiences pleasure with? For hundreds of years?"

"O-of course not."

" 'Of course'? That's a strange answer for one from Sivaraus."

"I … I mean … we don't …"

Lethrix stroked the loosened sheath with leisure. "I'm listening."

"I just …" She swallowed. "We don't own each other. That's why we broke from a Matron."

"Fascinating. Then why are you so concerned?"

"I'm his bodyguard."

"According to who? Rausery?" He read her expression before Jaunda could and chortled. "Ah, I see. That's amusing. I'm clearly not hurting him, and I shall not even once he leaves. That's part of his payment."

"I'll … I'll still guard him through this. I must."

"If you can stay awake. Are you jealous?"

She jolted. "Huh?"

"Do you wish to join with him? Have you ever?"

"Well … ah …" She nodded "yes."

"Ah, good. Do you wish to join with *us* while we fulfill his Bargain?"

Halena paused, her eyes drawn to Vik's impressively pliable netherhole caressing the length of the Dragon's slimy prick with ease. The Davrin only hadn't taken the knot.

Lethrix noticed the cait's gaze and made sure to slow down, withdrawing completely before reclaiming the bua's slippery, warm channel thrice more. Vik hummed in response, toes curling against the footrest just above the cave floor. His flaccid sex had begun to swell.

Lucky bua's getting fucked good.

"I could join," the cait asked, "every time you touch him?"

"If you wish it to be."

She was tempted. "Do … must I make a Bargain with you?"

Lethrix grinned, his tail wrapping around Vik's right leg. "I would, if I were you."

Halena watched her shadow-lover squirm under their host as Vik murmured something about "it" getting hotter.

"What about my including everything Vik asked for," she said, "plus one more thing?"

Lethrix shuddered, his breath coming harder through his teeth as he sped his tempo. "Name it," he growled, hips flexing.

"Uhm ..."

The bua may or may not have realized his guts would soon be filled with that same scalding, mind-blurring goop drying thick between Jaunda's legs, but his prick had reached full length.

"Hurry," he hissed. "Before I spill into your bua and my interest in this deal wanes."

"H-help the three of us spy on the Elder Mind conclave without being seen, and make sure we can escape safely to Sivaraus."

"Done." A snarl appeared on Lethrix's lips as he climbed toward his peak. Vik started grunting with the increased force. "You are nearly out of time, Halena. You may only enter this late into his Bargain if ..."

"Yes?"

"If you kneel beneath him and take his cock into your mouth. Accept his seed at the same time he accepts mine. Hold it. Do *not* spit it out or swallow."

Curious now, Jaunda rolled over onto her side to ease the crick in her neck and see the action better. Rausery's spy had removed her cloak, gloves, boots, and stockings a while ago, but stripped quickly out of the rest. With impressive speed, she followed Lethrix's direction and ducked into place on her knees and beneath Vik's taut abdomen.

Jaunda shifted on her platform and craned her neck to make sure she saw Halena grabbing the bua's resurged erection and putting it between her lips. Meanwhile, Vik's sack shone with Dragon spit as it slapped her on the chin. When the cait squeaked, the Lead wondered if all that skin was burning.

Halena stayed in place, gagging occasionally on Vik's prick as Lethrix's roar built up slowly inside his cavern. The coils of his tail and his hands tightened on his partner as he started cumming in the bua's ass. Vik's head and upper torso started thrashing immediately.

"Ah, Goddess — ! Oh, fuck, *fuck!* Halena! Yes!"

From everything Jaunda could tell, that now-familiar rush of heat and magic had forced another orgasm from the bua with the power of a collapsing dam. Vik jerked and spurted uncontrollably into Halena's mouth as Lethrix pressed his hips forward, holding the swollen base of his shaft flush between the bua's cheeks but without forcing it through the straining ring.

Heh. Goin' easy on 'im.

The Dragon had also retained the option to withdraw when he pleased — which turned out to be quite soon.

"Stay where you are, Halena," Lethrix ordered as he dismounted with a gooey slurp.

Vik jerked and grunted, and his netherhole spilled a visible rush of semen down his thighs moments before their host lifted him with care, setting him fully onto the platform over which he'd been bent all this time. His cait made a questioning sound of concern through closed lips as she watched their every move.

"Relax, bodyguard," Lethrix said, stepping around with a slowly deflating penis, tucking a crooked finger beneath Halena's chin and tilting her face to meet his eyes. "Now ... you may swallow."

She did, seemingly without thinking about it, for the next moment she appeared surprised. Then dazed. As if someone had thrown a concerning powder in her face.

Yeah, I know that feeling.

Curious how the bua's semen made her woozy, though, not the Dragon's.

Regardless, Vik and Halena were similarly affected when Lethrix laid the two next to each other on the platform. Neither seemed cognizant enough to be speaking with him.

Then, with a teasing chuckle Jaunda recognized, Lethrix turned Halena onto her back and lashed his tongue across her bare breasts and down her belly. She shrieked in surprise, and he had to pull her thighs apart when she tried to deny him access. Their host layered generous amounts of burning saliva between the dark, swollen folds of her slit and between her buttocks, then he walked away, leaving her squirming and fondling herself.

Lethrix approached Jaunda with a broad, satisfied smile on his face.

Ah, fuck.

He grinned wider. *That concerned?*

My asshole is throbbing. Not sure even you can make it feel good.

Thank you for the honesty. I'm not that brutish. The Dragon reached out and mussed her short, fuzzy hair with the palm of one hand. *Let's take a warm bath, you and I.*

She swatted his hand from atop her hand with a low growl, then blinked. "Warm?"

"Yes. A warm bath." His metallic eyes shone. "By the time we're clean and rested, you'll have your Feldeu and be ready to play the next game with me."

"Oh."

He didn't look remotely tired but … energized. *Still playful.*

"Right." She got up on one elbow with a wince. "Might need to hold an arm to walk —"

"Allow me."

Lethrix slipped his arms behind her and the crook of her legs, lifting her into his arms. He flicked out his tongue, missing her face only because she turned her head away. Scowling back, Jaunda hooked her arm on his shoulder and pulled herself up to retaliate.

She succeeded in licking his face. His scales felt *weird,* and whatever counted as Dragon sweat was worse.

"Bleh!" she said, spitting twice with regret as Lethrix broke into raucous laughter, tilting his head to the ceiling.

"I love a bold playmate, Red Sister. It has been too long."

The Dragon swung her around to take her to the far side of the cavern, away from her equipment and the Davrin couple on the platform. At an unfamiliar mewl, Jaunda looked at them over Lethrix's shoulder, admittedly shocked to see that Vik had pinned Halena to the platform.

The mewling had been from his penetration. Now, he vigorously plowed the sopping slit of a desperate cait. Halena clung to him without protest, lost in her throes, begging him to keep going.

Goddess damn …

"I told you," Lethrix said on their way to the hot spring hidden in a dark alcove. "Conversations after the first round tend to be few and far in-between."

JAUNDA REMEMBERED MOST OF EVERYTHING THAT HAPPENED OVER THE FOLLOW-ing span, except for her abrupt drops into desperately needed Reverie.

She'd experienced, multiple times, the oddly healing hot spring, sooth-ing her raw orifices and aching muscles while reviving her sensitivity to Lethrix's saliva and semen.

She'd sampled the unfamiliar moss, bugs, and roots the Deep Dragon collected and prepared to supplement the meat he caught for their meals, all of which he cooked and made more flavorful than anything she'd had outside Sivaraus.

She recalled the few times Vik and Halena came out of their rut-stupor long enough to talk like they normally did, although Lethrix was always there. She found out that they did, at least, remember their couplings.

"Better than that," Lethrix had commented. "They are fully present for each and every one. Time ceases to matter."

True enough.

While emotions had wobbled at times between fear and anger at the loss of self-control, each of them remembered their Bargain and, in the end, chose not to fight it. Truly, they had no other choice. The Dragon's den had no way out unless Lethrix wished there to be.

He most certainly did not.

"At least it feels good," Vik had murmured.

That it did. Beyond anything he and Halena had ever experienced. Even Jaunda was hard-pressed to pin down a fuck-fest in the Cloister as intense as these sessions could be.

Once Halena had learned to swallow her pride and jealousy, as two or three of them took turns in any mix, that was when Lethrix got creative with all four of them.

During the first writhing cluster, Jaunda had nearly passed out at climax, and Vik and Halena had collapsed. They'd been on their knees in a chain. Everyone had a cock in their ass but Lethrix. Vik tenderly broke in Halena's surprisingly inexperienced passage first; Jaunda shuffled up to plug the bua deep with her Feldeu; and Lethrix attempted to drive the Red Sister mad with his aura and fat spear pressing hard against her magic cock from the inside.

Could have fucked me down to a puddle of magma ...

That wasn't to say their *other* holes weren't of intense interest to their host, too. Each of them knew what he tasted like in their mouth, how much they could fit before gagging, and how it always burned down to their stomach after he came. Each also knew the feeling of an invasive tail surprising their netherhole or their mouth, depending on which was open at the time.

Halena's resilient slit had been opened by all three cocks, numerous times throughout the span. She even learned about taking two at once in the same hole. While she was in her throes, *they* had learned she was calmest when bound, for Lethrix had hoarded some suspiciously silken rope.

If Vik wasn't the cock enjoying her cunt or ass at the time, she grew much wetter for the other, she came easily, if he was in her mouth at the time.

She's game for anything as long as she can see him.

Oddly, Lethrix kept Jaunda's three holes to himself where full penetration was concerned.

Why is ... this ... ?

She was all fours and hung up with him on one of his platforms, with Vik and Halena watching and touching themselves. She grunted, gritting her teeth as the Dragon finished up emptying his searing load into her plugged and straining sex. They were left panting as they waited for the knot to shrink.

*Mmm. Wonderful ... * he sighed. *But, what was that, Jaunda? Why is what?*

She shook her head to toss off sudden dizziness. *Why ... do I only get you or my Feldeu in my holes? Never Vik's cock, or even Halena's fingers. You've directed them to serve me with their tongues, but that's all.*

He chuckled, testing their tie. *Do you want *the shadows to fist you, Red Sister? Or have Vik sample your skills three ways as I have?**

She thought for a moment. *If they could pin me in a contest of strength.*

*Exactly. *You haven't proposed the challenge to them as you did me. Until you do, that position hasn't been earned. Is that good reason?**

Yeah ...

With a steady tug, Lethrix's shrunken knot popped out with a wet squelch of trapped air, spilling jism onto her inner thighs. Jaunda couldn't remember a time she'd taken so much of a single male's seed. She knew she was gaping — to his apparent delight — but not as sore as at the start.

She stretched out her thighs one at a time as she watched Halena drop onto elbows and knees, offering their bua her damp slit. Vik plunged in without hesitation, gripping her hips, and riding her like a recruit in the Cloister.

Damn, they were hungry.

Meanwhile, Lethrix started massaging Jaunda's hips and ass before working up her tired back; the Lead groaned and let her head droop.

"Feels good," she mumbled, sucking in some drool that escaped.

"Even better that you still talk with me," he replied, admiring her with his words and hands. "You are worthy of your heritage."

"*Ungh.* That's uroan shit."

"How so?"

"I don't buy that 'House lineage' blather. I told you, never part of a House, never had a Matron. *Fff* —" She hissed as he worked on a stubborn point of tension in her back. "Fuck, I barely knew I had a Mother, sure as fuck don't know the pedigree of her spurting cock."

Lethrix chuckled, sliding rough hands along her flanks and briefly cupping her breasts before exploring her tight abdomen. "Perhaps 'heritage' is the less helpful word, Arytiss."

Jaunda lifted her head slightly, cracking an eye open. "What's that?"

"I speak the blend of life and magic which makes you what you are, regardless of your social rules. That connection to your home which speaks to you through choice, action, and the flow of blood."

She sighed. "If you say. Everyone breathing's got that."

"Yes, they do. And what greater purpose but to strive to be worthy of their life's gifts? For no Noble Matron claiming a grander heritage can take that away from you."

"Damned right," she muttered, groaning under his expert massage. "Hm. Wait, then what's the more helpful word?"

Lethrix caressed her ass, first one buttock and then the other, slapping it at the end to make her jerk. "In your specific case, that word is Arytiss."

"And what the fuck does that mean?"

She could hear his grin. "It means 'warrior.' And I've only met a couple of you in the Deepearth."

She squinted, turning her head to look behind her before carefully sitting on one hip to better face him. "We have a lot of fighters. A whole army answers to the Queen."

Lethrix was caressing his cock again, awakening it from its brief nap, though he barely seemed to pay attention to that as he watched her with a piercing gaze.

"One who fights isn't always a warrior," he said. "To seek and face conflict for decades or centuries, and learn from them? Many find out this is not what they are, not what they want. Those who find their place within areas of conflict are usually protecting something precious. They learn the value of greater discipline over their most brutish selves. They can choose when not to fight, to harm, or to kill, when no one tells them to except themselves."

The smug lizard hadn't blinked through that speech. Jaunda huffed, flipping her hand in annoyance. "Are you sneaking on about the blonde Elf on the Surface?"

Lethrix grinned. "A most interesting choice you made at the end of *that* conflict, and telling that you still dream of it. Several before her, weren't there? An acolyte among the Priestesses. The disowned son of a superior. A blue-eyed granddaughter of the one who inspired you to *seek* that warrior inside. Stories you'd never volunteer to tell Fadele if you could avoid it, correct?"

"Yeah, nah," she granted, biting off the bare minimum before she could speak that fear. "But … maybe too much I'm going to have to tell my Queen when I get back."

"Please, do." The Dragon's tail slithered out and curled around them like a giant arm around her waist. "I have more than this yet to give you, Arytiss, which you may work with." He reached for her Feldeu, picking it up from the mat and extending it out to her. "One more cycle, and then … We leave my den to complete our Bargain."

Chapter 13

The Deepearth Wilderness

Jaunda could tell from the frequency of Vik and Halena scratching an itch through their dark outfits that they felt strange wearing clothes.

The Davrin prepared to leave the Dragon's den. First, each went through their possessions, making sure their equipment was all there and not obviously altered. As Vik checked over his sword, Jaunda slipped the Valsharess's ring onto her finger before donning her glove, flexing her hands to adjust the fit.

It feels weird.

You'll grow reaccustomed to wearing it. Lethrix smiled, barely covering his teeth. **The same with the clothes.**

Just him *thinking* that had Jaunda itching.

My skin's really sensitive.

I assure you, Arytiss, that will settle.

Better than being too sore to walk, she supposed, let alone hike to Sivaraus. Taking it as a whole, Jaunda had to admit she felt good, strong, and fully healed from Lethrix's eager and frequent use during every waking mark. If the Davrin weren't sleeping, they had precious little time to wash or eat before their host's tail offered blatant hints at his next selection or combination to place upon the mats.

They'd done their part and survived. Now, the Black Dragon would fulfill his Bargains.

Lethrix began by approaching Vik, pulling his collar out to partially expose one shoulder, and digging a thumb claw underneath the bua's collarbone until he broke skin.

"Ow!"

Lethrix's tail flicked. "Hold still."

Vik cursed under his breath as he strained to do so. Jaunda smelled something odd, like metal and flesh heated as one, and when the Dragon finally released the bua, Vik had a new scar. He poked at it while Halena made a visible effort to keep her mouth shut.

When Vik looked at her directly, however, she asked, "I assume you asked for that?"

"Uhm, yeah," he admitted. "I did."

"Did what?"

Vik exhaled. "Asked for a way to use the jump circles if we didn't have Jaunda with us."

"Yes, you did," Lethrix said. "And now you can, Vik, anytime or anywhere you wish."

His eyes widened. "Any ... where?"

"Correct."

"I ... meant between the two circles that brought us here from the drake canyon."

"Ah. I'm afraid you didn't specify that."

"What?!" Halena yelped.

"Wait a fuckin' flick," Jaunda groused. "You mean you just gave the bua what not even half the Red Sisters have?"

"A Bargain made must be kept," Lethrix reiterated with aggravating calm, "and he earned it by similar measures as your Sisters, if I may suggest. I merely mimicked the mark you bear, Lead, though he'll need practice to use it, as you did."

"Great," Jaunda said flatly, hands on her hips. "My superiors are going to kill him when they find out."

The Dragon winked. "I believe they need to *find* him, first. I presume you've already decided."

She frowned. "Decided what?"

"You said your superiors would kill him. *You* could, and before they ever find out, if you truly didn't want him to have this tool."

The Red Sister hesitated, fully aware of how warily Vik and Halena were looking at her. She shook her head. "I need to talk to Elder Rausery before I do anything like that. Halena warned me at the start that he'd be missed."

Out of her periphery, the couple breathed out.

"Excellent. I concur." Lethrix looked at Halena. "Are you ready, bodyguard?"

"Oh, fuck," she said miserably, like she just remembered something.

"Indeed. You rather impulsively asked for 'everything' Vik asked for plus 'one more thing.' I'll be generous and give you a chance to trim this out of your boon if you wish."

The cait was shaking. "What happens if I change my payment?"

Lethrix tilted his head in thought. "Nothing worse than if you'd chosen to leave behind a chest filled with treasure."

"Does that insult you?"

"Only if you'd tried to renege on your own payment at the same time." He smiled. "I am satisfactorily familiar with *all* your assets, bodyguard, so it's up to you. What do you choose?"

Jaunda pursed her lips but kept her mouth shut, looking to the side so as not to influence her. Her crotch tingled to recall just *how* familiar they all were with each other.

At some point, Halena must have pushed through some block because she told Lethrix, "No, I'll take the jump-mark, too."

Jaunda looked and caught her gazing at Vik as she added, "Or I'll be a shitty tracker if we get separated."

The Black Dragon hummed. "Very well."

He approached the cait to do the same magical ritual, making her squirm through the pain, and soon enough she had a scar matching her bua's.

This is going to be interesting.

His tail flicked with humor, one eye glinting gold as he turned his head. *I hope so, Arytiss.*

"Grab your things," Lethrix said aloud, "and allow me to escort you out into the wilderness to complete the rest of our Bargains."

WHAT DID YOU ASK FOR? VIK SIGNED TO JAUNDA ONCE IT BECAME KNOWN they were looking for the Rin'oveaus first and the Elder Mind's conclave second.

Don't worry about it, the Lead replied, keeping an eye on the low sway of Lethrix's tail so she didn't kick or step on it.

After passing out of the Black Dragon's lair — a moment none of them recalled — they'd retraced their steps exactly to the river chasm, opposite where they'd first met him. This time, their guide didn't expand his form so far as to shove them off the broken ledge but merely sprouted the wings necessary to carry his bipedal form along with a passenger to the other side. He took three trips.

Couldn't you have done it all at once? she thought skeptically.

Certainly. He turned his head and showed fangs. *I did not want to.*

Explains the butt squeeze and their expressions. Glad you tucked the prick away.

The Dragon snickered.

Within the same time it had taken them to travel this tunnel before, the Davrin recognized the cave of ore veins containing the jump circle which would lead to the drake canyon.

"Wait, were we that close to them at the start?" Vik asked as Lethrix climbed up first.

"No." His tongue flicked out twice, tasting the still air of the cave before gliding inside. "This can lead to more than one place in the Deep-earth."

"Who built it?" Jaunda asked, climbing up next.

"Vuthra'tern."

"Vuthra-wha?"

"But they appear to have forgotten already."

The Lead climbed in and made space for the other two, watching the Dragon poke a few runes with one claw. Once she saw Vik's shocked face, she asked him, "Who are Vuthra'tern?"

"Not who," Lethrix corrected, continuing to crouch at the circle.

Vik motioned toward the circle. "What he said. Not who, it's where."

Ah, fuck.

"The other Davrin city," Jaunda said as Halena joined them. "Where the mercs came from."

"Yes."

"So Elder Rausery knows about this?"

"She does."

"How?"

"Well —"

"Do you truly think your Queen is blissfully unaware of them?" Lethrix rumbled with a chuckle. "Or your Drider Keeper, for that matter."

The Red Sister sighed. "And the Prime?"

"Unless she's willfully forgotten, yes, she knows."

"Elder D'Shea?"

"Hm." The Dragon seemed satisfied with whatever he'd adjusted in the runes as he stood up to look at them. "Now *her*, I am not certain. Her House has been kept on an extremely short leash for a long time."

Jaunda felt her face scrunch up. "She doesn't have a House."

"Sure she does. I've met others from House D'Shea."

"Well …" Jaunda realized then what should have been obvious. "Then she's the only one left."

"Oh?" Lethrix's tail stilled as he considered that. "Hm. Must have happened while I was Asleep."

And, Jaunda realized, *after I was born. I knew, in a way … Why haven't I thought about this recently?*

Gold eyes glimmered in the dark. *I can tell you why, when you're ready.*

The Lead clenched her teeth. *Not yet. Later. That's part of the Bargain.*

As we agreed. Very well.

Lethrix beckoned to Vik. "Come. You must learn what the jump trigger feels like."

"Wait, are you jumping without us?" Halena asked.

He smiled at her. "You'll learn next, and be quite motivated so you may follow him, yes?"

Staring at him, Halena signed she would. The younger cait had learned value in getting a quicker handle on herself. Jaunda was glad to see it.

The two females observed while Lethrix instructed Vik on how to use whatever sliver of magic he'd bound to Rausery's messenger. This took a few attempts but, abruptly, the two males disappeared.

"*Shit!*" the shadow cait whispered.

"Easy," Jaunda murmured, lifting her hand to sign. ★He has to take all three of us to the conclave.★ She smirked sidelong at the cait. ★Good thinking, by the way, to include me and Vik in that.★

"Uhm," Halena replied, glancing down but raising her hand. ★Thanks.★

Moments later, Lethrix reappeared alone. He turned around and smiled as he held out his hand for Halena.

"Your turn, bodyguard. He is safe and waiting for you."

JAUNDA HAD NO IMMEDIATE WAY TO TELL HOW FAR THEY'D JUMPED OR IN WHAT general direction. The unfamiliar scents and luminescent mosses were enough to know, like last time, that the distance was long. Despite the unique protection of their guide, the Davrin fell into hand-sign as their ears and noses went on full alert.

★So, what do you need to do when you see the Rin'oveaus?★ Jaunda asked Vik.

★Deliver a message,★ he replied, although he didn't seem confident about how it would be received.

★*A message from the one city they've strived to avoid,*★ Lethrix tapped Jaunda's mind privately, standing with arms crossed. ★*I can't wait to see this.*★

Jaunda squinted his way before refocusing on Vik. *And should Hal and I flank you while you do the talking?*

Vik replied, *That might be best.*

They'll recognize your uniform, Red Sister.

Jaunda's eyes slid to the side as she arched an eyebrow. *And what would that mean to them?*

Not much, I'll admit. I do not believe they've encountered the Sisterhood personally, only heard the stories and know who stands at the fore beside the Queen.

They know Fadele?

They know of her from some old stories. Because of her and your Valsharess, your options and loyalties will seem narrow and rigid by comparison.

Noted. I'll worry about it when it comes. Jaunda's thoughts paused. *You never said if these Vuthra'tern Davrin have wariness of the Priestesses of Sivaraus. Just the Valsharess and the Prime.*

A trickle of pleasure moved through their mindlink.

Mm. I'm glad you noticed.

Predictably, he wouldn't answer any other questions on that.

Reaching the Rin'oveaus required a long, downward crawl through rough channels set with trip-threads and toxic growths threatening their air. The passages changed between manageable travel and partially collapsed canyons perfect for ambushes. The three Davrin knew they didn't encounter living obstacles solely because of the Dragon taking a stroll; Jaunda found multiple stakeouts hastily abandoned.

Why are we taking this route? Halena signed during a brief rest.

You mean, Lethrix thought "aloud" so the three could hear him, *why didn't we skip this part?* His low chuckle scared off something with six legs. *Because the Rin'oveaus keep far from jump circles and maintain enough wards around their camps that my barging in would result in your deaths.*

The cait frowned as Vik asked, *How many jump circles are out here?*

In this area? Lethrix shrugged. *Not many, and nothing new for quite some time.*

Because? Jaunda nudged.

The Dragon revealed sharp teeth. *Because the founders of Vuthra'tern gave up on reaching the Surface once their next leaders took over.*

The Red Sister squinted. *Why would the Surface be their goal?*

Why wouldn't it? What better way to cut all ties with the Valsharess and her agents of the Spider Queen?

Oh. I see.

Jaunda wondered, then, if this had anything to do with Rausery's missions up top. Had some of them made it? Was the Valsharess still looking for them?

I doubt it.

She never sorted out which of her thoughts he'd been answering.

Over the next two cycles, they climbed up through some surprisingly fertile areas with enough food and water to attract a Yutogul clan and several pockets of primitive Pytes. The valleys were generally hard to reach, however, even for bold Deep Traders forging routes for others to follow.

Jaunda peered at the fish folk watching them from beneath ponds and behind a waterfall. *Betting the swimmers keep an eye out for strangers and pass it on to the Rin'oveaus.*

A certainty.

Would these wandering Davrin recognize you?

Lethrix's smile climbed slowly. *After a fashion.* He enjoyed her expression for a moment before adding, *They've only seen me in Sleep.*

Huh. Why is that?

Because I've been Asleep since they met me.

Jaunda rubbed her forehead. *Right. So ... Can you introduce us? Speed things along?*

No. What's your rush?

She pursed her lips. *I dunno ... guess I just want to go home. See if anybody I know is gone since I left.*

I see. Well, my presence will give them pause, and I won't allow them to kill you. But the rest is up to the Davrin to complete Vik's mission.

The Lead shrugged. *Good enough for me.*

THE RIN'OVEAUS WERE CAMPED AROUND THE NARROW SHORE OF AN UNDER-ground lake on the far side. There were two directions to approach the water, requiring either straight swimming or scrambling over rough rocks to discover the hints of a habitation behind a screen of jagged boulders.

We would never have found this place, Vik signed to Halena, who signed in agreement.

The Yutogul had warned them; Jaunda glimpsed the ripples caused by swimmers as they settled. Although nothing in the water resurfaced, the Lead detected quiet movement on dry land within the large cave.

Vik removed the sword from his back but kept it in its sheath.

Jaunda cocked her eyebrow. "Getting ready to fight?"

The bua jumped at her whisper, glancing at her and shaking his head. "Could have fooled me."

Halena smiled at her for the first time. "Come and watch, Lead."

Vik moved in the direction of the sounds, carefully choosing his steps across the stones while Halena and Jaunda followed behind him. Neither of Rausery's shadows had donned the black masks they'd worn when she first caught them following her.

Should I get in front? Jaunda signed. *In case they attack him?*

A bua in the lead is the first thing they'll notice, his bodyguard replied. *It's a signal.*

According to who? The 'indirect-Rausery.'

Halena smirked. *Yes.*

Alright, then.

Lethrix seemed to have vanished from sight, but something told Jaunda he hadn't gone from the area. She could hear the shadows' quickened hearts as they climbed carefully around the shoreline. Vik lifted the sword in its sheath above his head with one hand and kept it there as long as he could; several times, he signed to meet without conflict. So far, the Rin'oveaus hadn't overtly acknowledged him.

When they were about one-third around to the far side of the lake, Jaunda finally spotted three figures coming toward them. It hadn't been easy; the clothing they wore was smearing their outlines to her Dark Sight.

Meanwhile, I'm bright as a torch.

Yes, you are, Lethrix chuckled in her mind. **Be careful with the one to your left. He's a fire mage.**

The mercs had mages?

Shit.

The Davrin coming to meet them weren't hiding their faces; all three were scowling, and Jaunda was sure they were all male.

Hmm. Do they have a male leader?

Wait and see, Arytiss.

The Deep-fucker anticipated a show.

Once Vik had reached a larger and somewhat flatter rock upon which to stand — a clear and easy target if they wanted to shoot him — the bua signed *"No conflict"* again before gripping the sword with both hands and holding it aloft.

The three males approaching shifted their focus to Halena and Jaunda, who put up both empty hands with minimal finger movement. The Lead measured her distance from Vik to be roughly the same as his bodyguard but on higher ground. When they finally got close enough to make out some facial detail in the dark, Jaunda felt weird at what she was seeing.

Then the fire mage summoned a warm, orange glow in his palm.

Oww …

Not one boot scuffed the stone as Jaunda waited for her color vision to kick in, blinking through tears. Her "second sight" confirmed what she had glimpsed in Radiants.

Shit. They're my age.

She stared as it struck her: the one in front had gone gold at his temples like Rausery.

… or older.

Lethrix chuckled. **Is that rare, Arytiss?**

Jaunda swallowed. *Yeah. Only one I know of. The Headmaster.*

Interesting.

Meanwhile, that eldest bua — or whatever she might call him — bowed his head briefly to Vik and reached out both hands, palm up. The young one from Sivaraus responded by placing the sword in his hands.

It's not his, she thought. *That's his 'message.'*

★Very good, Red Sister.★

The elder male partially drew the sword while the fire mage offered him greater light by which to study it. Their expressions were skeptical, reluctant to accept whatever this was supposed to mean. Ultimately, they didn't deny it.

With a sigh, the eldest sheathed the sword and returned it to Vik with one hand, passing a length of cord with the other. Rausery's bua accepted both and peace-knotted the weapon before slinging it on his back.

"Your names?" the elder asked, his voice low enough not to carry across over the lake.

"Vik, Halena, Jaunda."

The elder stared at the Red Sister longer than the bodyguard. He nodded once, returning his gaze to the young bua. "How did you find us?"

He had a manner of speech which Jaunda had never heard before.

"The Black Dragon," Vik answered frankly. "We wouldn't have, otherwise. Probably fallen to one of those poisons or traps before now."

The skepticism left their faces; the two flanking males seemed amused while their leader appeared resigned.

"What do you want?"

Vik pursed his lips, breathing audibly through his nose as he hesitated, considering his answer. A fish splashed the water to their left, biting at something which had become visible under the mage's glow. The flanking males studied Jaunda's red uniform intensely.

Finally, the bua answered.

"A Davrin House may need to escape Sivaraus," Vik said. "We seek to hire the Rin'oveaus to help them disappear."

Jaunda held her face like stone despite the deep shock hitting her gut. The elder male was even harder to read; a good example of giving no tells.

"Which House?" he asked.

Here, Vik shook his head. "I cannot say yet. May we speak with your Commander?"

The old bua smiled like he'd expected that. "First tell me who sent you. A name."

Again, Vik paused, this time reciting from memory and speaking with confidence. "Hachyrr'ne of House Khelnoch."

Khelnoch?

There was no such House in Sivaraus.

"Brother of Jakrel," he added.

Whatever *that* meant.

Lethrix purred inside her head, and Jaunda worked hard to keep her face placid.

You know who this is, don't you?

★I do.★

Is he in Sivaraus right now?

★I believe he is, assuming he hasn't been killed since Vik and Halena left.★

Jaunda thought she heard his tail slither languidly across the rocks, but no one else reacted. Instead, the eldest male took a deep breath, letting it out slowly.

"Come with us," he said, motioning them to follow. "Keep the peace, and you may speak with our Commander."

"Do not keep it," the fire mage added with a widening smile, "and we turn you to ashes."

Vik turned to look at Jaunda, who smirked and said, "We're just here to keep the bua alive."

They weighed that response, didn't swallow it whole but considered it enough for now. Lethrix followed them at a slight distance; by every sign, he seemed to evade their detection.

★This gets better and better,★ he said.

THE RIN'OVEAUS CAMP REMINDED JAUNDA OF THE QUEEN'S SEMI-PERMANENT drill yards situated near the Fringe Houses, though smaller in size. The shelters, work areas, and small animal pens followed the shoreline, a long, narrow road with several projects in the works.

Unlike the Valsharess's Army, however, no one avoided eye contact with her. Everyone stared at her with awareness of the threat she represented. They all wore armor and carried weapons and equipment, but little of it matched. Among those individualized designs, Jaunda also spotted no obvious signs of rank among them, nothing to suggest in which shelter the leaders took their rest.

The Commander could be any of them.

The Davrin were as dirty as the Army generally was when they weren't parading for the public eye. They looked worn, too, with no permanency or central wealth to replace clothing, armor, and equipment as needed. The Elven faces also didn't *look* quite like those she was accustomed to seeing casually around Sivaraus. A few children were too curious for their own good.

I can believe they've been separate from us for centuries.

Indeed. Keep listening to all that you perceive.

How are they not seeing you?

Because I don't want them to.

Jaunda kept her head on a swivel. *Do you walk into Sivaraus when you want?*

It has been a while.

And the Valsharess doesn't know?

That depends.

On what?

The Black Dragon fell silent as three elder females approached their group, the rest of the company making room for them, all eyes turning inward to watch them in a large, loose circle. The elder in front could be older than Rausery; she had only a few white streaks remaining in her blond hair tied in a bun at her nape.

"Satisfied, Eallo?" she said, and it took Jaunda a moment to realize she spoke to the elder male.

"I am, Commander," he said. "The sword is genuine, and the bua knew three names from Vuthra'tern and how they connected."

"They're also not knowingly deceiving us," said the fire mage.

"Alright." The Commander turned her eyes on the three visitors, one at a time. "My name is Vian. Formerly House Dar'Prohn."

She paused as if awaiting a response or recognition. When Vik said nothing, Jaunda spoke up.

"Never heard of it."

That got an audible snort out of several Davrin around her, but she grinned and shrugged.

"It's truth," the Lead added.

"So it is." Vian looked her over, paying keen attention to the details of her uniform. "And you, enforcer?"

"Jaunda. No House."

"How is that possible?"

"Born in the slums of Low Gate. No Matron gave a fuck that I breathed until *after* the Sisterhood scooped me up."

"Ah-hah. And what is your rank in the Sisterhood?"

"A Lead."

Vian frowned. "A high rank to be wandering around the tunnels playing bodyguard with this youth."

Jaunda shrugged. "Matter of convenience."

"Hm." After a moment, Vian nodded to their bua. "I'm sorry, Vik. We can't negotiate with the Red Sisters, no matter what you need or have to pay. I'm sorry you came all this way. We'll let you go to convey the message to your superior.

The younger male was trying to think through imminent failure and dismissal. "Wait —"

"Rest assured we will *not* be here by the time you give your report." She began to turn away. "Escort them out, Eallo."

"No, Commander, wait. Is House Dar'Prohn related to Phaelous Ja'Prohn?"

Vian paused, exchanging a look with her flanking elders and reluctantly acknowledging this. "Phaelous? I don't know that name."

"The Headmaster of Sivaraus. He's … ah …" Vik rubbed his jaw. "Belongs to the Valsharess and teaches all the wizards —"

"Wizards?"

"Bua sorceresses."

That got a ripple of reaction. They'd never heard the word before.

"Why not call them mages?" Vian asked wryly.

"Because they're all locked in a tower. Wizards learn in groups." Vik splayed his hands as if helpless to have it make more sense than that. "But *are* you related to the old House Ja'Prohn in Sivaraus?"

"Why would that matter here and now?"

"Because my message has to do with Phaelous's son. The Valsharess normally keeps tight hold of the Ja'Prohns —"

"Of course, she would."

"But the House we want to help is currently boarding him, and they're in a precarious position."

The Commander took a slow breath. "Again, what would that matter to us? We're not a company that takes any task if the price is right. There isn't enough magic or equipment in the Deepearth to convince me to put what remains of my Davrin directly beneath your Valsharess's nose."

"You don't have to. Hachyrr'ne said he would meet you farther out. He needs your help to move that many Davrin once they're beyond the city limits."

"*No.*" Vian calmed herself. "Please. Take your lives and leave us. You'll not find us again, no matter what you tell them."

She glanced at Jaunda as she finished. All the Lead could think was, *D'Shea should be here, not me.*

I think not. I'm fairly sure she would make matters worse.

How? I just crushed whatever Rausery planned by standing here, and Vik was doing pretty fucking well —

"Who are you talking to?" demanded the Commander of the Rin'-oveaus, taking a few impressively intimidating steps closer. "I recognize your distraction, Red Sister. Speak."

Fuck.

"No one," Jaunda replied without thinking it through.

Aww. Don't start lying now.

A tail slithering sounded again, and Vian glanced in that direction, looked at Jaunda, then jerked her focus over the Lead's shoulder.

"*Sargt,*" she spat. "How dare you?"

190

"Hello, Vian. A pleasure to finally meet in the flesh."

As Eallo and the other elders collected defensively around their Commander, the entire company gasped and scuttled away as they spotted the Dragon. Vik and Halena blinked as if now recalling that he was with them.

"A pleasure?" Vian repeated, dressing down the Dragon in the center of her camp. The male she'd called Eallo grimaced. "You've compromised us beyond my greatest fear, Sargt. Why? Are we beyond *use* to you? Has it been too long since he left? You're *finally* Awake, so you would clear us out of your Deepearth like rachas?"

Jaunda heard an uncomfortable emotion in the Commander's voice, bordering on pain, but couldn't say where it came from as she spoke, fearless and familiar, with the beast looming over her.

"None of that, Vian, Eallo." Lethrix nodded to each of them, arms crossed and tail curving slowly. "Have no fear. I would not have brought them if this wasn't of some benefit to you. Even with the Red Sister, you can see this is truth."

"How is that?" she demanded.

He showed her teeth. "I still owe the Lead a boon. You'd like her as I do, I think, given enough time."

He stopped the exchange there, and the aggravated Commander — clearly worried for her company — turned her back on them to sign unseen with her officers. Vik and Halena shared a few as well, though they seemed confused, trying to catch up with the implied gossip. Jaunda didn't even want to try.

What the fuck is going on?

Wait and see, Arytiss.

Eventually, the eldest female of the Rin'oveaus turned around to face Jaunda, Vik, and Halena, lifting her eyes to Lethrix. Hands on her hips, wide open to attack, she asked simply, "How is he?"

The Black Dragon hummed with an odd drone. "I am not certain. Many changes lately. You will have to ask him."

Jaunda saw the Commander swallow, and something brightened in her expression for an instant before she turned and conferred with her five elders. When Vik looked at her, she could only shrug.

"Very well," said the elder, turning around. "Vik and Halena, come with me. Lead Jaunda, you will stay out here with Sargt while we talk."

"Fine with me, Commander. You got fresh water?"

Vian signed to one of her own to show Jaunda where to refill her waterskin, and the Red Sister let Rausery's shadows leave her sight in one of the drab tents she'd never take for a ranking meeting place.

Shortly after, Jaunda sat on a rock and sipped from a plump skin, surrounded by the eyes of suspicious mercenaries and their small ones. They seemed to have lost track of the big Dragon. Ruefully, she chuckled to herself and drank, glad for the rest and confident she wouldn't get stabbed in the back.

No questions?

She shrugged.

Not the least bit curious?

The less I know, the less I can spill to Her Majesty or the Priestesses.

Isn't that some form of treason?

So was letting the pale Elf go. They didn't kill me then. She sipped again. *Nomad Davrin aren't my concern. I belong in Sivaraus. That's why I did all this.*

Lethrix hummed, the tip of his tail wrapping and giving her ankle a squeeze.

A thought returned. *Although …*

Yes?

What was that part Vik said about Phaelous's son boarded at a 'precarious' House?

Heh heh. I haven't the faintest idea. His golden eye winked at her. *You will have to ask him.*

CHAPTER 14

THE ELDER MALE, EALLO, ESCORTED THE QUEEN'S DAVRIN AROUND THE LAKE-
shore a few marks later. As on their way in, he was flanked by his apparent
right-hand, who'd never spoken, and the fire mage, named Jahn. The
camp behind them had begun the process of breaking things down. As
their Commander had stated, the mercenaries wouldn't stay here to be
found later.

Lethrix had gone ahead before the meeting had ended. Jaunda didn't
know where he was or whether he'd bid the mercenary leader farewell,
but the Lead was certain of two things.

I'll leave here alive, and next we're going to spy on the flayers.

Then, hopefully, she'd be going home not too worse for wear.

The three males acted too old to really think of them as "buas," but
Jaunda didn't have another word in mind. She expected them to be cautious
about talking on the way out, but they were almost silent the entire time. If
not for the occasional gestures or slight smiles aimed at Rausery's shadows,
Jaunda might have believed they anticipated an ambush, and she was about
to get jumped.

Eventually, Eallo stopped and spoke softly, motioning ahead. "Back
the way you came." He smirked. "Best avoid the same traps than chance
new ones."

"Right," Jaunda muttered. She took a couple steps as Vik signed a longer farewell. She paused when Eallo abruptly asked a question.

"Has anyone from Sivaraus been to the Surface recently?"

She didn't have to answer that.

"Yes," Vik responded. "The Valsharess sent some. They're still there." *Interesting that he knows.*

Vian's male elder asked, "Was coming back part of the plan?"

Also something she didn't have to answer, but neither Vik nor Halena knew for sure.

Maybe I can say it? Jaunda consciously unclenched her fist and turned around. "Not really. Possible, maybe, if they stay lucky and remember their training."

Eallo focused on her. "So ... some of the Red Sisters have been there?"

Though not blank, the Lead couldn't really read his expression. "Yeah. I'm one."

"You," he echoed with awe as astonishment bloomed on her escorts' faces. "And you came back."

"Yeah. I wasn't running away." She shrugged. "Not too hard, either."

"What was it like?" Jahn asked, his tone cautiously eager.

Jaunda huffed. *Not the first time I've been asked.*

"Imagine the scents you notice most but twenty times stronger," she began. "Imagine that quiet is a state you can never find. Imagine the brightest mage's flare," she nodded toward Jahn, "and had a thousand like it. All that light and heat wrapped around everything you touch, wherever you stand. Then, night comes whether you're ready or not."

She grinned at their faces. "Take the heat and light away, hide it behind a mountain, and turn the air cold and constantly moving, whistling in your ears all night, when your eyes don't ache for once. But it doesn't last. It starts over another cycle later, and it might drop water or ice flakes on you instead of burning you. That's what it's like."

They all stared silently until she finished, even Vik and Halena, and Eallo showed a slight smile at the end.

"Thank you, Lead."

"Sure."

"Do you hope some of your Sisters will return?"

She arched a brow. "Why hope? They do or they don't."

He smiled warmly, like he'd seen that coming and would glide around it. "Would you rather they return?"

She sighed. "Sure. Yeah, it'd be good to see them make it." She took an impatient step away. "But I'd be a fool to want it too much."

"Hm. I understand."

"Oh, do you?"

Eallo bowed his head with respect but didn't answer. "Safe journey back where you came from, Red Sister. Shadows."

Jaunda nodded as the other two mimicked him, signing farewell to the Rin'oveaus. She had been leading the way around the known dangers and through rough terrain in near silence before halting their hike to scowl around for the Dragon.

So. Conclave now, or not?

He didn't answer. She sighed, looking at her two most recent partners and signing, ★You get what you need?★

Vik blinked at her, face carefully blank as Halena turned around. ★Enough to return, Lead.★

She smiled wryly. *Smart bua.*

They continued, each warier without their guide, yet all they could do was retrace their steps.

Back to the jump circle, if necessary.

In an area where Yutogul could be heard splashing in the next cave over, Jaunda signed conversationally.

★Hey, Vik.★

He blinked rapidly, straightening up.

★The elder merc called you 'shadows,' too. Where'd he get that?★

★What do you mean, Lead?★

★Our 'host' started that, didn't he? Said you were my 'shadows' for always following me. You used it for negotiations?★

★Oh … ★

Vik exchanged a look with his cait, who allowed a smile to creep up.

★I think he picked that up from our thoughts,★ Halena signed. ★We have used 'shadows' in negotiations before this. It is without rank.★

Jaunda shook her head with a growing grin. ★Got it. Yeah, that's been stuck in my head, too.★

The pair didn't seem to mind; in fact, they dared to look amused.

It didn't last.

★What must you tell Her about all this?★ Vik asked, finally.

The Lead started to purse her lips but bent it into a smirk. ★Ideally, that I found his den alone. That's all She really wants. I'll let my Elder handle the rest.★

They wanted to feel relieved, to believe her, but she knew where the doubt was coming from. *Don't blame 'em at all.*

Later, Jaunda estimated they were about halfway to the jump circle when Lethrix finally scared the shit out of them.

★*This way,*★ he said in their heads.

Fucking piss!

They spun around together, not seeing him. Somehow, his words tugged their attention toward the smaller, dead-end cavern on their left. Reluctantly, they entered, looking for trouble.

They found him.

Lethrix scooped them up off the ground into his arms. He was even bigger than before.

★*We're short on time,*★ he said, displaying rows of fangs in their faces. ★*But you should see this.*★

Jaunda groaned as she felt something magical overcome them, a trigger like the jump circle. Where they reappeared, however, had no runes carved into the ground.

That was all you, she accused.

"Indeed, it was," said the Dragon as he set them down on their feet. "Now, we are close enough to an Elder Mind that I require each of you strictly to speak aloud from this point on. Try to silence your thoughts."

They all had the same expression: *What?*

"No, no. *Words.*" His tail flicked like a whip. "Use only words. No looking at me to think your questions. No hand signs which require inner translation. I can better protect you this way. Understood?"

"Fuck," Halena whispered.

"Got it," Jaunda managed.

"Understood," Vik answered.

"Excellent."

Apparently, they would all trust him on this, especially now that the Queen's ring grew warm on Jaunda's finger. Lethrix's eyes glinted like he noticed before peering down a damp tunnel and motioning them to follow.

"Come with me. Upon Halena's Bargain, we shall see what some Ornilleth are up to."

Moisture wasn't truly rare in the Deepearth, but certain areas could be dangerously dry. Water collected in places which lay undisturbed the longest, leaving the schisms and rubble of recent collapses, quakes, or eruptions dry as fine dust.

Usually water seeped through rocks for a reason, trickling through cracks or carving out a trench in the stone one flushed grit at a time. Beyond streams, rivers, and lakes, other appearances could be a thin strip across one boulder, broad marks darkening most of a cavern's walls, or pockmarked puddles of mud and moss.

But Jaunda had never seen water thicken to the point of lining the inside of every tunnel in a system, one after another, for nearly a mark.

"What the fuck?"

She reached to touch what looked like soft, semi-translucent lichen spreading over a protrusion.

"Do not," Lethrix said.

His voice had no echo.

"What is it?"

"A message system." He smiled. "Which becomes a tracking system if you smear too much on yourself."

Jaunda glanced at him. "You mean like your straw squirts?"

Vik and Halena's eyes widened as their guide laughed unrestrained. Somehow, he didn't sound so large as when she'd been standing — or lying down — in his den.

"Not a bad parallel." Lethrix winked. "One reason you three are sliding by, at present."

The Lead snorted softly but looked at the underside of her boots anyway. "It's not sticking."

"For now."

Colors appeared in the odd, watery gel despite her Dark Sight at the fore, an unsettling trick to her eyes. Shades in many greens and pinks swirled through the passageways, sometimes flashing then vanishing like tiny bolts of lightning.

Jaunda slapped at her ear twice as an annoying buzz started pressing in around them. Her ring moved past the simple state of warming her hand; she could swear it vibrated.

"Talk to me," Lethrix prompted.

"I'm hearing insects coming out of my hand," she groused, shaking her ring hand as if to fling the creepy sensations out.

"Interesting way to put it."

"Or is it coming from the colored sludge?"

"What is your best guess, given our approach?"

"I think it's many thoughts at once," Vik said, peering around in awe. "Like they're streaming through space, but I can't tell if it's the tunnel itself or something ... larger."

"Very good." Lethrix's tail swayed as he walked. "While you are with me, the best counter against this distraction is chat."

"Chat," Halena repeated skeptically.

"Indeed. With me, or amongst yourselves. I know it goes against every instinct and word of advice about living in the Deepearth but, as a workaround, I quite enjoy its simplicity."

"Can no one hear us?" Vik asked, his voice thinning as if he was tempted to stop using his regular voice.

"I can hear you," the giant male answered. "So can your playmates, but nothing else at present."

"What about catching sight of us?" Halena asked.

"Not that, either."

"Wait a tick," Jaunda said, pointing up at their scaly guide. "Is this what you did when everyone in the Rin'oveaus camp didn't see you until the Commander called you out?"

"Mmm. Something like that. She has greater practice altering her sight and knows what to search for."

"Yeah, that was obvious. What did she call you? Sargt?"

"Ah, yes. She did, didn't she?"

"Another name?"

Lethrix shrugged. "A Word. Like Arytiss, actually."

The Lead blinked. "You mean she called you something in Draconic? What does it mean?"

He looked smug. "Guardian."

Jaunda paused. "You guard the Rin'oveaus?"

"Broader than that."

"Your treasure, then."

"Ha! True enough, though I guard all my territory."

"From what?" Vik interjected, abruptly uncomfortable with the worrisome grin on the Dragon's face.

"Those things the rest of you cannot handle," Lethrix said.

"Oh." The Shadows exchanged glances before the bua asked, "So, is the Commander a mage? Is that why she could see you?"

"Hmm," the Sargt considered. "The Ja'Prohn line all seem to have strong resonance with the Ley, I suppose, if not realized expression."

Jaunda shook her head. "Uhhh, doesn't answer the —"

"Wait, so I *was* right?" Vik broke in. "Commander Vian is a relative of the Headmaster?"

The Dragon rumbled. "Rather distant by now but close enough. Although, may we shelve this discussion to be aware of our surroundings?"

"You have shelves?" Jaunda snickered.

"I do. Just not where you could see."

"What about those coins we kicked? I imagined they're in a big pile and scattered around." A grin settled full on her face. "Or did you make your bed before coming to meet us? Scooped it all up nice and tidy."

Lethrix slapped her ass with his tail, making her yelp. His teeth were on full display. "You'd think I Sleep atop precious scrolls? I can be too restless for fiberstalk parchment to withstand, even the imbued type."

Jaunda rubbed the sting on her ass. "Do you drool on them, too?"

"Heh. A disservice to imagine my Sleep as mere unconsciousness."

"But you *are* out of the game for centuries at a time."

"I know others who would disagree with you. Vehemently."

Jaunda found she could do little more than squint at him.

"So, where do you get scrolls for your den?" Vik asked, looking around at the wild ruggedness beneath the translucent slime.

"I'll admit they are a newer addition, as the Davrin are the only race down here that bothers to create and preserve them. The Tragar have no interest and the Yutogul and Ornilleth have no need." Lethrix followed Vik's gaze with one extended claw. "Speaking of whom. We may talk but best pay attention to where we're headed."

Jaunda *had* noticed the air growing warmer, plus new sounds from movement. The damp coating in the tunnel had taken on greater colors and faster swirls. Ahead of them, the incline ended in a wide cave mouth which seemed to crest and descend on the other side.

"Wait, are we about to just walk into their lair?" Halena asked with concern.

"Only one relevant chamber," Lethrix answered. "Unless you'd like to go deeper?"

White teeth appeared underneath molten gold eyes in a deeply shadowed muzzle, responding to her horrified face. "Not to worry, bodyguard. Your auras shall harmonize with mine readily for some time yet. Thus, I can mask you from the Elder Mind and its conclave. This fragment is still young."

"Fragment?" Vik repeated.

"Wait, young?" Jaunda echoed, her face twisting. "These things grow up?"

"Of course."

"You'd never know it."

"Only because you don't recognize what you see."

"*How* young?" Vik interjected.

"Oh, let's see … your Elder D'Shea's age, I think." Lethrix grinned at the Shadows. "Or a bit older than Hachyrr'ne of House Khelnoch."

"That's quite a name," Jaunda remarked, noting Vik's wide-eyed response before he met her eyes.

"He doesn't like using it," Rausery's bua murmured. "Only when needed with the Rin'oveaus."

"Except a Red Sister knows it now," Halena said, "so it's pretty much worthless."

Jaunda shrugged, stepping into the steeper grade. "Yeah. Too bad." She glanced at the Dragon. "So, why do we have a 'young one' threatening Sivaraus?"

"Because it needed space and settled near Vuthra'tern, first. But the nest moved while I was Sleeping. I'm curious why."

Jaunda frowned. "Settled from where?"

His claw pointed at their feet. "Farther down."

"Wait, farther?"

"Indeed, where there are no jump circles or parchment." Lethrix's brow ridges perked up in surprise. "Have you never heard the Great Cavern rests much like the main guard room to your Queen's dungeon?"

"What? Uh. No?"

"Ah. Well, now you have." Another toothy smile. "I know Sivaraus seems far from the Sun, but you must admit you have achievable access to the Surface. You might as well be atop a mountain compared to everyone else when reaching for the sky."

Jaunda couldn't choose a question after that. Her ring hand started to quiver.

"Clear your mind if you have no words to calm you," the Guardian reminded them. "This would be an unfortunate place to get wrapped up in your own thoughts. They could strangle you."

Jaunda controlled her breathing, ignoring the tremors from the Queen's ring to sweep the haze out from behind her eyes. This technique had never been too difficult for her, fortunately. Words and thoughts weren't always needed to act.

In Lethrix's den, the Lead had rediscovered listening to her senses without some inner exchange making remarks at the same time. This was how it usually was for her in Sivaraus around her Sisters. Jaunda had developed that silent voice after so much time alone, and at times she'd wondered whether it soothed or enhanced the solitude.

Either way, Vik, Halena, and Lethrix had fixed that distracting habit. The Dragon had certainly offered a hoard of remarks to make instead.

"Why aren't there any guards?" Vik asked.

"The conclave doesn't rely on their eyes to detect or block intruders," Lethrix said as the Davrin followed him closer to the right-side wall. "The Ornilleth method of delegating tasks is somewhat different than you are used to."

Jaunda glanced at her boots, recognizing she *should* be slipping and sliding all over the jellied slope in this passage. "We would never have gotten this close. They aren't expecting us."

"Correct."

"So, we'll see them with their guard down?" Vik asked, fascinated.

Lethrix chuckled. "Good way to put it. Though I should clarify, I do not make the same Bargain twice. So, make the most of what you are about to see."

ONLY ONE "RELEVANT" CHAMBER, HE'D SAID.

Jaunda stood watching the foreign activities for what seemed a full mark, taking in the details though feeling generally lost with the strange, nauseating scents and subdued sounds. She hadn't the words to grasp what she was looking at, much less weigh a threat.

The dark chamber was riddled with eerie, dimly lit walkways and a startling number of steep stairs which allowed access up the walls. The Ornilleth could reach practically any part of a cavern about twice the size of a Noble manor in Sivaraus, all steps and tiers but without walls.

The luminescing colors decorated most surface areas and were consistent with the "message system" in their pinks, purples, and greens, some edging toward yellow. She interpreted different shapes into a possible function: supply cubbies, chests and platforms, tools and worktables.

Finally, she noted the bizarre water chambers, either vertical or horizontal, with windows translucent enough to glimpse an unrecognizable body floating inside. If they in any way observed a work area, then the Red Sister couldn't guess how they used all those tubes or scab-and-bone grips and levers.

The nearness of twenty mind flayers and double that of their warped thralls tested their nerves, even if they were convinced Lethrix would keep his Bargain with Halena. At the far end, something splashed and glowed but they couldn't see it over another rise in the cavern floor.

The entire place hummed with thought and modest shuffling yet stiffly quiet, to the point that the Davrin took turns muttering descriptions of their observations aloud, to keep the heavy density from laying over their minds.

"What are they working on?" Vik finally asked.

"Maintaining their colony," replied the Dragon. "What else is worth the time?"

"You said there was something we should see."

"Ah. Well." Lethrix looked at Jaunda. "Mostly, I meant the Lead."

"I don't like how you say that. Why me?"

"Well, we can't hurry them. It depends how long you are willing to wait."

"Wait for that?"

"For one of the vats to be opened."

"Vats? What the fuck is that?"

"I believe you called them 'water chambers.'"

"The ones with the bodies?"

"Indeed."

The Lead looked back, unable to read any sign of readiness in the body of the nearest one. She wondered aloud, "Does the rate the colors change mean anything?"

"Oo, interesting theory."

"Don't you know?"

The Dragon smiled coyly. "Each hive mind is, ironically, unique."

"So, no."

"Not with precision, but I do believe we're close to such an event, or I wouldn't have come and retrieved you."

Jaunda sighed through her nose and looked back, glancing at the Shadows. "Willing to stay a while?"

"If you are, Lead," the bua said.

"Right. Let's find a seat."

Lethrix warned them not to close their eyes or fall into Reverie.

"I may not be able to protect you unless I compel you myself."

"No fucking thanks," Jaunda growled. "I'll stay awake."

"I thought you might."

So they had to play a game or two. Or three. Making up the rules as they went along. The Dragon had the most fun, and the Davrin ended up losing one mundane dagger each to him.

Then the Valsharess's ring flared strangely on Jaunda's finger, returning her attention to the Ornilleth chamber and those large sets of lantern-like eyes floating around in the dim. The fact that the Davrin were just *sitting* here in what should be plain view to their deadliest enemies seemed unreal, but the flayers kept focus on their tasks while Davrin minds remained clear enough to talk.

"Why did it do that?" she wondered aloud, clenching the ring through her red glove.

"Do what?" Vik asked, leaning forward with interest.

"A pulse. Like when we used the jump circle in the drake canyon. Not the same as the warmth or tremors."

The Red Sister glanced up expectantly at the Dragon, who counted his three daggers for a third time, lining them up neatly on a flat stone.

His tail swirled contentedly around him as he looked her way.

"Possible indication of a Ley shift."

"Uh. A what?"

"Similar to when you arrived near my den."

Suddenly, activity broke out within the cavern. Six robed Ornilleth rushed to surround the same rectangular vat, one lying on a tier high from the bottom. Jaunda saw what had drawn their attention.

"The body's thrashing."

Even knowing nothing about the tentacle-faces' life in their own private quarters, they seemed flustered, communicating in silence. Their taloned, long-fingered hands splayed out in momentary indecision above the sealed chamber.

"Should they open it?" Halena asked.

Lethrix said, "Exactly what they're asking themselves, I imagine."

"Don't you know what they're thinking?"

"If I dug into hive thoughts now, I'd be threatening our Bargain."

Jaunda watched the flayers ultimately decide to open the vat, moving through ten or fifteen complicated steps as they pressed, squeezed, and twisted things nestled in between clusters of tubes. They drew out fluid through those serpentine ducts, allowing air to get sucked in as they pushed the lid to one side. The top didn't fall but hovered above the floor, attached to the whole apparatus in a way she couldn't see.

Four of them reached into the colorful, frothing fluid and drew up the first half of a hairless, tentacled body with smooth, light purple skin.

"Shit," Vik said. "A new flayer?"

"You could say that," Lethrix replied.

The Lead's ears perked up, for the Dragon hadn't sounded as playful as he'd been a moment ago. His tail had stopped moving. With an unnamed foreboding, she fixed her attention on the struggling Ornilleth drawn out of the thick, slimy fluid.

The tall, lithe form continued to struggle, acting as if they didn't recognize the place or who held them.

"Panicking," she whispered. "Why … ?"

"Can't it hear them?" Halena asked. "Their thoughts?"

"And why did they use their hands?" Vik pointed out. "Why not lift with their minds? We know they can."

All good points.

"They aren't treating it like another Ornilleth," Jaunda murmured.

"Very good," Lethrix said.

The tentacles draped oddly from the new Ornilleth, seeming deformed compared to the uniform sameness of the other six despite her flawless skin.

More of the conclave moved across the chamber, sending their thralls to the far side to ignore the activity. The thralls obeyed with utter compliance. Before this next group of gaunt gliders arrived, the vat's former inhabitant opened their mouth and screamed the most nerve-shredding sound Jaunda had ever heard.

"Shit!" Halena covered her ears as Vik shuddered.

Jaunda couldn't take her eyes away. She'd seen a mouth open during that scream. The white beak hadn't been obscured by tentacles around the jaw; instead, tendrils were growing off the top of the skull, curling and flexing like pincerworms. Very much alive.

"What the fuck ... ?" she hissed. "What *is* that?"

"Not what," Lethrix said. "Who."

"What do you mean — ?" Jaunda stopped and blinked.

The bony, purple creature had *tits*.

And hips, like a Davrin.

The legs and arms were too long and lean, and she had claws like the Ornilleth.

But the words crossed Jaunda's mind.

A deformed Davrin.

Or an incomplete Ornilleth.

The cluster of flayers seized her and tried to stuff her into the vat. She fought them, spitting fluid and screaming. Eventually, she would lose and be sealed back up, though not before several flayers gained mind bruises or tears in their robe.

The Lead's body shook with sympathy and horror. She knew who this was. She *knew*.

Reishel …

"Jaunda," Lethrix growled. "Speak it aloud."

"N-no," she wheezed, her chest feeling crushed by an avalanche. "I-Is that her?"

"Who?" Halena asked.

"No," the Sargt answered. "Not as you knew her."

You prick. The Red Sister gritted her teeth. *I didn't* need *to see this. I can't do anything to help her now!*

"We should leave while they are distracted," Lethrix said, grabbing Jaunda by the back of her armor and pulling her toward the exit. "Come along, Shadows."

They moved quickly, the Dragon pushing the Red Sister out front, their group running an impossible speed atop the slippery surface.

All the while in retreat, Jaunda couldn't get the images of the mutated Davrin out of her head. She couldn't take a full breath, and the ring seemed to burn on her hand. Her eyes blurred until she could barely see anything anyway, so she closed them, listening to the rest of her body to keep from falling on her face while she had strength.

Eventually, she recognized the impact and sound of boots hitting solid stone. They stopped, catching their breath.

Familiar scents entered her nose, her throat, her head.

Somehow, she knew this place, too.

We aren't far from the first caravan stop near Low Gate.

Correct, Lethrix answered. **I gather you and the Shadows may want to part ways here.**

Part ways. *Already?*

The Davrin opened her eyes, looking around and confirming Vik and Halena recognized this passage and its markings, too. They'd arrived farther from the flayer conclave at a faster speed than they had any business remembering it as a sprint.

"A Bargain fulfilled, Halena," the Dragon said. "The three of you are out safe."

"Oh … yes," she gasped. "Thank you …"

"Good. I shall see to the Red Sister and completion of hers. Might I suggest you take your charge where he must go next?"

Vik and Halena were reluctant to leave her at first, but then they saw the look on the Lead's face. After the conclave, Jaunda still felt like she'd been hit in the chest with a hammer.

"Um, a privilege working with you, Lead," Vik said, as Halena signed the same with sincerity.

Jaunda pursed her lips. "Yeah. Keep going, you two. Whatever you do next, don't get caught."

Rausery's Shadows didn't take long to vanish, but the Lead from Low Gate had a guess or two which shortcut they might have taken. She knew all the nooks around here.

But she had to wait to pick her own.

"So, you can do it, right?" she muttered, shock and pain turning to anger as she faced her biggest success.

"I can." His tail slithered normally. "Are you certain of the length of time?"

"No," she scoffed to herself. "I'm guessing. That's all I can do. Can't be too soon, can't be too long. Unless you have a better suggestion?"

"I do not. I think you know your relations to your superiors better than I do."

"Then ... I'm ready to go back home."

Lethrix smirked, bowing his head, and opening his arms. "Come, then, Arytiss. Let our Bargain be complete."

Jaunda approached him and threw a fist in his gut, making him grunt slightly, before she wrapped her arms around his middle.

Know I need to hold on. What next?

Lethrix answered by tilting her jaw up to meet his eyes, and the Lead felt his aura penetrate hers one last time.

When they separated, the Red Sister was ready to meet her Queen.

CHAPTER 15

THE PALACE OF SIVARAUS

HEADMASTER PHAELOUS WAITED WITH HIS USUAL PATIENCE, OUT OF SIGHT, ONE crooked finger parting the purple drapes. The Valsharess stood on Her platform, flanked by the Red Sister Prime and the Drider Keeper in her feral Davrin form. All faced the jump circle at the other end of the small, carpeted throne room.

His Queen sent Her voice beyond the jump circle.

Enter.

After a moment, Lead Jaunda appeared, surrounded by the colorfully strewn murals of the throne room. Her hair was much shorter than the last time he'd seen her, and she no longer appeared stunned by the intensity of the Queen's private meeting room.

"Approach Us."

Phaelous saw the young Sister's fear but also the courage which kept her shoulders level for all this time. Few in Sivaraus ever became the Left Hand to an Elder Sister; fewer still had braced herself alone against the pinnacle of the city's power.

Jaunda kept her eyes forward, never looking directly at her superiors. The missing station upon the platform was that of a Priestess, which was telling of some undeniable change.

Not long ago, Wilsira would be here as well.

After as many times as he'd stood here in the past, he acknowledged a deeply strange feeling to know the Conceiver would never walk into this room again.

The cost has been heavy.

The Valsharess drew breath to speak. "Red Sister. You have completed your mission."

Jaunda slowly took to one knee near the center of the circular chamber. She closed one fist and pressed it to the floor. "Yes, Your Majesty."

"You look different to Us."

The Lead ducked her chin. "The ... *Sargt* accepted Your offering, Highness."

The Queen's head tilted at the foreign word, Auranka hissed through her fangs, and Phaelous's heart surged in his chest.

Sargt.

It sounded familiar.

What does it mean?

The Queen's long, blonde braid moved with the golden embroidery on Her deep purple gown as She turned Her head to the Drider Keeper.

"Displeased?" asked the Valsharess placidly.

"Disssappointed, my Queen," Auranka cooed, narrowing eyes like glossy, black beads. "Had he refusssed, she would be palatable."

The Headmaster observed a familiar, regal shake of Her head. "Had he refused, she would have failed and died. Base though he is, We have never gleaned one taste of a fool. He bears a message in return."

"What message, Your Majesty?" the Prime rumbled, squinting at her subordinate as if she expected a tattoo on Jaunda's face.

"We cannot hear it, yet. The Ley hasn't yet settled within her."

The three peered at the younger Davrin from their periphery while they spoke. Two of them studied her aura at the same time. The Headmaster shifted his position to see between the Valsharess and the Prime, focusing on the Lead and her unique halo of colored patterns and threads.

Indeed, something had changed. A stark, metallic gold strand meandered, comfortable and benign, throughout her essence. What was not "settled" enough to read meant it lacked permanence.

She had not been born with it, as he had.

Amazing.

"I don't like this," said the Prime, planting fists on her hips, spreading her red cloak like wings. "What will we do with her until then, Majesty?"

Phaelous saw the Lead swallow, because he was watching for it.

I don't blame you.

"First," their ancient ruler extended Her arm, unfurling Her hand with palm up. "Return Our ring, Lead Sister. You need it not anymore."

Jaunda returned to her feet, pulling off her right glove at the same time. She didn't step forward but eased the gold ring from her middle finger to hold it in her bare palm. "Permission to approach, Your Highness."

"Granted."

The Prime tensed, watching like a pincerworm about to strike.

"Your Lead is under no geas, Eldest," the Valsharess said like a gentle admonishment. "Not Ours or his."

"*Rrm.* Yes, Your Majesty."

Jaunda bowed her chin to her superior, stepped up to the platform, and dropped the ring into her Queen's palm without touching or looking at Her. Curiously, Auranka took the smallest step back, the coarse hairs on her forearms flexing as if reacting to something unseen.

Then, the Lead stepped backward with her head bowed and fist on her chest.

"Well done," the Queen said. "Now, Jaunda, follow Us behind the throne. Auranka and Prime, remain here."

The Eldest Sister and Drider Keeper turned their heads his way. Phaelous stepped back, glimpsing twin glares before the drapes closed.

Reining in his heart, the Headmaster waited for his Valsharess and Lead Jaunda to join him in the small, dark room, empty but for a writing table and a warded jump circle only She could use.

The young leader was surprised to see him. "Headmaster?"

Phaelous bowed his head to her then turned to bow to his Queen at the waist, waving toward his writing supplies brought from the Tower. "I am here to create a record, nothing more."

"Sit."

That command was for him. He took his seat and prepared his ink, parchment, and drying sand.

"Lead, kneel facing him. You may meet his eyes if you wish. We shall stand behind you. Do not be afraid."

With a deep, steady breath, Jaunda knelt in front of his writing table, folding her legs and sitting on her heels. With back straight, she chose to look up, boldly meeting his eyes.

"Remove your Feldeu, first," said the Queen, a royal purple figure looming behind the older cait. "Place it upon the table near his hand."

With another swallow, Jaunda reached with one hand to the small of her back, detaching the false phallus and placing it within his reach with a soft thud. Phaelous momentarily forgot the scribe's tool in his hand, staring too long without speaking.

"What do you see, Headmaster?"

"Majesty," he acknowledged, barely above a whisper. "Um —"

"Is it altered from how you crafted it?"

The simple answer was "yes," but the change didn't appear deliberate despite matching the metallic gold in Jaunda's aura.

"The staff holds the seed of a new pattern, perhaps," he said, twiddling his writing tool, "but without a clear progression or design. The Lead would have to keep using it to discover that potential."

"Agreed," She said, studying the phallus with Her own keen eye. "This one is attuned to her stronger than before."

"If it proves advantageous," the Headmaster added with caution, "I may study and create something new for Your Sisterhood, Majesty."

His Queen stood in silence, gazing at the back of Jaunda's head, eyes unfocused in Her ancient face.

Then She spoke.

"Let it be done. Reclaim your weapon, Red Sister."

Jaunda's face brightened, her curiosity and relief mixing as she took her favorite magic item and secured it behind her.

Phaelous began some notes. "She is in high health, my Queen. Well fed."

"We noticed. The Black was generous this time."

"Uhh, well," Jaunda began, "Highne —"

"Yes?"

"Food, water, and rest were part of the Bargain."

"Hm. Perhaps We should start at the beginning of your last journey."

Phaelous felt Her reach out, touching him unseen. He recognized the abrupt hook first piercing then setting inside him. She gave it a tug; he knew not to fight.

The Valsharess then lifted Her hands to cradle Jaunda's close-cropped head between them. The Lead knew not to fight, he could see it in her eyes, but she'd only succeed after the pain peaked. The difference between them was merely that the Headmaster had practice silencing his aura before it could start.

When the agony crested, Jaunda wailed through one long cry.

On the other side of the drapes, Fadele chortled.

PHAELOUS'S HAND MOVED QUICKLY AND WITHOUT HIS AWARENESS. WHEN HE next came to himself, he would have filled his available space with a small, tight script and would need a few cycles to ease the cramp in his right hand.

Until then, he waded through Her whispers, Her commands, and what seemed important to describe in his own words.

Look, She said. *Take note. The Yutogul still breed there. Good. And here. This is where they find their sentry drakes. That canyon connects levels.*

Yes, my Queen.

And what is this? A jump circle hidden there ... Was this noted before?

I shall have to check the archives.

Do it. Ah, but he was leading her, testing her ...

The Black Dragon had accepted his tribute by that point but wanted to play with his dish first.

He's Awake.

Indeed, it has been more than five centuries.

Half my lifetime ago.

The Valsharess chuckled ruefully. *A fraction of mine and his.*

How did Your Majesty know to send her at this time?

That is between Us and him, Headmaster.

Yes, my Queen.

Regardless, even Lethrix had said She had chosen well. Jaunda bargained well, learned quickly, and held her own against a creature which should have terrified anyone. Jaunda had been too tired to be afraid, too lonely not to consider the Black's proposal.

Solitary this entire time, the Red Sister just wanted to come home.

His Queen turned Her inner eye away from the raunchier memories. Phaelous could sense Her revulsion, bearing witness as if he crouched at a peephole. He could hear and smell enough to know what happened, could glimpse body parts straining against each other in the nude.

But he couldn't feel anything.

Toward the end, the Valsharess gasped.

*Arytiss ... *

My Queen?

The Sargt named her. Arytiss.

Only through Her did Phaelous understand those Words. Their meaning flashed like faceted gems in his thoughts.

The Guardian named her.

Warrior.

Sivaraus has a new protector.

His Queen smiled where Phaelous could see it, so he recognized its importance.

At last, when Lethrix prepared to bring their Lead home, the two stopped by the Ornilleth conclave first. Jaunda didn't understand much of what she saw, but a tremor of fear arose from deep within the wizard and his ruler as they observed over her shoulder.

It failed, She whispered.

What failed, my Queen?

They lost the prisoner. Lost part of the Elder's mind.

Behind Her throne room, tawny, translucent eyes pinned him down in their trance.

The conclave shall come for Sivaraus. To extract payment for this loss from among Our own. He knew this. Why we were given the Arytiss. She is a warning and a weapon.

The Valsharess gazed into the nightmarish vision, as the manifestation of a brilliant unity fractured, broke …

And fell into insanity.

Foreboding moments passed before She brought each of them to the surface with one final thought.

We do not have much time.

PHAELOUS LEFT THE NEWEST SCROLLS WITH HIS QUEEN, AND THE VALSHARESS peeled Auranka away from the rest of them, insisting the Drider Keeper come with Her behind the curtain. The Prime and Headmaster were instructed to find the Elders Rausery and D'Shea and convey extremely specific information.

"Which you will use to prepare for war, Prime Sister. No harm is to come to your Lead before We receive the final message. The Headmaster shall report to Us later."

He glanced at the Eldest Sister once they left the throne room through its circle. Fadele was visibly resentful with having to haul the Lead and Headmaster with her for this next stage.

"So," the old Davrin growled, stepping out into the sixth-floor room with the wizard and Lead following her. "A giant magic lizard used you as a cock sock to catch his spunk and load you up with some riddle. Now our Queen wants you roaming free around the city until She figures out how to sieve the message out from the lumpy stew in your sloppy ass. Have I got that right?"

Jaunda pursed her lips slightly, managing to nod her head without bowing her chin too much. "Yes, Prime. As the Valsharess compelled my penance served for killing Kerse. I completed my trial and obtained knowledge about our enemies. Success."

The voice of an Arytiss is impressively steady.

"Until the other boot drops. A disgusting submission, Lead, don't know how you're gonna live it down. Almost as bad as Sirana getting double-ended by Kerse *and* the fuckin' flayer." Fadele spat on the floor and headed toward the exit. "*Bah*, but you're still alive and back in the Sisterhood."

Something unspoken hung in the air.

Phaelous thought, *For now.*

The sixth floor held most of the Priestesses' private chambers. Unlike the straight lines of doors in the infirmary directly beneath them, the entrances to each Priestess were well-separated from each other by recessed alcoves and blind corners coming off the main, elaborately decorated hallway.

The upside was greater difficulty in marking one's passing by putting an ear to the door. The downside was the entire floor was riddled with wards, alarms, and traps. This didn't affect non-mages like the Prime or Jaunda much, but Phaelous frequently felt his less-tangible senses overloaded when passing through.

The fifth floor had become as bad ever since the Priestesses Juliran and Irrwaer had passed. The two austere healers had kept their level ascetic, bare-walled, and clear of magical influence to better aid the deliberate mending of body and mind. Usually, Phaelous would take shortcuts through there for that reason.

In recent, stark contrast, the fourth floor once contained the Consorts before their maturity but was empty, devoid of these paranoid spell attachments. Despite this, the Headmaster didn't enter this level unless it related to his work with Lelinahdara and Elder D'Shea.

"Prime Sister! Headmaster! What a pleasant surprise to find you here."

Think of the demon, and it appears ...

Even Fadele's shoulders sagged as she lifted her eyes toward the ceiling. "Confessor. We're busy."

Tarra smiled at the elder as if she couldn't break her in half. "Oh, but

I have business with Phaelous."

"It can wait, web spinner. Back up. He's got a directive with the Elder Sorceress first."

"D'Shea?" Tarra blinked and smiled wider.

Uh-oh.

"Why, she's on the fourth floor this very moment, Prime. Allow me to escort you." The Confessor spun around, waving her arm, robes swirling elegantly around her. "She'll be delighted to see her Lead. She seems ... overwhelmed."

"*Baby cunt,*" Fadele whispered under her breath, jerking her jaw for them to follow the Priestess two floors down.

Phaelous, as always, quelled his disappointment at the unfortunate circumstances of meeting his fierce sorceress again.

"She left in a hurry," Rausery murmured, looking at the empty doorway where Tarra had excused herself.

"Shh," D'Shea shushed from down on the floor, peering beneath the empty bed using the light of a glowstone. Craning her head, she signed one-handed. ★Help me turn this on its side.★

The two Elders each took an end, lifting the bed quietly off its legs and turning it so they could see the underside, trapping the thin mattress between the frame and the wall. The General frowned at the unfamiliar script, though D'Shea's heart surged.

Wilsira's cypher ...

Phaelous had finally broken it and had given her the keys to transcribe it several spans ago. She could not read them at a glance, so she pulled out her leather-bound scrapbook and started copying while Rausery kept watch.

At one point, D'Shea tapped Rausery's boot to catch her peer's attention and signed, ★Qivni said this was the position where Wilsira's favored Consort slept, correct?★

"Yeah," Rausery breathed, signing once the Sorceress turned her head. *She knew him as Kino. I think he was purged as part of that first 'failed' crop. A different Consort was sleeping here during the recent purge.*

That fits. Thank you.

Rausery nudged her leg before she could start marking in her book. *What fits?*

D'Shea took the opportunity to stretch. *I believe there are multiple names here, as each have an additional mark against them except one. They might be the 'true names' held by the Sanctuary, no matter what the Nobles named them.*

The General emitted a soft huff. *So she scratched out his name as he was replaced with another?*

Probably. The Sorceress finished her notes. *Alright, now the next bed. Before Tarra returns.*

The Elders found and copied nine beds before they received plenty of warning that the Confessor was returning and brought unexpected company.

"What the fuck is she doing here?" Rausery murmured.

"Hurry," D'Shea said, hiding her book and motioning for her to take one end of the bed to right it.

As with the others, they returned the ninth bed to the exact position it had been in and moved together to a supply closet. D'Shea picked up a basket of embroidery supplies and shoved it into Rausery's arms before picking up a clean stack of bedding to place it on the nearest table.

They were fussing with these things when Tarra brought the Prime, Jaunda, and Phaelous in with her. As usual, Rausery broke the shell.

"Jaunda!" she said with a clear smile and welcome in her voice. "When did you get back?"

With a wavering smile, the Lead saluted her greeting to the General. And to D'Shea. "Just this cycle."

Her Left Hand's aura felt different, even from here. D'Shea glanced at the Prime, who was scowling and uninterested in catching them up right then.

"Heading out again?" Rausery asked.

"Uh ... no, Ge —"

The Prime brought her arm up, both slapping the Lead on the back and shoving her hard, forcing Jaunda farther into the Consorts' communal bedroom. Rausery and D'Shea freed their hands at the same time and paid attention.

"She's finished her mission," their Eldest grumbled. "Paid her penance."

D'Shea straightened and caught herself holding her breath. "She has."

"Yeah. And the next task you give her has to be something 'safe.'" she said with a sneer. "The Valsharess can call her anytime. She's not finished with her yet. Got it?"

Better than many possibilities.

"Yes, Prime," Rausery said as D'Shea bowed her head. "We'll find something for her."

Old eyes like scratched rubies fixed on the General. "What the fuck are you doing here, anyway?"

"What, me?" The General grinned, nodding to Tarra. "Ask her."

The Confessor cleared her throat as the Prime narrowed eyes on her. "The Elder Sorceress requested access to this room some time ago, related to our own task for the Valsharess. The Headmaster hasn't been available of late, but we have a rule in the Sanctuary that a Priestess and a Red Sister should not be alone together. I insisted on a credible witness next time. Varessa brought Rausery."

"What a massive dung drop," the Prime snorted, unclear in which part she meant.

During the exchange, Jaunda took her familiar place near D'Shea, letting out a quiet breath and ready to keep out of the way.

"Well, whatever's going on, web squirt," their Eldest continued, ignoring the slight shift in Tarra's expression, "you can't keep my General. Here's your Headmaster. And I need D'Shea to report to the Cloister as soon as fuckin' possible. We got something bigger to worry about than this spitting nest."

The Confessor nodded smartly, pushing out her chest as she straightened her shoulders before the taller Davrin. "Of course, Prime, as soon as may be. What about her Lead?"

"Need her at the same time as the Sorceress."

Yet the Prime looked at Rausery.

"I can use my escort again, Elder," D'Shea spoke up, peering at Phaelous and Tarra. "She will be safe enough. We can report together."

"Agreed, Prime," Rausery said, scratching her head with a tilt in her most disarming way. "I don't have any safe missions right now. Need to collect some reports."

"Fine. Jaunda, stay. Rausery, with me to the Cloister."

If only I could watch all three of you at once.

All for different reasons.

D'Shea felt colliding impulses to comb Jaunda for physical changes, read Phaelous's aura and the tiniest changes in his expression, *and* keep a close eye on Tarra as she searched for anything she had missed when she left to divert the Headmaster and Red Sisters onto the fourth floor.

The Priestess attempted subtlety this time by using directness to mask it. Not the Confessor's best trick, but the Prime's arrival on the sixth floor had been poorly timed.

For her.

"Do you need help determining who slept where, Elder? Is that why you came?" The Priestess smirked, hips swaying as she looked about the items abandoned on the shelves, which bore a distinct lack of books. "You could have asked me. I kept track of all that, or I wouldn't have uncovered their deformities."

The Sorceress counted on her and Rausery not having left anything badly out of place. She was also trying not to be distracted by the Headmaster watching Jaunda in a way he never had before. Why?

Her first unwelcome theory focused on the fact that her Lead was the same rank and age that D'Shea had been when the Headmaster had begun to look so appealing. When the temptation to risk conception overwhelmed her better judgment.

Jaunda wasn't a mage, and she rarely found buas tempting, but something *had* changed about her.

The Queen couldn't want a child from her, could She?

Now that Jaunda had satisfied her geas, had her worth grown that much in the eyes of the Valsharess?

D'Shea squashed down a galling rise of jealousy. *What is going on?*

"You kept track," she repeated, making herself sound quite interested. "That *would* save time, liaison."

Tarra smiled. "Why? What did you find?"

"Any pattern to the bua rotation between rooms." Which was mostly true, though her eyes scanned the walls and ceiling. "Whether Wilsira began sequestering a smaller number of demonblood Consorts at first. We need firm evidence when it started."

Phaelous cleared his throat quietly. Knowing the sound, the Sorceress paused to look at him even as Tarra kept talking.

"Oh, well, I believe it began before I gained my vestments," said the Priestess. "Wilsira was making deals with all the Priestesses when I was an acolyte."

Meanwhile, the Headmaster bowed his head and moved toward the far end of the long, narrow quarters.

"The last one was Juliran," the Confessor continued, keeping one eye on him. "You remember, Varessa, don't you? The healer-Priestess on the fifth floor who mothered that older Consort executed at House Itlaun."

Auslan.

She felt a trickle of cold.

Breathe.

Tarra turned her attention to D'Shea with a smile as the Headmaster ran his fingers along the far wall. "I recently visited Curgia Itlaunaduv in the dungeon, you know. She's close to birthing. It seems the sire had his Priestess-Mother's talent to an extravagant degree for a bua. Curgia insists he was still alive somehow, but there's no chance of *that*, is there? Too much blood spilled by the Sisterhood."

What are you sniffing at?

D'Shea welcomed the distraction as Phaelous found a seal and began to whisper under his breath. "Indeed. Unpleasant business, cleaning up the Conceiver's corrupted mess."

"Alas. Have you visited your son lately? Shyntre's been unusually quiet in the Palace rumors."

Damn the Abyss.

"I have not." The Sorceress smiled. "Far too busy chasing bloodlines and keeping the Nobles from doing something stupid without their bua toys to distract them."

Phaelous opened a hidden door. "Ah, here it is, Priestess. Elder. Not permanently sealed after all."

"What was sealed?" Tarra asked, surprised but eager for this revelation.

"A training room, as I understood it." Phaelous stepped away and allowed the Confessor to poke her head in first. "Consorts needed their fertility confirmed regularly and needed experience. Not every Priestess had the time or desire to teach themselves. I believe Wilsira used servant caits in such cases. This is where they'd sleep."

Like Qivni.

D'Shea frowned. She knew well the story of how Rausery's Right Hand had come to them. The daughter of an acolyte, and the servant in the Sanctuary who "soiled" the first crop of Consorts, leading to the first purge by the Conceiver.

Though it always sounded to me like they had soiled her.

"Sleeping right next to the Consorts? How interesting!" The Confessor summoned a gentle light, inspecting the dark, hidden space. Whatever she saw made her look out at them with bright eyes. "I know your superior demands your return as soon as possible. How about I investigate here and share my findings later?"

D'Shea looked at Phaelous, who seemed at complete peace with this. She swallowed her smirk and replaced it with a hesitant, thoughtful sigh.

"Perhaps that is best," she said reluctantly. "We should be briefed without delay at the Cloister."

"And you, Phaelous," Tarra asked. "Will you stay?"

He bowed. "My apologies, Priestess. I must check on my buas at the Tower. I've been gone all cycle."

"Very well. I'll take notes, and we shall reconvene in Wilsira's library?"

"As soon as may be, Priestess."

Smooth as silk, Phaelous got them out of the Consorts' quarters and left the Sanctuary without the bed markings or her book of cyphers being discovered.

As much as D'Shea still hated him, she could not deny the Headmaster excelled at what he did.

"Are you certain, Elder?"

"Yes. Take us to your quarters, Headmaster."

After three jump circles, Jaunda wavered on her feet, finding herself standing in a place she'd never been: the private quarters of Headmaster Phaelous at the top of the Wizard's Tower.

"We do not have time to waste," her Elder said brusquely, giving the wizard a stern look before switching to Jaunda. Her face softened. "What happened to you, Jaunda? Please be brief."

"Uh …"

"She was given to the Black Dragon as penance," Phaelous said. "I was there, but you are about to hear it from the Prime."

The Sorceress switched her gaze. "What do you mean, 'given?'"

"He woke up after five hundred years," Jaunda said, her voice hoarse. "He was fuckin' randy."

"What?!"

The Lead shrugged. "I'm trying to sort it out myself. Uh. The Prime talks like I'm a used stocking with a permanent hole, but I'm not against saying he knows what he's doing more than she ever has."

D'Shea pursed her lips with concern. "So, that is the change I see in your aura. You merged?"

Jaunda blinked. *Was that what that was?* "I … I guess?"

"Yes," Phaelous confirmed. "Typically such powerful auras take a while to fade. At least among Davrin."

Even Jaunda heard the hesitation in his tone.

"What else do you know?" her Elder demanded. "Say it."

"Are you sure?" he asked.

"Phaelous. After everything I've ever risked, you must ask?"

He exhaled, his direct gaze steady on her face. Jaunda always knew there was something between them, but the eldest wizard was making that clearer in his expression.

"I see the common thread in Rausery's bloodline which Wilsira must have been after. The missing piece."

"You do?"

The Headmaster glanced at Jaunda, nodding. "Yes. It's a Draconic influence. I don't know where it came from in Rausery, but your Lead confirms it by what I see in her after her return."

"What?! Wilsira knew somehow but the Queen didn't?"

"I don't know, Elder, truthfully. Either the Valsharess has missed it, or She turns a blind eye even now. It has never shown in any mages of Sivaraus, so does not compete with Hers."

"Compete with *Hers*? What do you mean *Hers*, Phaelous?"

"Look in my eyes, Varessa. What do you see? What do you see in our son's eyes?"

Jaunda had never seen her Elder look so shaken. She *looked* like "Varessa" as her ear tips greyed a little.

"The ... The Black Dragon?" she whispered. "He did this?"

Phaelous shook his head. "No. Of that, I'm certain. Not the Black."

"How else?"

"A ... Another Dragon. That is all I have ever been able to guess in ten centuries. One our Queen ... fled, perhaps? In some time long past. Long before I was born."

Jaunda's limbs had gone stiff listening to them, but her Elder stumbled to collapse into a seat while Phaelous clasped his long-fingered hands before him. The wizard's quarters were silent for some time.

"Rausery and Jaunda?" D'Shea murmured.

"The same influence. The Black. Exactly what Wilsira was trying to dig and exploit from commoners related to our General."

"Which means the 'influence' came sometime before her, and we don't know who this was."

"Correct, my Elder. There are no records."

The Sorceress swallowed. "But you ... and Shyntre ... ?"

"Not the Black. Another influence ... far older."

"And one our Queen keeps jealously close," she growled. "Which means Auranka at least knows about this. This explains why she's always taunted you and Shyntre over the centuries."

Phaelous hesitated, his eyes wavering. "Perhaps."

Jaunda knew that look. *Something else he can't say.*

"There is something else you will hear from the Prime," the wizard continued. "And, eventually, the Queen."

D'Shea looked wary. "What?"

"Jaunda was given a gift from the Black, but it hasn't manifested yet. The Valsharess is certain it will help us against the Ornilleth, who are sure to attack Sivaraus. That's why she wants Jaunda kept off dangerous missions for now."

"Indeed. That's interesting." Slowly, her Elder gathered herself and rose to her feet. "Well then, we should catch up to Rausery and the Prime in the Cloister."

Jaunda said, tamping down the weird revulsion thinking of her top leader. *Fadele.* "I'd ... rather not be there where the Prime can try to fuck with you, Elder."

The Sorceress frowned. "Rarely do we receive what we'd rather, Lead."

"I know. And I know *you* know more than anyone, Elder. But the Queen gave the Prime and Headmaster the information to give you. I wasn't instructed to do the same, and I think Phaelous dropped the big stuff on you, right?"

The ancient wizard agreed. "I will see you get a fuller report via bloodstone, Elder. You can compare to the Prime's report."

"That would be crucial," she agreed, tapping her lips in thought. "I grant it would be easier to handle her if you are not under her nose, tempting her to take you away from me again."

Jaunda smirked. "Gone from sight, gone from mind. How she often is, right?"

"Agreed." D'Shea studied her again, contemplating the massive, intricate web of links ever-present in her mind. "Hm. I have my first 'safe' mission for you, Lead."

She straightened up. "Name it, Elder."

"House Thalluen."

"Again? Um, you want me to guard the healer?"

"Him and Shyntre, yes."

The Lead jerked. "Wait, Shyntre's there?"

"He is. He should be retraining the healer for combat, but I don't expect much progress to have been made yet. Just remind him."

Jaunda frowned slightly at D'Shea's sudden look of amusement.

"Work with Matron Thalluen," she continued. "Watch everything you can, keep my buas safe, and I'll join you as soon as I can."

My buas.

The Lead had never heard that before, but Phaelous seemed incredibly pleased about this turn of events.

"Yes, Elder," Jaunda said. "Count on it."

"Thank you. Now, I shall give you a head start through the jump circles, but I must get to the Cloister."

"Yes, Elder. I'm ready."

D'Shea smiled. "You were born ready. Let's go."

Jaunda sneaked unseen through familiar territory easily by now, having done this three times before, going to the same place.

She remembered carrying a shrinking Auslan, bruised and abraded by the Sisterhood, to the Matron's House in secret. She remembered the pretty bua's warm hands as he healed her in the bath, mending worn muscle, swollen joints, and minutely fractured bones.

She thought of Sirana's disciplined Matron, Rohenvi, nursing the new infant heir while keeping watch on the friendly little cait who lurked near the healer. What was her name? *Natia.*

Now, Shyntre was there, too, of all buas, on some kind of mission for his Mother. That was a change between them she thought she'd never live to see. Now, Jaunda would be there, too.

Ready to get them out alive if something strange went down.

Crouching down as a cart passed by, she frowned to herself. Why think about something "strange" going down at a middling House that rarely drew attention during these last decades?

Until Sirana tricked the First Daughter into breaking her own neck.

Maybe things were getting interesting there again, like during Matron Siranet's reign.

Looks like I'm about to find out.

All the while as she approached, the Lead had the quiet, persistent feeling she was forgetting some important connection in all this.

Something that just happened …

What was it? Or who?

Eh, I'm sure it'll come back to me.

CHAPTER 16

KERUT RIVER MOUNDS – THE SURFACE

"*I don't feel well,*" JAEL WHISPERED IN OUR NATIVE TONGUE.

I believed it. Her face had greyed, her lips and the tips of her ears paling while I watched. Just like Mourn the moment before he collapsed in the middle of this underground redoubt.

I was impressed how well the general noise was muffled from the hundreds of sentients which might be packed underneath the Kerut hills at the moment.

"*Here.*"

I claimed one of the empty pallets for us, pulling Jael to kneel upon it, though I didn't force her to lie down yet with so much tension and activity around us. I let her slump against me, wrapping my arms and cloak around her to keep us warm.

"Thirsty?" asked the broad, grey-bearded Dwarf watching us.

Did I have water? I checked my empty waterskin and cursed softly.

"Truden, pass out th' spares, will ya?"

"Aye, *Oltere.*"

A younger brown-beard approached Jael and me, carrying four full waterskins with another four slung over his shoulders. He handed two to me before turning and hesitantly offering one to Gavin.

The tall Deathwalker still had those strange growths, like black flint, poking holes in his robes around his shoulders. With a familiar frown set and ice-black eyes unblinking and peering down at him, he shook his head once. Truden didn't offer twice but moved on.

Overlapping voices in at least three languages, none of them mine, rang in my ears. I slaked my thirst before getting my Sister to take slow sips.

"Is he wounded, *Tentente*?" Krithannia asked one of the Templars, standing tall and unguarded between the Manalari and the Taiding Dwarves hovering over our Dragonchild.

"Blooded, *Gremia*," answered the man with the red-gold beard, who'd helped carry an unconscious Willven Isboern through the jump gate. "Not deathly."

"We have a healer." The dark-haired Elf bowed her head toward the red-headed sibling with the bouncing curls. "Ragura of Clan Baradum. Well respected in Augran and Taiding."

Ragura stood up from kneeling by the unconscious Mourn; she bowed without speaking, showing her medicine kit in a strong grip. The Manalari men eyed the short, buxom woman warily, though little more than the tall, willowy Tamuril and her fussy falcon.

As if they haven't figured out Pilla is the same bird of the 'falcon boy' working with their Captain to defend Jael all this time.

"Got someone else in mind?" Talov asked bluntly, folding thick arms, breaking the awkward silence. "An' say ya do, know where they are?"

This was enough of a prompt. The *Tentente* removed his helm, darker reddish hair plastered to his skull, and bowed his head once. "We accept, Baradum."

He motioned the Dwarven healer closer, saying something in Manalari which encouraged the other three soldiers to make space for her. The large pieces of Willven's armor had been wrangled off, so Ragura got to work: requesting assistance to remove clothing, inspecting, cleaning, and dressing various minor injuries about his body.

I wasn't sure when the psion had gotten them. Abrasions from the armor itself or those times he'd fallen or been knocked down. Or maybe that final, hard fall into the river during our escape.

Gavin seemed interested in what Ragura was doing and stepped closer to observe. Predictably, this unnerved the Templari.

"Why do you stare?" said the eldest with the dark beard. "Does death draw near?"

My ally's gaunt form shifted its focus. "No. I see nothing like that."

"Then ... *nomilu dergo*, take those eyes from us, *hom'grios*. At least until we have regained strength."

The Deathwalker straightened when a third Templar made a surreptitious gesture. "These eyes may see more of what wilts, *hom'sol*, but cause no greater harm than yours in what they witness."

Ragura glanced over her shoulder at him, cleaning and salving another wound. "Hm. So ... can ye see disease or fester, too?"

Gavin looked at her, and the Templari visibly relaxed. "Only advanced enough to affect the strength of the life aura. Probably no better or sooner than you can detect by other means."

"Ah. Aye, tha's honest. Why look, then?"

"Noting your methods. Comparing."

"Ye have skill with wounds?"

"Some. As a chirurgeon might."

She finished covering a large abrasion with a pale, clean cloth. "Like removin' arrowheads?"

"Yes. And setting bones."

"Huh. Good tah know." Ragura looked behind her. "Uncle?"

"Ahead ov ya, lasschen," Talov said with a grin. "Guild's offerin' ya a private room, Deathwalker, right now, if ya trade some ov that skill fer the really bad ones this first day. They'll be drugged fer pain. They won't care if yer lookin' at 'em."

"Hm." Gavin didn't think long. "I accept. As long as I am given time alone without patients."

"Ya will. Great!" Talov turned to a younger blond. "Kellan, check on the progress an' come back."

"Aye, *Oltere.*"

I wondered what progress the greybeard meant, though Gavin's private room didn't sound like the place to get something to eat.

I noticed Tamuril had turned away during this. She was wringing her hands, eyes flicking between Pilla hunched on her shoulder, me, and Jael, Krithannia in the center, and the bundle of Dwarves milling around the black lump of scales, trying not to step on his tail.

Everyone but Willven.

Her calm sister approached her, gently taking the Druid's hand in both of hers, standing opposite the falcon, and spoke softly in yet a fourth language I could barely hear. The blonde Elf's slight ease in tension reminded me to check on Jael, who'd pulled her lips from the waterskin. She was awake but not as alert as I was, her copper eyes dull while she stared across the room at nothing.

"*What's wrong?*" I whispered in Davrin, gathering her closer to me.

Admittedly, I didn't expect her to tense up, and I was further shocked to see her eyes start to shimmer. She banished the tears with a blink and scowled before looking away. "*Nothing.*"

Lying.

Only then did I check where her hands were in relation to Soul Drinker. She growled in annoyance when I reached to pull both her hands where I could see them.

"*You really thought I'd lift it from you?*"

"*Not you. I'm being cautious. Remember what Mourn said about it.*"

"*Tch.*"

My Sister pouted and said nothing more, so I loosened the pouch to let my two surviving guardian spiders out, lest they be squeezed. As the pair crawled up to my nape, my stomach gurgled, for once drowned out by the noise of the crowded room. Only Gavin looked at me. I shrugged and drank more water, studying the room.

By action and appearance, I guessed the two groups were preparing to move both Mourn and Willven at some point. Each had been rolled onto a litter with handles, one reinforced with double the handles for the Dragon's son. Was it necessary? Here was as good as anywhere to rest, wasn't it?

"Um, Talov," I asked.

His pale green eyes turned to me, crinkling at the corners. "Aye?"

"Where will Jael and I stay? With Mourn, I hope. We have an agreement. I can help keep watch."

In my periphery, Krithannia looked our way at once, while the elder Dwarf scrunched his hairy face in a way I couldn't read.

"We'll get tah that, Sirana, promise. Let's move Gavin an' the Templari tah settle first."

The old Dwarf didn't want to discuss it? Did he think I would stab his "kid" while he slept?

"I hope we're not staying here," I said.

"Fer a li'l bit, aye."

I sighed. "May we at least have some food?"

"Soon." Talov glanced at my expression. "Apologies, lasschen. We weren't expectin' the delay."

"What delay?"

"Need more information 'fore we can say."

My stomach grew tenacious in its complaints until I was edging on nausea and about as distracted as Jael. As soon as Ragura stood up to rejoin her black-bearded brother, however, the Dwarves erupted into a bustle again, working quickly to transfer Gavin to his own quarters and the Templari to a "secure" location, each separately.

Clearly, from the way the Dwarves surrounded them and created visual obstacles, they wanted minimal witnesses for these two strangest of men from Manalar. Although I tried to catch Gavin's eye before he left, his ice blue pupils flickered in and out, unfocused on any one body as he followed his band of escorts out.

Well, damn.

Maybe he was eager to get started digging metal out of bodies and setting some bones.

Tamuril watched the Manalari leave next, her eyes intent and obviously distressed, but she remained silent as the *Tentente* led the others, two carrying Willven out on a litter while the last man guarded their rear. Pilla squawked in an oddly quiet way while Krithannia rubbed the Druid's back through the doeskin.

Talov was the only Dwarf in the room for a few moments until another five joined us, closing and securing the door. All were older than those who'd left with the Humans; some bore streaks of grey and white among the black, red-brown, and blond. The greybeard had been looking at Mourn somberly but peered at the new arrivals, bewildered.

"Did ya find him?"

"Nae," the older blond in front admitted with a red-cheeked shake of his head. "He's hiding from us."

"Whaddaya mean 'hiding?' "

"Not where we left 'im. Slipped out. Room's empty."

"*Ach*." Talov made a face and looked at the Naulor. "Krithy?"

Thoughtfully, the Guild Mistress rubbed a knuckle beneath her chin. "Hm."

Then she tilted her head and leaned, bracing her weight on one leg as if to look underneath the wide, low chair Talov had been sitting in when we arrived. I followed her gaze, and a pair of familiar, hazy red eyes appeared, looking at me.

Graul.

"There you are," Krithannia said with an obvious and welcoming affection.

Talov turned around to try and see for himself. I could not tell if the airy hiss was from annoyance or laughter.

"Awright, *grumpus*, will ya come out an' help us assess?"

"'Course," the shadow drake replied, snapping his jaw on something bulky before dragging it out with him. Objects inside clinked together, sounding like a pouch of coins.

"Where in the Hells ya get that?" Talov asked as Krithannia chuckled. "Didn't steal it from the refugees, I hope."

"Not this time," Graul answered, dropping the bag long enough to grin. "I leap before we jump, remember?"

"Ah. Had a feelin', huh?"

"Felt close, not sure."

"Bah."

The elder Dwarf made room and motioned for Mourn's companion to go by, which Graul did without hurry, dragging his bag in his teeth.

No one seemed to think it a good idea to "help" him with it.

The soft grunting and jingling brought Jael out of wherever she'd been. She frowned at the drake inspecting the large half-blood lying partly curled up on his side. We watched Graul stuff the coin pouch against Mourn's chest, nuzzling until the pouch was pinched in place by the muscular arm.

"*What the fuck is that?*" my Sister whispered.

Graul paused in waddling around Mourn, neck stretching up stiffly. He looked straight at her.

"*He understands Davrin,*" I murmured, noting how Krithannia's eyes flicked our way. "*Mourn's beast companion, like the pale one's bird.*"

Her eyes remained fixed on the drake, a stubborn edge coming to her jaw as Graul refused to look away. "*That's ... from the Deepearth.*"

"*Yes. That's Graul. They left together.*"

The ancient shadow drake squinted beady eyes at us, his throat pouch fluttering in vague threat before he broke the stare and continued his investigation on the state of his friend. Graul had some trouble pulling himself atop Mourn's shoulder, grunting like a tired wolf, partially stretching up his wings and swaying his tail to keep balance. He moved too stiffly for Jael not to notice.

"*And he's how old?*"

"*I don't know. Four centuries? A little more?*"

"*Step on my fucks ... you mean that nook lizard is older than Qivni?*"

Graul glanced our way again, tail bending in slow mischief as a brief chortle escaped mid-snuffle.

I almost hushed her against speaking so freely but paused. "*Wait, how old is Qivni?*"

"*Huh?*" My Sister blinked. "*Oh. Upper three hundreds.*"

That's all? Half a century younger than Jaunda. The stern Collector had certainly fooled me.

Still, it felt good to have Jael back and talking. Her curiosity was a good sign.

My stomach cramped up again, and I took to sipping from the second waterskin, watching as Graul settled down atop Mourn. His short legs were tucked close to his body with his head draping down toward the coin pouch and tail crossing the hybrid's shoulder blades as it reached for the floor. Easier, at least, to confirm the Dragonchild's breaths as the shadow drake rose up and down.

I glanced at Talov and Krithannia, who had turned away. They watched each other, probably speaking privately through the Dragon pearls. The five mature Dwarves waited patiently, their faces either too bushy or too placid to read, while Tamuril finally settled onto a pallet with Pilla on the opposite side of the room.

I'd grown near certain Graul had fallen asleep by the time he finally snorted and groggily lifted his head. It took several moments before he found and focused on the tall dark-haired Elf.

"Gone deep," rumbled the small beast, clouded eyes blinking at the Guild partners. "Baenar's hum sleeps."

I raised an eyebrow. *What? But we're right here ...*

Talov took a deep breath and let it out slowly, looking at me then my Sister. "Was afraid ov that. Gonna hafta ask fer yer cooperation, Sirana. An' Jael."

She narrowed her eyes with suspicion but let me ask the obvious.

"Cooperation about what?"

"Yer not gonna be able tah stay with 'im while he's asleep. We'll getcha a room somewhere else."

"What?!"

"No one can stay," Krithannia broke in, her arms crossed, nodding toward the drake. "Except him. We must place Mourn somewhere alone. Graul will alert us if there's trouble inside."

I didn't like my position and climbed to my feet. Jael sprang up with me, and Tamuril swiftly abandoned her seat, eyes wide like a deer while Pilla flapped to keep her balance.

"Why the isolation?" I asked, grappling with confused irritation. "He made a Bargain with me —"

"And it's because of that Bargain," said the Guild Mistress, "that we're trying to help him keep it."

"The kid doesn't always know where he is or who we are when he goes deep," Talov grumbled. "Can't risk you getting hurt as he tries tah come up."

"It could undo all the good work you've done together," the Naulor added. "Please believe us."

"Baenar hum sleeps," Graul repeated, shaking his head slowly in the negative. "To'vah will wake up first."

The greybeard nodded firmly. "An' we don't know when. Gonna be hard tah be prepared."

All of this sank in, and I could not doubt how earnest they sounded. *Oh ... that's what that meant.*

Krithannia chuckled wryly, her tone softening toward Talov. "I wonder if we've ever been prepared for the To'vah. But we must be immensely cautious with this many people all around." Silvery grey eyes focused on me. "And especially those with whom he hasn't settled his trade."

"Aye," Talov agreed, following her gaze to me. "So, Sirana, will you an' yer sis stay here while we move 'im elsewhere? Will ya wait with us till he awakens?"

In the center of a Dwarven stronghold without my bodyguard, for some unknown length of time.

Meanwhile, we'd left an entire army behind far to the South. The aftereffects hadn't begun to catch up for all around us.

"Only if we get some food," I said, my voice firm. "Now. More than you think we can eat from looking at us."

The Dwarves laughed softly amongst themselves, one of them motioning agreeably with his hands to his elder, presumably volunteering to be the server as he turned to leave.

"Awright," Talov said. "Hang tight. A big tray's comin'."

ABOUT A QUARTER MARK LATER, THE DWARF RETURNED WITH A HANDLED TRAY piled with bread and vegetables around a large, steaming bowl in the center. Whatever was in the bowl was warm and savory.

Before he could place it in front of us, Krithannia touched his shoulder to stay him and cast a small spell above it where we could see her. She leaned above it, sniffed delicately, and nodded her satisfaction.

"Tamuril," she said. "Would you partake with the Davrin while I oversee the transfer? I want to be sure you and Pilla have eaten."

The Druid seemed to pale at first, then her cheeks flooded with color. "Ah … of course."

"Thank you."

I hoped Jael didn't miss the clear statement that the food would be safe. After a week as a prisoner, resisting torture for a night, followed by a large battle, she needed the food as much as I did. Regardless, I would be eating as much as I could get my hands on the instant that they set down the tray.

"Here ye are."

Jael and I leaned over the shared meal with Tamuril and her falcon opposite us. The vegetables were at least boiled rather than raw, and a third pile of dried meat nearly hidden among the small, dense loaves. The bowl itself was filled with a salty, brown broth.

"Soften th' meat in the soup," the Dwarf instructed as he backed up, preparing to help the others lift Mourn and Graul off the ground. "Dip the bread. Eat the veg how ye like. Fill up."

Tamuril glanced at him, her face still warm, and gathered up the strips of dried flesh to place in the broth. Meanwhile I claimed a loaf of bread and several small tubers, shoving the latter in my mouth to chew while I tore up the bread for dipping. The "soup" turned out to be some mushroom and animal stock.

Jael watched me with stark disbelief when I moaned aloud in pleasure, drawing some chuckles as they carefully lifted Mourn's litter off the ground. I arched an eyebrow at her and took my next, large bite of soggy bread.

"*Start or I eat it all*," I said with my mouth full.

My Sister wrinkled her nose at me. "*You're going to choke.*"

Then she dug in, doing a poor job hiding how good it tasted.

Meanwhile, Tamuril had gathered some vegetables and bread in her lap. She let those sit while she claimed a small, dripping handful of the softened meat from the bowl and started to feed Pilla a piece at a time.

Watching them, I added some of that tough meat to my next bite of bread and chewed for quite a while before I could swallow and grab a sweet, dark purple root to chase it down. Far more rustic fare than Yong-wen but still excellent. *Firm and fresh.*

I watched Krithannia pick up Mourn's tail from dragging on the floor as the Dwarves followed Talov to the door. Graul shifted from his perch to look at us, flicking out his tongue shortly before losing sight of us as the door closed.

"*Little pucker squirt,*" Jael muttered, chomping deep into her sagging loaf with a slurp.

"*I don't disagree,*" I replied with a smirk, "*but antagonize him at your own risk.*"

She tilted her head. "*Oh? Looks too old to fight anymore.*"

"*He can still shadow jump.*"

She paused in her next bite. "*Jump?*"

"*Mm-hm. Like what you and Mourn were doing. The Dragonchild might have learned it from him.*"

"*Well. It's a good cheat.*"

I grinned. "*Ask about his breath attack.*"

" ... *Breath attack? Stinks that bad?*"

I laughed. "*I don't know, truthfully. But he can knock a man against a wall or suck the air from his chest when under threat. Or so I'm told.*"

"Hm." She finished another bite. "*Might've heard of that.*"

"*You have?*"

"*Yeah. Some shadow drakes beyond the Fringe, near my House. Er, former House. Anyway, yeah, I've heard they can blast with a gust to knock your ears out if you do something stupid.*"

Interesting.

I meant to keep eating and encouraging a chat like this but noticed Tamuril's expression and the fluffing of her companion's feathers. Both had stopped eating.

"Something wrong?" I prodded.

"Hm? Oh ..." The Druid plucked at her bread and shrugged weakly.

"Nothing."

Now *she* was lying.

"Please, eat," she murmured, shredding meat to offer her companion. "Soon, we will rest."

I watched Jael weigh the food with the temptation to poke at some obvious weak spots. As she watched me return to filling my belly, however, she did the same with a shrug.

Good.

We cleared the tray of everything edible shortly before Talov and Krithannia returned alone, so the awkward silence didn't stretch too long as our eyes began to wander. The elders let themselves in, quickly shutting the door, and faced us in a room that felt too empty.

"Gerrit's Balls, it's all gone?" the greybeard said as he tromped closer to inspect the tray. "D'ya need more?"

"We're full," I said. "Thanks. Very good."

"Aye … sorry I missed th' show." The old male eyed the three of us. "Now yer lookin' like ya could use a nap."

I yawned at that. "True."

"Excellent. Let's get you three to a smaller place so we can use this hall fer something else."

"Near Gavin? If not Mourn."

Talov made a face as Krithannia rubbed her neck. "Might not rest well with th' sounds right now. Maybe later?"

"Good point."

Tamuril made a small peep as she stroked her bird, green eyes fixed on the floor.

"I am loaning you my quarters," Krithannia said. "The three of you will need to share."

I grimaced, and the Guild Mistress fixed on that.

"Protest?" she asked coolly. "Speak it."

"Not protest," I replied, "only that I wonder if your sister will get proper rest with us."

"Huh?" Jael asked, more confused than surprised.

The Naulor exhaled, offering Tamuril a hand to get up and holding her close by the arm while the Druid stood, meek and obedient though her lips were pursed.

"I hope she *can* get some rest despite circumstances," Krithannia said, squeezing Tami's arm, giving her an encouraging look before refocusing on me and Jael. "Space is precious. We are working to transport all able families to Augran as fast as we can, but the wounded and those Guild needed for operations must stay. Additionally, we and the Templari must stay until Mourn awakens. The next few days, at least, will be a turmoil. So, I must beg you."

The Guild Mistress paused for effect. Jael raised one brow.

"Please do *not* wander around the halls at will. Take your rest while you can. Do not risk yourselves or make the work of others more difficult. There are many yet who may not survive the escape from Manalar."

Fortunately, not even my youngest Sister scoffed at that declaration.

"Agreed," I said for us. "We'll stay in your quarters and —"

Though I tried to hold it back, a forceful yawn came over me.

" — cooperate."

Krithannia smiled, and Talov chuckled, stepping to offer me a hand up. I accepted, feeling the strong grip and powerful warmth through my glove.

"Bit o' envy here," he said with a glint in his eye. "Take an extra nap fer me, will ya, lasschen?"

My grin felt lopsided. "Easily done."

"Heh! I knew I liked you. Let's go."

CHAPTER 17

THE TRUE STRENGTH OF OUR BODY ODOR DIDN'T STRIKE ME UNTIL JAEL, TAMURIL, and I crowded into that smaller, unused room intended for us. Krithannia stood in the doorway, checking the intricate halls behind her, before handing each of us a warm-light glowstone.

"Use anything necessary to get your rest," she said, having no special attachment to the furniture here. "I shall lock and ward the door from the outside. This entry bears nothing visually remarkable over the others. If necessary, you can open it from the inside, but the ward will be broken and I will know about it."

"Just like home," Jael murmured in Davrin.

Krithannia's lips quirked, and she bowed her head. "Forgive me, I must go but will return to check on you." She smiled at her blonde sister. "Perhaps join you for a while."

Jael and I nodded as the other two made some private exchange in Naulor, then the Guild Mistress closed the door.

I turned my attention to our new space. The wide, low bed was strong enough for two Dwarves, though unmade with two blankets folded on top. Next to the head, against the wall, was a roomy chest; at the foot, a tiny table with a wash basin and pitcher with one chair.

Lastly, we had a spot in the far corner which I guessed would help us eliminate waste. My bladder had filled quickly after our large meal, so I was first to investigate and use that area.

Beside the liftable metal grate at the center of a depression in the stone floor, the three buckets: one empty, one with clean rags. and the third with a scoop and that same white powder in Alran's public privy. Across the corner was an apparatus which reminded me of a tiny water pump. The entire corner was nicer than the closet Mourn had in his private library in Yong-wen.

Jael watched me with a smirk while Tamuril turned away.

"*How in the Abyss did they build that?*" she asked as I dabbed and finished up.

"*Deliberately.*" I grinned and switched to the Trade tongue. "This will be nice to have. We shouldn't be forced out of the room too early."

"It is missing a curtain or a screen," the Druid said, setting her glow-stone upon the chest, where Pilla hopped to stand guard over it.

"It's a room for one Dwarf. Or a pair, maybe."

She shrugged, and I couldn't see her expression as she took a seat on the floor opposite the bed. I collected some water from the spigot into the wash basin as Jael used the corner next.

Neither Jael nor I bothered with our glowstone for now; Tamuril's light was plenty. I managed to slip my spiders high up on the wall without Pilla watching and started stripping down.

It would take more time and effort than I had to remove every layer of the last week — and especially the battle — from my body and equipment. I could manage a rough scrub before lying down. As Jael joined me at the washstand, I measured the width of the bed with my eye.

"Must you?"

"Huh?" I blinked, one leg out of my leathers and barefoot on the floor, my cloak, belt, boots, and stockings off to one side.

Tamuril was blushing again, legs crossed and knees up with her arms wrapped around them. "Could we not just get some rest?"

"In armor?" Jael asked with a smirk. "Bad rest. Get filth in bed of sister."

I sighed and sped up my getting naked and starting my cursory wash with cold water. "We've been here before, Druid. I do not care if you watch or look away but I will clean my wounds."

Tamuril sighed, and my Sister looked at me, wide-eyed.

"You have been 'here?' " she asked.

I grinned. "You saw the thorn vines she summoned against the Ma'ab?"

"Yes. Effective."

"She first summoned them against me."

"She what?!"

"I was afraid!" Tamuril cried, Pilla seconding her with an annoyed screech that made us wince. "You invaded our valley."

"I needed water," I countered. "I said so. You didn't believe me."

She opened her mouth.

"*But* I grant that you had good reason to be afraid." I scrubbed harder. "I didn't know who you were or that you were alone until after. Had I known, I would have chosen differently."

"You would have?" Her soft voice sounded doubtful.

"Yes. I might have avoided the place, or at least not charged you. I am glad we didn't kill each other."

Green eyes moistened before she looked down, choosing not to reply. Jael looked between us, her expression approaching astonishment.

"So," I finished for Jael's sake, my tone becoming wry, "I had to strip down in Tamuril's hut to clean the thorns' pokes. She's seen me naked before."

And I've seen a bit of her.

I hoped the glass needle hadn't left too large a scar in her buttock.

"Oo," Jael teased with a smirk before her curiosity returned. "What was 'good reason' to attack?"

While I was pleased that my Sister followed along, she'd already forgotten what I told her.

Jaunda attacked first, remember? I signed pointedly.

White brows lifted above wide, copper eyes. She mouthed, "*Oh.*"

I paused. "Krithannia has seen me like this, too, for the same reason."

"The night-hair injure you, too?!"

Heh, Night-hair.

I should remember that.

"No!" I laughed, holding up my rag. "I needed a wash from boat sailing for days."

"Hm." Jael squinted.

"Thinking back," I continued, "the Guild Mistress did not enjoy my scrubbing naked while we talked, either. Why is that, Tamuril?"

"Why?" she echoed, her face scrunched. "I don't ... understand. You *expect* us to enjoy it?"

I made a face. "No, not enjoy. It's just —"

"Sign of weakness," Jael interrupted, nude and washing, too. "If female will not look, she be surprised. Davrin just laugh."

True enough.

Tamuril's mouth opened along with her eyes, but she didn't look at us longer than a moment at a time. "That's ... unnecessary where I am from. And rude."

"Rude?" Jael asked, shaking her head.

"Insulting," I translated.

"Insult? To look when naked? *Pfeh!*" Jael waved her cloth. "Either beauty to see or scarred from fight. Look away and stupid takes blade in back!"

I couldn't stop grinning. "Ah. I missed you, Jael."

She blinked with surprise but grinned back. "Me, too. You."

In contrast, the Druid held her knees in her hands. I waited a bit before asking, "Will you wash before sleep?"

"Wha — ?" The Druid shifted away, her knees closer to the wall. "Uh, no."

"We won't look," I offered.

Jael's blatant incredulity almost forced an ill-timed laugh.

"No, thank you," Tamuril repeated.

No, 'thank you.' Hm.

"Will you sleep on the bed? There's room for three if we're on our sides."

I received quite the territorial look from Jael, which I was glad the Naulor didn't see.

"No," said the Druid, voice firm this time.

I waited again.

Just 'no,' apparently.

"You want the floor?"

"I will be fine, Sirana. Just ... let me be."

I sighed. "How about a blanket?"

The pale Elf hesitated and glanced over her shoulder at me. Reaching to grip one of the heavy, folded covers, I tossed it gently toward her. It landed near enough for her to drag it closer, the thump and waft of air causing Pilla to beat her wings a few times.

After a pause, the Druid murmured, "Thank you."

Jael gave me a look, subtly rolling her eyes, but her tiredness visibly returned with mine as we finished our task with rags wrung and drying, dirty water sitting for now, and our smelly gear barely sorted beyond separate piles.

The one piece I could not leave beyond my reach was the relic, which I stuffed out of sight between the mattress and the bed frame.

Finally, my Sister and I crawled onto the firm, stuffed mattress and shared the one remaining blanket. I positioned myself close to the bed's edge so that I'd feel the jostle if someone tried to get at the dagger. Jael preferred her back to the wall anyway and snuggled her belly and breasts against me, draping one arm across my hip and tucking the other beneath her head.

I lay facing Tamuril against the opposite wall, my eyes closed but aware when she finally wrapped herself fully clothed in her blanket and lied down.

The room filled with quiet breathing, the soft light remaining to cast shadows as we each slipped into Reverie.

WIND WHISTLED MOURNFULLY IN MY EARS. GRAINS OF SAND FLUNG THROUGH rain-starved air. I closed my eyes tightly lest they lash my eyes in their rush.

Champion. Too long it has been.

The words seemed to form from the hush of the moving sands, a whisper without a voice.

Blind, I turned around, listening with more than my ears. I barely felt the pressure of my feet inside their boots, and a lightweight cloak flapped around me.

Warrior ... Welcome.

Once the wind was at my back, I reached to pull up my hood so I could open my eyes. The moonlight was a silvery blue. So were the dunes. This was not the Red Desert at night.

"Elsewhere," I whispered, my words lifted by the wind and joined with the shush all around me.

A multitude answered this time.

*Yesss, wielder ... *

"Am I beyond the demon's gate?"

You stand among us once again.

That I was, but I hadn't tried to. My eyes lifted to the clear sky, searching for a hint of the vortex which led to the gatekeeper. How had I passed by the black throne covered in crystal?

"Did you summon me?"

*We have been calling ... *

Only now can you hear the call.

Only now? Why?

Then a deep chill pricked me.

My first Reverie without Mourn to watch over me? My first trance with the relic without my bodyguard to protect others from Soul Drinker ... I'd fallen asleep with Jael and Tamuril close, unaware, with no one else around. The guilt stung like an echo of the laughter from the relic's cruel gatekeeper, trying to worm its way in.

~No. Not here. That voice stays silent.~

I closed my eyes again, breathing like Willven had taught me while awake. The laughter unraveled, fading behind a shield of crystal.

The wind returned.

*Wielder. Come ... *

Holding my hood to shield my eyes, I turned into the wind to follow the voices of the victims and past wielders.

One of them was Innathi.

*Yesss ... *

Come ... find your lost queen.

*We have been calling ... *

Why? And why now? What could I have done to delay this? Lock myself alone in a closet and stay awake until either the Dragonchild or the psionic Captain woke up to shield others from my sleep?

~Doesn't matter. I'm here.~

I would find her.

The blue dunes became blurry and level when I chose a direction and started walking. My feet disappeared into the sand up to my ankles, though I felt no drag. The landscape didn't seem to be changing.

I moved from a walk to a jog, and when this didn't cover any discernible distance, I sped up. Breathing deeper. Letting my hood fall, pumping full my arms and legs.

Abruptly, I hit a crest.

"Whoa!"

I began skidding down the tallest dune of them all. My foot hit a buried stone, and I tucked and rolled, gaining speed and soon unable to stop. My feet slammed down together, my body fell backward ...

And a new dune loomed in front of me, ready to be climbed.

On the other side.

I regained my feet and scrambled upward, cycling my breath until it sounded continuous in my ears. I focused on the one I'd seen in both places, in dreams and trances. Cris-ri-phon, Innathi, and the golden-eyed bua all knew this place.

Koorul.

I descended the massive dune and entered a canyon cutting deep into the Desert. Its sheer walls and high cliffs boasted many shades of blue, the trails lined with grey mist. It lacked all the banded colors of the sunset, and there was no firebird leading the way to a golden-eyed bua's prison.

Instead, a waterfall would be hidden within its labyrinth. One created from ancient memory and pure will.

She would be waiting there.

I searched, avoiding the swiftest and thickest flows of mist lest I become lost. I relied on keen hearing instead, following the muted trail of falling water until a vanishing stream appeared. Tracing it back, I reached the source: the pool at the base of the falls, in which Innathi had first coupled with her Human sorcerer.

There, I saw her.

Barefoot, wearing a stark white gown and shining bracelets, bands, and rings. The long-dead Desert Queen smiled, her bright scarlet eyes the only warm color apart from my uniform. Her ancient dialect caressed my ears.

★"Khalithan.★ You live. Welcome back."

I smirked. "Were you expecting me this time, Your Majesty?"

"Truth? Yes, *khali*, I was."

After a pause, I asked, "Do you remember my name?"

She laughed with familiar, regal poise, her gaze admiring my uniform from top to bottom. "You have grown stronger since our first meeting, Sirana."

Hm.

"How so?"

Her smile lowered. "You appear ... clearer to me. More than a pair of wilder eyes wearing red. I see your face and ... an unfamiliar aura."

Again, her eyes trailed over me, and I could believe this might be true. "You said that before, I recall. What are they?"

"Hm?" The Queen lifted her stare and blinked at me.

"Wilder eyes."

"Wha — ?" She laughed with a touch of disbelief. "The offspring of the Druid exiles? Do you not know them?"

Hoo bua.

"No, your Majesty. That knowledge is ... gone."

Innathi frowned. "As must be all those with the mixed skin?"

"The ... what?"

She scoffed with a shake of her head stepping closer to the pool to glance upon its surface. "*Hmph.* I never did know what to do with those refugees. Cris-ri-phon brought them with him into my Queen-dom, though I did not know it for many decades."

"Brought who? The Druid exiles?"

"Yes." The Desert Queen turned to face me. "They were from the Naulor lands and had forsaken their Queen Yivon. Some protest or punish-ment I never confirmed, but they were skilled with all plants and animals, quite useful to my subjects living far out from V'Gedra.

"Over time, they interbred with my Davrin. I never saw a Wilder enter the capital until long after I'd married my General and borne our first children." She scoffed. "Only when he could not deny their appearance did he seem to remember them."

"From where?"

"From Nalari to the East, while on his quest for my hand."

Nalari. I'd heard that recently. Where?

"The Naulor Druids had governed the magical pool there for some time, apparently," Innathi continued, "but then were forced out by the Dwarves and Humans. Some of their children followed Cris into the Desert when he returned." She smirked. "They seemed not to need each other after that."

I jerked with surprise. "Magic pool? You mean Manalar?"

Her face pinched in confusion. "I do not know that name."

Nalari. Nalamar. Manari. Manalar …

The names flowed through my memory, cooed by the male Elf with auburn hair we'd confronted at the sacred pool during the battle. The "merchant" who'd bargained to close the rift to the Greylands.

Toushek. The deal broker.

"Were the 'Wilder' Elves brown-skinned?" I asked.

Innathi lifted an elegant eyebrow. "Oh, yes. They were easy to see among my own. Do none exist now under your queen?"

I heard the derision in the last word. "No, Majesty. We're all Davrin now."

She looked me over. "Not without the barest touch of Naulor remaining, it seems."

I swallowed.

"I accepted them as Desert Elves, like us," she said firmly. "Yivon certainly wouldn't have them. Born and raised among my dunes, keen on learning all they could of my lands and ostensibly loyal to the ruler of their new home. They joined my army, wandered my borders, tended the land. They even mimicked the animals if they so wished."

"Mimicked animals?"

She crossed her arms, disapproving. "Is this talent lost as well?"

The only mimic who came to mind was Auranka.

"Yes, Majesty."

Innathi exhaled with frustration. "Where are my people? Squatting in a hole somewhere?"

I laughed but might have sounded caustic, then considered the meeting of those ancient figures Cris-ri-phon had recognized at the pool of Manalar. Toushek certainly had some control over him even now, which was concerning for Innathi's time. This Wilder was *not* easy to see among Davrin if he didn't wish to be.

Then, there were the others who'd stepped through the rift to protect the pool. One had shaken the Deathless more than the rest.

"Do you know the name Houda?" I asked.

The spirit of the Desert Queendom looked shocked at the sudden turn in our conversation. Then shock shifted to discomfort. "Where did you hear it?"

"From a Deathwalker's summons."

Innathi relaxed, nodding. "Yes, she was a Deathwalker. One of the first to be welcome in my Mother's reign. But she did not live among us long. A few decades."

"Welcome ... because of Cris-ri-phon?" I asked. "I thought she was his tutor."

Innathi frowned, "Why would he tell you that?"

"He was shaken to know she walks the Greylands."

"Ah. So you know about that."

I sensed when she mentally backtracked.

"And Houda answered a … another Deathwalker's summons, you said?"

I nodded.

"Death mages exist in my sister's queendom," Innathi continued with a touch of bitterness, "but the Wilder do not?"

I grimaced. "Ah, no, your Majesty. I met the Deathwalker on my current mission. Far away from my queendom. I was the first Davrin he had ever seen."

"Hmph. How far we've fallen. *Everyone* knew who we were when I was Queen."

She looked behind her, drawing my notice to the dim cave leading into the nearest cliff. Others waited there, blurred, and grey. I could barely see them.

"Although, I do not recognize *them*," she said, jerking her chin toward the vague figures. "Yet they seem to recognize the magic of the Davrin, albeit wrapped in talk of demons and parasitic hunger."

She paused as if recalling something, eyes sliding to one side.

"Does that sound possible?" I prompted.

Innathi shrugged it off, tossing her head. "As the envious have always accused us, *always* something they do themselves."

"Hm." I glanced toward the cave. "Who are they?"

I'd prompted another laugh from her. "Who are they? The last two you sent here, *khalithan*. They seem to be of the same blood. Once big men in life."

My mouth opened with surprise. "The Ma'ab?"

"If you say," came the blithe response. "I never heard a whisper of their supposed 'empire,' so they must be an infant queendom in the ice lands."

I bit my cheek. "You've been talking with them?"

The Desert Queen's expression shifted then. "Only long enough to teach them who rules here."

"May I see them?"

"Not a good idea, my warrior." She bowed as if to tease me. "The newest among us cling hardest to what they've lost, and there is reason to cling to you. Speaking of parasites, as it were."

I shook my head. "I do not quite understand, your Majesty."

Innathi gave me a look that reminded me of my older sister when she'd found my hiding place. "The same as your mind and will, Sirana, your tether to your body has strengthened as well. I see you lied to me about losing your child. Why is that?"

I shrugged that off like she did, though the lump of ice in my gut was significantly heavier. "Too many have tried to manipulate me through my belly on my mission, Highness. A defensive lie when not knowing your intent."

"You think I would threaten you through your baby? Me, a mother of twelve children?"

"How would I have known? After confining the gatekeeper, I was exhausted and did not recognize all that was real. I apologize, your Majesty." I covered my belly. "Yes, I still carry. The demon did not starve it out, though it tried."

She seemed mollified, straightening her shoulders. "Well, that is acceptable, *khalithan*. But for that reason, you should not approach the new souls here. They would strive like mad animals for a chance to be pulled out through that tether and be reborn."

The lump of ice became a boulder.

"Oh."

Her chin lifted. "Not to worry. I would never allow a lesser soul to attempt such vile usurpation."

I wished that were more reassuring. The thought of one ghost holding a line with the rest within the same condemned place suggested motives less trustworthy than a Deathwalker protecting me from the same swarm. I just wanted to leave.

And she said my "tether" was strong.

I turned and looked up into the sky, believing I could make out the gossamer threads she must have seen so clearly.

I want to wake.

"Sirana," she said, sensing my doubt. "Worry not. You *are* the wielder. I acknowledge this. Visit me again, and I shall tell you about our lost queendom. Evade recapture by my former Husband, and you will know *all* we used to be by the time you return to our people."

Evade Cris-ri-phon.

The ancient Queen made this sound like a simple matter, as if others hadn't a vested interest in where the Deathless wandered or what he did. Even Houda had nearly convinced him to stop seeking Innathi and the relic. *Almost.*

The ancient Deathwalker had tried to give him some other hope.

"Do not follow that path, Cris. After so long, let her go. Let all the River children go. Your children need you more. They are here. They remain … They need a guide. They have been waiting for one out there, in your home."

The Zauyrian had chosen to believe her. He'd turned to leave the Temple of the Sun, to begin a new search. One for his daughter.

Someone had stopped him. I remembered his scathing remark to the Grey Maiden's emissaries.

"Your Cris is gone. Your time is dead. For all our sakes, do not reveal what does not belong to you again."

"Toushek," I said.

"Hm?" Innathi coaxed. "What did you say?"

"Do you know that name, your Majesty?"

"Toushek?" She frowned, touching a crooked finger to her lips as she reflected.

Even before she shook her head, I could tell she didn't recognize it. *Not good.*

How else might she know this Elf? Because she *must* have. I couldn't imagine a male that poised and well-spoken, manipulative and accustomed to coaxing things his way, yet *not* visiting the Queen of V'Gedra at some point.

"Who is this?" she replied.

"Someone I need to evade along with your old Cris," I murmured, frowning as I glanced off to the side. "But what if Houda suggested, perhaps …"

"Perhaps?"

"Your children may not have all died? Which would you rather find, given the chance: your daughter or your sister?"

Brilliant scarlet eyes widened, and Innathi took a step back from me, bejeweled hands lifting in a suggestion of defense. If she'd been living, I might have heard her heart racing.

"They were all murdered," she said.

"But they are not here."

"So? They did not die by the relic. This only means my assassins knew not to pick it up."

"Houda told us —"

"Houda was Human! She was *dead* for centuries by that point!"

"Bearing witness to your husband's actions over many lives," I counted, "by word of her Grey Maiden. Say she brings us truth beyond her death. Who would you want to search for?"

Innathi's eyes narrowed with resentment, slowly shaking her head. "You *know* where my sister is. You do *not* know where a daughter of mine may be." She looked me over before staring into my eyes. "You also do not know how long you may be the wielder of this blade, warrior. A child unborn can give you strength or take much of it from you. All this considered, we shall find my sister. Do not be distracted by this tease from the Grey, *khalithan*. It is not your quest to take. Understood?"

I took that in to think on later. "Understood, your Majesty."

The Desert Queen paused, smiling coyly. "You are hungry."

She motioned to the glimmering lines leading from me into the sky. They seemed much brighter to my eyes.

"Time to feed the child, or you may never see her face."

"As you command." I bowed, backing up a few steps. "I shall visit you again."

"Do not wait so long next time."

"Apologies, your Majesty." I grinned. "I shall try to avoid landing between two Human armies. It's not a pleasant smell."

Reluctantly, she chuckled.

~*Now.*~

I could wake up.

CHAPTER 18

I OPENED MY EYES, DRAWING A SLOW, SILENT BREATH. BLUE LIGHT AND WARMTH rose from my chest, though I resisted the urge to cover Shyntre's pendant with my palm.

I lay on my side with Jael behind me. My hand had slipped beneath the mattress until my fingertips touched Soul Drinker. Not unexpected, and I was glad such communion still required touching the blade.

At least this Queen's will can't leap through vast distance to compel me.

Cautiously, I withdrew my hand, leaving the silent weapon behind. A falcon's curious chirp marked my movement, and I looked to Pilla nesting next to Tami's calm, goldish glowstone as the other source of light in the room.

At least she didn't screech.

Next, I confirmed Innathi was right again. I was hungry, but Jael and Tamuril still slept.

Damn. What should I do next?

Pilla's head twitched between me and the door enough to draw my attention. Then, finally, I sniffed the food on its tray upon the floor. Someone had poked their head in while we slept, leaving more of what we'd been fed before, but neither Pilla nor my spiders had been bothered.

Interesting.

255

I got up to eat. I wouldn't bother to dress until after I'd quelled the feeling like a gnawing rodent in my gut. In the near silence as I consumed my share, my ears picked up vague, distant screams and wailing elsewhere in the Dwarven redoubt.

This didn't harm my appetite but reminded me that Gavin might be "working." Talov had said the first day would be most intense, and Krithannia had suggested others might die over the next few.

What would we do until then? Would we be informed when Isboern was conscious again, or was he already?

Mourn certainly isn't.

Then what? What would the Manalari soldiers plan next at this underground fortification?

I put my ear to the door and heard the murmuring of voices, feeling the curiosity rise along with the boredom. Keeping my word to stay out of their way — both to Krithannia and to Innathi — might be harder than I thought when I was tired.

Don't be stupid. You've no escort, no bodyguard ...

I wanted to find Gavin. He was the next best thing, and I could talk with him about Houda and Innathi, maybe even Cris-ri-phon's daughter.

I sighed, craning my neck at Jael. I couldn't leave her behind to wake up alone, not after everything it took to save her. But how long would she be in Reverie? She hadn't so much as shifted her weight on the bed since I got up.

My gaze drifted to the Druid's corner.

And stopped.

Her leaf green eyes were open, bearing a stark fear like when I'd stood above her, her body fighting spider venom and struggling to breathe. I swallowed, the surge palpable even before Pilla squawked and opened her wings as if to beat me with them.

I truly doubted I'd live to see beyond that reaction from the falcon, but I wished for a moment I didn't feel so stuck with the Naulor. I was aware of my nudity and how consistently it conveyed greater threat to her while I'd always taken it as less, or sometimes better than, like beauty, strength, or flirtation.

I touched my finger to my lips in a shush similar to what Humans had used around us, including a smile and a wave of my hand in the same flavor. She was confused, but at least her fear lessened. I pointed toward my pile of clothing and gear before moving.

Her eyes followed but perhaps not her thoughts.

Will have to do.

I shuffled quietly over to my days-worn clothing and pulled on my shirt and bottoms, lacing up the sides and glancing Tamuril's way. This gesture granted her some ease as she sat up and rubbed her face. The next helpful action was bringing the tray of food to her.

I took care not to awaken Jael since she hadn't jolted upright with that one blurt from the bird.

"Hungry?" I whispered in Trade, putting it on the floor within her reach and sitting back, crossing my legs.

Tamuril licked her lips before speaking. "Th-thank you."

I watched her soak some of the shredded meat for Pilla again, feeding her first before selecting vegetables and bread for herself.

"Do you eat meat?" I asked curiously, keeping my voice low.

Her eyes flicked up briefly. "Sometimes. I do not need much."

That might explain why she was so slender.

"Can you …" I hesitated, which she noticed. "Um, change shape? Like Mourn? Or mimic an animal?"

The blonde Elf frowned. "Why would you think I could?"

"Is that a 'no?' "

She shook her head. "I cannot. Some *Odad* can."

Odad. I had to scratch back to my conversation with Krithannia on the river boat for that meaning. *Father druids …* While she placed herself beneath them as a *Guded.* Interesting that Tamuril spoke it aloud like that.

"If you could change shape, which animal might you mimic?"

Her frown deepened. "Why do you ask?"

I shrugged at her tone, deciding to drop it at her clear suspicion and resistance. I considered the old spirit's library as the source of Naulor Druids guarding the sacred pool at one time but decided against it. I didn't understand the consequences of putting that responsibility on the

Manalari if Tamuril were to tell her Queen someday.

Making 'suggestions' like that to the Druid might be how I got Jael captured …

"Do my eyes seem unusual to you?" I asked instead.

This only confused her. She finished chewing her soft root. "Um, well … you are the … only Davrin I have seen with blue eyes. But I have not seen many of you."

"Do most Naulor have blue or green eyes?"

Slowly, Tamuril shook her head. "No. We have dark eyes, brown, or grey like Krithannia. Or some mix of these."

So, more like Humans and Dwarves than we were.

"But no red or copper?"

She drew in a deep breath. "No. The stories said that was your color."

The unspoken suggestion that this was undesirable or indicative of some danger sounded loud to me.

"I was … surprised to see yours," she admitted.

And quite possibly why she would even settle in to talk with me, as it had been with many Surfacers who'd met my true face. They didn't seem to hold Jael's eyes for as long, nor did she do the same with them.

"Any ideas," I prodded, "why some of us have this color?"

The Druid shrugged. "Magic?"

I grinned. She wasn't wrong, there. Some of the Consorts had been bred to have unusual eye colors. But where would Wilsira have pulled those colors from, anyway? Could she simply summon them? Change us so easily with a little extra demon blood? I didn't see why not, but also knew I wasn't a product of the Consorts.

Mother had left Court by then and stopped chasing them.

Was I proof of our distant relations with Naulor Druids who'd come to the Red Desert? Had my line not always been one of Nobility, but living far out from V'Gedra? Walking the borders, hearing about those at Court through travelers looking for water.

Something about this suited us at House Thalluen.

"Back home," I began, "did you ever hear a story about … ?"

Then stopped until Tamuril had given me her attention.

"About what?"

"A band of Druids exiled from their queen."

She leaned away from me; without thinking, I leaned forward.

"Yivon, is it? Queen Yivon?"

The Druid flinched like I'd struck her. "Oh, *please*, do not say the Wife's name!"

"Why not?"

"Just do not!"

Jael shifted on the bed, grunting, and Pilla clucked calmly on swallows of air as if to balance her mistress's agitation for once.

I'd paused but when my Sister didn't open her eyes. "Alright, I won't say it again."

"Where did you hear it?" she hissed. "You knew nothing at all when we first met!"

I smiled. "I have been listening to many mouths for months."

Horror entered her eyes. "Did Krithannia tell you?"

"No. She is blameless. I have other sources."

Her heart started pounding. "The Deathless One. The sorcerer Willven helped to stop. *He* told you."

"He is one source, yes, but I don't know how much of what he says is true. That's why I ask you."

Tamuril watched me warily until I prompted her.

"Druid exiles. Any knowledge from a time when the Davrin lived in the Red Desert?"

Her face paled further until she shook her head in the negative. "I have not heard this story." Her cheeks flushed as soon as she said it, and her eyes flickered with hesitance.

Lying.

Or truth by omission. She'd never heard the full tale nor had much knowledge about it, an answer for which I couldn't blame her, though the idea may not seem impossible to her. Regardless, Tamuril feared consequences speaking freely about her people, a shared, self-protective mindset with Krithannia, Mourn, and myself.

We're a cautious bunch of pointy-ears.

Suddenly, my spiders chimed at me, a shrill alarm which raced up my back. I gasped and spun around to face Jael on the bed. Her eyes were closed, body in repose, but her arm was outstretched, her hand reaching over the edge of the mattress.

Fingers digging between it and the bedframe.

"No, Jael, wake up!" I shouted, lapsing into my native tongue as I sprang at her.

Her eyes flew open, tense readiness overtaking her body as her mouth curled into a teeth-baring snarl. I clamped both my hands on her wrist to wrench it away from a fate worse than death.

I didn't know if I made it, if I was fast enough, because she started screaming nonsense. Her free hand grabbed me, fingers digging in without mercy as I rose up to claim the upper position.

We fell into a fierce struggle on the bed, and my guardians twitched above us, preparing to join me.

~Don't jump!~ I commanded. *~Not yet!~*

"Lemmeooouuut!" Jael shrieked, blocking the third of our mutual attempts to pin and hold the other.

Echoing off her cry, a high pitch filled my ears which had nothing to do with Pilla's flustered flapping behind us.

*Wieeelderrr ... *

~Be still.~

A hollow silence followed my command as my Sister's skin grew *scalding,* as if she were suddenly ill, and she thrashed against me as if in seizure. I shivered, squeezing my grip harder, trying to hold her down so she didn't hurt either of us; so she couldn't dive for the dagger. My eyes blurred with tears as her resistance started to weaken and she stared blankly up at the ceiling. I was losing her.

If only I'd been faster.

Or never turned my back on that foul thing in the first place.

"Sirana?" Tamuril's distress filled the brief lull. "Should I get help?"

I bit my lip, wondering what the Guild Mistress could do now that I'd broken my promised guardianship of the black blade. "I-I-uh —"

Jael's copper gaze blinked.

Then refocused on me.

"O-oh, Goddess, Sirana," she whispered, eyes tearing up.

I stared at her, struck dumb, and afraid to hope.

More likely to be fooled.

Her body was burning, thighs squeezing one of mine hard enough to bruise. Then suddenly, she relaxed.

"Sirana. You're here."

The swell of relief threatened to weaken my hold.

"Yes," I whispered. *"I'm here."*

Her hips tilted tentatively, undulating in a familiar way, like she tested the connection with her own body.

She hadn't taken her eyes off me. *"Am I ... awake?"*

"I think so," I managed, resisting the urge to drop down and hug her. *"What did you see just now?"*

Her eyes blinked rapidly. *"Storm ... made of sand. No ceiling. No trees ..."*

Shit.

"What is your name?"

She squinted at me, baffled and annoyed. The expression was perfect.

"Just tell me," I said. *"Who are you?"*

"Jael. Aurenthin. Your fucking Sister."

I started to smile for real. She moved against me, grinding her mons in a way I knew she liked. I answered with a push, dragging my leather-clad thigh teasingly along her naked mons.

"Ohhh, yes," she cooed, looking down at her fur patch, opening her legs wider. *"Sirana ... ?"*

Yes.

I lunged to kiss her lips, running my tongue along them as she opened her mouth wider, then we deepened the kiss, grips softening to hold and caress. She was fevered but the scent was *hers*, a musky, mouth-watering arousal wafting up from the junction of her legs. Her slit grew wetter as I pressed my thigh against her. Beneath my squeezing fingers, her nipple stood up firm. She fumbled to loosen the leather thongs at my hips, and Tamuril spoke behind us, soft and hesitant.

"Wh-what are you doing? Do you still need someone?"

Jael had bared my ass by that point, nudging my pants down until cool air hit my crotch.

"Uh …" I shuddered as my Sister's familiar hands gripped both my buttocks. "N-no, I think we are —"

She strained her reach until two fingers glided along my bare sex from behind, spreading my juices around.

"Ah! … good."

"You're … good? Is anything wrong, Sirana?"

"No," I panted. "Safe."

"Safe? C-can you stop now?"

Fuck, no.

Not with the increasing desperation with which Jael ground against me, building toward her climax. At the same time, her fingers sank the smallest way into my cunt, and my asshole twitched like it anticipated Gaelan or Jaunda's Feldeu at any moment.

"Ah, fuck," I murmured.

"Can you stop, please?"

"Shut it, bird Elf," Jael growled. "Been waiting long enough!"

That was true.

"Tamuril," I managed, my hips finding a rhythm. "I've missed her."

"And y-you'll just … just *do* this in front of me? Can't you control your impulses?"

Not an impulse, but this *was* urgent. Even if it were, why should I refrain?

My younger Sister agreed, pulling me away from the Druid into another full kiss. The angle between us changed so that her fingers slid up to my netherhole which practically kissed her in greeting.

~Oh, Goddess, yes, Jael!~

Ha! You always liked that tease, huh?

Her voice flowed, eager and perfect in my head. My worst fear vanished in the clarity of our mindlink.

~It *is* you.~

Of course!

~*Ah, yeah! In a little more!*~

My cunt smeared her bare thigh as I writhed harder against her, my back-hole giving way to her familiar and welcome invasion. We could have been home for how *real* all of this felt—

Until someone slammed the door on her way out, taking the falcon and glowstone with her.

I jumped. ~*Ah, fuck!*~

Now my heart pounded from lust *and* fright.

Pfeh! Forget that cringing willow.

~*Yeah, but the ward's broken.*~

Jael's eyes glimmered wickedly in the blue light of my pendant. *At least we're staying where the Guild Mistress said.*

~*True.*~

And at least the Druid had closed the door.

She and I stayed entwined on the bed, rocking against each other, stroking and squeezing each other's flesh, and kissing hungrily.

~*Arrrrgh, goddess!*~

When I finally came against Jael's hard thigh, her fingers teased my asshole continually, from the start of that delicious climb and all the way through, coasting down …

She felt it, too.

*Wow … *

~*Yeah … *~

Uhm. So … ?

~*Hm?*~

How can I be in afterglow but really *need to come?*

I chuckled, shifting my hips so her fingers popped out of my bottom before drawing my body downward.

I croaked out loud, *"Let me finish you."*

She rumbled coyly. *"How ominous."*

"Then we've been too long out of the Cloister."

I kneeled on the floor, pulling her legs and hips to me near the edge of the bed. Soul Drinker was out of sight beneath the mattress and farther to my right. If she tried to go for it again, I had enough space to respond.

And if not …

I breathed her in, pushing her legs apart, exhaling hot breath on glazed netherlips. Her cunt was so swollen and aroused, waves of heat rising up, that I fervently wished I had a Feldeu to attach and fuck her senseless.

"*Teasing,*" she whispered, an accusation and plea.

"*Heh.*"

Tongue flat, I took my first, luxurious taste of her in far too long. She squeaked, toes curling. I closed my mouth on her, drawing on the stretchy skin, and making her writhe. My lips chased hers to land clusters of kisses across those fragrant folds.

"*Awyiss,*" she grunted, gripping my hair to ground herself rather than mash my face in like other Sisters. ★"Ah! Hahh, aieeyah★ …"

The mindlink remained between us, but the boundary of our bodies was not as blurred. I recognized the clearest signals of pleasure I'd ever known from her and used them to give her *more*. They enhanced what I knew about her, suppressing doubt to heighten every excited gasp and foot twitch, until she was caught in her own private rapids of sensations tumbling over each other.

Until she clamped her legs on my head like a Tragar trap.

"*Yesss! There!*" Jael announced her orgasm with abandon, her voice devolving into a series of sharp, heaving cries while her flushed, pulsing sex seeped moisture between our skin.

I forgot to breathe but held on, flicking and pressing my tongue, relishing every sound while my cunt ached for its reward. My thoughts rushed to imagine large, rough hands — equally hot as Jael's skin — gripping my hips.

~*Oh, yeah, do it …* ~

The memory was sharp enough to feel it, Mourn pulling me up to a proper height, aiming his unique cock against my slit, and stretching my netherlips wide. Ready to rut me deep.

~*Knot and all.*~

Jael smothered me in another thrashing rush of pleasure as she curled up and crossed her ankles.

"*Mmph!*"

"Whoaaa, oh fuck, yeahhh!"

I came with her that time.

We must have blacked out briefly, because I came to myself with my chin on Jael's bush, gasping for air while someone knocked loudly on the door.

"Sirana, I'm coming in!"

~Oh, Hells.~

Disoriented, I lost my balance and landed on my naked ass, my pants caught around my knees, and my shirt scented with Jael's juices. My Sister was flat on her back, arms stretched out and legs flopped open, her chest rising and falling quickly.

That was how Gavin and the Guild Mistress found us.

"Oh," said the latter, pulling herself up short. "Um. Are you alright?"

"Fine!" I gasped while Jael moaned in slight annoyance. "Shit. Sorry, did Tami send you?"

"She did." The elder Naulor motioned Gavin inside and closed the door , her composure under remarkable control despite her concerns. "She mentioned Jael touching the relic in her sleep."

"Almost, but, uh —"

Gavin's inhuman gaze was tightly focused on us; not our nudity but our auras. He still wore the newer, grey robes given to him by Ada and the others, though his hands were stained with blood which had been quickly scrubbed dry before he arrived. Those random thorns of black flint jutted through in places but looked to have shrunk. His icy pupils slid to the precise point where Soul Drinker was hidden, held a moment, then turned to me.

"That seems to have been avoided this time," he said.

I expelled the breath I was holding, and Jael sat up then, propped on her arms and glowering. "What do you talk about?"

"If a connection was made," Gavin said to Krithannia rather than answering Jael, "it didn't hold. Sirana must have severed it. I see nothing of concern."

"Ah. Good news." Krithannia motioned to me. "May I see it?"

I sighed, deciding to push my pants off the rest of the way rather than pull them up lest they stick to my crotch. I crawled over, took a breath, and reached under the mattress. The dagger was oddly cold but quiet.

Withdrawing it, I held up both hands for the Guild Mistress to see. Jael reacted as though she saw a pincerworm and backed up farther on the bed. A good sign of her instincts toward the relic.

Krithannia indicated her satisfaction. "Alright. We're ... sorry to have interrupted."

"We finished," Jael said with a self-satisfied grin.

I smirked. "Only need to get clean."

"Hm." Krithannia looked at our equipment then. "I may be able to arrange a thorough washing, but you must be ready to use the space upon your turn."

Our turn?

"Until then," the Guild Mistress said with chagrin, "Tamuril has volunteered to assist some of the Manalari women until Willven wakes up."

Translated, the Druid wouldn't return here.

"Do you wish to stay in this room, or shall I find a secure area where you might assist us?"

"How long we sleep?" Jael asked first, perplexed.

"A long time," Krithannia said warmly. "Easily ten hours."

More than Humans usually slept on a good night.

"Could we stay near Gavin to assist?" I asked. "He's the only one besides you awake *and* aware of the relic's voice and threat."

"I would agree," she said, turning her head to the Deathwalker. "Are you willing?"

"If they can be quiet at least part of the time," Gavin said. "I still need to meditate."

"Pfft," Jael scoffed. "Sivaraus Sisters always quiet."

The death mage watched her with a dry tilt of his head. "Feel free to prove it."

"Give us a few to scrub down and gear up," I said. "We'll be right out."

"Very good," said Krithannia. "We'll wait for you in the hall."

266

Chapter 19

Outside our borrowed quarters, the scents and their accompanying sounds of discomfort grew potent and all around unpleasant. My nose could hardly expel the scent of one body fluid drifting out from beneath the door of one room before we passed another. It all entwined with dirt, metal, leather, and days-old ripening.

Krithannia noticed our expressions when Jael and I looked at each other. "The aftermath will improve."

"It has since last night," Gavin remarked, his stride long and slow, the thurible chain jingling at his belt. "The Dwarves haven't stopped in their goal to catch up on the influx from Manalar."

"True. This quadrant of the redoubt contains those gravest wounded and the upper officers. The rest is filled with Guild and Manalari soldiers in better shape but recouping from the last days."

"And all the women, kids, and elders?" I asked.

"Outside," Gavin answered flatly.

"What?"

"We're forming caravans to escort them to Bor," the Guild Mistress clarified with a smirk at the Deathwalker. "There aren't enough rooms here, and a lasting camp in the hills will inevitably draw hostile attention."

"From that Witch Hunter fort off the Big Kerr?"

"Them, also Ma'ab assassins and spies. We weren't planning to use that jump gate until we confirmed Jael was held captive, so our hope is no one down south knows the area it leads to." She shrugged as we turned a corner. "Still, the Kerr Rivers help to speed all news regardless of intent."

As if in response, a familiar, young Yungian poked his head around the next corner.

"Sho'shien. Yunze." Deshi was relieved to find them, waving his hand. Then he blinked to see me and Jael just behind, smiling. "Ah, Janshi and Jiji. You are wake!"

"What," Jael replied, her voice flat.

"Jiji means 'sister' in Yungian," Krithannia said, answering Deshi's bow.

"That me?" Jael made a face when we all nodded. "The other?"

"Janshi means 'sky warrior,'" I answered with a teasing grin.

"Pfft. *You* get strong one?"

"I earned it."

"How?"

"I sparred with twenty buas in one evening." I held up all my fingers, flashing them twice.

"Nineteen, Janshi," Deshi corrected.

"*Wen-yung* does not count?" I countered.

The young man straightened, eyebrows lifting, and bowed. "Ah! Correct. Twenty!"

"Excellent."

Jael's eyes were close to bugging out as she understood the number but scoffed. "Human bua must be weak."

"Novice fighters," I grinned, tilting my head toward Deshi. "Except him. He was faking."

"Faking?"

Deshi's face had flushed remarkably deep. He looked to Gavin and Krithannia for guidance rather than attempt to explain.

"What is it, Deshi?" the elder Naulor prompted.

"Something is wrong with my brothers," he said earnestly, looking to Gavin. "I plead you will look at them, Maiden's traveler."

Krithannia and Gavin seemed confused, the former saying, "They were not bad off. Did the Dwarves not tend to their wounds properly?"

"They did well!" the youth exclaimed, horrified at the thought of offending the Dwarven clan. "We thought all was well, yes. But something becomes bad. New bleeding, though they did not move."

The Deathwalker grunted. "Is there new pain?"

"Yes, Sho'shien. Salve does not help, tonic barely. I worry."

"Why?"

The Yungian hesitated, and Krithannia prodded him gently. "Tell us why you seek a death mage instead of a Dwarven healer, Guildsman."

Deshi explained with caution. "A disturbed feeling in the aura. Like bad magic from Ma'ab ... or the rift in the Temple. I am not certain."

That seemed enough for Gavin. "I left my chirurgeon kit in my work room. Let me retrieve that and a few things. I will meet you there. Make sure we have hot water."

"*Shi'sheh, shi'sheh.*"

I looked at Gavin once Deshi had vanished around the corner. "Should we go with you and stay in your quarters, or ... ?"

"I could use spare hands if you are not queasy at the sight of blood."

Jael snorted before I could.

"While I cannot stay this moment," Krithannia said apologetically, "if you both would stay with Gavin and assist him, I would be grateful."

"Definitely," I said as Jael shrugged with indifference.

"I will circle back soon to check on you." The Naulor bowed her head to the Deathwalker. "We welcome your insights in this unexpected matter, Herald."

"I shall have some," he replied. "I am curious to see what's changed."

JAEL AND I STAYED OUT IN THE HALL AS GAVIN RETRIEVED HIS THINGS FROM HIS "private" quarters. I caught only a glimpse inside but took in morbid details all the same.

A large, broad table stood in the middle must be his body bench, a work surface clear but stained despite a recent cleaning. Dark drops and streaks on the floor led between it and the door, suggesting several times when an injured body had been moved in and out by various means.

In the corner were a spigot and floor drain much like the one we'd used to relieve and wash ourselves, but Gavin's was spattered with diluted blood and surrounded by used buckets and basins. A stack of clean rags, towels, and bandages sat in a single pile upon a smaller table nearby. I wagered the cloths were recent replacements, for the basket underneath the table held those damp and stained, having been emptied at least once before.

I didn't get a chance to see if Gavin had anywhere to sleep or write before he exited his room and closed the door. He'd been given a metal key to lock it behind him but set his own ward, too. He carried his pack, the Temple thurible, and his spade.

"Uh," my Sister said, indicating the sharp tool. "Expect to cut off heads?"

"Not expecting," he murmured, "but one never knows with the Greylands."

I smirked. Wasn't he the perfect example of that?

If Cris and Amelda had known what was coming, they might've tried to cut off his head before he could sit up in that shed.

Jael's look reminded me that my ease and good humor with most things to do with the Deathwalker was atypical.

Gathering steam greeted us as we arrived at one of many cot-filled rooms in the "gravely wounded" quadrant. All these doorways were wider than I was used to, and the air within each room was far fresher than it should be if these were just holes dug in the ground.

I paused inside the door, astonished by the larger chamber.

Deshi was filling a deep, standing sink with the spigot high enough to imagine it as a bathtub intended for a Dwarf. Underneath was a dense, polished piece of granite marked with runes and emitting enough heat to warm the water Gavin had asked for. Next to him, a similar table of supplies with a dirty collection bin underneath, as I'd seen in the Deathwalker's quarters.

The room itself was large enough to hold fifteen cots, each with a man covered in a blanket with a bedpan on the floor near his head. One corner was curtained off in a way to make me think of Tamuril's lament in what had been "missing" in our waste-water corner.

Lastly, at the rear was a deeper alcove with standing storage cabinets, a worktable, another two cots, and several chairs. Overall, the area was breathable, clean, and well-stocked for whomever would be tending the men. Right now, that seemed to be Deshi, Tak, and a blond, male Dwarf I didn't recognize.

Moments later, I jolted to recognize the rest of Deshi's "brothers." Beyond Torch, Peng-lok and Nianzu, the latter having been struck by Ma'ab arrows while trying to reach the gate, all the rest were part of Reprisal.

I met Tak's eyes first, his concern deep for the pallid man in the cot next to him. Their Hand, Brian Wolf, was white-faced, sweating, and shaking. A spot of bright red blood had soaked through and dripped slowly onto the floor underneath him.

What the fuck happened to him?

The Head of the teams had sounded fine the last I'd heard his voice through the Dragon pearls.

"Herald?" Tak said, standing up, caught between dread and hope.

"Not here to guide him," Deshi reassured from the hot water sink.

"Not yet," Gavin agreed.

The Guildsman glanced at the thurible at his waist, its function well-known by now. Tak swallowed.

"Deathwalker." The Dwarven tender bowed his head. "I'm Welden. Clan Gherudum. Deshi said ya were comin'."

He glanced at Jael and me. Apparently, we were deemed neither a help nor harm as he continued.

"I've never seen somethin' like this, but it's affectin' 'em all at once like somethin' delayed. Hope ya can see what he's been tryna describe."

Gavin scanned the room of wounded men, some sleeping or resting uneasily, others awake and watching intently. "How many at once?"

271

"Five. Wolf is the worst off due to th' location."

"Leave the door open," the death mage said to me. "Guard it, if you would."

I cocked a brow. "Alright."

Deshi hauled over a bucket of gently steaming water and cloth while the Dwarf and Tak helped to roll Wolf so Gavin could set his spade against the wall and take a knee by the cot to wipe the skin clear of blood. He didn't seem to care about the fact that he was kneeling in the puddle; there were plenty of older stains from the day past.

Those new robes didn't last long.

"Thoughts?" Welden asked.

"Greylands," Gavin murmured, setting down his chirurgeon's kit to unroll it before plucking up a thin pair of metal grippers. He placed them precisely, using them and his fingers to pry the wound open a bit.

"From the rift?" Deshi asked with dread.

"The Malok, yes. Just a sliver, it seems, but that can be all it takes."

"Sliver of what?"

"Shh," Welden touched Deshi's shoulder. "Let 'im work, first."

I couldn't see anything but blood and flesh where I stood, but my death mage seemed to be seeing far more. He pressed one thumb on a spot below the wound and Wolf cried out, his voice breaking from pain and his face flushing deep red from the sallow white it had been a moment ago.

Tension swept the room as some men woke up. I noticed Peng-lok shifting on his cot as if he couldn't move one leg, trying to see what was happening. Torch and Nianzu were nearby; though each bore some injury, they didn't seem as weak as their brother.

"Too close tah th' kidney?" Welden asked with apparent concern.

"Yes," Gavin replied with little inflection as he intently studied the wound. "And working itself deeper. Interesting …"

The Dwarf quirked one bushy eyebrow. "What's interestin'?"

"The barb draws on his will to live to burrow through, disrupting his life aura as Deshi said."

"*Shyit.* Can we get it out? Or neutralize that draw?"

"Hm." The death mage considered, a tendril or two of ice blue light moving through the flinty black thorns on his shoulders. "I can neutralize it, but the sliver must be removed. Otherwise, chance is strong it will spontaneously animate again, and I know not yet how quickly that can happen. You will need powerful magic healing on hand to repair the damage, or he will bleed to death before the organ has a chance to fail."

"*Fuck, fuck ...* " Tak said under his breath, holding a distressed, muttering Wolf in place when he would have rolled onto his back.

The Dwarf stayed focused. "Buying time might be enough until we get hold ov stronger potions an' some more healers."

"How long?" Gavin asked.

"At least a couple hours."

"Not ideal for this one to survive."

"I know. What d'ya need tah draw out the essence?"

"I have what I need."

Gavin demonstrated by lifting his wrist, aiming the sharp tip of one black protrusion, and nudging it into the bleeding hole. Wolf jerked, sucked in a breath, and howled in agony.

"*Freishenkryt!*" Welden cursed, covering his ears moments after Jael and I did.

"Stop!" Tak pleaded.

Gavin lifted his wrist and inspected the hole again. "The movement has stopped. For now, at least." He looked over his shoulder, focusing on Peng-lok, his eyes subtly glowing. "Shall I assist with the other four?"

Peng-lok flinched, and I easily picked out the other three men of Reprisal who must have similar "slivers" inside them.

"No, 'm good," muttered one Guildsman, whom I recalled placing bets at our planning table in Alran.

"Are you?" Gavin asked, his unnerving eyes shining. "The barb is still moving."

"Ya can see it that far?" Welden asked.

"I can. Based on the rate, in a few hours, it will come out the front of his shoulder and puncture his lung along the way."

The blond Dwarf glanced around his infirmary, his face flushed and deep brown eyes worried. "And if some got it in a limb instead ov the torso?"

"Given enough time, these slivers will burrow through bone. The men will suffer longer but have a chance at surviving without intervention, though it will cripple them."

"Fucking Hells, Deathwalker," Tak said through gritted teeth. "I see why they brought only the unconscious ones to you."

Gavin grunted without offense. "The outcomes will be poor ones unless I neutralize and remove them now."

"W-well, then, finish what you started with Wolf!"

The Deathwalker looked at Welden. "Have you no way to close the wound quickly once I do?"

The Dwarf exhaled. "Can't stop a bleedin' kidney fast enough, an' I used my best potions before these things started movin'. Need time tah make more."

"He won't last." His tone was a statement of plain fact. "Does your Clan have any life mages?"

Welden looked confused. "What, you mean a midwife?"

"No. One who shares their mage's aura to strengthen health rather than weaken it. Perhaps with touch as their focus?"

"Ah ... no, sorry. That talent is dashin' rare among us."

Rare, indeed.

Ruefully, I thought of Auslan. Healing me was the only reason he avoided the purge. Given I'd looked worse than Wolf, I imagined the Consort would not have cringed away from helping had he been here.

"Hm. To be expected." Gavin pondered the issue further, glancing at Deshi. "All death mages can hypothetically take life from one to strengthen another, but the addition of further death magic in this operation would complicate things and possibly negate my neutralization."

I cocked my eyebrow, not quite following as the Dwarf winced.

"Yeah, no. Let's not go there. Gotta be somethin' else we're missin'."

Jael tugged on my sleeve, and I looked away from the discussion.

The mind-reader healed me by touch, she signed, making some effort to hide her hands from the men. *In the crypt when we found the shield. The Queen's compulsion would have killed me. He kept my heart beating, I know it.★

I remembered. ★But he is down as well.★

★Do we know that? The pale Elf said we slept ten marks.★

True.

★Would you guard while I sweep this quadrant?★ I asked, expecting reluctance but watching her balance our separation with the fact that it was her idea.

★Yes, but hurry.★

I signed that I would, saying, "Gavin?"

"Hm?"

"I will see if Isboern is awake."

The Deathwalker twisted his neck to peer over his shoulder, one eye glowing blue. "Good idea. Best hurry."

Then he turned around, calmly terrifying another wounded man.

Smirking, I squeezed Jael's shoulder and left to scurry down the hallways, pulling up my hood before I passed Dwarves carrying supplies. The first group stared but didn't try to stop me while I kept ears and nose open for familiar scents, voices, and languages.

Krithannia had said this was the "officers" quadrant, so the Templars must be close. Counting my corners and curves, I encountered two checkpoints staffed with Guildsmen and Dwarves. At least that confirmed I was on the inside of a perimeter with greater security.

Both times, I turned around before they could challenge me and kept searching.

Finally, far from either checkpoint, I picked up Manalari spoken aloud and paused at an intersection. Two Templari stood guard in a dead-end hall. At the same time I spotted them, they recognized me and weren't pleased about it. Regardless, I approached, showing both my hands low and palms up.

"Is your Captain awake yet?"

One man pursed his lips while the other said, "No, *signala*."

Was that right? I didn't quite believe him.

"Five Guildsmen are dying from helping you fight against the Malok," I said. "They need the Godblood's healing."

The Templari frowned, one offended by my statement.

"He recovers like us all, *signala*."

"Will you ask if — ?"

They shook their heads, stubborn jaws fixed.

"But just tell him —"

"Go rest, *signala*. We are sorry for the Guildsmen."

My spiders responded to my annoyance, shifting in my hair. Once I'd mentally calmed them down, I tried one step farther.

~Willven? Can you hear me?~

His calm, confident touch was immediate. He was awake.

~Sirana. What is wrong?~

~Five of Reprisal have some Greylands thorn inside them. It's digging deep and draining their life, how Gavin described it.~ I let him see my memory of the death mage by the bloody cot. *~Brian Wolf will be dead in the next hour without magical healing. We need your help to save him.~*

~Of course. I'm coming.~

"Do you hear us?" asked the Templar, leaning down in front of me. "Clear away, *pin'fave*."

I blinked, smiling up at him. "No, I will wait."

Behind them, movement and voices rose behind the second door on the left. Their Captain exited with his *Tentente* and another Templar, each wearing about half their full armor. The color had returned to Willven's face, his blue eyes shining and alert.

Hmph. Lying curds.

The guards turned their backs to each wall and saluted; Isboern responded with a calm command and a hand motion of his own. I could assume he'd announced his intent to leave with me and his flank men, and that the others should remain behind.

My two obstacles were unhappy but obeyed.

"Lead the way," the Godblood said to me in Trade, his smile tinged with sorrow.

Nodding, I set a quick pace to bring the three Manalari the way I'd come.

We arrived not a moment too soon.

ODD AS THEY APPEARED TOGETHER, AND DESPITE THE CONTRASTING BEDSIDE manners, the two deity messengers and the infirmary Dwarf worked well together on Wolf.

Without speaking aloud, the psion offered an encouraging smile to Tak as the younger man moved away to give them space. Isboern then closed his eyes and levitated the injured man off the cot without touching him, rolling him to one side. This made it easier for Gavin to perform his incisions just beneath Wolf's ribcage while relieving the strain of the world's pull on the patient's body.

At Gavin's request, Welden held a bright glowstone close to provide the light he would need to cut and prod his tools into the living body. The Dwarf also helped wipe away blood when it obscured the death mage's work.

I could hear my ally muttering in the dead tongue as Gavin stared deep into a bloody opening that he'd made larger. As he reached for the barb with his tools, a second blue glow appeared deep inside Wolf, flickering and reacting to his voice inflections.

"So much for our extra hands," Jael whispered in Davrin.

I smirked. *"Just as well. I don't want to get closer to that white glowstone."*

The room was quiet despite all the men awake, at least until Gavin started his extraction in earnest. This was when Wolf regained enough consciousness for the Guildsman's screaming to escalate with every pull of that sliver closer to the surface.

"Shhh," Willven soothed, his eyes closed, everything about him intent on easing the suffering. *"Dalme a duelet, irmon. Sancto insengi ..."*

"S-Sancti seng-guron," the Guildsman replied.

Finally, the pain left his mind.

Jael frowned at me. *"Did the infiltrator speak the Sun tongue?"*

"He did. Many do. Some were once from the Sun City but left because of the

male priestesses."

"*Huh.*" She scratched her chin. "*Guess many in my House would have, too, if there was another city to go to.*"

I bit my cheek as, right then, Gavin finally removed the barb.

"Got it," he said.

"Good, good," Welden murmured, withdrawing a small bottle from his waist. He removed the stopper with his teeth and slowly poured the clear liquid across Gavin's incision and whatever he'd caught between his metal grippers. Once empty, he offered it. "Put th' barb in here."

"Do not throw it away," said my scholar sternly. "I must study it."

"'Course. I wantcha to."

The white light dimmed at last, and we all watched Gavin drop in an insultingly small piece of Malok weaponry which had wreaked such havoc on the Guildsman's body. Welden couldn't seal the bottle fast enough.

"He's still bleedin'," the Dwarf observed.

"Down, down," Isboern whispered, lowering Wolf onto the cot as quickly and gently as he could.

The room held our collective breath. The Godblood didn't have a lot of time as the Guildsman had turned snow white in color and slightly blue around the lips. The psion gathered up the wounded man in his arms and murmured into Brian's sandy-colored hair, yet another language I hadn't heard before.

That isn't Manalari.

Jael reached out and gripped my arm.

"*This,*" she whispered in Davrin, briefly drawing the eye of the other two Templars guarding the room. "*He did this, so I'd live through the geas ending.*"

If that was so, then I felt the same gratitude that Tak showed on his face.

Interestingly, my Sister reacted to the rapid swell of power before I did. She squeezed me harder until I put one arm around her, covering Soul Drinker's grip with one hand. The magic wasn't threatening but easily overwhelmed our hidden senses. I blinked when my vision blurred.

"*Sancto insengi,*" Isboern chanted.

To my surprise, Brian answered again, "*Sancti senguron …* "

The glow of the Godblood's hands became as bright as the Sunlight outside, causing most of us to look away and cover our eyes with an arm.

"*Argh*," Jael groaned. *"Don't know if this happened before …"*

I couldn't see a damned thing but grinned, my gloved hand over my eyes. *"Either way, glad it did. Gave us a chance to grab you out of Keros's tower."*

She fell silent, possibly brooding on all that happened afterward. While I waited for the healing to finish, my thoughts drifted to the *second* time she was in that crypt.

With me and Mourn.

She said earlier she didn't feel well … How is she now?

When the light died down at last, Brian was sleeping peacefully, his color normal. The wound looked entirely healed, although the blood stains remained. Welden rushed over and checked his vitals as Isboern leaned tiredly against the wall, shaken by the intensity of his own healing trance.

"Sister Sora," the Dwarf murmured with awe. "Well done, Godblood, well done."

"No," Isboern shook his head with a half-smile. "Brian did it. He wanted to live."

"Well, I think he's gonna be fine," Welden said, addressing the room. "Better an' we coulda hoped."

Tak released a shout of joy, leaping into the air as if he could not contain the burst any longer. Another man in a cot clapped as several others of Reprisal started laughing and hooting with relief.

Gavin cleared his throat, and the noise died down.

"Who is next?" he asked.

Of the four sweating, shivering men, Peng-lok was first to meet his brothers' eyes and sigh. He threw back his blanket and tried to straighten his unresponsive leg with his hands.

"*Wo'zhuyan, Sho'shien*," he volunteered with a strained bow of his head.

Our strange but fascinating trio got to work.

CHAPTER 20

Each man screamed in some measure while Gavin removed a solitary, spiny, otherworldly fragment of black glass from his flesh.

Not long before, we'd learned that the Godblood would not remove their awareness of the pain, as he had for Wolf, while each man was "communicating" and conscious of what they were doing.

Isboern didn't say that he couldn't. He *wouldn't*.

"Why not?" Welden had asked, curious but retrieving his medicines.

"The method is … not without risk," the Captain had admitted. "When the foremind has no control of the body, or its sole awareness is the pain itself, I can be confident all function and sensations will return upon waking. If I separate alert minds from their bodies, I wrest that control from them to numb the pain against their will. The numbness could remain despite my intentions. I cannot decide that for someone else."

"I see," Welden said, looking through his bottles as several men swallowed with worry. "So, we either wait on a sleeping draught or they stay awake and take a blur syrup?"

"Correct. That is safest for a man to remain whole."

To my surprise, all four Guildsmen refused to take a sleep syrup; they opted for the "blur" one where they'd be awake while Gavin worked.

The cries ended up loud enough to cover my ears, but only because each intoxicated Guildsman had tried hard to be silent for as long as possible before their will broke.

Interesting. They're safe here, and everyone's awake. Why hold back?

Most injured Sisters I'd ever seen had strained for silence through pain because we had *not* been in a safe place. Why would something like this be imperative in this circumstance?

Thinking back, I recalled how I sometimes heard another crying out in private Palace Court chambers or in the Cloister's barracks. I did, too, but often a sound ward had been put in place to hide such moments from listening ears.

Does that have anything to do with this?

Did the men in this room feel vulnerable crying from too much pain?

With Torch's and Deshi's support, Gavin had removed the second Malok barb from Peng-lok's thigh. The Yungian proved the first to politely decline Isboern's offer for a healing trance like Wolf's.

"I will … accept next Guild potions, *Capitan*." Peng-lok sweated and gasped, his leg trembling as Welden got to work cleansing and wrapping the wound. He motioned toward the brown-haired man with the Malok sliver buried in his back. "Save your Temple magic for Duan."

Gavin had described it moving toward his lung, and I believed this from the way Duan was jumping and jerking in his cot despite the syrup, unable to sit or lie still.

"Probably a good idea," the Deathwalker had said, cleaning his hands thoroughly yet again before changing patients. "We should focus on him next before the barb shifts."

Duan screamed the least of the Guildsmen because he ended up passing out before Gavin got too deep. Isboern granted him as long of a trance as Wolf to aid in repairing his shredded torso.

The last two Guildsmen had been hit like Peng-lok, with the barb caught in one of their limbs and headed toward bone. Only one of them accepted Isboern's healing afterward.

"I'm good," said the other, trembling from pain. "I'll wait for Welden's potion."

Jael and I glanced at each other, and she signed, *Three of five?* When I shrugged, she added, smirking, *I think those two are insulted.*

I glanced at the Templars. She wasn't wrong; their faces were easy to read. First, they hadn't wanted to share their Godblood, but now they took offense if not every man wanted his magic.

I snickered and shook my head, startled when my stomach grumbled loudly in answer. The familiar, empty ache swept in to seize my attention *and* middle with two fists.

Damn, I'm hungry …

How long had this sequence of surgeries taken?

"*Shhf*, Sirana!" Jael commented aloud with a laugh, her arms crossed.

At the same time, Gavin and Isboern turned to me. Their expressions were in stark contrast, but each understood what had changed.

"We're nearly finished here, I think," the Captain said with a smile. "I could escort you to find some food. I am hungry as well."

Gavin grunted, helping Welden to clean up after claiming the bottle of Greylands barbs from the Dwarf. Then he spoke to Peng-lok and the two conscious Paxians.

"Describe how you came to know you'd been struck by one of these small weapons."

I supposed he had no protest and wanted to keep working. I would have enjoyed staying to listen to their answers, but my baby wouldn't let me. My appetite had been suppressed during the height of the tension, but soon, I would be teetering on nausea or faintness.

Speaking of vulnerability.

"Let's go," I agreed, motioning to the Manalari, glancing at Jael. "Unless you want to stay?"

She made a face and shook her head. "Hungry, too." She poked my arm with her finger. "Not leave you anyway."

Captain Isboern smiled wider hearing that as he joined his men. "Do you know the way?"

I shook my head. "Food was brought to us before."

"Ah. Us, too."

"Out left an' straight four intersections," the Dwarf interjected, "right one, left four again."

"Not bad," said the Godblood. "Thank you, Welden. Shall we bring you anything?"

"Nah." He tossed his beard toward the alcove. "Got supplies there, an' cot meals comin' soon with my back-up."

"Very well. Thank you for sending Sirana before I'd be too late to help."

The short, blond male straightened up and blinked. "Uh, no, that was them. The dark sisters thought ov ya. I had no idea."

The three tall Manalari looked at us in surprise. I showed my teeth in a smile and Jael frowned, shrugging.

"We eat?" she asked.

"Ah. Of course. Shall we lead?"

"Yes," Jael and I said together.

With a chuckle, Isboern turned out into the hallway first, his flank men sticking close to protect his back from my Sister and me.

Better than those long metal strides stepping on our heels.

On the last leg of Welden's directions, several important details caught my ears well before I could see on either side of the Templars. Up ahead was another checkpoint, beyond which I smelled the food. Before that was an open door with women's voices drifting out ...

Aaand Tamuril, Krithannia, and Talov standing in the hallway.

My hopes to obtain food quickly stopped in our tracks.

"*Oh, no,*" Jael muttered as the greybeard craned his head and nudged the Guild Mistress in the waist.

"Captain Isboern," Krithannia said with surprise. "Is anything wrong?"

Tamuril appeared like a startled deer, and Talov leaned far to one side, peering around the Templars and catching my eye with an enormous grin.

"Lasschen!" he crowed before Isboern could answer. "What's been happenin'?"

Predictably, the Naulor needed time to consider the oddity of two Davrin walking alone with three Templar, including their Godblood.

"Plenty," I replied dryly.

"No crisis, however," Isboern interjected with a bow to the non-

Human trio. "We come from Reprisal's room, helping there for a while. Welden of Clan Gherudum directed us to the kitchen for some food. Are we headed the right way?"

"Ye are," Talov answered, cocking an eyebrow toward the tall night-hair. "But … ?"

"Reprisal and Welden?" Krithannia picked up, pouring concern into her face and tone. "Have you seen Gavin?"

"We aided him just now. Do not worry, your men are stable and shall get better with time."

Krithannia and Talov looked at me as if to confirm.

"Deshi saw tiny body cripplers," I said, showing them the size with my thumb and forefinger. "From the Malok, suddenly moving deeper. Gavin had to cut them all out, but Welden didn't have enough potions and Wolf had bled too much. He needed a life mage to live through it."

"Oh!" Isboern's cheeks turned pink. "I am not a life mage, Sirana. Musanlo's favor allows me to give of myself to one whose mind is open to it, but it is different from a mage whose heart and nature makes them a healer or bringer of life."

As precise as Gavin about magic.

Then I noted the blond man's eyes drifting to Tamuril as he finished, causing her cheeks to pinken.

Wait, is he saying … ?

"Well," Talov said with a sober beard stroke, "either way, sounds like th' right time an' place. Thank ye, Captain. Good men in that group. Would hate tah lose 'em after the battle."

"Reprisal fought alongside us in the Temple, and not all made it. It is my honor and my oath, Grandfather Baradum, to help those in need."

My stomach protested the delay once again, and I breathed out against the nausea, returning one Templar's frown when he glanced at me. Jael couldn't decide whether to snicker or gape in astonishment at how loud it was.

"Oh, yes," said their Captain ruefully. "The kitchen. We're quite hungry."

"There is food here for the women," Krithannia said in an odd tone I didn't recognize.

"Yeah!" Talov said with unusual exuberance. "Sirana, ya don't hafta wait. Look just inside th' door." Then he clapped his wide, dry palms and motioned forward. "Come with me, Templari. I have questions while we get a meal."

"Very well," Isboern accepted, motioning to his flank men, who suddenly seemed at ease.

Aha.

This suggestion had tidily removed all the men from the women's quarters, with Jael and I no longer at their backs. Whatever the meaning, I accepted the Naulor's lead to step inside and help myself to the cold but hearty fare atop several covered platters; Jael followed with caution.

This room was as large as Reprisal's and contained more candles and glowstones yet seemed dimmer due to areas sectioned off by curtains hanging from pole frames. The segments numbered greater than any space I'd seen thus far.

Moans and soft weeping rose among the gentle sway of draped cloth which ranged in their colors from cream and tan to dark blue and earth brown. One woman moved among them, who neither dressed nor acted as Manalari, assisted by another red-haired female Dwarf.

Not Ragura.

"I thought the women were outside awaiting caravans," I murmured quietly to Krithannia as I chewed.

"The healthy ones are," she agreed. "These are the injured who still need care."

Jael blew through her lips before eating a shriveled sun-berry. "From fall while climbing?"

"Some of them. Others were unlucky targets among Ma'ab or Manalari." Krithannia hesitated when Tamuril's eyes pitched her a worried warning, yet she continued. "Still others are like the Lady Verina you assisted to the wall."

Jael frowned as I asked, "What do you mean?"

The Guild Mistress's eyes looked like storm clouds as she focused on my sister. "The eruption of the sacred pool awakened mage auras, but these women we've collected are untrained and alone. The Guild can help them."

And get first pickings of their potential talent.

"Is Verina here?" I whispered curiously.

Krithannia's bright grey eyes flicked toward the curtains in answer. "Soon we will take them to the showers. I was coming to get you if you'd like to join."

"Showers?" Jael repeated before I could.

The Guild Mistress smiled warmly. "Standing baths. Warm water and soap. An attached area to wash and dry your clothing or work on your equipment."

Hm. "Was this what you meant about needing to be ready when it's our turn?"

"It was, indeed." She smiled without showing her teeth. "Will you be ready soon?"

Jael rolled her eyes before darting a look at Tamuril. "They will all scream seeing us without clothes."

"I have a stall in mind to give us privacy," Krithannia explained, "but all females, Human and Dwarf, must go together once the showers are cleaned from the last seven groups of men."

I blinked. *Seven?*

"Us, mean 'you?'" Jael asked as if surprised Krithannia had to bathe.

"Yes. Tamuril and I shall follow the schedule and join you."

My Sister glanced at the bright-faced Druid, who stood next to her own sister in silent acceptance, and smirked, copper eyes scanning the elder Naulor head to toe as if seeing through her clothes.

I tried not to grimace at the spark of minor discomfort. *All of us together in the sluicers like the Cloister. Whewf.*

This would be interesting.

"Now, Sirana," Krithannia prompted, changing the subject by taking hold of her earlobe and giving it a pull. "If you would give me a brief report on what happened with Gavin?"

Gavin, she'd been saying, not Deathwalker or Herald or death mage. Probably for the sake of the women who understood any Trade. Likewise, she didn't explain the "how" of giving her a report, but when I mimicked her gesture and touched Mourn's pearl attached to my ear, the Guild Mistress nodded.

"Will it work while he's asleep?" I asked.

"It works for us," she replied. "Give it a try. I am open. I will try to guide you."

Alright …

Staring into the Stormseeker's eyes, I did manage an odd sort of mindlink with her. Not the same as Isboern's psionics nor my practiced link with Mourn, but it recalled my message pellets among the Sisterhood. Krithannia could hear me, and replied with an exploratory question, but I couldn't *feel* her mind and presence as I had with the two males.

Or with Jael.

This must have been the same when the Guild Mistress's voice had sounded through the Dragon pearls at Manalar: a strong mental voice but a quiet and shielded mind. Precisely how the elder Naulor wanted it, I wagered.

Rather like Gavin that way. The two certainly get along well.

Nonetheless, it worked. I gave her the full details of the Greylands barb extractions along with Gavin's insights and methods, all of it without Tamuril or the Human women overhearing.

"Excellent," Krithannia said with a somber nod. "Thank you. We shall stay alert for those symptoms among the wounded. Perhaps we can send Deshi to search for this with his death mage eyes."

"Good idea," I agreed, watching her face to catch that moment where she passed the information to Talov or some other Guildsman through her pearl.

"But next," the elder Naulor continued, turning to her sister, "we must organize the women to have their showers and clean their clothes."

Tamuril exhaled, resigned, and glanced at her falcon roosting on a high wall shelf.

Neither of them made a sound.

Chapter 21

Jael stared with open incredulity, shaking her head in disbelief, while we stood behind Krithannia, who was talking with a group of Dwarven women.

No, I decided. *Nowhere near as simple as the sluicing room.*

It could have been. The Tundar Dwarves had designed the showers to be open and capable of washing many bodies at once with efficiency.

One half of the impressive underground space had no segmentation, with multiple waterspouts lined high on the walls, reasonably aligned with spigot controls and multiple drains in a slightly depressed and downgraded floor.

The other half had built-in benches around the perimeter and standing sinks and drying lines or tables for washing items other than one's body. Nearby, cabinets held stacks of towels, rags, and soaps.

Finally, a few stalls recessed from the main space, measured along the segment of wall between open showers and the benches and sinks. Inside each was a small, built-in bench and enough space to include those unable to stand plus their helpers. The female Dwarves were setting up temporary privacy curtains as I watched.

The design was for all Dwarves and Humans, I could see, be they undergrown, pregnant, injured, hale, sick, or old. Luxurious in that way compared to the sparse and austere Cloister. The apparent requirements of the Manalari women, however, destroyed any hope that this group of fifty could be clean in less than two or three hours.

No wonder they followed behind hundreds of men.

I imagined the Dwarven women might be finished long before the Humans wearing their many layers and head veils coupled with the need to segment the showers with temporary curtains the same way they did their cot room.

Curtained or not, the concentration of scents was pungent and mixed. Somehow loud, too, despite that none shouted or shrieked over something.

Yet.

I wasn't looking forward to this if we were required to remain here in any capacity after we were finished.

"Do they want *to be surprised?"* Jael whispered to me in Davrin. *"So much blindness, and it's intentional!"*

I sighed, noting the tense, concerned looks from a few females close by when they heard her in Davrin. Like Gavin watching the Templars, the women made signs of protection from their Sun God.

Subtly, I motioned with my hand, *Maybe the Trade tongue or hand sign?*

Jael read that and rubbed her eyes in frustration. "Krithannia?"

The Guild Mistress paused her discussion, turning to blink at her. "Yes?"

"Where we wash?"

"Oh." She smiled. "I'll show you. We're just finishing up."

The elder had mentioned privacy for us — Tamuril, especially — which had me eyeing one of the stone stalls with room enough for two or three Dwarves to use the bench inside. It would fit four Elves and the falcon if the blonde insisted on bringing her.

And she doesn't mind wet feathers.

Krithannia indeed led us that way, but first we stopped at a cabinet in the far corner. There, we could remove towels, pucks of soap, and scrub sponges before storing our unique sets of boots. Jael and I also stashed our cloaks, armor, packs, belts, and weapons, including Soul Drinker.

The Guild Mistress closed the doors and settled the small metal brace in its cradle which kept them closed. She then displayed a metal loop-lock which slid neatly through a cross-space intending to keep the brace from being lifted.

She snapped the lock shut and handed me the key with a smile. "The Dwarves agree you have the possessions best protected from ill-advised curiosity. Rest assured it would take much force and noise to break into it now, and we will stay close. Test that you can open it."

I glanced around the large room. A few were watching us from a respectful distance, mostly the three female Dwarves Krithannia had been speaking with. The multiple curtains offered an unexpected boon of not attracting someone's gaze every moment.

I exhaled and used the metal key how Gavin had on his door. After securing a neat fit with one piece of metal inside the other, I found I could slide a heavy rod through the semi-hollow body in a circle to create a gap, allowing me to remove the lock and reopen the cabinet.

"Very good," Krithannia said.

After a nod, breathing in the steam as I listened to water spattering skin and curtains, I coaxed my guardian spiders inside before closing and locking the cabinet with the rest of our dangerous things. When I turned back, the Guild Mistress's expression had changed.

"Oh," she admitted. "I'd forgotten."

"*Psht*," Jael muttered with an eyeroll, "they hide so well, *I* forget. Well made by elder."

Despite Tamuril turning to hide her expression, some of Krithannia's smile returned hearing that. "This is a show of goodwill, Sirana, and I am noting it. On behalf of everyone's safety, I thank you."

"Better to avoid further misunderstandings," I agreed with a slanted grin, including Tamuril in the message even if she wasn't looking.

The tips of her ears turned deep red, but she said nothing.

Perhaps she imagined, like I had, Pilla snapping at my spiders, either trying to eat them or repay them for the bites suffered by her mistress. Whether the falcon became sickened from such an attack or not, it wouldn't be worth it. I didn't want to risk it. Such reactive, territorial skirmishes couldn't end well for any of us.

The Druid had been luckier than me to live through two of them.

When the elder Naulor motioned toward the stall we would use — also the one farthest from the rest of the room and with a new temporary curtain put in place — Jael started tugging on her leather ties at her hips.

"Oh, let us step in, first," Krithannia encouraged, motioning toward me and the Druid.

My Sister squinted as we moved in. "We standing in wet clothes?"

"At first. Easier to wash them without taking up a sink, then you may take them off. We have methods for quick drying when we get out."

Reasonable and hopeful. Jael's clothing had waited the longest since its last full cleansing, anyway.

We stepped inside the stall, Tami barefoot and the rest of us in stockings. When Pilla stayed outside atop the cabinet and Krithannia drew the curtain closed, I was astonished.

The stall had one spout for the water to drop, and I watched the Guild Mistress seem to initiate it from rune-marked gems installed in the wall itself.

Jael jumped when the water struck her first, soaking into her scalp and shirt. I laughed to see her eyes widen with shock, reaching up to catch some in my cupped palm.

My grin faded. "Hot."

"Pleasantly so, I hope?" Krithannia asked.

I turned my hand to let the soothing liquid run down my arm. "Very."

The water for sluicing in the Cloister had always been cold.

"Good timing," she continued, adjusting the rune-gems. "Heating the cisterns takes magic and time. The flow may cool before we are finished, so enjoy it."

With a mischievous grin, Jael pulled me under the stream to get doused, too. I chuckled, closing my eyes as loops of soggy hair fell over my brow, reaching to start unraveling my braid.

"No sex, please," Tamuril murmured softly, earning an instant scowl from Jael as I pushed my hair back.

"I agree," Krithannia said. "We don't have a luxurious amount of time before this space must be cleared and cleaned for the next group."

Luxurious. Heh.

"Please use this opportunity to revive your uniforms to their finest," she finished, speaking to soothe some of Jael's ruffled nape.

"Fine," she growled. "No sex."

After she and I were soaked through from hair to stockings, Jael offered me hard soap and a sponge. "You scrub my uniform, I scrub yours? Then we strip and scrub again."

"Deal," I accepted, taking the wash tools.

I started with her front, alternating between rubbing the slippery bar over the sponge before creating a lather of suds on the tough, black cloth with small, circular motions. She sighed in pleasure as I worked in some early massaging of her muscle.

My hands industrious and my touch firm, I worked one area at a time, from her shoulders and chest down to her taut belly and thighs before moving around to start over behind her. Saved her hair and scalp for last, I made sure not to push lather into her eyes while gradually removing the layers of sweat and dirt from her captivity and the battle.

Even seeing evidence of what she'd been through and having witnessed her fight with Mourn against the Ma'ab, I was still surprised how much grit and grime rinsed down the drain.

Krithannia shared the shower in a similar fashion with Tamuril, though her touch was light and tentative; her sister didn't lean into it like Jael did. In fact, the Druid fussed with some of the spots herself, filching her sister's sponge to scrub near her crotch or across her breasts. She seemed calmest letting her elder cleanse that long, golden hair.

The moment I had helped to pull off Jael's stockings for thorough washing, she decided then to strip out of each piece, lightly wringing then hanging her clothing on hooks out of the raining water.

"Now you," Jael said, her eyes shining with refreshed glee.

I submitted to my Sister's ministrations in water which seemed to have cooled but was not a frigid mountain stream. My smile never wavered as I relaxed into it, focusing on her fond, familiar touch in her efforts to get me clean.

I paid little attention when Tamuril and Krithannia exchanged places, a side note to my ears. Jael was as thorough with me as I had been with her. My crotch had begun pleasantly tingling through it all.

Mmmm …

"Okay!" she announced, catching my attention with a breast bounce as she rose to her feet. "Stockings and clothes off!"

Her fingers plucked at my thongs before mine could, and we chortled together trying to get them undone. Soon enough I was nude except for my pendant and setting my lightly squeezed clothes where they could drip for a while.

I was privately pleased when Krithannia began to undress.

That's a lot of pale skin.

I might be blinded if the tall Stormseeker stepped outside on a sunny day. She'd be easy to spot in a forest. She even had plump, pink netherlips like Tamuril, though the curly mat of her mons matched her night-dark hair. I found her startlingly easy to imagine with Mourn, naked.

At one point in their history, those petals have given way for his Davrin-dark, purplish pole. *Whew.*

"Like what you see?" Krithannia asked, crossing her arms beneath small, pink-tipped breasts.

I blinked, her Davrin-filled slit lingering too long behind my eyes to think of a good reply.

"Not bad," Jael said with a light grin, lifting her chin.

She'd been looking, too, appraising, for certain curious, but without the confession I'd heard from the Naulor's own lips about initiating the half-blood's dick.

I tried smiling without speaking.

The Guild Mistress lifted her eyes and chuckled before turning to her sister, murmuring gently, "Here, let's get these off."

Outside, Pilla flapped her wings, chirping at her. Tamuril swallowed and took a deep breath, her heart audible to Jael and me as she whispered above the splashing water.

"I have a … bottom layer that I must keep on."

"Bottom layer?"

This was new to Krithannia.

"Yes. From, ah, Willven. S-so I could wash in the city, um ..."

"Ah. I see. Well, if you wish."

The Druid bared only her arms and legs, a bit to my disappointment. The rest of her was covered in thick, plain, and rough cloth which covered her from shoulders to mid-thigh. The garment was heavy enough to obscure her breasts and the curve of her waist even when wet.

This Human idea doesn't suit the wilderness Elf at all. Did Isboern insist — ?

"*Ugh,*" Jael grunted in comment. "Ugly."

Krithannia darted a look so sharp that I straightened up and moved slightly between them. "Don't you dare make such remarks, Red Sister. One of yours was the catalyst for this added shield."

Jael's eyebrows lifted in astonishment. "*You* insist we undress all in here!"

The Naulor breathed in through her nose, filling her chest with patience. "Necessary to conserve. We're in a war refuge, for God's sake."

"You are right, Krithannia," I said, absorbing my Sister's expression as I shook my head. "I admit the bottom layer is not flattering for an Elf of Tamuril's elegance but wonder why Human women wear it?"

"To bathe," the Druid said, her voice too small a response. "Flattering is the *opposite* of the intent."

Jael's and my face scrunched in confusion, and Krithannia sighed.

"Let us finish the final lather and rinse, Ladies. We waste water."

Each of us scrubbed our own body with more focus, fine for me as my breasts had grown sore after Jael's handling. It didn't take long to get fully clean. My Sister was eying me, however, and I paused at her wry expression as she focused on my middle.

"What?" I said with a knowing smile.

She shrugged. "You need privy next?"

My smile dropped. Maybe I didn't know. "What?"

"Your gut." She pointed. "Too full. You eat much earlier."

Both Krithannia and Tamuril stilled, and my Sister wasn't so focused not to catch it. Jael tried to read their faces, then mine.

"What?" she asked.

Tamuril covered her mouth with a gasp. "Can't you see it?"

I groaned inside as the tension in the stall spiked.

"What can't?" Jael leaned toward my face. "What *can't* I see?"

"The aura," I began in our native tongue, annoyed with them both.

"What aura?"

"A second aura."

"How the fuck do you have a 'second' aura? Are you a mage now, too?"

"What?" I touched my belly in a way all females seemed to recognize. *"No, I caught —"*

"You caught?!" she blurted loudly. *"Is that what's been winking at me? A baby?!"*

"Winking at you?" I exhaled, exasperated. *"What in the Web does that mean?"*

She flipped her hand. *"Here and gone. A tease. A glimpse of colors. It's been confusing, but now I ... I see it."* She swallowed. *"S-so you're carrying an unborn?"*

The idea was twisting her up. *"Well, yes —"*

"Was it him?"

"Him ... ?"

"Him! Did he do this? That's the 'bargain' you had to make with him?"

My mouth hung open as Krithannia finally turned off the water. *"You mean the Dragon son? No, he's not the sire —"*

Jael looked even more troubled as she glanced at the two Naulor who had known about this before she did. *"Then who is?! Who did you ... did you find someone stranger to fuck on the Surface?"*

"No, I didn't! Count back." I held up seven fingers. *"I am over a half turn carrying. Who could it have been?"*

Jael jerked in shock. *"Shyntre? When you visited the Tower?"*

"No! ... Well, wait, that's a good guess —"

"Oi-aye? Ya alright in there?"

We froze in place, realizing the Dwarven woman had sneaked up on us.

Damned curtains.

"We are well, Dula, thank you," Krithannia said. "A necessary debate between the dark sisters is all. A storm passing, is all."

"Ah. Very good. Jus' checkin'."

We waited as the wide, soft-soled boots padded away, and Jael and I brought our voices down as we faced each other.

"Auslan is the sire," I murmured. *"When he healed me. After you and Jaunda … um. Killed him."*

Her copper eyes grew round as coins. *"Does … who knows?"*

"Oh …" I shrugged. *"The Valsharess. Both Elders. Jaunda. Not the Prime, fortunately."* I paused. *"And Shyntre."*

Jael's smirk twisted. *"Not surprised with how he acted in solitary. I can't believe you didn't say!"*

Another shrug. *"Didn't know if I'd find enough food up top."*

"Well …" She eyed my middle again and glanced at Krithannia. *"You definitely have. Gonna keep carrying?"*

"For now."

The discomfort and uncertainty hovered between us long enough for Jael to exhale and look down. *"Got it. Sorry. A … surprise. And I've been looking but didn't see it with your clothes on."*

"I understand."

Soft whispering from the corner filled our space then, and I glanced at the Naulor sisters, expecting them to be staring at us, waiting for a signal that the argument was over with no fists thrown. Although I'd intended to give it to them, I blinked to see instead Tamuril huddled and facing a corner with Krithannia coaxing her to turn around.

"Letima, leimana seur," the elder murmured, touching the blonde's hunched shoulders.

"Now they *speak their home tongue, "* Jael murmured.

That they were. I couldn't understand a word of the musical speech, but whatever the subject, the Druid was horrifically apologetic.

And the Guild Mistress was …

Terrified.

I glimpsed Krithannia's left eye when she looked off to one side, staring into a great distance before turning away.

"Leimana seur," she whispered again, tugging on Tamuril's shoulder as

if to turn her around. "*Leimana seur …*"

Jael had the sense to hand sign. ★What's going on?★

★I don't know.★

Krithannia succeeded in coaxing a quarter turn from her sister, tucking her finger into the high collar of Tamuril's sleeveless shift to catch a glimpse down at the cringing Druid's breasts. The elder pale Elf paled further as a strange, green tinge swept her face.

Like the sky on the Midway that brought hail.

Was she going to hurl?

The Stormseeker seemed caught in between powerful emotions: fear, anger, horror. She said something in Naulor, her voice breaking, teeth clenched as her face threatened to collapse into a sob, and she stumbled to catch herself against the stall wall.

Tamuril tried to flee. She grabbed her sopping shirt and pants, slipping into them before any of us could think to dress.

"No!" Krithannia said with crushing pain and dismay. "Don't leave — !"

The Druid would have abandoned her sister, would have left her boots locked in the cabinet and collected her bird to run off somewhere in the redoubt.

I stepped in the way, braced to stop her.

"*Rishelna!*" she shrieked as we collided, trying to twist free.

I gripped her clothing harder, pulled us closer until I had her firmly in a Cloister wrestling hold. She cried out again, I assumed a demand to be released, and Pilla cried out shrilly, attacking the curtain.

"Tamuril!" Krithannia broke from her cacophonic shock and scrambled over to us. "Calm, please, I'm sorry! You're safe, I promise! I'm sorry!"

Jael and I flinched when talons tore through the curtain behind us, wings furiously beating the air with another screech. Manalari women were calling out, worried and confused, as several Dwarven women spoke with clear intent to lead them away from panic.

"Tamuril," the Guild Mistress breathed. "Please, assure Pilla you're safe. We shall never hurt you."

"L-let her in," came the whimpering response. "Or she won't ... believe you ..."

"Will she attack?" I asked.

"She rip drape down first," Jael said dryly, crouching low to pull the heavy, wet fabric to one side. She ducked when the falcon darted inside.

Pilla landed on the stone bench, squawking at us with baleful, tawny eyes as she took in the scene. Once Tamuril said something to her in Naulor, the bird reluctantly settled down, earnestly grooming her feathers.

"Close the curtain all the way," Krithannia said to Jael, who obeyed but couldn't resist peeking out.

"I keep guard," she replied, standing up with her naked back to the wall.

Meanwhile, I kept my arms wrapped around the first Surfacer I had ever met, holding her tight in her soggy leathers, though she no longer struggled to escape the stall.

Beside us, Krithannia brushed her hair from her temple, sometimes pressing her lips to it in a soft kiss, murmuring comfortingly in their native tongue. Mostly, Tamuril did not respond, though once or twice I caught her hand squeezing Krithannia's as she leaned against me, accepting where she sat.

Admittedly, I was entranced and uncertain how to feel.

I didn't want to leave but wasn't sure how long I should keep her restrained. I could see Auslan comforting a child or another bua like Krithannia was doing but couldn't think of a place in Sivaraus where I might see this.

I *had* seen this in Yong-wen, though, for Dandan and that grand-mother's sick child. Hints from Mourn and Krithannia, both.

I swallowed. I'd *felt* this as well. *Twice.*

First, on the boat sailing down the Big Kerr, when Mourn witnessed the Ornilleth prison in my mind, then underneath the Manalari Temple when he scented the Sathoet and chose to warn me. I'd fallen against the wall, and he had squeezed me so tightly, as if to keep me from falling apart until I could pick myself up.

She is shamed, Krithannia had said to him through the pearls. *She *need not be.* ★

Shamed.

An emotion painfully clear in the Druid in my arms. I squeezed Tamuril harder as Mourn had for me, my cheek resting against her head. She didn't protest.

Didn't even tense up.

Finally, Krithannia asked her, "Would you please come with me, cherished one? We may rest in my quarters."

Tamuril swallowed, green eyes glancing up fearfully. "Do you … take back your words?"

The hint of stone in the Guild Mistress's face told me she didn't.

"Take back which words?" I asked curiously, ignoring my doubt that it could be done.

Krithannia straightened up and took a deep breath, watching the Druid's face before looking to me. I could have sworn storm clouds rolled in her eyes.

"I said … I would kill him."

Him?

"And I am sorry I said this to you, Tamuril."

"Kill who?" Jael asked, glancing outside. "No worry. Clear. Avoiding us."

"Her … my … A Priest at home."

New tears appeared in emerald eyes. "Not *any* Priest. My brother, Krithannia."

Brother? Shit.

"Oh?" Jael glanced outside again. "Why kill brother? What he do?"

That odd green pallor appeared briefly.

I frowned. *She'd looked down her shift …*

"Did he … mark her?" I asked.

The Guild Mistress blinked in brief surprise as the Druid tensed up in my arms, but they both nodded.

"B-because of what happened," Tamuril murmured. "In the cave …"

A rock fell in my middle, nausea bubbling out in waves.

"With the Red Sisters?" I asked.

"*Yes…*"

Barely a whisper.

Swallowing, I looked at Krithannia. The anger remained in her eyes but was better hidden on her face.

"Penance scars," said the elder. "The … closest translation I have. Ritual cuts, stained with a powder that cannot be washed out for seven years."

What?

"Ritual cuts … ?" I echoed.

"They also dampen magic and joy. Suddenly …" Krithannia swallowed, leaned to kiss her sister's brow. "I understand why she has not found comfort in the wilderness as she always had before. Why she has not spoken to me about …"

"C-can't!" Tamuril whined. "I cannot speak of it."

Cannot speak …

Jilrina.

I felt sick. "Her brother did that? To punish her?"

Krithannia nodded.

"For what?"

Her expression, at once so poignant and bitter, seared into my memory. "For not escaping the Dark Elves. For 'allowing' herself to be soiled by them. She needed 'purification' on the altar."

I grew dizzy, a high pitch overtaking my ears. *Huh bua …*

My arms loosened from around the Druid so abruptly that she nearly fell. Krithannia caught her as I scrambled over to the drain and started vomiting into it.

"Sirana?!" said all three at once.

"Sorry …" I hurled again. "M'alright … sorry …"

Pilla was closest as I heaved my last meal out and down the drain, but the falcon didn't take advantage of the moment to claw my back.

"The baby?" Tamuril asked me quietly, having shifted into Krithannia's embracing arms.

"No —" I shook my head and retched.

"She, ah," Jael began uncomfortably, "purified on altar, too. Left marks."

Tamuril and Krithannia fell quiet.

Close enough.

I could somehow see the Druid traveling home after Jaunda threw her out of the underground alive, only to fail to save the Human boy, and then to be marked and thrown out again ...

Until I found her two years later, living alone with a bird in that hovel.

We both knew what had happened then.

I spit out excessive bile and spit, gasping for breath on my knees. I was glad I hadn't dressed yet, though I needed to wipe down the saphgar for sure.

"I'm sorry," I rasped, an abrupt sob escaping my lips. "I'm sorry ..."

Tamuril blinked at me. "What's wrong, Sirana?"

"Why so much 'sorry?' " asked Jael, baffled.

I shook my head. "I'm just ... sorry, Tamuril. I am sorry for the pain. I wish ..." I swallowed, my tongue sour. "I wish I could have stopped it. Somehow. I didn't know ..."

I didn't understand anything.

And Tamuril had *still* helped keep Jael alive. Perhaps she'd sent the message Krithannia had received. The Druid could have done so much worse to my Sister for revenge.

Or she could have done *nothing*.

The Druid is like Isboern.

Mourn had been trying to tell me. In the broad web of the Surface, harming sentients one after another only made one's own misery last longer.

For decades ... or centuries longer.

Until misery was all we knew. All *any of us* knew, with the eldest forgetting the rest.

Forgetting the Sun, moons, and the sky.

And it goes on and on without change.

"I am sorry, Tamuril," I muttered, quivering, exhausted. "I will *never* hurt you or watch another. My ... oath, I will stop it first ..."

"Your oath?" she echoed, cautiously disbelieving.

"My oath," I repeated, finally twisting my neck from the drain to look at them. "Never."

I must start somewhere with this new world, apart from Sivaraus.

She didn't respond. The quiet stretched for a few moments inside the stall while other females rustled and murmured outside.

Finally, Krithannia got up to turn on a small stream of water for me to rinse out my mouth, wash my pendant, and flush the contents of my stomach down the drain.

"Let us go outside," she murmured.

Outside?

"You mean, trees?" Tamuril asked, sounding hopeful.

Her sister turned to her with a tender smile. "Yes. Trees. And sky. And mice for Pilla to hunt."

"Day or night?" I asked.

"Late in the night. Or ... very early the next day."

I smirked.

"Come with us," Krithannia invited. "Your eyes shall be comfortable, and many in the camps are asleep."

I nodded, willing before glancing at Jael, seeing her eager grin.

Apparently, I'd accepted for both of us.

CHAPTER 22

JUST AS THE DWARVEN REDOUBT NEEDED NO DAVRIN TO HANDLE THE ARRIVAL of this gaggle of women, we also weren't expected to see them out.

Jael and I took the opportunity to hang wet clothes in the "drying stall" operated by two Dwarves, which vastly shortened the time before we donned our uniforms only slightly damp. Unlocking the cabinet, we collected our armor, tools, cloaks, and boots, my spiders sneaking out along with them.

More women had ventured out from behind their curtains to watch us leaving after the noise we'd made. Jael and Pilla openly scowled back, the latter opening her wings on Tamuril's shoulder to appear larger. I wasn't sure which of the two was more intimidating. Several women retreated and hid again.

Some, not all.

One in particular made me look twice.

A Human with a pale, speckled face, dark eyes, and curly dark blonde hair held a towel to obscure her front, though she pressed it so tightly that her breasts seemed like they might spill over her arms. She stared at me and Jael as if she knew us.

Or at least has seen us before.

Then I glanced at the light blue pile of fabric and veils on the bench next to her, which I presumed to be hers.

And recognized the pair of boots Jael and I had stolen from a walking corpse to replace her sandals.

Aha.

"Lady Verina," I said with a surprisingly easy smile.

The way she jumped in fright made Jael chuckle but stand down at once. She glanced at me and then took in her own view of the woman we'd escorted from the Temple courtyard.

Lifting her gloved hand, she circled her face. "Good to know."

Verina's face flushed as if to break into a sweat as she mashed her chest further with the towel.

"Not ominous at all," I murmured to Jael before adding in Trade, "She means we are glad to know you escaped, Lady."

"And strong climber," she interjected, flexing her arm before pointing at the Human's feet. "Many signs."

Jael referred to the scrapes, bruises, and blisters on her feet. It might've been her first mountain, for all I knew.

I lifted my arm in a flex. "True. Strong."

Verina and several women near her stared mutely at us. I glanced at Krithannia, whose fingers rested on her chin.

The Guild Mistress blinked at me and smiled slightly. "Don't look at me. You're doing fine."

Whether that was true or not didn't really matter. Verina bowed her head briefly to us and slipped behind a curtain, her movement followed by a swell of whispering.

Oh, well.

I hadn't the time to coax Manalari women like sheltered buas; this was not the goal tonight.

I leaned closer to the Naulor, my voice low. "How about those trees?"

Tamuril's once morose expression brightened, which was most certainly the signal that pushed Krithannia into action.

The night-hair tied things up with her Dwarf contacts and showed us an unobtrusive way outside.

"We shan't go far," Krithannia reassured the sentries, her tone placid and unassuming. "And *Oltere* Baradum knows where we will be."

"Aye, very good," said one sandy-bearded Dwarf as he stood up from his workstation. "I gotta clear it, first."

He'd been mending tools on a table shared with a second Dwarf in the hall, which had been placed right next to a ladder recessed into the wall. Now, he climbed that ladder while his similar looking brother motioned for us to wait.

"Minimal noise while he does," he murmured, glancing at me while I chewed on a large piece of bread. "Anything bigger than a rat notices, and we gotta call someone."

I imagined a gem somewhere nearby that allowed him to do it.

The four of us and the falcon stood quietly, not wanting to wreck our chance of breathing the night air. Even Jael kept quiet after quirking an eyebrow at how humbly Krithannia had approached them.

No exit from the redoubt could remain unwatched, no matter how small or inconveniently placed. Like the first time I'd arrived with Mourn ahead of Reprisal, those who'd lived here longest decided whether and when they'd open a hatch hidden beneath sod.

I was glad, truth be told. The Guild and their Taiding allies remained alert to all that surrounded the escape of this portion of a city's population from Mount Sonai. Had one narrow chute been unguarded, I'd have wondered about an oddly negligent gap.

Krithannia also wasn't lying. Talov had met us on our way here, smiling and handing me a bag of food with a wink. "To replace what didn't stick."

If the Grandfather Dwarf knew about my losing food down the drain, he truly *would* know where my feet were as long as I stuck with his Naulor partner.

Meanwhile, at the top of the climb, the sand-beard crouched on a sturdy platform built to one side of the ladder itself, taking his time to quietly release the shadowed mechanisms keeping the hatch sealed. Jael and I stared up at his hands since he used no additional light than what his brother held for him at floor level.

Interesting design.

"Light off."

The glowstone in his lantern dimmed. The turn and shift of the hatch above us was impressively quiet. Crickets chirped over any possible squeak of a hinge, and I spotted not a sliver of daylight.

We waited as he looked around outside.

Finally, he whispered down, "Clear. Climb slow."

Krithannia went first and Tamuril behind her, who carefully balanced her shoulders for her feathered companion. Jael motioned me ahead, and she brought up the rear while the second Dwarf observed in the dark.

"Gherudums been gatherin' anythin' useful in th' hills," our scout said to Krithannia when she got on level with his perch. "Goin' in an' out this way the most. Try not tah scare 'em or mash their mushrooms underfoot."

"We shall be careful," she answered, sounding amused, and proceeded to climb out of the ground.

My face scrunched in thought while I climbed the ladder. *Gherudum ... Hm. Oh! Yes, Welden.*

The blond Dwarf aiding Reprisal alongside Gavin and Isboern.

Sounds like there's more than one healer from that Clan here.

Once Tamuril was out, I paused when level with the sand-beard. "How do we get back in?"

He blinked in surprise before smiling with teeth. "The first one knows, but in case ya get separated ..."

I watched him reach up and touch his thick fingertip to an unassuming stone half-embedded near the hatch, soon realizing it *wasn't* made of rock. *Bone, maybe? Or pearl?*

"Tap like a woodtapper. We'll hear ye."

This matched how Mourn had brought me here the first time, though I'd been blindfolded. "Any secret rhythm?"

"Heh. Fast as ya can is good enough. We're expectin' ya before sunrise."

True enough.

"Noted. Thank you."

"Welcome, Elf."

Jael didn't pause to speak to the hatch-keeper, and soon enough we all stood outside, the way sealed behind us. This exit lay at a higher elevation than the previous entrance Mourn had found, the Kerut Hills thickly forested with plenty of tall grass framing the network of tree roots.

Tamuril had headed into the trees, weaving among them with a light step, while Pilla had taken off into the sky to stretch her wings. I caught up to Krithannia where she stood with her arms crossed, looking after her sister with concern. After surveying the area myself, I was sure no one was nearby.

"Will we stay together?" I asked.

She sighed. "Not if you don't wish it."

Krithannia glanced at Jael and me, and I looked at my Sister, who shrugged.

"You still eating," she said.

That was true. Having finished the bread before climbing, I was digging into the bag for a handful of nuts and cheese curds. Meanwhile, my Sister took a deep breath and a good stretch, noticing the lack of Moons as I did.

"They've already set," said the Naulor, as if reading our faces.

Jael sniffed the air through her nose. "Smell water."

"There is a remote lake nearby, mostly filled by rain and snow," Krithannia answered. "And a healthy stream moving through here. Where we get the water for the redoubt."

I smiled. *So we might've showered in heated snowmelt.*

My Sister and I turned our ears the same moment, listening for the stream to judge its proximity or direction. The Naulor waited until we'd made our own determinations.

"Falls," Jael murmured, confused, but pointing in the direction Tamuril had gone.

"Impressive," Krithannia said, and it sounded genuine. "The streams fall at a few points on their way down. Not large, though they create a few pools. We're near the top one."

"How long we have?" she asked next, squinting at the half-covered sky.

"More than an hour, less than two."

Jael stared at me. "You gonna talk more?"

I finished chewing a salty curd and swallowed. "Probably. At first, not the whole time."

She breathed out. "I go ahead? Follow stream. Keep watch."

I signed agreement. I could trust her in that.

And she doesn't want to stay and twist her fingers in boredom.

Like Tamuril, Jael moved off on her own into the trees, and Krithannia remained where she was, watching me. Patient but expectant.

My lips twisted with my first thought. "*Would* you kill him?"

Her folded arms grew tighter. "I shouldn't have said that."

"Not what I asked."

Krithannia touched her forehead, grimacing as if waiting through a brief stab of pain. She sighed. "No, I would not kill him. It wouldn't help. I would heal her if I could, undo his marks upon her. Perhaps …"

Her eyes lost focus for several beats, then she blinked and focused on me. Her throat flexed in a swallow. "Did you mean what you said?"

My turn to sigh. "You mean my 'oath?'"

"Yes. That is not something Tamuril takes lightly, knowing Willven his whole life."

I could believe it.

"I mean it," I said. "I have lost any appetite to see her weep. I feel sick to imagine watching. Like …"

Krithannia tilted her head. "Like what?"

The image was clear in my head. The fear of having left Auslan in solitary within the Cloister.

"Like I'm standing aside while a group of *caits* torment a single *bua* for their entertainment," I said, creeping too close for comfort. "We all know he is not a warrior or a mage for battle. Not enough anger or any bloodlust at all. He *cannot* fight them, but he could *heal* them if they just kept him safe."

The Naulor listened without interrupting, watching the nearest tufts of grass blow in the night wind. "Have you ... seen that before?"

"Yes," I growled, seeing Curgia trying to strangle him in his quarters. I cinched my rations shut rather than risk losing a second meal.

"So you ..." Krithannia began with caution, "would protect Tamuril instead? Not to 'see her weep.' It's the same impulse as this *bua*?"

I didn't consider long before affirming. "Yes. The path is clear but still looks strange to Jael."

Krithannia smiled like she wanted to chuckle. "I understand. But you are experienced in making such decisions."

"For whatever reason, yes."

Going back decades. *To Micraen lying passed out on the floor.*

"Admirable to see so clearly, and I am glad you said so."

The Guild Mistress contemplated a while longer as we enjoyed the breeze and scents of sleeping flowers.

Then, "How is Jael? Have you had much chance to talk?"

I shook my head. "No. When we got here, she said she felt ill after Mourn first fell into sleep, but this passed after she rested. Nothing since. She's ... just watching."

"What about your struggle with the black blade?"

The niggling discomfort increased. "She hasn't spoken of that, either. I don't know what she saw, if anything."

"How is *your* bond with it?"

"Not broken, I promise."

"I believe you. Has anything unusual happened?"

I shrugged. "Dreamed with some of the souls inside, no gatekeeper. They're still cooperative. I am the wielder."

"Interesting. Anything else?"

"Not for now."

I think I should talk to Gavin first ...

"Hm. Very well." The Guild Mistress motioned ahead. "Shall we walk after them? Perhaps we will catch up."

"Yeah, we probably should," I agreed, ready for a good stretch of my legs.

Each of us was competent walking through the woods at night without tripping over rocks or snapping branches. For a while, the peaceful outing felt strange but ... familiar at the same time.

The reason struck me in a memory.

Rausery training us for the Surface.

At all other times these last few months, I'd walked alone or with non-Elven males, often riding horses or boats over water's waves that made much more noise. Here I stood once again, in a quiet forest with females, each of us with good reason to avoid disturbing our surroundings.

Krithannia and I didn't stay shoulder-to-shoulder; our chosen path through the trees diverged and swayed though we remained in sight of each other. We wouldn't glimpse Jael easily unless she wanted to be seen.

Or Pilla gives away her position again.

How well could the falcon see at night without the Moons? I'd only seen this type of bird during the day, while the night-hunters on silent wings appeared much different in the shape of their swiveling heads.

Jael should be safe from Pilla's gaze this time, unless her Druid granted her some magical gift to overcome the limitation. The blonde Elf's passage had certainly proven difficult to track by any of my senses, and I wasn't convinced the skill had come from pure physical training.

No tracks, scent, or sound ...

The sound of a modest waterfall reached my ears as we drew closer, with a cool vapor drifting through the air. It made me thirsty and seemed like a place to go with purpose.

I made my way closer to the Guild Mistress and signed on impulse, *I want to drink there.*

Krithannia looked where I'd indicated and seemed to deduce but not actually read my message.

Water, I signed. *Water.*

Her eyebrows lifted, and she signed the Guild's affirmative. This gesture was close enough.

The climb grew steeper following the fast-flowing stream to the first pool formed by a fall. Approaching the crest, I smelled a small campfire on the air as a low voice murmured. Then something splashed in the water which was not the falls itself.

At once, I crouched low. *Shit.*

Krithannia signed, *Ear?*

I smirked and indeed tugged on my ear, making another motion like my voice leaving my mouth. *Male talk.*

She pursed her lips. Then she sniffed; she smelled the smoke, too.

Fire, I signed.

That one received a solid grasp as she returned it perfectly.

Water. Fire. Makes sense.

I will spy, I signed, pointing at my eye and above us.

Krithannia frowned and shook her head, touching a finger to her chest and pointing above us.

Both of us. Fine.

We climbed up and closer together, finding a spot to witness the pool without revealing ourselves. The male voice rumbled again, and I thought it must be a Dwarf.

Another Gherudum, perhaps.

Then another replied, revealing her location near the water while the male poked the small fire with a stick.

My body froze in place; my ears prickled.

Cannot be … I misheard.

Krithannia noticed and reached out to touch my wrist; I grabbed hers firmly instead and leaned in, my breath leaving in a Deepearth whisper competing with the breeze.

"I know them!"

My heart pounded thrice as the Naulor showed blatant interest. "Who?"

"Rithal." I stretched up far enough to glimpse the blazing red beard and ducked out of sight. "And Osgrid, the eve witch from Troshin Bend."

Her face brightened like the Big Sister Moon. "Wonderful. Go say hello and introduce me."

"What? But should they be here?"

At once, I recognized the look of the Guild Mistress. "Absolutely. Osgrid is Gherudum Clan. And Rithal was born in these hills."

I remembered the latter now, but was the eve witch linked to the redoubt's healers?

Makes sense.

"Does she know Welden?" I asked.

Krithannia shrugged. "Probably. Ask her."

Above us, a crow cawed brashly, drawing the Dwarves' attention, and I palmed my face.

"Who's there?" Rithal called, standing up.

"I forgot about her bird …" I muttered. *Again!*

The Naulor chuckled, nudging my shoulder. "Introduce me."

"As *what?*"

"As your Guild ally from Augran, of course. Tell her that Roewn introduced you."

Roewn.

The face Mourn wore when he last spoke with Osgrid.

But Rithal would have seen Mourn's *actual* face, the creature killing Castis and chasing off Mathias and Amelda, before "suggesting" that the Dwarf escape the warp rot forest himself.

Huh bua.

"Keep it simple and true," she added. "Like you saw in Yong-wen."

"Right," I whispered dryly, pushing myself off the ground and coming up slowly. "Rithal! No threat. It's me, Sirana!"

Quiet followed; not even the witch's crow spoke.

I climbed until my upper body could be seen above the grass.

"Putting down my hood," I warned, showing both hands before pinching the hem and exposing my hair and ears. "It's me, Sirana."

"*Cas du'ifrein,*" he muttered in disbelief. It sounded like a curse.

The redbeard didn't blink and couldn't seem to move at first as Osgrid hauled her dripping basket from the pool's edge and set it down by the fire.

"Sirana!" she called, beckoning. "Yer here! Come closer!"

Rithal broke through his stone face and leaned to whisper something to which Osgrid folded her arms beneath her breasts and gave him a patient look. He glanced down and never saw it.

"I have a friend," I responded. "From Augran."

"Sounds good," she replied without hesitation, tight black curls bouncing in a nod.

"Well," I added, "her and two others, but they're hiding somewhere in the hills."

Osgrid laughed, prompted by Rithal's befuddled expression as he looked around and at the top of the waterfall.

"Aye, so be it," said the eve witch. "Come along, then!"

Krithannia seemed quite pleased as she made herself visible next to me, her eagerness greater than made sense to me. Although she waited for me to lead the way and grant her that introduction, I began to think she wanted something specific from one of the Dwarves, whichever one had sparked the interest in her eyes.

In contrast, I wasn't sure which one I was more glad to see. Each one had helped me save my freedom when I hadn't been prepared to leave either my search for Gaelan or Gavin's body in Troshin Bend. Each had taught me critical things about the Surface and helped me get out of bad places while, like myself, had also effectively saved themselves when the time came.

As Krithannia and I approached the poolside, the redbeard's eyes grew rounder staring at the Naulor. The eve witch's pale, smiling face took on a touch of awe.

"*All* th' legends are comin' out now," Rithal muttered.

"These be interesting times," Osgrid agreed, glancing up as her crow flew in and landed on a nearby bush. She motioned toward a kettle hanging over the fire. "Some hot herb tonic?"

"Yes, please," said the Naulor, touching her chest. "I am Krithannia from Augran. Sirana's friend."

Chapter 23

Osgrid's tea was indeed hot, fragrant, and a strange mix of plants and their various parts, floral, bitter, and something oddly bright. We found rocks on which to sit, blowing on and sipping from wooden cups. Rithal had made one bench so far, barely large enough to squeeze him and his darkly dressed companion.

"Not enough time yet," he rumbled. "Just got settled here, out o' the way."

The two certainly were a far distance from the camps. The wind moved such that I could neither smell nor hear the camps from here. I had yet to lay eyes on them.

"Did you answer the call from Clan Baradum?" the Naulor asked.

"Ah, ye know 'bout that." Osgrid said firmly. "Aye, I answered. Rithal agreed tah help me with th' medicine makin' needed here."

Her partner shrugged with visible discomfort. "Seemed as good a time tah come home as any ..."

A pause, and Rithal's blue eyes met mine. He caught me thinking about what he had said in the shed, about the exchange as Gavin had pulled Jacob's soul from his body.

"Let your offering seal this prison behind his soul," said the Deathwalker. "Cut the threads with your grief, and the Bishops shall have no defense against their own

corruption."

"*Fer Brenna,*" Rithal said, pulling off a glove, touching the tears on his face. "*Gone this last century an' ten but still loved at night. Fer li'l Hancet and Pitrel, ne'er seein' their craft come tah their hands. Fer Nabrin, Shoana, Deacon, an' Quir. Bridges burned, sheep slaughtered, stone walls an' garrisons built on yer graves. M'sorry I couldn't do more, or sooner ...*"

"Is ... ah," the Dwarf said now, "what of Gavin?"

I blinked in surprise before my lips twisted with amusement. "Oh, he's still with us." I pointed at the ground. "Below your feet, providing aid in the redoubt."

Rithal's ruddy cheeks darkened a little. "Aid?"

"Yes. The Guild discovered he has skill as a chirurgeon."

A pause.

"Aye," he mused with comprehension, glancing at Krithannia rather than Osgrid. "I guess th' monk always was polishin' that scalpel after cuttin' meat at the campfires, wasn't he?"

I grinned. "Best kept precision kit on the Surface."

"*Heh!* Think that dulled Kurn's stupidity fer a bit, too."

We shared a mutual chuckle, though this reminded me of Innathi and her oblique reference to the two young Ma'ab nearby in a misty cave. One fake Hellhound and the real one, still within the dagger attached to my belt. I said nothing more and sipped my tea.

Krithannia, Osgrid, and Rithal each drew breath to speak.

"When did you — ?"

"How long — ?"

"Why are you — ?"

I stopped sipping, coughed, and laughed as Krithannia apologized.

"You, first," she said to Rithal.

I knew neither the reason nor precedent involved here, but the red-beard took the Naulor's offer and focused on me. "How did you and Gavin get here?"

"We came through the jump gate from Manalar," I said. "We joined the Guild to break the Bishops' hold on the sacred pool and escaped with the refugees."

"At th' expense of the Ma'ab takin' it over?" Osgrid asked frankly.

I welcomed the ready smile I had for her. "Almost. Not quite."

Krithannia touched my leg, and I stopped talking so she could add, "That remains to be seen, *Hekcai* Gherudum. We shall continue to aid the Guild to avoid this outcome."

Uh-oh.

What did that mean? Was she including Gavin and me? Or Jael?

The eve witch's paler blue eyes watched the Naulor steadily, twinkling in the dim firelight as smile creases showed at her eyes. "Lotsa rumors whirlin' about on th' northside 'bout the city they left behind. No idea what tah make o' what really happened inside th' Temple."

"Agreed," the Naulor responded smoothly. "One should always treat such shock and confusion with care."

"Sounded like some real magic fights happened."

"For certain, there were. The Templari are exemplary battle mages."

"Speakin' of, heard the Godblood got out," Rithal interjected. "Is it right? That's what folks at the base really wanna know."

Krithannia bowed her head. "Captain Isboern made it out, yes."

"I believe ya, but ... so you know, some ain't leavin' yet. They wanna *see* 'im."

"I believe the Guild is aware but I shall pass it on in case they don't."

The redbeard looked between us. "Yer both workin' with the Guild of Augran?"

"For now, yes."

"Ye have stakes," Osgrid stated, finishing her cup with a mild smile.

Krithannia answered with one of her own. "I believe we all do when a war involving this many begins. If pain is not felt at once, it shall be soon enough."

"Aye. True." A brief pause. "Speakin' o' feeling somethin' at once ..."

"Yes?"

"A worrying number o' mages got their spells off since yesterday. Includin' mine." Osgrid waved her hand. "Why I'm out here, relearnin' some o' it from th' waters."

"Ah." Krithannia shared a look with me. "Yes. That was the moment the Bishops lost control of the sacred pool. A Ley surge."

"Ah! Gotcha. Hm, felt those before."

The Naulor tilted her head. "Oh? Have you?"

"Aye. More common than ye think 'round the Archipelago."

I failed to keep the shock from my face, and Osgrid noticed, grinning at me. "Heard something interestin' 'bout my home, Sirana?"

"Your home," I echoed, my expression fixed. "Well, I ... sailed through there. From, uhm ..." *What was it called?* "The weeks port?"

Osgrid laughed aloud. "Oh, aye! Port Fortnight."

"That's it."

"Ye sailed from there tah Augran?"

"I did! Um, a Guildsman called Roewn got us on board."

She recognized him. "Roewn! Well! Glad he was hangin' around tah findja, if he was gonna help one o' us."

Rithal was instantly suspicious. "Guildsman helped ya?"

I nodded. "After the warp rot was dealt with, we were taken to meet him."

"Ya were. By someone else, ya?"

"Uh, yes. We both saw him."

He narrowed his eyes further. "Can I ask *what* that hunter was that found us?"

Keep it simple and true.

I exhaled. "Another legend with a stake in things, tracking the Ma'ab. He used powerful magic and wasn't going to let the warp rot spread. We were in his way ... at first."

"Then?"

I smiled. "Then he read Gavin's aura. Lucky me, as the non-mage."

Rithal and Osgrid looked at my belt at the same moment.

Oops.

"Might not be a mage," Osgrid said, "but ye have th' equivalent in yer possession."

I shook my head. "But it's not too long before the cost is too high."

"She knows the danger," Krithannia interjected, her tone and expression pleasant, "and has handled it wisely while I've worked with her. She has a strong will."

"That she does," Rithal agreed with a rare smile.

"Good tah hear," said the eve witch as if tucking that subject away for later. "I'm curious. Why was this other 'legend' hunting the Ma'ab who came to Troshin Bend?"

I would enjoy answering that one. "The two murdered a Ma'ab noble woman. Her family tried to track them, but the Guild interfered when Kurn and Castis passed through Augran." I shrugged. "The family was smart and offered the job to the Guild instead. And, somehow, they found *him*."

"Whew," Rithal exhaled, shaking his head. "Glad he wasn't after any o' us."

I bit my inner cheek.

"An' then he introduced ye tah Roewn?" Osgrid guessed.

"He did. Gavin and I needed to reach Manalar. He suggested we talk to Roewn, first." I turned my head northward as if I could see the refugee camps. "From the Deathwalker's view, that worked exceedingly well."

"I bet," rumbled the redbeard with a morbid laugh.

Osgrid kept her eyes on me. "An' ye, Sirana? Didja find what ye sought at Manalar?"

I straightened. "I did."

"Now can ye say what 'twas?"

I could but looked around the trees first with the Dwarves following my lead. Frowning, I called, "Jael? Will you come out?"

She sighed behind Rithal, near the falls. He cursed again and stood up, turning around.

"Friend!" she said grouchily from behind a tree, waving her hand vaguely in my direction before leaning out. "Sirana friend."

She's been listening to us a long time.

"'Nother one?" Rithal uttered.

"She was in the Manalari dungeon," I said, looking at Osgrid. "I went to get her out."

Jael crunched branches louder than necessary as she stalked the long way around Rithal and closer to me, choosing another tree to lean against. She kept her hood up so they couldn't see her eyes.

"Tea?" Osgrid offered.

"We don' have a fifth cup," Rithal pointed out, less generous toward the Davrin who'd been crouched behind him.

"I can wash mine."

"No," Jael said, holding up her freshly filled waterskin, still dripping, and taking a deep swig. "Cold melt. Like better."

Watching their expressions to realize she must have filled it behind them and while I wasn't looking, I grinned so hard it seemed fixed to my face. *You little slit. Well done.*

"'Nother Red Sister?" Rithal asked at last.

"She is."

"Why was she at Manalar?"

Jael and I both shook our heads. Though we *could* answer that now, we weren't going to.

"Interestin' times," he muttered.

Osgrid reached over to squeeze his hand, smiling in agreement. "Hm. So, tha's three. An' the last?"

We sat quietly as if wondering if she would appear.

"Not here," Jael said with confidence, her arms folded, one boot heel up and braced against the bark.

Krithannia looked to agree; worry passed over her face.

"She has Pilla," I murmured.

With thoughtful sadness, the elder sister replied, "I know."

Her mood shift and expression seemed strange at first. She had allowed Tamuril to leave and hadn't seemed concerned until this moment. But then she asked the eve witch a question.

"Might you be considered a mage-healer among your own, Osgrid?"

The Dwarf's dark eyebrows lifted; blue eyes bright in firelight. "Aye, through mentorship more'n a strong affinity."

"But you learned magic through nature upon the stormy isles? The Archipelago?"

Stormy isles? Appropriate name.

"Mm. Aye. May I ask why yer askin'?"

The Naulor smiled softly. "Have you ever aided to break a harmful spell placed by another mage, *Hekcai*?"

Well. Now I knew which Dwarven presence had enticed Krithannia at the start. Good to know some webs were the same everywhere, even on the Surface.

Osgrid seemed wisely cautious in forming her answer, first glancing at me. A nod from me seemed a reasonable response; I knew where the Naulor was going with this.

"Wouldja call it a 'curse?' " asked the eve witch.

"Yes," Krithannia answered at once. "Precisely."

Osgrid rubbed her thumbs around the smooth outside of her empty cup, peering down into it for a few moments. Finally, she nodded. "Aye, I might've done. Curses be a personal sort, though. Not like makin' an antidote or numbing agent."

Krithannia seemed to hold her breath a moment. "What about ritual magic?"

Rithal frowned as Osgrid subtly tensed.

"Rituals tend tah scare a lotta Humans 'less they're theirs," he said with impeccable accuracy.

"While Dwarves have seen great variety without blinking," I agreed with a nod. "Some in the strangest of places, like a shed behind an inn."

All but Jael understood that reference.

"Point taken," Osgrid replied, smirking.

"The curse was placed by ritual magic," Krithannia explained, "and can only be undone the same way. In any case, she isn't Human."

"Hm. But she's willing?"

"I do not know yet. I wanted to speak with you privately on the matter, at a time comfortable for you."

Osgrid looked at me. I didn't know what she might have seen in my expression, but she lowered her chin firmly with a slight smile. "Awright. Dawn be as comfortable as dusk fer an eve witch."

Dawn?

Glancing above Rithal's head and the short waterfall to the treetops, I confirmed the sky grew lighter.

"*Shit*," Jael said in Davrin.

Chuckling, Krithannia turned to us. "Would you be willing to return without me?"

"Dwarf guards expect four," my Sister stated.

"*Oltere* Baradum knows I shall be late."

Rithal jerked in surprise. "*Oltere?*"

"Yes." The Naulor smiled pleasantly. "Why the shock? Have you met him?"

Another bite to my sore inner cheek. As if Krithannia didn't know the answer to that question. She must have certainly expected that response.

"Uhm," the redbeard hesitated. "Aye. I know 'im. Didn't know he'd come this far tah oversee things himself."

"Interesting times."

"Aye, been so a while fer me."

"Would you like to speak with him while you have the opportunity?"

Rithal stared into the fire then shrugged. "I'll think about it. Thanks."

Now I was staring. This unseen connection had always been there, from the first time we'd spoken at the Ley Tower, when he'd told me he knew old stories about Elves.

Just no way to see it until now.

For the first time, I weighed the possibility that, despite his shorter lifespan, Talov's contacts outnumbered Mourn's and Krithannia's by far as a "Grandfather" out in the open.

Purple sky gave way quickly to pink and blue, and Jael straightened up off her tree. "We go inside?"

I confirmed by handing Krithannia my empty cup and gain my feet. "We'll be with Gavin," I told her but with a side smile at Rithal.

The Guild Mistress replied. "Thank you."

For introducing you to the eve witch, no doubt.

I bowed my head, thanked them for the tea, and bid them well.

Jael hustled to the hatch as if to outrun the day, and I had to catch up to her. Taking on the decline, placing my feet with care, I thought over the reason we were leaving Krithannia alone.

Can they help Tamuril?

Would removing the marks lift the shame? Not on its own, I didn't think, but maybe in some way this was like my surviving Jilrina.

It might give her a place to start.

The hatch-watchers allowed us in and seemed to have gotten the message to wait longer for the pale ones.

Jael had been paying attention to the layout of the redoubt, showing few hesitations retracing our steps. Although we found the area Gavin had been working in, he was gone from Reprisal's room.

Most of the Guildsmen had fallen to sleep, including Deshi, and Welden wasn't visible. His replacement saw us poking our heads in, swiftly covered her surprise, and put a finger to her lips, dark blond eyebrows drawn down in stubborn slopes.

We quietly closed the door.

Back to his room? Jael signed.

If we can find it, I replied, trying to "see" the pathway he'd taken us to retrieve his kit before attending to the Greylands barbs. I hadn't been paying as much attention as I should have.

Ask or explore?

Reasonable to think many awake knew where the Deathwalker resided, given how much help would have been needed moving the unconscious and injured in and out of his quarters.

Explore until we can ask.

I took one wrong hall, apparently unable to rely on the heaviest scents of blood, which made things harder because the passages had become quieter since we left. The space was also an odd mix of square intersections like a Surface city and curving ramps like the Cloister. I'd had as much trouble finding the removed corner of rooms where the Templari had been settled.

While I was turned around, I had time to wonder where the Dwarves had placed Mourn. Could I reach out to either ally with my thoughts, as I had Isboern? At once, I shook my head. Gavin disliked the intrusion and Mourn had gone "deep" according to Graul and might not recognize his closest friends.

Out of reach, then.

And concerning for whenever he awoke. I couldn't imagine what we'd be doing next to move in the direction of the Ley Tower. At least the geas wasn't bothering me while Mourn slept; magically enforced impatience was the last thing I needed in this place.

Finally, a blonde, female Dwarf with tight curls like Osgrid padded softly toward us. I scraped my boot on the stone and waved to get her attention. She stopped, her grip on the laundry basket tightening.

"We're lost," I said, as Jael glanced at me like I should at least try to save face. "Seeking the Deathwalker?"

She blinked, her eyes an interesting mix of brown and green, then motioned us to follow her down the passage the way she'd come. Two curves and a left turn later, she swept her broad hand down to the right hall. By that point, we'd been following aging blood stains since the first curve.

"I remember," Jael said, nodding.

So did I. This hall came to an abrupt stop yet wasn't as far from the gate room as the Templars' rooms were. Gavin quartered somewhere central in the redoubt, not its fringe.

"Thank you," I said.

The Dwarf nodded and went her way without speaking, which made me wonder if she was related to those assigned here permanently. Perhaps she was just tired.

At last, I knocked on Gavin's door, turning my ear to it. Utter silence inside; he could be in a trance for all I knew, and the quiet in the hall seemed too thick to be wise breaking it. I tried a mental push.

~Gavin? It's Sirana.~

The legs of a chair dragged on the floor. Jael tensed.

Gavin opened the door only a crack, as he had in the Ley Tower and Brom's Inn, though the single eye peering down at me had starkly changed in that time. He said nothing, his body hidden behind the door, and my Sister shifted in discomfort.

"May we stay in here a while?" I whispered. "Until Krithannia finds us. We weren't given a room after she locked hers to find you."

"Curious oversight," he remarked.

"She warned us the first days would be disruptive."

"Indeed."

The death mage stepped back, opening the door wide enough to let us through one at a time, closing it behind Jael. He seemed more comfortable placing a ward than he had been in the past.

I stopped to stare at him, and Jael bumped into me.

He wasn't wearing his robe or boots, only the braies covering his pelvis and thighs. I had no thought to speak at first, and Jael's eyes got rounder.

"I was attempting to document the changes," he muttered, some of his mortal tension touching his face from the few times he'd needed to show any skin beyond his face and hands. "While you're here, perhaps you can assist."

Changes. Quite the understatement.

"The black spikes are gone," I said.

"Yes, I've noticed."

Gavin returned to his writing desk, wisely situated in the corner most obscured by an inward-swinging door. His chair also faced the entrance with his back to a solid stone wall. In the opposite corner was the water corner and wash sink.

"I need better descriptions of details I can't observe directly," he said, moving his seat out from between the desk and the wall. He placed it at one end, presumably for an accessible view of his back. "Your command of Trade is more than sufficient for the task."

Heh.

Jael glanced at me, annoyed but noting my smile.

"I can study my front from the chest down, my limbs, hands, and feet," Gavin said, lifting his second favorite precision tool and dipping the tip in his ink bottle. "There is no mirrored surface. I need descriptions of my head and my back."

"Not his ass?" Jael murmured in Davrin.

I elbowed her, arching an eyebrow. *"He has strict boundaries with his body, for reasons like you, and we are in his room."*

She sighed through her nose. *"Sorry. You step lightly."*

"Good ground gives way at unfamiliar moments up here."

"Yes, quite the shit."

"Some remarks I should note?" Gavin asked, staring without a living twitch. I could tell Jael suppressed a shiver.

"Sister talk," she said. "Learning."

"Hm. A habit best used daily."

Her mouth twisted. "I stay back and quiet."

"Very well."

His gaze shifted to me. Abruptly, I realized he was waiting.

Alright, then.

Jael folded her arms to wait as I approached Gavin's desk. Taking a breath and letting it out slowly, I studied the details of my death scholar several times over. Where to begin?

"Well, your face is still familiar to me, as are your eyes from when you sat up in the shed. The pale blue on black."

"Good to confirm," he said, beginning to write.

"Your hair is the same length and black to the root. Seems to have ... well, a sheen?"

"Sheen? Like oil?"

"No, not oil. You don't seem to sweat anymore. Like glass or a polished stone. But tangled in places."

He grunted, making notes. I waited until the scritching paused.

"Your ears are slightly smaller and darker around the edges," I noted.

"Darker? What shade?"

"Bluish-grey. Oh, and you knew your teeth were black, correct?"

"Correct. Same as my fingernails and toenails. Why are the ears smaller?"

"Oh ... shriveled?"

He wrote that in his book.

"Your skin is white out of the Sun, stretched across the bone, doesn't have much padding. Your … nape is … um."

Gavin paused as my eyes trailed down. He turned his neck, and it popped.

"So, your entire spine," I began, "is … showing? Or maybe armored? It doesn't look like bone, though it's bumpy. More like black glass, same as the spikes earlier."

"Interesting. Would you confirm the texture?"

My eyes widened. *He's … asking me to touch him?*

He noted my hesitation. "Too distasteful?"

"Uh, no … nervous."

"Why?"

I blew out quietly through my lips. "You said at Manalar … your bones acted like a soul trap. Like the Malok hunters."

"Ah," he said with a nod, as if that explained everything. "You are safe to touch it, Sirana Although I *am* laced with pneuma flint, I bear conscious control of what essences I draw in, unlike those traps. As an added note, Elven essence is far more resistant to this pull than Human."

"Really?" I asked, frowning. "How do you know?"

"Observation during the battle. The Malok tried several times to draw on Krithannia from a distance. She barely noticed. Then you, Jael, and Mourn fought them directly, and even with added urgency, none of their traps worked on you. That could be different if you were to travel the Greylands but here, on your home, pneuma flint is ineffective against you."

" … Wow." I tugged off one glove. "So, you want me to touch you."

"Please."

I still felt a tremor of nerves. *Ridiculous.*

Drawing a step closer, I reached out, tracing my fingers lightly along the shiny, uneven bend of his spine. "Can you feel that?"

He didn't answer immediately, his face drawing down in concentration like he wasn't sure. "Hm …"

"It is hard and smooth," I confirmed rather than await a detailed answer. "But not like glass, flint, or some rougher rock."

"And not porous enough to be bone," Gavin muttered, writing to catch up on the details. "Like a beetle, perhaps?"

How well that matched. "Yes. That's a good description."

A nod. More writing.

"And you noticed similar lines like a black beetle on the undersides of your ribs?" I asked.

"I did. Do they continue?"

"They do."

"Each one? Visibly connecting to my spine?"

"Only the lower ones. Your shoulder blades seem to push higher ones under your skin, and they do not resurface."

"Hm." He wrote that down. "What else?"

"Well ..." I looked over both shoulders to be sure, all the way to his waist. "I can't see where the spikes once jutted through your skin. They left no holes or marks."

He nodded; something he'd expected.

"And ... the sunburst brand is gone."

"What?"

His surprise was genuine.

"The brand is gone," I repeated. "As if it never was. Same with the lash marks borne from the monastery. You have no scars at all."

His quill didn't move at first. Had my choice of words annoyed him? Accurate in a physical sense, but perhaps presumptive.

Gavin reached up to touch his opposite shoulder as far as he could. His fingertips searched around as if they hadn't explored where the brand had been for a long time. Pushing and brushing along his dry skin confirmed for me that the rough, silvery tissue hadn't simply faded with his paler skin to be hard to see.

They were just gone.

Had Gavin still been a young, living man, he might have exhaled in his quiet astonishment or taken a few breaths as his heart beat in his chest. As he was, the room was eerily quiet until his quill started scratching his book.

"Anything else?" he asked.

"Those are all the changes I see."

Behind me, Jael shifted her feet and took a breath; I looked.

"I ... see," she began. "Something."

Gavin turned his head to peer at my Sister with narrowed eyes. "Speak it, if you will."

"Blue glow in beetle back," she explained, "when Sirana said no burst or lash mark. Glow appear, brighten, then gone when you start write."

The Deathwalker frowned until he appeared angry.

"What?" she said, crossed arms tightening. "I see!"

"Indeed. Sirana? You saw no such glow?"

He didn't *sound* angry.

I shook my head. "No."

"Interesting." He recorded that, his expression easing. "Anything else?"

"No," Jael said.

"Very well. I thank you both for the assistance."

I stepped away as Gavin rose from his chair to retrieve the torn, stained robe from a hook on the wall. We watched him don that and his belt before pulling out his seat to sit and replace his stockings and boots, both of which were in better shape.

The Deathwalker looked at me when he'd finished, focusing on my middle in a familiar way for several long moments, then lifted his gaze. I read a subtle question.

"She knows," I said, motioning behind me.

"Hm. In that case, the life aura has grown brighter since the first jump gate to Manalar. I see a potent white in the middle, and a new purple shade visible in the corona."

I swallowed. "And does that mean anything in your knowledge?"

"It does not. Merely an observation."

"Alright. Have you communed with your Lady as you wished to yet?" I asked.

"Not yet."

"Will that be delayed while we're here?"

"Not necessarily. I may leave myself open to her but do not choose the time."

"Ah."

"You have your pendant?"

"Of course."

"Then feel free to hang your belts on the wall and use the towels for padding if you wish to lie down. Even sleep. I shall be writing for some time."

"Right."

One look at Jael, and I knew she was going to be bored.

Chalk game? I suggested in sign.

She smirked and shrugged to acquiesce.

We had some time to wade through somehow.

CHAPTER 24

I ATE THE REST OF THE PORTABLE MIX TALOV HAD GIVEN ME WHILE WE DREW small marks on the wall. I offered some to Jael, and she reluctantly accepted the snack. Despite our quiet shuffling and hand sign, Gavin gradually seemed to forget we were here; he never turned his head or stopped writing.

At one point, Jael signed wryly, *So, no sex here, either.*

I considered it. *If he goes into a trance, we could try.*

She made a face. *Ew. No. You fingered me while we were squeezed in-between Human bones. That's enough.*

That was true.

The Human burial pit was the only safe place we could take you, I signed, apologetic. *Not the most alluring place to welcome you, but I'm grateful you *did* come back … *

She flipped her hand, her face darkening in a flush. *Oh, I wasn't complaining. Glad to wake up after … all that shit with the Bishops.*

Shying away from specific wounds. Wasn't that familiar?

The next chalk mark was hers, but she stared at the wall for quite some time.

Something else? I prodded.

Her face shifted toward an odd, unguarded expression I'd never seen before she covered it up. She shook her head. ★Not important. Maybe thinking pain will start again if that half-blood doesn't wake up to teach me something.★

That sounded fairly important.

★Has it hurt since you last woke?★ I asked. ★You said you felt sick before.★

Jael turned the splinted chalk over in her fingers, the leather wrap keeping pale dust off her black gloves. She shrugged. ★I don't know. Like him,★ she motioned toward the Deathwalker, ★my body isn't the same since Manalar, but I can't ask you what it looks like. At least when you touch it, that's familiar.★

I tilted my head. ★Familiar. Not the same?★

Her shoulders slumped. ★No. But I don't know if that's me or you.★ She frowned. ★Or something linked with *him*.★

The slant of her hand on that last gesture reminded me of when she'd asked if *he* was the sire, forcing me into a bargain like that.

A Bargain baby … heh, no.

Given that Mourn *was* one, conceived and traded by the Deepearth Dragon, and killed his Mother in the process, I doubted he would ever want to make another.

Dragging focus to my Sister, I signed, ★You seemed to enjoy how he taught you to fight in the battle.★

★Yeah.★ Jael smirked. ★Easy to ignore pain and confusing things. Have to trust you everywhere else, even here, since you seem to know all these Surfacers.★

A dart hitting center target.

★Do you have any new questions for me?★ I offered. ★I can try to answer them.★

★I don't know,★ she said again, making her chalk mark like a cat swiping a bug and passing the piece to me. ★Other than seeing things I didn't before, I don't feel like a mage but a conduit for someone stronger.★

Like Gaelan or Reishel.

Or like me.

I grimaced. ★You might not feel like one for turns. You need to survive the change, first. Then practice. I changed four turns ago in the tunnels, yet I haven't felt like a psion until ... well ... ★

Jael narrowed her eyes with a sly smile. ★Until you met a tutor who needed your cooperation more than he needed to be in control.★

★Right. I think we are in similar places.★

Her lips thinned. ★I don't think we are.★

I arched one brow. ★Does Mourn need to be in control?★

She snorted audibly. ★Did you miss it? You made a bargain exploiting that need, Sister.★

Had I? I squinted in thought, shaking my head. ★You don't know how difficult it was to come to an agreement with him.★

★Proves what I'm saying.★

★No, it doesn't. I didn't exploit him, he won't tolerate it.★

★See? Needs control.★

For rutting's sake.

My stomach squeezed from tension as I tried to hold on to what had felt like some of the most honest negotiations in my short life. If anything, the Valsharess's compulsion exploited *me* in preventing me from walking away or telling the Dragonchild exactly how he was involved.

I wasn't in control on either side, whether I wanted it or not. I could only bend as each allowed me to.

I touched my fingertips to my forehead, forgetting the chalk in my hand. ★You and he stepped outside the gate room and talked. You came back, borrowing his weapons, and said you would obey us if he taught you magic. Did you make a bargain with him?★

★No, and I am glad,★ she replied, slightly pleased but more annoyed. ★Your bargain spilled over onto *me*. He said if I stayed, his agreement to protect you included defending you *from* me as an untrained mage. So, in his 'best interests' to teach me.★

That sounded like him. In fact, he'd said precisely that before I "chose" Jael's magical affinity for her in the crypt to heal her aura.

They warned me, Mourn and Krithannia ...

And Jael still didn't know that's why it had to be the Dragon's son to teach her.

Shit.

Are you saying you don't want to learn from him because of my bargain? I asked. *Or his stating a strict duty for its duration? It won't be much longer.*

I think.

She shrugged; her face seemed too cool. *I'll take what I can get to survive the change, like you did. But we will make no bargain. I don't trust him.*

I breathed in slowly. *Why not?*

It's too convenient he was there. It's suspicious.

How so? I don't understand.

How can you not?! Her face fell into a scowl as she looked at the marks on the wall. *Remember what I told you about the gold eyes? The presence who spoke to me about a 'bargain' fulfilled and I was fucked on that account?*

Oh, right.

I remember now.

Your bodyguard knows whoever that was! Her gestures were pointed and strong. *He spoke like that other Dragon to the Godblood! But he told me nothing when I agreed to stay and learn.*

Alright, that part was worrying. We hadn't had time to talk, not myself with Mourn nor anything involving Jael.

Did you ask him about this? I signed curiously. *Specifically.*

No, she signed irritably. *He told me I had to cooperate if I wanted to stay. And I … he did take some of the pain away, doing something with his aura, proving he could help, so I … we didn't have much time. I didn't ask about it, but I also didn't bargain like you did.*

I sighed. *Mourn gives little for free. He must trust first, and then I must ask for what I need. The habit to keep connections hidden from others is deeply woven in him, which is no different from us in Sivaraus, right?*

She sneered slightly. *I suppose.* Then she arched one eyebrow, looking at me askance. *So, he trusts you?*

The past weeks of constant engagement and feelings of mutual exposure passed behind my eyes. I signed with clear certainty: *Yes, he does. Or I think the way we fought the Malok in the streets wouldn't have worked.*

She remembered that; the discomfort and uncertainty was stark for an instant. Her face warmed, though her expression smoothed out, and she fell still for a time. Then, *If you were to ask who that was in the crypt, or about anything he knew about a bargain that changed me like this, would he tell you?*

Probably. If I approached him like a discussion and not a demand.

Jael's face twisted. *The big male doesn't like females making demands of him, does he?*

I smirked, shrugging. *Not Davrin females, at least. Although he has fought for a Davrin commander before, respected her. It's acting like a Noble Matron over him that gets his spines up.* I winked at her. *Like you insulting that Fifth House healer on the battlefield.*

Such a public act of defiant disrespect had resulted in both the Sathoet and the Sisterhood coming after the youngest Aurenthin Daughter. I could see my point hit when she made a face.

Fine. Understood. She fidgeted with her glove, choosing her next sign. *In that case, which House was he? I don't see something like him born from a commoner.*

I leaned forward so she'd meet my eyes. *He was once of House Dar'Prohn.*

Jael frowned. *Never heard of it.*

I know. But ... Sivaraus did once have one House named Ja'Prohn. Wager they're related.

She was intrigued. *How do you know that?*

My smile grew tighter. *It's Shyntre's House. Or at least his sire, Headmaster Phaelous.*

What?!

*Yeah. I recalled that recently."

From where?

During the Sisterhood trial, after we'd executed Kerse.

She looked wary.

★Wilsira claimed 'Ja'Prohn and Varessa D'Shea' were the most 'potent pairing' in centuries, because we are 'losing' mage strength somehow.★ I shrugged. ★I know Phaelous and Elder D'Shea made Shyntre, and also this weakening in mages is why the Consorts were made. My Matron opted to try for them at Court, to revive a mage line at House Thalluen. That's what *all* the upper Houses competed for.★

Jael stared at me, unblinking. ★But we never had any mage line at House Aurenthin. Why am I suddenly … like *this* after surviving the geas?★

I offered a look of sympathy. ★I don't know. But if it is related to an older bargain with Mourn's sire, then … maybe we can negotiate a question or two to ask him. Or perhaps your Matron would know something?"

The latter idea made Jael lean back; I couldn't tell if she was surprised or wary.

★In any case,★ I continued, ★I wager that's why Phaelous and Shyntre are kept so close to the Valsharess. They cannot join another House if the rest of their house escaped to Vuthra'tern and became Dar'Prohn.★

Which certainly had potent magic, based on the memory of Mourn's first squad taking on Ornilleth by themselves. I imagined something similar or related with the vanished House D'Shea, otherwise it made no sense for my Elder to hold that name as the last one.

Truly, no wonder to me that the Queen's geas commanded me to bring home *any* half-blood sons I encountered. I'd thought for months She wanted Vesram, who was free after enslavement with the Ma'ab for a hundred years and supposedly headed toward the Ley Tower.

I couldn't see before how anything else would be relevant, yet She *must* also know about House Dar'Prohn in whatever form.

The web grows tighter than I could ever see before.

I glanced at Soul Drinker hanging on the wall, a weapon containing enough of the past to destroy that same pattern in a blink.

Hoo bua.

Our conversation wound down, not altogether satisfying for my Sister. Jael had too many concerns with too few answers for which she should be wary, but she at least stopped laying *all* of them at Mourn's feet as she contemplated what extra insights I could provide.

When she suddenly grew tired and laid down on the stone, I got up to retrieve the clean pile of towels to make a pallet for us to share.

I paused on my way back, realizing Gavin had stopped writing. His body was in the same position, he wasn't moving. His eyes were open but had gone void black.

Hopefully Jael wouldn't turn over and look too closely.

We cuddled together for warmth, fully dressed, with layers of towel below us and our cloaks laid over. I felt for my saphgar pendant beneath my shirt and checked the hooks on the wall for the third time, making sure our belts were *well* out of reach of both of us.

My spider guardians were nearby, but I didn't want them to attack anyone in this room who approached the dagger. I'd told them to wake me but couldn't be sure it would work. I wished I had a trunk to lock the dagger inside, so I could be sure I wouldn't lose my Sister after too many close swipes.

Part of me thought I shouldn't Reverie at all until Gavin came out of his trance, but I was having trouble keeping my eyes open after Jael fell to sleep. I didn't know if a full day had passed, yet so much had happened since I'd last seen Innathi, *not* including that eight-legged battle on a mountainside.

Sigh. Mourn, when will you wake? I could relax with an extra guardian while I sleep ...

Despite my thoughts and worries, my eyes slid shut and my body stopped listening, falling quiet for a time beside my new mageborn Sister.

I stood upon a border at dawn, somewhere flat with a cold wind driving down from the North. Beneath my red leather boots was a hard, yellowish sand with dry, rustling grasses pushing through in coarse patches. My cloak flapped around my legs, the corners snapping the air.

To the West the sky was dark. The long slopes and hills held firm by large stones and stubborn, scraggly plants. To the East, the Sun approached from behind endless red dunes. Not far from me was a rippling, shallow river.

Water.

On the edge of the Red Desert.

There, something splashed as if in mid-struggle: grunts and hissing, in pain or in threat, followed a long, predatory growl.

Uh-oh.

If I was awake, I'd be headed in the other direction.

If I was awake ...

Through all the other dreams in which I'd been aware while on the Surface, especially the last one where I found my buas in need of help, when had running away from the noise or the figure ever happened?

Never. Eventually, I'd always walked toward it.

Perhaps something or someone drew me to what I must witness or where I should stand. I turned North and West to answer, stepping lightly toward the river bank and the loudest noise in this Reverie. The cold wind pushed back and smelled strange, a foreign scent to the Desert.

But not ... unfamiliar.

I breathed in slowly, trying to place it. The closest match which came to mind was the tallest mountain Rausery had led us to in our training. It had been cold that day, threatening us with tiny flakes of snow before the skies decided to rain instead.

Cold and miserable.

Meanwhile, broken rows of thirsty trees and scrub clung as close as they could to the river's edge. Whatever drew me lay just on the other side. I slipped behind a trunk when another round of snarls masked my footfalls, waiting for the thrashing to follow before peeking out. Several moments passed before I could be sure of what I saw.

A ... winged drake?

If this was a shadow drake, the body was massive compared to Graul, easily the size of Nightmare and not including the wings or tail. Muscles in its back flinched as if reacting to stabs of pain, causing all its limbs to twitch and quiver.

The dark body lay there huffing from what seemed like exhaustion. The damp sand had been scarred by the raking claws and a lashing tail over a fair amount of time. I couldn't tell at once what fight or injury had tired it out.

Finally, it opened its eyes, and I froze.

Gold ...

Not pure gold. Something darker obscured that distinct sheen at this distance, but the shimmer must be in response to the rising Sun. The muzzle was long and feral, the head earless and hairless, yet the shapes of the eyes, brow, and horns were familiar.

With a surge of recognition, I studied the scales again, spotting the subtle, purple sheen within the onyx black in that better light. The armor covered his *entire* body this time, unlike when he was awake. Those wings were entirely new, but ...

It is him. It must be.

With a swallow, I stayed where I was, heart pounding as I prepared to gain his attention the same way I had Gavin.

~Morixxyleth?~

He jolted alert, talons digging deep, four legs preparing to launch toward me, wings spreading wide.

He eyes on me, purple mixed with gold.

And distant.

Like when we'd been trapped atop Mount Sonai, when he'd summoned the magic to jump port us down into the river at the bottom. His eyes had lost the metallic gold and looked like the stars at night.

~Morixxyleth!~ I shouted before he could sprint. *~It's Sirana!~*

He kept his stance, lavender tongue extending to taste the air, relentlessly focused on my location. His tail moved hypnotically.

~Sirana,~ I repeated stubbornly, sensing my opportunity draining away. *~Sirana. You know me! Kiabil! Companion!~*

*Kiabil ... *

His tail stilled behind him, wings folding down as the muscles in his haunches relaxed. His tongue extended again, curious to confirm, but I stood downwind from him in this chill.

Trelkilt, he said.

If he'd been speaking aloud, I wouldn't have understood him. However, I saw glimpse of me approaching him enter his thoughts. I could see it.

Closer.

He wanted me to come closer.

What was the Draconic word for "bargain?" Did I need to remind him he couldn't hurt me? Because this *wasn't* Mourn watching me so intently; this wasn't the hybrid bua raised by the Davrin.

Trelkilt, Kiabil.

Oof ...

Slowly, I stepped out of the screen of vegetation, watching his feet for the first hint of an incoming pounce. Nothing like that appeared, and his tail further relaxed. *So far, so good.*

Morixxyleth didn't rise or move, keeping his belly to the ground in a four-legged form even less Elven than I'd seen before. Once I was close enough that he could have reached out and struck me, he dipped his head once, tongue flicking out and his eyes drooping as the earlier sense of threat drained away.

Now he could smell me and seemed to relish it.

Stharl mrith've, he whispered, showing me kneeling to sit by his head.

The soft sense of much-needed rest encouraged me to get comfortable on my backside, legs crossed, while the To'vah blood shifted closer, Stretching out his neck, he settled his jaw across both my thighs.

"Whoa," I muttered. He was larger than a riding horse.

Morixxyleth looked up at me, gold coming into his gaze as I watched. He took a deep, deep breath and released it slowly. At the same time, my belly heated up; he tilted his head to rest his cheek against it, closing his eyes.

I touched his scales for a while, exploring the texture; he rumbled quietly as if to encourage it. Questions appeared, one at a time, until I finally had to pick one.

~*Were you in pain earlier?*~

Jennu loerchik, he agreed, his tail slithering to one side, smoothing over some of the rake marks in the sand.

Great pain.

At last, I stood close enough to see how disrupted the patterns of scales were between his shoulder blades. He had hard, larger ones alongside small, tender ones. The flesh underneath seemed swollen, hot, and I found streaks of red reminding me of blood.

~*You grew these wings recently?*~

Axun, he thought with a tired sigh. He had yet to part his lips to speak or show me his teeth.

I'd heard that response before, between him and Graul. It felt like a simple affirmative.

~*Do you need them to reach somewhere? Like when you shift to run or swim?*~

One eye cracked open, colors glinting like a coin flipped into an evening sky. *Thric.*

A negative? What did he mean? He hadn't tried to grow them or had tried though he knew he didn't need them?

That eye closed again, his head resting in my lap while I traced the short, ivory horns which seemed longer when he had no hair.

~*Are you falling asleep?*~

Thric.

~*Alright, then.*~

Irisvir ...

I waited for any insight on that word, spying a glowing aura enveloping us in my mind's eye. The purple outline I assumed was his ... until I realized it centered on me. Or rather, on my womb.

An intense, pearl white like Gavin had said, with purple in the corona ...

~*Is it ... comforting?*~ I asked.

Zi.

More than ... More than what?

340

More than I understood, apparently.

As the North wind swept in regularly at my back, I pulled up my hood and wrapped my cloak tighter, sharing the heat rising off the Dragon's head. The rest of him wasn't visibly affected; now that the pain had seemed to pass, he hadn't so much as shivered.

This wasn't Mourn resting in my lap, I reminded myself, hearing Graul's small voice speak in the back of my mind.

"Baenar hum sleeps. To'vah will wake up first."

Did this mean he was close? What happened then? I didn't even know where they'd taken him within the redoubt.

Meanwhile, the dawn passed slower than it should have; our shadows reached, long and thin, to the West for some time. I sat in the sand as my belly warmed pleasantly with the To'vah-krav's head resting against it.

Morixxyleth's thoughts settled; he never spoke though was aware, and answered my questions in the shortest of Draconic descriptions. A single word, if he could get away with it, and never enough to understand why I'd found him like this, why he was here, or why *I* was here.

Or when we'd wake up.

This Reverie ... I was lucid, like Gavin described, with all my recent memories at my disposal. Was this how the Deathwalker was in his trances? Where did he walk as he sat unmoving in his seat?

Something blew onto my cheek.

I expected the sting and tickle of a grain of sand, but then it melted, gone immediately in the dry air. I spotted another one attempting to land on Morixxyleth's back, but it vanished before it reached his scales. Then another three swirled in, two turning to vapor between large, black wings and the third alighting upon my red cloak.

~*Snow.*~

To'vah eyes opened abruptly, color returning to a solid, metallic gold. His pupils narrowed as he lifted his head above us, twisting his neck to look North. I did, too.

Dark clouds had appeared on the horizon.

Morshin wer niarhaanin, he rumbled in my head as he rose to all four feet.

A clear image of me entering the Red Desert, dripping wet.

Cross the river.

Morixxyleth paced away from me, tongue extending out time and again to taste the cooling air as his wings stretched and practiced motions of flight.

~*Are you leaving* — ?~

Morshin wer niarhaanin, he repeated before taking off in that startling sprint I knew him for.

I watched his form shrink in my vision while he picked up breathtaking speed. He launched off the ground in one giant bound, his new wings unfurling like banners before beating the air in powerful strokes to keep himself aloft and climb higher.

Flying right for those clouds.

Goddess shit.

Despite thinking I should feel awe in what I'd witnessed, I first took this as a sign he wouldn't be waking up just yet.

Crystalline flakes still floated around me, and the wind had grown colder such that I hesitated to simply dive into the river and cross it. I'd be freezing with no way to warm up if that early Sun didn't grow any hotter.

I think the danger has passed, and I don't have to —

"*Sirranna* ..."

The chill rushed up my back, and I turned around and started jogging South. My sole thought was to escape that wind!

The day finally moved forward as I did, though little of the landscape changed along the river border. The heat of the Desert finally spilled over onto my side of the banks, tempting me closer to the water, and snowflakes hadn't appeared around me for quite some time.

I stopped jogging, turning in place, breathing in warm, dusty air. I was getting too hot. The urge to remove my cloak had me reaching for the clasp, but my hand froze when the hooves of a galloping horse touched my ears.

Nightmare?

It whinnied, loud and clear, and I frowned. Could Nightmare call like that at all? I'd never heard it. I turned to look across the water as the horse slowed, trotting along the bank before stopping.

Sitting astride a blood bay stallion, without a saddle or any tackle at all, was a familiar and welcome face.

I smiled, lifting an arm and waving. "Auslan!"

My Consort slid off the beast's back, approaching me as he had in previous dreams — astonished, shy, yearning. I got close enough to sense his familiar presence in this dreamscape, to *know* his mind was real, his form not an illusion or a trick.

The relief was pure bliss. He still lived.

I embraced that drive to cross that river.

"Sirana! Sirana, wake up!"

I opened my eyes and, at first, I thought I lay in the Cloister, peering up at my Sister after another restless Reverie. Jael stared down at me, concerned and confused, but not terrified. A good sign?

"Did you come in your sleep?" she whispered, her hand resting on my shoulder, eyes flicking over to the other side of the room. *"Twice?"*

One corner of her mouth twitched in a hint of humor.

Did I just … ?

Oh.

My crotch and heart together spread the afterglow in a resounding yes. My body was coasting but began to relax. I needed time to make my mouth work.

"This is not the first time," Gavin said.

I jolted in surprise, squeezing my thighs as my slit remained sensitive. Finally, I remembered the Dwarven redoubt. I wasn't in Sivaraus, despite my bed underground.

The Surface, not the Deepearth.

I turned my head to make sure Soul Drinker hung on the wall.

Yes.

Then I lifted it until I could see the Deathwalker sitting in his chair, writing in an open grimoire. He didn't seem *too* annoyed.

"I take it you did not share her dream in some way?" he asked Jael directly. "I realize you had awakened before she found her pleasure."

"Uh … Share?" She frowned, waiting far too long before adding a hesitant shake of her head.

"Hm. If that is true, your control may be increasing, Sirana."

I listened but kept my eyes on Jael. Controlling who I mindlinked with *was* something I wanted, especially in dreams. But we had been lying right next to each other, *touching*. I didn't think I'd gained that much control.

"Did you dream?" I asked her in Trade. When resistance passed over her face, I added, "It's important to me. Gavin has been helping me understand psionic changes. His observations are helpful. Will you say if you remember standing somewhere strange?"

Her eyes narrowed though her expression softened. "Strange how?"

I shrugged. "Somewhere you've never been while awake?"

She couldn't hide the affirmative but chose her description with care. "Surface. Hard ground. A river."

Oh, shit.

"What color was the ground?"

She shrugged. "Mix. Brown. Yellow … and red?"

"Any trees by the river?"

"Yes. Shorter."

"Was it dawn? The Sun about to rise?"

She looked suspicious. "No. Night. Many stars. Moons, no Sun."

That was different.

"Did anything happen?" I asked. "Did you see anyone, or were you alone until you woke?"

She looked away and sat on her backside; I detected a slight increase in her scent.

"You did," I prompted, sitting up.

An uncomfortable shrug. "Mm. Made mistake."

"A mistake?"

She exhaled loudly through her nose, a familiar, practiced annoyance trying to hide the rate of her heart. "Saw a creature swimming in the river. Reflect stars first, on back and eyes. Look like shadow drake, but no wings."

"*No* wings?" I repeated.

She shook her head, and I believed her even as I struggled to reconcile that with what I'd expected to hear.

"It talk, asked me closer," she said, "and I did not feel awake. I was curious, moved closer."

Out of my periphery, I noted Gavin making a few subtle notes. I waited, reaching for her hand, but she pulled it back, flexing and frowning at it.

"I touched it," she said. "Mistake."

I waited, but she offered nothing more, looking to the side. "Did it hurt?"

She swallowed, nodding. "It roared at me, tried to use claws but missed. I ran away, expecting chase, and … woke up."

Her heartbeat told me it had been an unpleasant waking. I sat in stunned silence, my mind still putting links together.

Nighttime, starry eyes, and no wings. Dawn, with wings, golden eyes returning.

But not before great pain. Perhaps that was why he didn't chase her, thank goddess.

Was it me or him who dragged her in?

Probably me. I put her in danger.

Again.

The body pleasure of my dream's finish faded as unspoken concerns filled my waking mind. How much should I say? Did we need to sleep apart? As if *that* would lower my overall concerns for her safety.

She wouldn't leave anyway, and I didn't want her to.

Fuck.

"What?" Jael asked. "You think. Lots."

I shrugged. "I … did link you into my dream. Psionically. I just didn't see you."

"Agreed, and again," Gavin interjected, "this is not the first time."

Our eyes snapped to him. "Huh?"

"Your experience at times seems to be a sort of projection or travel," he said, making marks with his stylus. "From listening to Krithannia, I understand this is a potential talent of Reverie for Elves as a race, not a unique function of psionics. In contrast, I can state that sharing memories in an unconscious state feels quite different from such travel, as the two are 'locked together' in the same moment in time."

From Jael's expression, she might have understood half of that, though all of it made too much sense to me.

"You dream with death mage, too?" she asked, mouth tight like she'd suppressed a grimace.

"I have," I said. "When we slept close in the warp rot forest and on the ship in the Archipelago."

"Strange places, too," she noted, peering suspiciously around the redoubt.

"It can happen anywhere," I explained. "It happened in Augran, too. If I sleep near another who sleeps."

Her mouth got tighter. "Like blue sand? You woke me in fight. Hold me down."

Ah, fuck.

"I am sorry," I said, my stomach tightening up, sick and empty. "The black dagger was too close to your hand."

She frowned as if trying to confirm this in her own mind.

I had to ask. "Did you ... see anyone there?"

Jael shook her head, blowing out the breath she'd been holding. "No. Heard voices, never saw what lay on other side. Nothing happen. No pain, and alone."

Chance held one small favor, then.

My middle gurgled as a powerful hunger pang made me wince.

"Would you like to retrieve your food or attempt to have it brought?" Gavin asked, unsurprised and preparing for a change of task.

"We should get," Jael nudged me. "See where prepared."

Indeed, that's what I would have done as a guest in any House in Sivaraus. Now, the only reason I didn't have it brought was for the desire to stretch.

"Let's find that kitchen."

CHAPTER 25

THROUGH OUR NEXT WAKING PERIOD — ALWAYS LONGER THAN THE HUMANS and the tellingly exhausted Dwarves — Jael and I didn't talk substantially about anything we might have been brooding about. I counted myself lucky I'd coaxed her to tell me about her dream by the Desert river while the memories were fresh and that she'd brought up the mage's aura herself.

But those remain intensely relevant to her present.

My youngest Sister sometimes talked about recent encounters if something about them bothered her, but once she'd chosen her lessons, after they had passed to retreat a certain distance behind her, she shut the stone door on them. She quickly grew impatient or silently hostile if anyone tried to bring it up.

I'd discovered this shortly after her trials into the Sisterhood, in a mention of the Sathoet. By every indication, she *never* wanted to talk about that aspect of her trials. The same seemed ready to happen with any talk about the Archbishop or his Inquisitor: they were dead or gone and she was out of their dungeon. In her view, what had happened was irrelevant to her once she'd survived it.

But it wouldn't be that way forever. Knowing myself, knowing Mourn, Krithannia, and even Gavin, Archbishop Keros and Inquisitor Kegyek would come back into discussion.

As will Vesram, if we'll truly see him again.

I'd have to wait and see if anyone else could pull information out of her beyond the point when she decided she was done with it. I didn't have a way between us that worked.

In addition, I'd wanted to speak in depth with Gavin about Innathi and the souls in the red rune dagger. Once Jael and I were outside his room, she dragged her feet about returning and was willing to tell me why.

"You two just talk and talk," she said. *"I don't have anywhere safe to go or anything to do, only too many Humans to scare by breathing. I'm bored and ignored if I'm not spilling 'interesting' things for him to write down in his fat book."*

I tried not to grin. She'd meant "fat" as an insult, though Gavin had made it that way himself. But her point was also difficult to argue with.

Krithannia and Tamuril were out of view. I didn't know if they'd come inside yet, but her door was still sealed and warded. We didn't have another room besides Gavin's for privacy or safety, and we couldn't leave the redoubt without letting anyone know.

Well, we *could*, but it would cause trouble and I'd be breaking my agreement with Mourn not to fling myself into stupid situations from boredom or lust, especially when he couldn't guard me.

Ironically, I had to keep Jael in check for those same reasons.

Perhaps the discussion about Innathi and the Ma'ab souls can wait.

Gavin hadn't spent a lot of time alone since Yong-wen, largely because of me. He was probably enjoying the spacious quarters after fixing and stitching up bodies for the Guild.

For the first part of the next waking cycle, Jael and I wandered around the halls. We could get plenty to eat and drink once we followed the directions to the kitchen from Reprisal's recovery room, all of whom were doing well enough.

From a somewhat rested Welden, I learned Deshi had been visiting every room and some of the camps outside, searching for those sharp, black splinters only his eyes knew how to see.

"He spotted another four just as the strength-sapping bastards started twitchin'," said Osgrid's cousin. "An' we saw four Manalari soldiers quickly into a private room. Between the early warnin' and an *extremely* responsive Godblood, we didn't need tah drag th' Deathwalker out of his room again."

My amusement mirrored Welden's face. If Reprisal had been unsettled by Gavin's brusque evaluations for their teammates, then Isboern's men might have tried to break down the walls.

"What has the Captain been doing since?"

"Healin' who accepts," the blond Dwarf said with a dry smile, "while expressin' desires tah go outside an' reassure his people, 'specially after the barbs saw four ov 'em dragged inside. *Oltere* has been lettin' 'im pass messages tah his officers outside but holdin' back showin' him or the Templars in public yet."

"Do you know why?"

The lead healer shrugged. "Guessin' they need a plan with enough Guild talent tah protect the highest target we got during a speech."

That made sense.

Mourn's inability to vet those around me was why Jael and I had stayed with him during the battle rather than leave earlier for the redoubt. Without him, this concern became stronger since we'd arrived.

I'd spotted Mathias in the crowd at the Temple before he'd run off; before then, Cris-ri-phon was inside waiting for us. I had no idea where Amelda, Ma'ab Noble and Daughter of the Deathless, had gone after Troshin Bend.

Nyx's protection over the sacred pool would end if a lucky bolt hit the Godblood in the right spot. The Guild could not know a fraction of all those who'd passed through the Dwarves' gate, yet some waited outside who "refused to leave." Some could easily be connected to the Ma'ab.

As a last thought, Rithal's and Osgrid's presence was proof enough that one could follow us with enough gossip and information.

A lot of Dwarves know we need help here.

I hoped Mourn didn't sleep for weeks or months, as he'd mentioned doing before. I'd seen how Humans could panic or grow hostile over rumors, with or without a confirmed threat. The sooner the Guild resolved this sticking point which kept too many refugees here, the better for all of us.

But if he takes too long to wake, Talov and Krithannia might have to think of an alternative before the Manalari start defying all good advice surrounding their Godblood.

How far could Isboern be pushed in that direction by his own men? He had the ability to bend their will, I knew, but Willven used his psionic insights to persuade through action and speech instead.

How often might the young man be tempted to manipulate them beyond what their own willful choices might have been? After the way we'd shared information and honesty, I couldn't imagine him pursuing it as any but a last resort. If someone dear to him was threatened, perhaps.

Like Tamuril.

If Isboern hadn't set eyes on her since we'd all stood in the hall, before all the women had gone to the shower, then he seemed to have his concerns under control. Or I wasn't around to hear it.

Where was she?

For an hour or so after our second meal, Jael and I returned to Reprisal's room, largely because the men there were accustomed to our appearances. Welden offered a few tasks to help with, and I was glad to see Brian Wolf with his eyes open.

"Ah, good," he said, looking from Jael to me. "She made it."

"With much thanks to you and your teams," I said, maintaining the reflective and solemn air.

Wolf smiled slightly, and my Sister looked at me strangely, as if she thought I might be manipulating a social ritual like a Noble at Court. Although this *was* a ritual, I was not pretending. Most men in this room felt the absence of those who'd fallen like I felt Gaelan's and Reishel's absence.

I still feel their absence.

While they lay recovering in their cots or strengthening their bodies, there might not be a lot else to think about.

"Hey," said Tak nearby, "I've noticed you two sign to each other, but I only get bits of it. Is it special group slang, like ours?"

"Some," I answered my one-time city guide. "Most of it is known by all in our city."

Wolf's eyes widened as Tak's mouth opened. "The *entire* city?"

"Yes."

"Like, the kids, and everyone?"

I grinned wider. "Correct. There are enough sources of danger that it benefits us to learn young."

"Brazen balls, can you imagine?" Hawk said to one of his brothers, who laughed and shook his head.

"Would sure make it easier if anyone lost their hearing, aye?"

"Oh, yeah!"

"We could use a few new code names," Wolf said to me with a tired smile.

Not a bad distraction to cover some time.

Jael scowled at me for teaching them any signs about the underground until she learned to enjoy their reactions when I explained pincerworms, tunnel runners, blind sprays, and drop hooks in finer detail.

A little too fine. Heh.

"Oi, lasschen, there ya are!"

I fully expected a specific greybeard at the door when I turned around, smiling. "*Oltere* Baradum."

Talov grinned. "You an' Jael got some time? I wanna go over somethin' with ya."

Certainly vague, but maybe he had an update about Mourn.

"Of course."

I signed farewell, which several Guildsman picked up immediately, and saw myself out with Jael and Talov. He chatted on our way to wherever we headed.

"So, *Oltere*, hah?" he chuckled. "Ya been hearin' that."

"Almost nothing else," I replied. "What does it mean?"

"A practical term, means 'Over-Father.' When more than one Clan Hall decides tah work together on a problem an' they want one experienced Grandfather tah make th' calls on the ground."

Interesting.

"You have 'Over-Mother?' " Jael asked bluntly, sounding skeptical.

Talov's cheeks bunching in a familiar smile. "We do. Called *Udstere*."

"She here?"

"Ah. I meant we have th' title. No specific *Udstere* here in the redoubt at this moment."

"Why not?"

He shrugged. "Sometimes a Grandmother is the better choice to lead, especially the long goals, but most Clans acknowledge any aftermath ov Humans fightin' each other goes better with an *Oltere*."

That suggested a lot about how Humans "fought each other," and I didn't enjoy how easily that was flipped in my head if the Tundar Dwarves ended up ever working with the Davrin.

Or they once knew from trading with the Desert Queendom.

"I know at least two Clans answered the call," I said, recovering another thought I'd had after learning Osgrid's Clan. "Baradum and Gherudum?"

His pale green eyes twinkled as he walked unhurried beside me with Jael watching our backs. "Aye. An' two others, Yelkardir an' Tildrinush."

The Dwarves seemed to like that triple beat in their clan names.

"Yours and Osgrid's two have the same sound at the end," I pointed out. "Are your Clans related?"

"Aye, very good!" Talov smiled. "Distantly. The Cl'dum can trace their Halls tah the Great Lake 'round Taiding, the oldest ov active Dwarven cities up top."

"Up top?" Jael interjected.

The ancient male had to twist his torso more than his neck to look at her. "Aye. Our ancient Halls are underground." He winked at us. "But we don't tend tah show those around tah one an' all, ya know?"

"We know," I answered with a smirk.

He chuckled. "But yeah, families might reach far across th' lands but ye'll meet Cl'dum near anywhere if ya live long enough."

That pulled a laugh out of me, which surprised Jael and made Talov comb his beard in thought.

"Usually say that tah Humans as a jest," he reflected.

"I imagined so," I replied, grin in place.

"'Tis true that yer still a kid tah me," he winked, "but I'm gonna rethink my intros fer older races, rare as ye are."

As we turned down a curve, I recognized we were somewhere in between Krithannia's and the Templar's quarters. I was about to ask if we would see Mourn, but Talov seemed to know as he tapped his first finger to his lips and signed in our tongue.

He sleep. Hold questions.

Ah, damn.

I also wasn't surprised Mourn had taught his Augran partners some of his own hand sign. Talov had certainly lived long enough to find it useful.

We arrived at an iron-banded, wooden door with some Dwarves either loitering or stealth guarding, and other doors partly open with a lot of Tundar talking inside. This room sounded to be surrounded by all working Dwarves not performing a task elsewhere.

Talov retrieved his key to unlock it. No wards, I noticed.

"Come on in," he said, motioning us in behind him.

Jael and I exchanged glances, and I shrugged. I had no idea what he might want to talk about.

"Do we go in?" she asked, suspicious.

"We agreed to talk, and he was there when I confirmed the Bargain. He won't trap us."

"Better not," she muttered, waving me ahead of her.

I stepped in to a surprisingly thick and welcome scent of hot stew and Dwarven bread. A covered, earthenware tray was sitting on a flat heating stone, and had been here long enough to have filled the entire room with the mouth-watering scents of the kitchen.

"We ate," Jael said, watching me sniff the air.

"Hours ago," I added, frowning at her.

"It's fer me," Talov said with a bushy smile, laying down a cloth mat on his work desk before retrieving the tray by its wooden handles. "But I'll share if ya want some. Grab a chair an' sit across from me."

Jael and I looked around. In addition to his small counter with the heating stone, a small sink next to it, and the heavy chair behind the broad desk holding his meal and piles of parchment, the office contained four more chairs and a long table plus something which looked useful for posting or sketching quick designs.

No cot, pallet, or waste corner lay out in the open, so I assumed Talov didn't sleep here. However, there was a smaller door in the corner opposite of where we'd come in.

Jael grunted trying to lift one of the chairs; she ended up dragging it, and I moved to help her. Then she moved to help me drag mine.

"Eh, you know you … um," Talov began, watching us stubbornly get it into place. "Alright, so, you both might fit in one, like a bench —"

Jael took her seat, sitting center between the wide arms, boots flat on the ground, back straight, and face scowling. "Why so big? This even too big for you!"

The *Oltere* guffawed, watching as I took a seat, and fell into a mirth that made his whole torso shake. He lowered his head, palms down, and let it out.

Jael looked at me. "What?"

"Um, well," I began helplessly.

"Sorry, the two ov ya look so cute and tiny in those chairs!" Talov explained, his eyes moist at the corners as he straightened up. "Oye, *heh heh!* Ah, *ahem* …" He took a deep breath. "So, tah answer, Jael, they're wide enough tah hold a Dwarf in full armor, an' strong enough tah bear a Kurgan man fallin' in it without crackin'. Just the way we build 'em fer places like this. Sure ya don't wanna share with Sirana?"

She shook her head, settling in and reaching out for the chair's arms. She connected with a thump, back bowed, her bottom too far forward, and elbows floating off the support on either side. I bit my lip as Talov enjoyed another round of chortles.

Then, finally, he lifted the cover on the warm meal. "Want some?"

The portions seemed generous even if he intended to eat alone.

"Yes, please," I said.

He handed a large spoon and what was either a small bowl or an empty cup to me. "Take whatcha need. We can get more."

I resisted no part of that, scooping in plenty of roots, greens, and broth into my bowl and claiming one of the three small loaves. Sitting on the edge of my seat, I tore into the hearty meal, once again unable to hide my enjoyment of the flavors from my Sister.

Jael stared and shook her head. "Now making sense."

"What makes sense?" Talov asked with interest, tearing a piece of bread off to dunk.

She stuttered at first.

"He knows," I muttered between bites.

Jael exhaled, exasperated. "Do *all* know?"

Talov and I shook our heads, but he paused eating first. "As far as I know, me, Krithannia, Mourn, Graul, Gavin, Tamuril, and presumably Pilla in some bird way."

"And Isboern," I added, not truly pleased.

"Oh, aye? From th' mindlinks?"

"Yes. But I asked him to keep it secret, and he knows why."

The greybeard thought that over. "Alright, noted. Thank ya."

"And Cris-ri-phon. Or Brom, whoever."

Talov grimaced. "Oh, right. Him."

Whoever that bronze-skinned Elf had been, making a deal with Nyx's Deathwalkers. Whatever the Deathless knew, that ruler must know, too. I chose not to speak that part aloud.

Jael exhaled. "In time and food, it show anyway."

"Ya got some time yet, as I understand." He looked between us. "Not obvious through clothes fer maybe half a year still?"

"True," said my Sister, sounding confident as she rubbed her chin.

Wait ...

"Have you learned much about carrying?" I asked. "Or birthing?"

Jael smiled a bit. "Could not avoid. Some *cait* in our land carrying or sucking tit every year. Mother has six, just her, may have others. My sisters look for sires, too."

Oh my fuck ...

"Oh," I said, attempting to smile. "So, you could help me?"

She frowned. "Help how?"

I swallowed. "Tell me if some change is expected or worrisome?"

"Like what?"

"Well, my tits ache. Always."

She grimaced with sympathy. "Expect."

Great.

I glanced at Talov eating, watching us, and looked to see Jael frowning again. *That didn't last long.*

"You can't go home with belly showing," she said stubbornly. "They throw you in Bishop cell."

"Throw you in what?" Talov asked, sounding as surprised as Jael looked.

"She means *Priestess*," I said, quelling my stomach. "We have a … temple prison, too. Red Sisters who catch kids stay in the temple prison until birth, so she doesn't kill the infant during a mission."

"And Priestess keeps infant!" Jael barked, showing teeth in a snarl. "She go back, she gives them new one and never sees again!"

Between my head and my middle, I winced. *Ow …*

"Oh," the Dwarf breathed, looking between us, nodding slowly. "Thank ya, I didn't know that. If I may ask, what are yer options? I know ya thought 'bout it."

"Stay up here two years," Jael said, "and hide infant into city, or end early."

Uh … no. My eyes teared up as my throat began to hurt. *No.*

"Queen knows," I rasped.

"So say you lost it."

"After two years? She's not stupid."

Jael tapped her heel on the floor, pursing her lips. "Then … maybe end early?"

I set down my spoon and breathed deeply. I didn't want to lose my meal. "Do you know how? I have nothing but starving or poison."

Talov stopped eating, folded his hands and placed them in front of his mouth.

"Well … uh …" Jael looked pained for a moment. "I don't know mushroom or potion up here. And … rare, not a lot. Mother helped if needed, I never there. Just saw them live."

Damn.

Tears threatened to spill out the next time I blinked. My throat ached more than my tits as the pain creeped into my head. I clutched my skull as the Valsharess spoke in my memory.

"For the sake of Our people, We shall let you live. But you must destroy the tainted death mage at the Ley Tower then return to Us without delay ..."

"Sirana?" Jael asked, her hand hovering near my shoulder.

"Do not disappoint Us. We have infinite ways to punish you and all for whom you care ... There is no place you can hide from Us, Sirana, and you will not reject what We've laid upon you."

"I can't stay up here," I whispered, gasping, my cheeks damp. "Not long enough to ..."

Not long enough to see my baby's face in that dream both Innathi and Krithannia had mentioned for Elven Mothers.

"Why not?" my Sister demanded, motioning toward the wall. "I in no hurry to go back."

Because Isboern broke your geas ...

But the spell had almost killed her in the crypt. The Captain had needed a trance like the one he'd given to Brian Wolf to overcome the full torment, thus far only hinted at.

Worse than losing it by starving, I wager.

"You mentioned returnin' tah the Ley Tower with the Deathwalker," Talov said, his voice softer than it had been at the start.

"What? Why?" Jael responded, her tone a solid gripe.

"Arrgh!" I barked, needing to release the tension as the headache increased. "Because ... I *must!!*"

I dared not force eye contact then; I didn't know what would happen. But Jael and Talov stayed quiet as they watched me shudder through a few painful sobs and catch my breath.

"I can't wait until winter, Jael," I managed. "That's too long. I must go back ..."

She gasped as if a revelation had struck. "Oh. I ... understand."

Thank goddess ...

"I go with you and the death mage," she continued, earnest and apologetic. "I go back with you."

A small nod was all I could offer right then. The headache and high pitch in my ears continued as if another voice tried to push through.

"Ah, Sirana?" Talov said.

"Hm?"

"I have a box fer th' dagger, if ya need it. It locks, an' I'd give ya the key."

I lifted my head, squinting through the pain, trying to read his face but avoid his eyes. "H-huh?"

"The saphgar glow," Jael said.

"And yer hand is on th' hilt," Talov added.

Oh, shit.

"Yes, please," I said in a whimper.

With a nod, the *Oltere* reached under his desk and brought out a lockbox large enough to fit more than the dagger. He took a key from within his cloak and turned it in the hole, opening the lid for me.

Other items were inside, but the halo in my vision kept me from seeing much before I fumbled my belt loose, removing Soul Drinker in its hilt, and dropping it into the box. Talov closed the box firmly and secured it before holding the key out to me.

"Maybe tuck it in yer glove?" he suggested.

I took his advice while he moved the box itself into a far corner, brushing off his palms as he walked back unhurried, stopping by his counter to pour water from a pitcher. He brought us each a wooden cup, setting them down before us. I drank gratefully, soothing my aching throat and cooling the heat in my head and face.

"Heh, hold on," Talov said, getting up to retrieve the whole pitcher so he could refill it.

Jael finished her first cup as I finished my refill.

"Better?" he asked.

We nodded.

"Alright. Then, Sirana, I have a question, but only ask tah know where ya stand. May I?"

I frowned in confusion. "Alright."

"Would ya like my Clan's help tah end early? I know an *Udstere* I'd trust with me own blood. She could help ya survive it with less sufferin' an' time ta recover."

I couldn't sort my body's response to that offer. Like a stone in my gut, ice in my fingers, and a fire in my chest. I doubted I could stand or move my arms in those moments.

"Forbidden," I murmured.

"Not true!" Jael said. "Only for Red Sisters, and it's from blood-sucking *Priestesses*!"

She was right, of course, but …

The tears restarted. I was afraid; afraid to try, to explain, because it wasn't all mine to decide.

"If Queen knows," my Sister said, "She sent you here. She have *no say* if not-born lost on mission, double-strong if you must reach mountains before winter. Need to *live* to come back!"

Goddess, she was right again.

"I know. I have thought this … so many times."

The two watched me shivering for a few moments.

"Still no?" Jael asked, sounding wary or worried. "Even if given to *Priestess*, you, then your infant?"

The Sanctuary, or possibly the Queen Herself. Like the centuries of D'Shea and Shyntre repeated.

"I don't want that …" I croaked.

"Red Sisters never keep kids," she stated. "We soon stop carry, or kid stay in temple when you released —"

"I *know!*" I repeated harshly.

Jael closed her mouth tightly. My hands were shaking.

Behind my eyes, I kept seeing Auslan and Shyntre as they'd been watching me in my dream. I recalled Morixxlyeth's head resting in my lap, seeing my baby's aura so vividly through his eyes, the aura which Gavin had described so perfectly.

Auslan waits for me to return. I just told him I would …

Because the Valsharess demanded it, and She may still believe the sire was D'Shea's son. Plus, I was the only psionic Davrin in Sivaraus.

Oh, Goddess, is there another way?

"Waiting make it worse," my Sister said.

"Not what I'm hearin', Jael," Talov replied.

"She no win against temple, Dwarf!" she retorted, her temper rising. "That why we up here!"

"I hear that, too," the greybeard said. "But we're not tryin' tah win against another temple this moment. We're jus' talkin' after wreckin' one." He smiled wryly. "Let yer sister be. 'Tis already a hard choice she faces, an' not you or me gonna make it or demand one too soon."

She snarled at him. "You know nothing what we face! You sit in chair, served food, lead around! You never under boots, watch your house under boots, never a laugh piece strapped to stone and eaten by hungry void!"

"Sounds bad."

"Worse. You beg die first!"

Talov remained calm, meeting her eyes with pale green ones. "Sounds like yer house don't beg."

"No! We fight!"

"But ye said ya can't win against th' temple."

"Don't care," she spat. "Still fight."

"Interestin'. Even if it gives them the 'laugh piece' they want?"

Jael was gripping her chair, giving Talov her meanest snarl. "That or die first."

"Why?"

"Mess up magic, mess up void eating. Or die before void comes. Then you win alone against temple, even if they laugh."

I shuddered at the memories that brought up. But how did she know that if she'd never been to Court?

Oh, wait ...

The Sathoet and her trials.

Shit.

"Ah," Talov breathed, keeping his voice soft and gaze steady. "Wow. That how ya stood up tah Keros an' his Inquisitor?"

She blinked. "Wh-what?"

"Ya lasted a night alone against 'em, after findin' th' shield in the crypt an' livin' with Isboern's help."

Jael shot to her feet, breathing hard. I jumped in my chair, lifting my chin to her and forgetting my looming tasks for the moment.

Talov kept talking, meeting her eyes. "I have no doubt they were torturin' you, but ya were th' strongest woman they met. They had tah pull out every trick tah 'strap ya to the stone' and eat, right? The Bishops were weak like yer void, fer th' same reason, I think."

"Bishop want clean magic! Same as home! They ... th-they —"

"Greedy? Can't stop eating?"

"*Yes!*" Jael shoved her chair out of her way, causing it to scrape loudly along the stone but failing to turn it over. "Never stop! Not better, not above us, just make stupid rules to trick and eat more and *more!* I show with magic, men kill me before I break!"

"Your temple doesn't know you have magic," Talov said, watching her pacing the room. "What now? They have 'stupid rules' fer Davrin like you?"

My Sister froze in place. Terror and rage at war on her face.

Shit.

Jael had been focused on me returning pregnant and hadn't imagined herself as a mage in Sivaraus until this moment. I swallowed, unsure what to do but keep my trembling belly under control.

"I-I don't ..." she croaked, copper eyes shining with real tears. "Yes, rules, but ..."

"But ya could stay up here. Never go back."

"No!" she barked, waving toward me. "Not if she must!"

"But ya can't make th' magic go away, so ya know the void will eat ya. An' she don't yet want that fer her baby, either, but she knows what happens."

"Just grind salt in cut, Dwarf!" she sneered.

"Not my intent. The Deathwalker wants tah work with th' Guild, an' the Guild wants him in that Ley Tower, with the 'tainted' death mage gone."

Jael's expression changed quickly, like she'd spotted a fresh trail to track while Talov continued.

"No matter what yer Queen forces Sirana tah do, we can help with that part 'bout the Ley Tower. Ya got time, an' ya will learn more magic yet. Enough time an' knowledge, options open up. Ya hearin' me? No decisions that far out need tah be made tonight."

I started to breathe again, taking that in, my cheeks wet. Even with Mourn asleep, I held hope that Talov would convince him to come West with me. *As a start.*

Then what? What might happen if I returned home then, before winter, and obeyed my geas …

Bringing a Dragonchild and Soul Drinker with me.

We didn't have any "stupid rules" to cover that, either. It would be an explosion of a fight, even if I never saw …

I sucked in a breath. "Vesram."

"Hm?" Talov asked, bushy brows drawing down.

"Mourn told him to find the Ley Tower."

"Oh. Yeah, I guess he did. That's interestin'."

"Who is Vesram?" Jael asked.

My stomach squeezed into my throat at the wrong time, and Talov beat me to the answer.

"A half-Elf, half-demon, enslaved by the Ma'ab. Sirana ran into him lookin' fer you, right? An' helped free him —"

"*Sathoet?*" she screeched when the impossible dawned on her, pinning me with scorching eyes. "*You freed a Sathoet and sent him where we're headed next?!*"

"*I had to!*" I barked, my fingers forming claws from the strain of forcing that out.

"*I'll gut him if he sticks his ugly nose where I can see it!*"

I had no doubt she'd try.

"*If he sticks his ugly nose where we can see it,*" I said, lips tight, "*he must go home, and I must stop you from hunting him.*"

"*How could you … ?*" Her voice was ragged with insult. "*After my … a-after Kerse? Even after what he did, you won't fight this? You wear the collar?*"

I gripped my head. "*Shut up! You're making i-it worse!*"

"*I can't even —*"

"Jael, you're free," Talov said. "She's not."

363

"I *not* free!" she barked, her voice breaking as she punched the back of the Dwarven chair. "*Not* free! Dragon *bua* holds my magic on a rope, like Queen hold Sirana's baby! He use us to fight Malok, like three in one, and she cannot fight, she *help* him bond, like she cannot fight Sathoet but help him try to kill us!"

Oh, Goddess ...

"Ah, well, I'm glad ya said somethin' on that," said the greybeard. "Mourn'll speak fer himself when he wakes but know he don't like temples any more than you and Sirana. He suffered the void trap, too, and he *had* that magic fer them tah suck on. It got bad, how I heard it." Talov paused. "He can teach ya how tah fight back. Like ya did the Malok, together. Only do me a favor an' ask yer sister why she helped."

Jael stiffened, jerking her head to me in suspicion. I stared back, wondering if she would ask.

Finally, "Why you help him link us?"

I spoke slowly. "Because he asked me to help."

"And that different than demon?"

"Entirely!" I barked, noticing when Talov smirked at the comparison of his "kid" to a demon. "The bond was earned, and mutual. I helped make it strong, and he helps keep it balanced. It's *not* forced, not like with Kerse. Perhaps I forced *myself* in how badly I wanted to find you, and witnessed enough proof that his help gave me the chance to succeed."

The room quieted but for our heartbeats.

Flexing the hand she'd used to punch the chair, Jael grimaced. Clutching her good hand around it, she asked, "Earned mutual ... So, earned how?"

I shrugged. "Time. Proof in action. Talking."

"More talk," she sneered.

I tried to suppress an unexpected smile as my chest loosened up.

"Yer hand's swellin' up," Talov said, pulling out a drawer. "I have a kit. Let's see if ya cracked a bone."

She wrinkled her nose. "It's fine!"

"Don't be a rock-head, now," I countered. "You need your hands working to do magic. This is why no one damaged *bua* fingers in the lead tutor's tower."

Jael looked surprised. "I never heard."

I smirked. "Harsh punishments for breaking a mage's hand, Sister."

"Good twist if ya might've broken yer own," Talov said with amusement, coming around the desk and opening the kit so she could see inside. I could see salves, potions, splints, wraps, and more. "Come on, Jael, sit. Arm restin' with hand off the edge. Need yer glove off, too. I agree with Sirana, we should keep these new mage hands from gettin' warped before ye learn tah cast yer first spell on yer own."

This was enough to convince her. Jael sat but had trouble removing her glove. She had likely broken it; the shape was off.

My Sister held still for the elder *Oltere*, watching as he took her hand gently between his broad, rough ones. First, he applied something he said would keep it from "puffing up" and numb the pain. Then he used what appeared to be a knowledgeable touch to find the point of fracture. Jael yelped when he did.

"Hm. Gonna hafta set that. Here, bite down on this an' hold Sirana's arm. It's gonna hurt."

Neither of us questioned why he didn't offer a magic-based healing potion. The supply had been exhausted in these first two days after the battle. I had Shyntre's pellets if she needed a slower boost, but for now, Talov provided an expert's job splinting and wrapping Jael's hand so that it wouldn't move.

"There ya are, lasschen," he said, his voice pleasant and soothing. "All done. Keep it dry an' close tah chest level as ya can."

Jael sighed as it sank in that she'd be working with one hand for a while, at least until I could negotiate some magic to speed the healing.

Eventually, Talov sat down and resumed eating his cooled meal; I did the same but also recalled why we'd come here in the first place.

"Uh, Talov?"

"Hm?"

"What was it you wanted to discuss when you came to get us in Reprisal's room?"

His eyes brightened, the corners crinkling as he chuckled softly. "Well, two things. First thing was askin' if there was anything either of ya wanted tah heave off yer chest. I'd say ya both got it done, an' well, too. Proud o' ya."

I blinked, swallowing as Jael arched an eyebrow. "And the second?"

Talov's smile didn't waver. "I know ya don't have a place ov yer own and room's tight right now. Graul is hintin' Mourn might come up soon, but this room will be empty until he does. There're a few cots through that door behind us, includes a waste closet, an' I can give ya the key. Wanna stay here fer a while?"

"You leaving?" Jael asked bluntly.

"Yep. I prefer th' family quarters nearby."

So we could sleep off the floor, relieve ourselves, and have sex without anyone complaining. It sounded good.

"And meals?" I asked.

"That an' extra, so ya don't hafta come out fer a while. Ya both look tired."

I met Jael's eyes. We were. It hit us like a falling arch.

"Thank you, *Oltere*," I said.

"Yep," Jael echoed, gingerly touching her stiff wraps. "Thank."

The greybeard chuckled. "Yer welcome, Sisters."

CHAPTER 26

Jael and me more than I dared imagine through the next day on the Surface.

We knew where to get food, but we also knew where to stay out of the way. We didn't require the communal shower room, getting by with the small water sink and waste closet. My spiders found insects chased their way by the activity around us, and Soul Drinker wasn't within reach while we rested.

That first day, we'd enjoyed slower, careful servicing of each other as Jael managed her fractured hand, what was truly needed — still — was a deep Reverie without any view of sand dunes, blue or red.

Talov's office gave us that, somehow.

Wearing my pendant and with the rune dagger far away, I avoided falling into or drawing anyone into that lucid state for a full rest. Jael slept without disruption, with her arm strapped to her chest, and I had a chance to recall what a "dark sleep" had been like before the Tragar.

Before Auslan.

Odd.

Wasn't I close to enough minds, active or resting? Did the Tundar Dwarves surrounding me have some different quality of sleep from Humans which better shielded them? Or was this room protected from scrying in a similar way as Mourn's underground library?

If Gavin were here, I'd be asking him.

Jael yawned and began to stretch, alerted by the restraint of one arm. She muttered a curse and turned her head to watch me while I sat in my shirt and bottoms, inspecting and cleaning my gear. I wasn't sure if her eyes lingered so long on my hands or on my belly.

"Sirana?" she began.

"Hm?"

"I'm sorry I pushed so hard. When you said you couldn't birth the infant up here, I didn't want you to miss your chance with the Dwarf."

One corner of my mouth lifted; I kept my hands busy. *"I grasp that. D'Shea gave me a vial to take if I needed to stop it early to survive. As you said, need to live to do the Queen's bidding."*

Jael carefully got up on her good elbow, intrigued. *"She did?"*

"Yes. Though we're not supposed to, the Sisterhood does it anyway. Sanctuary's gotten nothing from us since Shyntre."

She smirked, sitting upright. *"I knew it. Or was willing to wager on it. The Sorceress is as pragmatic as the General. So, you have something, then. You wouldn't need the Dwarf's offer?"* Jael saw the look on my face. *"What?"*

"The sorcerer who attacked us at the Temple?"

"Yeah."

"He found the vial and smashed it," I said. *"So ... no, it's gone. I've been afraid of getting trapped the same way the Sanctuary would ever since."*

"Another reason you made the Bargain with the half-blood," she said.

"Yes."

"So what makes him different? How do you know he won't ... I don't know, try to keep you or your baby, too?"

I smiled at how easily that answer came to me. *"He can't break his promise without losing some of his magic."*

"He what?"

"You know how the Priestesses never put their sons in real harm's way, because the demonbloods augment their magic? And how weak Wilsira looked after Kerse died?"

Jael appeared ever-so-briefly smug. *"Yeah."*

"Mourn doesn't make promises he can't keep or change his mind about them midway through, because there's a consequence if he fails. That's why he took so long to come to a formal agreement with me. He had to be sure it would be worth it to him."

"Hm. Weird. Is that a Dragon thing? It's clearly not Davrin."

"I think so, yes. He's mentioned his sire making Barg —"

I stopped, looking at Jael with a strange, apologetic shock.

"Wait a fuck," she said, frowning. "He's mentioned other Bargains with his sire? Was it before I told you about the crypt?"

I grimaced. "Well, at least one. The Davrin in the second city had Mourn because of a Bargain. An agreement to help one of them catch from him and give birth to a half-blood."

And die doing it.

Jael snorted. "That must've turned out badly for them. I get the feeling half-bloods of any type aren't the best idea as a path to power."

"Yeah," I breathed, thinking of Innathi and Cris-ri-phon's astonishing number there, wiping my damp cloth against a stubborn smear of grit. Houda's voice returned from when she'd pleaded with the Deathless to leave the Temple.

"They are not lost. The Grey Lady knows. You need only to find them."

What had she meant? Another thing I should ask the Deathwalker down the hall?

Jael cleared her throat. "So, you might need the Dwarf's help."

I blinked and looked up then breathed out. "I might. I was thinking, if it's as he says, then ... I'm not as scared."

She rubbed her chin. "But you aren't sure?"

I shook my head.

"Why not? Can I ask? I just want to understand."

Sigh.

I wasn't ready to talk about the dream-bond I seemed to have with the sire while I was up here. I also didn't understand enough about the "tether" Innathi had mentioned, about leaving the Elsewhere when I wished.

But I'd thought about it before those had become a factor.

"My sister at House Thalluen left me barren before I ever went to Court," I said, changing out my dagger to clean another. *"Gaelan knew. She was there, kept me from bleeding to death."*

Jael's shoulders hunched, like she expected my bland tone to take on the appropriate anger and pain. I just felt tired.

"Jilrina mimicked an altar ritual she'd heard about from someone in the Sanctuary," I continued. *"If it had been real, it wouldn't have cut me, but it did. The dagger went deep, and the healing couldn't mend everything. My Matron found out I couldn't catch, I couldn't bear an heir, and that's why she sent me to Court. I needed to hide it from the other Nobles, too.*

"When the Sisterhood came for me, my trials included reliving that ritual. But it was true this time, and it made me fertile." I smirked with a dark edge. *"Because the Priestesses would rather the Sisterhood not be a horde of barren cock-wielders."*

Jael snickered, rolling her eyes briefly.

"So, not only did the Sanctuary first take any chance I might've had to become Thalluendara, but they also gave that fertility back when I dared not use it. I'd lose what I'd gained with the Red Sisters while also losing any right to raise or place my blood anywhere in Sivaraus except the Third Floor of the Sanctuary."

My younger Sister hummed with a nod, like she was beginning to see it.

"Add on top of that," I finished, my neck and tone tightening, *"a Consort I wasn't supposed to touch, dangled in front of my face, while the Conceiver and her son continued playing their centuries-old games with fresh meat, many times worse than Jilrina, until ... until ..."*

"Until it all fell to shit," Jael finished, spreading out one hand, *"and here we are."*

"Exactly. I don't ... I don't even know if I'll have another chance to carry, or if I just won't make it as far as Jaunda. If I expel a strong healer's seed to spite the Queen and Priestesses, but also despite myself, with no other reason? If I do it before I've glimpsed all possibilities while I'm up here ..."

Jael's face grew sober. *"Like the Dwarf said. It would be worse because it's just Braqth forcing you into a corner again. Like it's always been. Even when you're far away."*

"Yes." I swallowed a hard lump. *"Yes, it's like that."*

Jael stood up, stepping closer, and lifted my chin to kiss my lips. She smiled impishly afterward. *"Alright. So we'll try to cheat the cunts first. I am your spare hands."* A wince as she lifted one good hand, wiggling her fingers. *"I mean your spare hand."*

I chuckled. *"With magic, one spare hand might collapse caves."*

Her face lit up with a mischievous grin. *"Can't wait to surprise a few choice slits back home."*

Although I couldn't yet imagine what that might look like, an equally young and defiant part of me wanted to live to see it.

I ESTIMATED WE'D BEEN HIDING OUT IN TALOV'S ROOM FOR TWO DAYS, GIVEN enough peace and quiet for several stress-relieving orgasms each and for Jael to begin wondering what else was going on in the redoubt.

"None coming to bother us," she murmured as I helped wrap her hand and wrist with fresh bandages. *"Not the Godblood or the Pale Ones, not the Dwarves or even the tiny old drake. At worst, we get stared at when we get food, but they keep away and make no faces or gestures. They don't follow us."*

I shrugged as we finished, speaking in Trade so she'd keep her ear attuned. "I think everyone is exhausted. Over four days have passed since the gate was sealed behind us, four Clans working shifts, day and night. Caravans leaving, messages passing between here and Augran, no doubt."

"And your guard sleeps, still," she answered back, her enunciation getting better as we'd practiced alone.

I exhaled through my nose. "Yeah. I don't know how long that will last."

If Graul had been hinting it may end soon, he hadn't meant by the next dawn or dusk. What did he sense? Next week or month?

Certainly not next year ...

That would do interesting things to my geas, no doubt.

"You never told what cautious Mourn took as pay," Jael said in a clear attempt to start a new conversation.

I looked at her eyes. She was genuinely curious but lacking the suggestion I'd expected. She also seemed not to have connected that Mourn had been there with us in the crypt, didn't realize that he'd been fucking me as I'd slipped my fingers inside her ...

Hoo bua.

Was this worth mentioning before he woke up, or wait until he could be included in the explanation? Recalling his embarrassment to accept sex as payment for the first time in his life, I was hesitant to gossip to Jael about it before he could speak for himself.

Hmm.

Someone knocked on the door.

"Sirana?"

Talov.

The greybeard spoke through a peridot gem, so he didn't have to shout through the thick door. "I brought Krithy and Tami tah talk about somethin'."

I grinned when the Naulor murmured something. Their tone protested something, maybe the short names.

Krithy and Tami. I liked them.

He added, "Got two others, too. Ye know 'em, Osgrid an' Lady Verina."

The eve witch wasn't a surprise. The Manalari woman, however ...

Jael and I passed expressions between us before I approached the door, pressing two fingers to the peridot and answered, "Unlocking."

Inserting the key, I was glad I kept the lock box containing Soul Drinker out of sight by habit. All five of them slipped in quickly.

Krithannia closed the door, motioning to me to secure it, which was enough to tell me they weren't inviting an audience to note their comings and goings with whatever they had to say. Interestingly, Verina wasn't wearing her veil; her springy, blonde curls contrasted Osgrid the same way Tamuril's straight locks did Krithannia.

Jael was on her feet, her arm out of the sling for now, though she kept her hand loosely fisted across her chest, elbow braced in her other hand. We counted the oversized chairs, including the two in front of the desk.

"Must move own seat," she said, waving her good arm.

Talov chuckled. "Yer hand doin' okay?"

She shrugged, ambivalent. "Okay."

"Good start." He looked between us. "We got a question, an' we might not hafta move seats if yer answer is quick enough, one way or the other."

"A question?" I asked, noting the mood of each arrival.

"Answer quick?" Jael echoed, doing the same with eyes narrowed.

Neither Tamuril nor Verina were looking at us; their eyes were down and wandering. Krithannia was hard to read, as always, but Osgrid maintained a warm expression for me, as if she anticipated a positive outcome when she took the lead.

"We've two deep wounds needin' a somethin' stronger tah mend," said the eve witch. "Yah both are aware o' their making, aye?"

The making of Tamuril's wound, certainly, but the odd one here …

"How woman wounded?" Jael asked first, coming to the same conclusion.

"Lady Verina's mage aura was awakened by the sacred pool," Krithannia said, "but she has no training, no affinity, and this hurts her. She cannot sleep enough to be well. Soon, mind and body will start declining."

My Sister fell silent with a slight nod. Everyone except Verina herself grasped how Jael related to that.

"We have a place fer ye both in a ritual," Osgrid said, smiling and presenting empty hands palm up. "An' this could even help yer sister, Sirana."

Looking at the eve witch's strong, bare hands, the realization struck me that neither her crow nor the falcon were present.

"My only question," the younger Dwarf finished, "an' why we're here, is wouldja help us *drive* our magic? Wouldja *want* tah see these two hale with hearts mended? No lies, no halfway answer. A full-throated *aye*, or we leave an' make do."

I noticed when Tamuril's face flushed beyond her control; it happened the same time mine warmed. We were probably thinking about the shower. About the oath.

At least I was.

"I will never hurt you or watch another do it. My oath, I will stop it first ..."

I hadn't promised to heal her because I didn't see how I could. But where in Osgrid's request could I refuse to help? Was standing back, especially as I loitered about, the same as watching harm done to the Druid? In that view, I'd break my oath and hurt her by choice, whether that required action or not.

A surprising tangle of thought.

I began, "I want to see them mended, but —"

"But?" Osgrid repeated, mildly astonished.

"Does Tamuril in return *want* our help? In some genuine way? Or has she been informed she must accept to receive your help?"

I included Krithannia in the question with a look, and both sets of dark eyebrows shot up. Talov chuckled softly next to them.

"Tol' ya," he murmured in a lean.

Krithannia exhaled with careful patience, and Osgrid smirked, darting a playful warning at him before she motioned to the Druid. "Tamuril? Speak on this, please. Honest words only. Tainted motives spoil rituals an' may even change yer curse."

Another interesting thought which seemed to frighten the tall blonde. I'd have to turn that over later and compare it to our Abyss.

"I-I believe Sirana *would* help me, yes." She spoke with soft cheeks and throat turning a delicate pink. "And ... I believe her sister would help *her* if asked."

Osgrid glanced at Jael, who gave that a weigh before nodding.

"True. I am her spare hand. She leads, I guard."

My chest warmed as much as my face. I hadn't expected her to say that aloud around others. Speaking it essentially mimicked an Elder and her Right Hand in rank: D'Shea and Jaunda, Rausery and Qivni.

Me and Jael? Oi.

Nonetheless, her confidence made Krithannia and the Dwarves smile.

"Whatcha say then, Sirana?" the eve witched prompted. "Seems Tamuril an' Jael wait on ye tah decide."

A strange feeling, for sure. Meanwhile, Verina's eyes wandered between us without enough comprehension.

"I have helped … drive ritual magic before," I said with care, glancing at Krithannia, "but some of them were tainted."

"Not in my observance," said the Guild Mistress as she picked up what I'd subtly laid out. She lifted her chin. "Your focus at Manalar aided us, especially Mourn and Captain Isboern. If you are willing, I know we can help them."

That unraveled some of my tension.

"Alright. Then our answer is yes."

KRITHANNIA SET A POWERFUL WARD ON TALOV'S OFFICE SINCE WE WOULD BE leaving our equipment behind, including Soul Drinker and my spider guardians. She didn't say so, of course, but we made eye contact, and I knew.

"Where now?" Jael asked.

"Back tah th' showers," Talov answered, jovially leading the way.

I encountered quite the surprise when we got there, for standing within the broad passage and blocking the entrance to the mass washing space were a group of males as mixed as the females.

I recognized Rithal at once, and easily spotted Willven Isboern even without his armor and weapons. Beside each of them was another of their kind: one bearded, red-blond Dwarf whose name I didn't know, and a helmless, sandy-haired Templar I thought I recognized from the library in Manalar.

Deshi and Tak had come as well, standing near the final man with skin dark enough for a Zauyrian.

"Ah, excellent, yer all here," Talov said, pressing hands with each of them while Osgrid stepped forward to give Rithal a hug.

Willven and Tamuril met eyes before he and his man bowed their heads to Lady Verina, speaking to Verina in her native tongue which seemed to reassure her. Meanwhile, Deshi bowed in familiar Yungian fashion to me while Tak self-consciously waved at us with one hand.

Jael arched one eyebrow as high as it would go, awaiting an explanation.

"Short answer," Osgrid said with an expression approaching excitement, "these are our counterparts. They agreed tah help protect us, but no worries, they aren't goin' inside. Each also has the talent and skill tah help if somethin' goes wrong. Then we call them in."

"Goes wrong?" I repeated.

"Just good plannin', Sirana," she replied, blue eyes meeting mine. "I always think what could go wrong but hope it doesn't."

Reasonable.

"So who are they? What skills are available?"

"Let's scooch closer tah the end," Talov suggested. "Let Krithannia set a cloak ward tah muffle us."

Also reasonable.

Once that was set, the Oltere introduced the males present.

"This is Rithal Hobgaer, Osgrid's companion," said the greybeard, "an' her cousin, Kellan Gherudum. Both are prepared tah tend her if she needs it afterward. Our Captain Isboern and his Lieutenant Sohl will help Tamuril an' Lady Verina if needed. An' ya recognize Deshi an' Tak, I take it?"

Jael watched a smile appear on my face. "We do."

"I'm afraid we're kinda short o' male Elves to be your counterparts," Talov said wryly, "but ya know these two, both are well in their minds, strong in motive. They agreed tah help if needed. Extra hands, if nothin' else."

I glanced at Krithannia first and then the last, dark-eyed man. "And him?"

"He is Sha-rish Urudre from Ahj-Zayr," the Naulor said forthrightly, enunciating well to make the dark man smile. "Presently in Augran working with the Guild, and a sorcerer capable of influencing the elements, water, fire, earth, and air. A skill we could need."

Sha-rish bowed at the waist, placing one hand over his heart. "*Bandrin shaku.*"

He'd faced Krithannia but repeated the action for Jael and me, and then Tamuril and Verina. Quelling my impulse of suspicion in the vague suggestion of Cris-ri-phon in his name and appearance, I looked him over without peering into my memory.

He was dressed differently, in higher quality clothing with shades of color suggesting many of those elements; even his cloak was an earthy reddish-brown. He would have fit in well in Alran during the midnight festival when we'd left by boat.

"You speak Trade?" I asked.

Sha-rish smiled. "I do, dark warrior. Quite well."

I had to agree. "Well, Krithannia says your motive is good. How?"

The Sal-Zayrian straightened up, bowing to the men and Dwarves. "I search for those suffering the consequences of magic growing beyond their ability to manage, and I help the Guild find solutions for them."

I noticed Tak nod out of my periphery. *Ah.* "Perhaps you noticed Lady Verina?"

"I did. I brought her to the attention of the *Oltere.*"

"Quite a strong motive, then."

"Absolutely."

His poise hadn't shifted in the slightest during our exchange, and he seemed like one quite comfortable in a large, busy city meeting many contacts. I could imagine he'd worked with the Guild Mistress before and guessed he may be here because Mourn couldn't be.

I bowed like Deshi, though not as deep and kept my eyes up. "I am Sirana. This is my sister, Jael."

Without reluctance, Sha-rish bowed a second time. "*Bandrin shaku,* Sirana, Jael."

Jael bobbed her head twice then addressed Talov. "These are guards for shower room?"

"Tha's one way tah see it."

"Hand-picked," Osgrid added, squeezing Rithal's hand. "Even if all is well, if no one tries tah get past 'em an' they only give us a hand tah our rooms. Gotta be th' right ones fer this."

"*Janshi,*" Deshi reassured me with a bow. "Trust us. If any trouble, I will call the Deathwalker as well. My promise."

If Gavin needed to come help, we were having a worrisome amount of fun.

I glanced at Isboern with a smirk. "You're not easily ignored if anyone glimpses you."

His Lieutenant covered a smile with his hand as the Captain shrugged. "I can be, and I shall. This is necessary."

Does he know about the marks, then? Or was he referring to Verina and the Sal-Zayrian's stated mission? I wasn't sure but thought Isboern must have *some* sense of Tamuril's pain, or his motive could be "tainted."

"Thank ya much fer that, Captain," Talov said, looking at Osgrid. "If ya don't need me this moment?"

Osgrid grinned. "Fly free, Grand Cl'dum."

"Heh." He patted her shoulder. "Do right fer 'em, as always."

After Talov had left and Osgrid seemed satisfied, she instructed the females to come with her and the males to "keep their wise," whatever that meant.

Although Krithannia, Jael, and I had stepped beyond the guardians' line, Isboern touched Verina's shoulder and offered encouragement in her tongue. The girl jerked dark brown eyes up to him and listened as if the word quenched her thirst. She shuddered and spoke something with nervous, reverent awe, and the Godblood responded by bringing both her hands to his brow.

"*Syras forche,*" he assured with confidence.

"*Grache, grache ...*"

When Verina finally came forward, tears upon her cheeks, Tamuril tried to slip by. She blatantly hesitated, however, swallowing and allowing herself a glance at his face.

Willven gazed at her for a moment, neither reaching for nor speaking to her aloud, yet his cheeks blushed deeply. He blinked, seeming to recall his place, and bowed his head.

"*Syras forche,*" he repeated, his tone much softer. "*Natridria.*"

The Druid didn't reply but, like Verina, came to us with tears in her eyes.

Osgrid waited patiently for each of us, but the moment all the females were out of sight of the males, she drew the heaviest, darkest curtain I'd seen so far, closing off the shower room as Krithannia lit a few glowstones set high in the wall.

The rest of us watched the eve witch hook heavy metal rings to the wall, stretching the curtain to prevent a peeking eye should any be tempted. Then she withdrew chalk from her belt and drew remarkably crisp runes on the dark material. Verina made a familiar gesture across her chest and head.

"Awright, our voices won't carry," the Dwarf said, "an' this is a mild warning."

"Warning?" I asked.

"Dissuader ward. Not unbreakable fer our cohorts outside, just protects our privacy here fer the next while."

"How long?" Jael asked.

Osgrid shrugged. "Depends on us, really."

"Does anyone wait on us to use it?" Tamuril asked, pensive as Krithannia put her arm around the blonde's shoulders.

"Do not think about that, my sister," she said. "We are here as long as needed, Talov has seen to it. This was planned. There is another place they may go."

Two utility rooms like this in one redoubt? Luxurious.

"What is our first step?" I asked.

Osgrid pulled a stack of pale circles out of her laden satchel and handed them out to me. "Take off yer boots an' lay these over drains in th' most circular space, then start the warm water on all th' spigots. Make sure they stick an' don't float away."

"I will help," Krithannia said, sitting on a bench to remove her boots and stockings.

"Me!" Jael added, claiming another to do the same.

This task went quickly with three of us. We stopped up two drains each then attended to three spigots, though the Naulor first had to teach us the "push-and-twist" trick to get them started. With nine warm sprays in action and entirely open without curtains, we moved quickly to get out of the water in our clothes.

"Floating away!" Jael pointed.

"Strip down if ya want," Osgrid called across the way. "Tha's the next step. Grindin' some stuff first."

The Naulor and Manalari were shocked how fast Jael took the Dwarf's suggestion. Soon, my nude Sister was catching drifting plugs in the sluicing space, resetting them to block the water from escaping by using its own weight.

With a small smile on her face, Krithannia began to dress down. She was graceful, unhurried, and calm in removing her fine, loose white shirt, simple breast wrap, and dark blue pants.

I stared for a few moments at the tiny, pale small pants hugging her pelvis; I must have missed them the last time we were in the shower. The Naulor kept them on for now but sat with her pert breasts out in the open.

I began to do the same, just without small pants, and quite aware that the two blondes stared at us with slowly escalating worry.

You'll have to undress eventually.

Even though I didn't yet know what the ritual entailed, nakedness seemed necessary when dealing with water. Or blood.

"Hey, Jael."

"Hey, Osgrid."

"Add this heating stone tah the showers, please? We need steam."

"Ooo," my Sister cooed, going to retrieve the smooth, unassuming brown stone wrapped in an insulating cloth.

"How may I assist you further, Osgrid?" Krithannia asked.

"You an' yer sister, both of ye come here an' grab a pestle."

Sounds like we're ingesting something.

"Sirana?"

I blinked at the Guild Mistress. "Hm?"

"Will you show Lady Verina where she can undress?"

She motioned toward the familiar stalls where this endeavor had begun. What good would that do?

"I can show her," Tamuril said, sounding slightly annoyed. "I am right here."

"And I need you over here with Osgrid, please."

"Yes, please," the Dwarf echoed. "Wanna double-check th' plants with ye."

Oh.

Well, I was accustomed to escorting nobles and waiting outside the door. Usually male, but this felt similar enough. The parallel had slipped my mind before, but I really should keep it in mind for Verina and any other Manalari women I interacted with.

I frowned. How might Auslan react to an abrupt confrontation with a large, nude, pale man watching him step naked out of a bath … ?

Hmm. Maybe not so easy.

Fortunately, Tamuril told the girl what to do in her own language, making her sister and the eve witch wait, gently nudging Lady Verina toward me. I could have waited on stripping down, but …

Too late now.

Verina's eyes dropped to my blue pendant but flickered about as if trying to avoid my breasts, her cheeks growing red. I smiled and lifted it in both my hands, letting her admire it as we walked, my palms providing a shield between the necklace and my tits. She seemed to appreciate this, using the distraction to study Shyntre's jewelry work as she moved into the stall.

"*Herdinsa?*" she asked, her hand on the curtain but not quite drawing it closed.

"Um."

"*Agasyo,*" Tamuril answered for me with Krithannia gently taking her wrist to draw her closer to Osgrid's workspace. "*Di'seu amantio.*"

Verina's face brightened with a pleasured surprise. Taking another moment to admire my necklace, the Human said something with a gesture that suggested she'd be out soon, and closed the curtain like she was indeed used to having someone waiting on her.

Huh.

"What'd she say?" I asked.

"She asked if it is an heirloom," Krithannia answered.

She and Tamuril were grinding two separate mortars and pestles while Osgrid laid out and measured ingredients.

"Heirloom? What is that?"

"Something which has been passed from parent to child for at least two generations."

"Only two? Half century?" Jael asked, unimpressed. "Pass from mother to daughter be 'heirloom' at once to Humans."

I nearly snorted — she was right — and the Guild Mistress shrugged as she kept working in her underwear. "Well, yes, that could be anything from a century to a millennium, couldn't it?"

"Got some o' those in Taiding," Osgrid reflected, weighing some large, brown-green leaves in her palm. "Humans lose track o' theirs quicker."

That they do.

I bit my cheek rather than make a remark about Soul Drinker and Cris-ri-phon. The dagger can't have been made by Humans, so it certainly wasn't an "heirloom" of *theirs*, even if they stole it over and over. Where had it come from?

"My necklace," I said, "is not an heirloom, so what made Verina smile like that?"

The Dwarf and two Naulor looked amused and too pleased.

Uh-oh.

"Tamuril said it was a gift from your male lover?" Krithannia responded, seeking confirmation.

I jolted slightly, looking at the Druid before recalling how she could know that. "Wait, you remember that?"

"Of course," she said, blonde eyebrows drawing down. "You said you earned it from him, in a game where you did not know who won. Is it not true?"

"Is true," Jael answered for me, chortling as she winked at me. "She in contest with older mage, very stubborn."

"Smart and tempting, wasn't he?" Tamuril added, using my words against me. The pink in her cheek refused to lighten one bit.

She remembers that, too. I sighed.

"So someone ye like made that fer ye?" Osgrid asked.

"Uh … yes, he made it. Though I think his, um, father was the one who insisted he give it to me."

Though Shyntre had returned it to me twice more after that.

The three pale ones were obviously curious, though Jael kept her mouth shut and, for whatever reason, the trio chose not to ask details about our unfamiliar rules back home.

"It's pretty," the Dwarf said, breaking the pause. "Not imbued with magic, which is interestin', but pretty."

I was clutching the blue and silver pendant when Verina peeked out of the stall, holding the curtain against her like another towel. She was mostly undressed, wearing the same sleeveless sack as Tamuril, and didn't look ready to come out.

Meanwhile, Jael and I leaned casually nude against the walls. My Sister seemed to be enjoying some of the early heat from the brown stone in the water gradually rising over the shower floor. I noted the small rise on the floor at the entry way, a lip separating the circular space from the dressing area and designed to prevent easy overflow. We looked to be about half full.

Until now, I'd been working to hear through the loud, multi-sourced shushes of the spigots spilling onto the smooth stone. Once we stopped talking, the room seemed to fill with that constant roar. Whenever Osgrid or Krithannia murmured something to each other, I couldn't make it out.

They seemed close to finished with whatever compounds the eve witch needed, however. We watched her line each one up atop a wooden tray with legs and handles, the blends and pastes separated either in a small bowl or tiny pouch brought from her loaded satchel.

"Is this a ritual you have performed before, Osgrid?" I asked.

Her bright blue eyes blinked at me. "Ahm, full truth, Sirana. No."

What?

"Osgrid and I have worked something out between us," Krithannia said, one eye looking over her shoulder, "based on our experiences, which should get around the priest's anchor chaining my sister."

Tamuril tensed; I recognized the shame but also her fight against panic. The glimmer of hope. Krithannia pushing me to be introduced to Osgrid certainly made sense, though no wonder this had taken two days for her to arrange.

Unless this is incredibly fast for working out a new spell.

"If I may ask," I began, waiting until the dark-haired females had turned ear or eyes toward me. "What is Verina expecting? And how did you convince a veiled noble unaccustomed to showing her face to trust standing undressed with no other Humans around?"

"Tis actually *not* havin' other Humans around that makes it easier for her," Osgrid answered first. "She saw enough at th' Temple and th' climb down, how I understand it, she knows the three o' ye were fighin' the Ma'ab an' defendin' Templars against the ghosts overtakin' the pool. It made an impression on 'er."

Krithannia agreed. "She's also been in a 'woundless' pain without any other Human understanding what she's going through. Some of the other Manalari women whisper she's possessed by a demon or becoming a witch."

Jael scoffed and pantomimed spitting on the floor, her breath puffing without spraying, the contempt clear on her face.

"Indeed," Osgrid chuckled. "She's been swayed to do this out of their sight."

"They worry about a taint following from Manalar," Tamuril added softly, "like with the deadlands barbs in some of the men. We must help her realize her magic so she can do good work among them and change their minds."

"An' earn a better place, I'm hopin'," the Dwarf added. "Lotsa shuffling places, new tasks up fer grabs among th' Humans now that the Temple city has fallen."

Made sense.

"In that case," I continued, "does she expect *any* focus to be on Tamuril, or just her? This is a double-healing, right?"

The Druid's shoulders hunched; their expressions were interesting. A gut feeling said they weren't entirely honest with the girl.

"We always need healers," Krithannia said, "so we are attempting to help her realize this affinity as we heal Tamuril's marking. The Lady understands she is part of this. She believes if she helps heal the 'golden grower' who assured so many of her people would reach the bottom of the mountain, then Musanlo will 'see' her prayers have been true. She in turn heals her own pain and can go forward to help others."

Ah. A clever way to "assign" a desired affinity to a mage lacking one: focus her will on it as if this were already the case. "Aren't there other untrained mages also awakened?"

"Each must be handled with care," Krithannia said, firm but nonspecific. "Lady Verina is best suited to *this* solution. You and Jael need not worry about the others."

Alright, then.

"No healer in witch hunter, hah?" Jael said with a grin.

Osgrid suppressed a smile, and Krithannia glanced back again, narrowing her eyes. "Hm. Correct, Jael. Most Human mages have an inborn leaning, and Lady Verina is the only one with a healer's potential. Like with Deshi discovering his death magic around Gavin, we shan't waste this opportunity for her."

I bobbed my chin. "Got it."

"That is why Willven is called the Godblood," Tamuril said, not realizing how familiar that name sounded coming off her lips. "He is a mage but has realized more than one talent."

"Very difficult fer Humans tah balance," Osgrid agreed. "Main reason is they grow too fast an' don't live long enough. Those who do tend tah make a big splash whether they keep their sanity or not."

Keeping their sanity. *Huh.*

Quite different from how Krithannia had described Jael's lack of an affinity. The Naulor had made it sound as if my Sister could take on *any* affinity which might have been available through the Elves around her.

I'd chosen the To'vah through Mourn for her while, unbeknownst to me, the abrupt rise of that open mage potential seemed linked to his Sire somehow. The Black Dragon of the Deepearth.

Hoo bua.

"Awright," Osgrid announced, brushing her broad palms together before climbing to her feet. "Let's get into it."

Chapter 27

We turned the showers off. The sound of a few drips followed the gentle splashes of Krithannia's shuffling feet.

Jael and I welcomed the comparative quiet while she checked over the area, bare feet submerged in gently steaming water reaching her ankles.

Meanwhile, Osgrid disrobed outside the pool we'd made of the floor. Gradually, she revealed equally pale skin beneath the dark layers, causing me to reflect on how Rithal was ruddier and had more color overall, like many of the Paxians who traveled frequently.

Tamuril reluctantly followed her lead, removing her worn boots, tanned top and bottoms, but pausing at the unflattering short shift obscuring her torso. She didn't wear small pants like Krithannia and Verina; I glimpsed the rounded curve of her buttocks peeking out.

Next to her, Osgrid and Verina were quite plush. The Tundar's overall shape wasn't a surprise to me; the cut of her clothing had offered enough insight to expect the impressively full breasts and exaggeratedly round hips and backside.

The hidden details nonetheless added to the reveal: much larger circles of rosy color surrounding prominent nipples compared to the Naulor; and far greater definition in her arm muscles compared to Verina. Osgrid bore a thick, dark bush crowning her startlingly powerful legs, even though she hadn't been forced to work her whole life like Lana down below.

The fleeting thought that the eve witch might be capable of breaking someone's neck during wrestling passed behind my eyes. *Whew.*

In contrast, Lady Verina was as soft in her arms, legs, and belly as I would expect someone who's life had been like a kept Consort. She was well-fed with plenty of padding in places a male didn't tend to have, and her breasts easily equaled Osgrid's in volume despite the taller stature, so that wasn't a unique quality of the short and stout races. She also had little silvery-red lines visible where the flesh seemed heaviest.

Interesting.

Jael stood close enough to lean in and murmur, *"Pregnant?"*

My eyes flicked to her, confirming she was looking at Verina. *"Possible, I suppose."*

A Manalari man had been quite intent on hauling her alongside him at the Temple courtyard. I didn't know who he'd been to her.

"She is not," Krithannia said in heavily accented Davrin. *"Magic confirm. Only one mother here."*

She'd used the wrong word for "mother," implying I'd given birth before and had living children. Nonetheless, we understood.

"So she is fattened up finding endless food on the Surface?" Jael asked.

Looking at Krithannia's face, I winced inside.

"Food not endless, and she survive beyond you through dark cold time," the Guild Mistress replied with an elegantly arched brow. *"No chill wind below, yes? Stay warm without clothes."*

All true. We'd both wandered the wilderness of the Deepearth nude and survived. Freezing to death had been the least of our concerns.

"We haven't seen winter yet," I murmured in Trade. "Our leader said the food vanished under snow and too-short Sun."

Jael's mouth twisted and for a moment she seemed pensive. With a shrug and a sigh, she let it go. "I see. Different up here. Need different."

The Guild Mistress smiled and looked satisfied with that, bowing her head to Jael and motioning Tamuril and Verina closer while Osgrid moved her standing tray of herbs and pastes into the shallow water.

Krithannia chose that moment to hook her thumbs into her small pants and drag them down her long legs, stepping out of them and hanging them on a nearby hook. Jael and I were staring as she gently coaxed the other two.

"Come. It's time. You are safe. *I'nora. Isti saveli.*"

Their hearts sped up, and Verina seemed to be gathering courage as she lifted her shift to follow her strange elders' examples. She pulled it off over her head all at once, holding her breath and scrunching her face as if she were diving underwater. The motion briefly lifted her generous breasts and dropped them with a jiggle.

Again, Jael and I stared, but at a quite different form. Verina wasn't ugly; I could tell she was healthy and wagered those mounds were better than the softest Noble cushions. Recognized by some part of me who still felt like Kain.

Tamuril had begun to weep softly, hands shaking as she plucked at the hem of her shapeless cover.

"Tami?" Krithannia asked.

"*Ithluniden*," she whispered to her sister, going on to explain something else too quickly to make out. She received a soothing response and another hug from the night-hair, but her glittering green eyes landed on me and Jael.

"I am not here to hurt," I said, forming the tender, new promise with deliberate thought. "I will help stop the hurt, if possible. Krithannia believes I can help."

"And I follow her," Jael agreed by bumping her shoulder into mine as she kept her arms crossed. "On the Surface, if she help, I help. I learn and stay alive, like her."

I wasn't sure Tamuril appreciated my Sister's honesty as much as I did, but Krithannia was satisfied. Osgrid waited on us patiently without speaking, kneeling in the warm water at a point she seemed to have chosen with care. Her fingers were loosely entwined and resting on her thighs, strong arms framing her bare chest.

"They are ... ugly," Tamuril exhaled, pained and reluctant to allow the loose fabric to outline her breasts.

"We know," Krithannia murmured. "As ugly as the jealous hand that made them."

"N-no, no, I didn't mean —"

"He *is* jealous, Tamuril." The Guild Mistress's face firmed up. "He did this because of *his* weakness, not yours. He had you believe you brought it upon yourself, didn't he? He told you this while you couldn't move, couldn't leave the room, and said you could return in seven years after you've abstained from all which gives you joy, correct?"

The Druid stammered, unable to speak, and the tears began to fall. Astonishingly, she managed to nod. *A confirmation.*

"That's why we will cleanse these markings from you, my sister. On behalf of the Davrin, Sirana regrets what happened. She cannot change what her Sisters have done, but she can help atone for it. We can lift a penance forced upon you, a punishment which was not earned and reflects only the fear and shame of the one who did it.

"This is *his* shame, Tamuril, not yours. Show us what he's done. We do not blame you. Let us help you shed this unjust weight you carry."

Jael's eyes were wide while listening, flicking to me as my heartbeat quickened with the earnestness of Krithannia's speech. Verina was making a conscious effort not to wring her fingers, her concern genuine enough to have forgotten that she was naked.

With Krithannia's help, Tamuril finally pulled the cover off over her head. Verina gasped and covered her mouth with both hands, dark eyes glistening while Jael squinted and scrutinized. A moment later, my eyes made some sense of what I was seeing.

Unfamiliar runes and a flowing script had been carved then stained black and green into the white breasts, starting around the nipple and spiraling outward. The lines themselves were thin and precise but the edges puffy and red as if they were fresh.

Not created more than two years ago.

"Words?" Jael asked, frowning. "Say what?"

The Guild Mistress nodded. Now that I knew what signs to look for in her face, Krithannia couldn't hide the effort required to manage her anger in front of Tamuril.

"Roughly translated," she said, reading the left breast, "it says 'public vessel' and 'interfere not in those natures not of your own.' And …"

"And," Tamuril hiccupped through tears, covering her right breast. "Find strength in Him alone, or die alone, and None sh-shall mourn."

The Human girl did not understand our words but responded to the Druid's distress and began to cry as well. The sobs flowed into a brief denial when Krithannia translated for her, too. Verina earnestly shook her head, speaking something to try to comfort the pale Druid.

Meanwhile, Jael made a face that reflected my initial confusion, though I had more insight after meeting Jacob in the shed. The Witch Hunter had submitted to be beaten and marked by Mathias because he *wanted* to be that "public vessel." That had been clear to me.

Yet he'd blamed *me* for his situation every step of the way. He'd blamed Gaelan, too, when she hadn't been involved in the slightest.

If Naulor Priests are anything like Davrin Priestesses …

"Not true," Krithannia whispered after a brief, private exchange, holding her sister's wet face in both hands. "It's a lie, Tamuril. *I* would mourn. Until my final breath."

"Th-hey have forgotten you."

"They have *not* forgotten me, even if they refuse to speak of me. I carry value none of them can forget and still be what they are. They are *wrong*. One of us would mourn until the end of all. But I would rather *not*, and *he* is lying, too. He would not forget his sister while he breathed."

Tamuril did not argue this, her body sagging into her touch as her eyes closed, lashes damp with tears.

"What if home in seven years," Jael began hesitantly, "and marks healed?"

Krithannia granted us a sly, all-too-familiar smile over her shoulder, the look of a sorceress who had uncovered the weakness in her rival's bedchamber. "The marks fade in that time regardless. If she does not go home before then, he will never know. She need not suffer or have her magic dampened when there is so much good for others she wishes to do instead."

The Druid nodded, slightly.

"Dampened?" Jael said then, sounding astonished. "Thorn wall stops

Ma'ab, protect us all, and your magic be *more* without marks?"

I took that opportunity to grin and chuckle. "I see why her brother is jealous."

"Hm?"

"Imagine a *Priestess* with a brother who had greater magic than her."

Jael blinked, her lips forming a circle. "Ohhh."

"That is too simple to be *wholly* true," Krithannia said with a wry smile. "But partly, and I appreciate the thought on her behalf. You are correct in that she has chosen to help many more with her gifts than he has."

"Krithannia," the Druid said in mild rebuke.

The Guild Mistress responded by putting an arm around her, opening the other toward the silent and observant Osgrid. "Shall we, my friends?"

Osgrid and I nodded at once.

"We shall," the eve witch said, beckoning us closer before instructing us where to sit in a circle.

We sat within touching distance and faced each other in the shallows. Until the water settled, I was aware of the gentle waves and ripples lapping at my crotch. I glanced around.

Much of the room wasn't used, but the steam and warmth made it feel far less like empty space. Sounds within seemed muffled, like an early grey morning, with not a single hint that a large handful of men waited for us outside nor that anyone traveled the halls.

We could have been alone in this whole redoubt.

Osgrid struck a flame from a tiny stick against a whetstone. "We start by lighting th' candle, an' I'll be burning somethin' tah help us relax. Ya might float, but don' be afraid. Just breathe. Focus on why yer here. Pure motive, pure ritual."

Krithannia quietly translated for Lady Verina, who appeared more determined than she ever had.

Don't taint the ritual.

"An' Sirana?" Osgrid picked up a compressed, dark brown bun I hadn't noticed on her table. "Please eat this."

"Why?" Jael asked, lifting her hand to take and pass it to me.

The Dwarf smirked. "Will keep her stomach settled in th' smoke."

Sounded like a good idea.

I bit in, surprised to discover the bun contained finely ground, cooked meat and vegetable in the middle, as flavorful as the Dwarf pies in Alran. I gobbled it down.

"We'll have a grander meal later," Osgrid promised, her cheeks bunching in pleasure. "Now, follow Krithannia in the pace o' yer breath, listen tah my voice. We're surrounded by earth, air, fire, an' water. The protection of our heart-kin is with us. We build up th' will an' focus, an' we gift our strength an' wisdom when our sisters need us most."

She paused as the mist grew thicker, the flame somehow brighter, lighting up innumerable floating droplets and adding colors not visible before.

"We wish tah grant a new view, a new song, a new grasp on life that others may see its power and warmth and come as they yearn the same."

My saphgar began to glow, dimly at first, but strengthening as Osgrid and Krithannia chanted in at least two languages, maybe more. They paused and opened their eyes, the Dwarf more astonished than the pale Elf in what they saw.

"Deepearth stone," I murmured, not wishing to disturb the mist. "My mage made it to glow in the presence of magic but is not magic itself."

"Harmful to ye?" Osgrid asked. "Or meant to cause harm tah others?"

"No," I answered honestly. "It provides awareness and protects me from … ah, mind spells."

"Hm."

The eve witch shared a look with the Guild Mistress to weigh this, and I waited to see if they'd ask me to take it off. I didn't want to.

"Mourn suggested I always wear it when others sleep around me."

"I was going to say the same," Krithannia confirmed. "I didn't know it would be so bright, but she speaks the truth as I know it."

"Ah, a focus piece?"

"Very much."

"Alright." The Dwarf's round face was friendly. "It stays an' offers its light. Let's get back tah breathin'."

The tension within the circle faded, and my mind began to drift in the quiet as a low hum seemed to strengthen beneath us like a distant gathering storm. The candlelight and blue shine of my pendant illuminated the flowing, swirling droplets suspended in air until it felt like morning with the fog ready to lift at any moment.

I didn't know how much time had passed, though I thought someone changed position nearby.

Jael groaned softly.

I opened my eyes, though hers were closed, her first noises followed by a growl both odd and quite like her.

"Easy, Jael," Osgrid whispered. "Only what yer willin' tah give us."

My Sister reached for her swollen folds with her good hand, thighs wide as she sat cross-legged. She touched herself, swirling the water as she stroked her slit and its nub, knuckles churning the water into soft, quiet ripples.

"Ah. If that's what it takes, go on."

Osgrid looked at me next, and our eyes fixed on each other like a current drew us together. The Dwarf gasped softly, drifting with me for a few moments as a link formed.

"Yer ... are ye alright?"

~A thrall fully aware,~ part of me answered. *~Floating and anchored at once.~*

"Hm. Impressive. I have somethin' tah ask that we need from ye."

~What is it?~

"Look in th' center."

I followed her gaze and confirmed that all of us had changed position some time ago. Tamuril and Verina lay together in the center of a four-point shape created by Osgrid, Krithannia, Jael, and me. We'd expanded our circle to accommodate them, though the only one who hadn't moved was the eve witch with her table, now half empty of its components.

~What's happening?~

"Helpin' tah find a new pattern fer Verina's aura, based on what me an' Krithannia know. But we could use yer help."

~How?~

393

"Wasn't clear before. Ye have th' mystic's spark fer a healer."

I laughed without opening my lips. ~No, I don't.~

"Okay ... How about yer carryin' one?"

I blinked.

"The father is a healer, ain't he?"

~ ... He is.~

"He passed his gift, an' it could help us. Would ye lie down between them an' let us continue? We won't stress or take from ye. Let the spark guide the new song to its rhythm."

About then, Jael felt her first peak; she grunted, and her toes curled. We all gasped at the wash of colors sweeping through us.

"Wow," Osgrid said with renewed respect while Jael started digging for a second rush like the first. "Whew! Awright. Sirana? Lie down in th' center?"

I bent and crawled forward, stretching out my legs as I walked on all fours through the water and into the space between the two blondes, catching Krithannia's smile, her Stormseeker's eyes roiling.

The Naulor invited me to lie down, but I paused, peering at her, listening harder to the thoughts on the edge of my senses. She drew away until I couldn't hear them.

Lie down, Baenar, if you would help at all.

On my right, Verina lay curled on her side, cradling her own breasts like a child, one ear submerged. She licked her lips as water touched them. On my left, Tamuril was on her back, her blonde hair floating around her shoulders. Both points of her ears dipped into the water without reaching the canals. Her hands were folded on her stomach, the ugly, stark marks marring her breasts, writhing like worms.

Jilrina's face flickered in my mind. ~Blood filth. Shattered youth ... ~

We shall comfort, and keep her safe.

~That we shall.~

I lay down on my back, wedging myself between the two, soaking my damp hair. At least my spiders were safe.

"Good, good. Now breathe, Sirana. Breathe with us ..."

I did, detecting a newer smoke added atop the others. The space remained quiet and unknowable, the hum and drone underneath constant and strengthening, rising like a shield.

Verina shuffled closer to me, pressing her incredibly soft chest against my arm. The Human girl reached to place her palm on my belly. Her eyes never opened; she seemed to be moving in her sleep, but I noticed when the hum changed around her.

I leaned closer to listen, wishing I could *see* how it made that song. Something suggested the possibility.

A gift. A new sight open.

Verina hummed as if she agreed, slowly rolling away and taking her hand from my stomach. She gained her knees and elbows, moving toward Krithannia to answer some silent call. I could see her blonde, furry folds as she moved away, peeking out from between plump cheeks.

So close …

Jael must have climaxed again, because a familiar wave struck me.

Oh!!

On impulse, I reached out, tempted to chase after the Manalari girl to touch her.

"Nay, nay, *down*. Stay with Tami, Sirana. Stay with Tami, she's not h-healed …"

Osgrid sounded as though she might've peaked, too.

I slumped into the water, giving up my prey. My head rolled, the water waving all around me, cooling my hot skin. When next I opened my eyes, I gazed into the deepest emeralds I'd ever seen.

No … Too warm to be gems.

My drifting gaze saw too much dancing to be a hard, polished object fixed as someone's trophy. Leaves caressed by a fragrant breeze, rippling on the branches of a tree, or flowers weaving in a meadow.

~Tami.~

Her eyelids fluttered in response, eyes and face bright with color but drifting. Still, she tried to push a clear thought forward.

I am not … angry. With you. Never was.

Angry? The Druid felt anger?

*I was afraid … * Tamuril reached to touch my belly like Verina had,

though Naulor's fingers were gentler, warmer, and refined. *I am sorry I threatened pinn'ionne with my thorns ... I didn't know.*

My smile felt lopsided as I pressed her hand firmer into my gut. ~Forgotten. Baby is still here.~

At that, she giggled then seemed embarrassed at the sound. Her thoughts felt soft. *I am thankful. Babies are so rare ... I wish I could stay long enough to hold your newborn ...*

I squinted. ~Rare? Not ... really.~

She peered at me, amazed, and then saddened as she realized its truth for me. *They are rare ... for us. I have never given birth, though I look forward to the day.*

A sense of unknown, empty expanse lay behind that statement.

~How many centuries are you?~ I asked, curious.

Oh ... She reflected on this. A number did not come easily. *Beyond five hundred, I think. Halfway beyond, at least ...*

Older than every Red Sister beneath D'Shea? Possibly older than Mourn? Fuck, she didn't look anything like that age!

Tamuril felt my shock, eyes widening, staring. *How old are you?*

I swallowed. ~A hundred years.~

Oh my God, you're just ... just a youth? You seem older ...

Silent and dry, I chuckled. ~Jael is twenty years younger. Her Mother is less than three and a half but with six children.~

Tamuril's lips parted with astonishment. She never blinked as she stared at me, though soon she felt far calmer than she would have been if we were sober having this conversation.

Conversation, she repeated, a tiny smile touching her pink mouth. *Yes, I ... have done this. Many times. I am comfortable. Feel safe.*

~What do you mean?~

With Willven. With his father and grandfather. His family in the mountains ... Finally, she blinked, new knowledge filling brilliant eyes. *He knows ... you're a psion like him?*

Uh-oh.

~A mischance,~ I thought, fear trickling in despite my attempt to shut it out. ~Not by birth but misfortune.~

396

*Oh ... *

~But I mean my oath. I am no threat to you, though I am ... alone among Davrin.~

Her eyes turned limpid, her golden brows arching with concern. *I understand being alone. You are braver than I with how far you've come ... *

"Sirana."

A hand on my shoulder.

"Sirana?"

~Hm?~

"I need your help."

~What do you need?~

"Take this bowl. Spread what's inside it over the priest's marks. Make sure they are all covered."

Tamuril lay docile as I pushed myself up by my arms. Once on my knees, I reached for the clay bowl placed within my field of vision by an elegant pair of pale hands. Once I held the bowl, my body weaved on my knees, and Krithannia caught me by the shoulders.

"Let me help you," she murmured. "Come. Perhaps straddle her, sit on her belly."

~Why?~

"Because she'll easily feel your baby. It will help."

~Alright.~

Settling onto my knees and tucking them close against the Druid's flanks, I found it much easier to keep my balance. I hadn't anticipated how comfortable this position would be, however, with an impossibly delicate abdomen rising against my wet ass and slit as she breathed.

My face heated as Tamuril glanced up at my eyes and then reached with both her hands to cover my womb.

"Ohhh," she breathed, eyes drifting half closed. Her nipples hardened as I watched, tattooed breasts framed and pushed closer together by her biceps.

Hoo bua.

~Cover the marks. Get them all.~

I dug a finger into the bowl, tested the dark green muck inside, and used three fingers to scoop a blob and start painting the Druid's tits. She flinched, and I paused until she stroked my belly as if to calm herself.

*G-go on ... *

She *wanted* to heal. She wished to know a day of joy walking in the Sun with a companion again. She didn't believe her brother would find her on the Outside to punish her in time.

I kept painting, fingers returning to the bowl to gather more muck to spread around. I used all of it, shifting her arms here and there to make sure no rune or curled script peeked out on the sides.

She chuckled. Hesitant.

I smiled without showing teeth. ~*What?*~

*You look so determined ... *

She smiled. Shy.

~*I think that's all of it.*~

"Good. Thank you."

Krithannia took the empty bowl, and the chanting began. Two voices, at first. Then others.

~*Several.*~

And some of them sounded ... male.

~*Unfamiliar.*~

"Don't worry. They are helping. Continue your kindness."

Tamuril reached up and took my dirtied hands, entwining our fingers and squeezing them like she was hungry for contact. Her elbows braced against stone beneath the shallow water, the Druid helped me balance and stay upright as the ritual went on.

Another surge of magic passed through us, and my pelvis moved, undulating against her. I didn't mean to climax but felt the pleasure shush along my slit anyway.

~*Ohhh ... shit.*~ I dragged my sensitive netherlips along her belly. ~*I'm sorry ... *~

You ... enjoy touching? Gentle, like this.

~*Yes. Maybe more? Depending who ... *~

Depending who it is?

~*I have my favorites. Best way to keep living ... *~

I had left a small, slick smear behind that time. The blonde Elf blushed, her mouth wavering in a hesitant smile, and I caught a glimpse of her thoughts.

A blond Paxian man who looked like Willven. He was about the same age but wasn't the Captain of the Wall. No armor, no helm, or any sign of the sunburst.

Blue eyes and thick bristles of golden-brown hair covering his lower face. A lot of dirt such as one would find working with soil, occasionally with a pine needle or two stuck in his rough woven shirt or hair.

He *was* a psion, and he could barely speak aloud without stuttering. But he didn't need to. He could make himself understood without words, without a common language at all between them.

I sucked in my breath, squeezing Tami's hands, as she relived what it had felt like to welcome him, to *receive* him while lying in the grass. Deeper than words, he'd loved her before his staff had penetrated, and pleasured her in the way which had been too-long denied.

He had a name and a familiar bond.

Camden Isboern. Willven's grandfather.

~*Oh, Goddess. He was your first ... ?*~

Not with another Elf. But she'd been entirely willing. The guilt she should have felt for not waiting for her husband had been nonexistent.

"Oh, God," Tamuril gasped aloud. "Yes ..."

She breathed deep and quick, as though her secret forest lover had just withdrawn after making love for a good long time, leaving her slit soggy and throbbing. The muck on her breasts dried as they rose and fell. Despite the multi-colored mist, cracks began to show.

More ... please.

My mouth hung open as I rubbed my crotch along her tensing stomach, our hands interlaced. I touched another memory where Camden had kept his mouth on her for much of the afternoon, both of them fresh out of a lake, as the trees swayed and sheltered them from the Sun. She'd never known she could experience such pleasure that way and had never denied opening those flushed, reddened petals for him afterward.

He had been the awakening and the salve for intense solitude, a loneliness which had begun long before she'd been named Observer to the Outside.

I remember! Her mind cried with joy, hands squeezing again. *Oh, thank you ... I remember. He was real, Camden was real! Not a desperate fever dream whose face I barely knew ... *

The man long dead, from a time when Pilla as an egg was decades away. I was stunned.

~You are ... welcome ... ~

I tried to catch my breath, unsure if I'd peaked or not, peering at the cracks on her muck-painted tits. I tilted my head as if trying to read the obscured script underneath.

'Interfere not in those natures not of your own ...'

Tamuril had continued despite the curse, leaving the West mountains to warn Willven about us and saving Jael from immediate capture by Witch Hunters.

There *had* been a time when she'd borne no regrets, none offered by the Outside. Only once she went back home.

Tamuril had fallen into a light sleep; her mind was quiet. So were the hums and chants. Krithannia crept closer.

"Now. Please, help me."

I jumped at her voice, looking as she knelt beside her sister. "Help?"

"Help me draw out the poison so it doesn't recur. Here, watch."

The night-hair leaned down and clamped her mouth on one tit, drawing in hard. *Doable.*

I shifted, leaning down to take the left tit, cupping it, ignoring the flaking paste, and started sucking on the Druid's nipple. Krithannia seemed to get something out of hers, which she quickly leaned over and spat into a bag Osgrid had ready for her.

Not sucking hard enough, maybe. I tried harder.

Suddenly, something vile squirted into my mouth. It tasted like the juice from rotting fish guts. I reared back, grabbed the bag from Krithannia, and ended up retching into it rather than spitting. My lips and tongue burned.

"Here. Swig, swish, an' spit. Don't swallow."

I obeyed, taking the cups as Osgrid handed them to me, rinsing out my mouth several times with water, my head growing clearer with each pass.

Soon, I realized the mist wasn't as thick and the candle had dimmed. My blue pendant's glow was low and subtle, though I sat astride the Druid's body with my ass nudged up against her thighs.

"What in fuck ..." I gasped.

"Well done," said the Naulor, sounding to mean it, and the eve witch echoed the sentiment.

"Aye. Well done."

I stared at the dried and cracked paste covering pale tits, at the sore, red nipples poking up. Although we'd grabbed and massaged them around, the dry, fractured layers remained stubbornly attached.

As soon as Osgrid snuffed the candle, leaving the glowstones in the dressing area for light, my vision flickered in and out between my Dark Sight and color vision.

Something about the texture had changed quickly in the moist room. I reached out to run my finger along the rehydrated cap of one mound and gasped in fright as her skin seemed to peel away.

"Fuck!"

"No, no, wait."

Krithannia moved next to me and plucked at the lifted edge I'd disturbed, pulling a thick flap away to reveal new, clear skin beneath a spot I'd known earlier to be covered in marks. The Guild Mistress laughed, tugging stretchy strips of tough, dark green bits from Tamuril's right breast, the paste and old skin coming off in equal measure.

As the Druid opened her eyes, I began on the left breast, helping to remove every speck of the curse-breaking paste that I'd put on. Incredibly, though her skin was pink and blotchy now, Tamuril's tits would be as pert and smooth as Krithannia's once it evened out.

The blonde Elf watched us, alert, not drifting now, her eyes tearing up as if she was afraid to hope despite the smile on her elder sister's face.

"Did it work ... ?" she asked, her voice cracking.

"How do you feel?" Krithannia asked, grinning.

She swallowed. " ... Well. I feel well. And I remember my greatest joy. What that time was like."

"Then it worked," the Guild Mistress said with delight.

"Oh, God ... !" the Druid cried. "Let me rise, please ..."

I crawled off stiffly toward Jael, who saw me coming but seemed bleary. Still, she welcomed me with a pleased chuckle when I put an arm around her and held on, nibbling my earlobe.

At the same time, the Druid sat up and finally dared to look down at her breasts again, gingerly touching them, studying their color and the lack of carvings and hurtful words. She wept again, which was not a surprise, but this had a *different* sound to it. Much different.

She got up to throw her arms around the night-hair and held on tightly. "Oh, thank you! Thank you so much!"

Krithannia kissed her cheek and squeezed back, her broadest smile stuck on her face. "Tami, I'm so glad ..."

Verina was awake, resting against Osgrid, who'd moved away from her tray. A fearless curiosity seemed to rise as she crept forward closer to Tamuril. The Druid looked at her, and the girl seemed quite surprised how different the Elf's face was when she smiled. Rich, brown eyes dropped to look at the healed breasts; she covered her open mouth with one trembling hand.

"*Musanlo Sol,*" she breathed.

"*Gracona ayuthmain,*" Tamuril said, her smile starkly beautiful compared to everything I'd seen before.

The young Human seemed transfixed by stunning, green eyes.

In my periphery, Jael wiggled her toes, and I looked. "What?"

She grinned. "Anyone else's feet turn to wrinkled 'shrooms?"

I hadn't lifted my toes to know, but she sounded drunk. Then again, the room hadn't turned to stone for me, either. I snickered, and so did she. Then we laughed louder, I didn't know why.

We chortled over the wrinkles on her toes until we noticed the water growing cool and thin. Osgrid had taken her tray outside and unplugged the drains.

"Whenever yer ready, kids," said the Dwarf, offering Jael a hand up, who reached to clasp hers with the one she'd broken.

My Sister noticed long after I did that the bone in her hand had been healed as well.

We held some clarity while Osgrid repacked the items she had brought with her, minus the bag of poison, puke, and strips of green-spelled skin, which she dumped into the latrine. That surge of energy and excitement began to recede as the water drained, once we'd dried off and tried to dress.

Verina collapsed first, caught by Tamuril, and I reached for Jael when she nearly fell off the bench.

Krithannia sighed, putting a hand to her head and breathing carefully. "I think … we need help getting to our … rooms."

I agreed, nauseated on an empty stomach. Once Jael had laid down along the bench, I slid to the cool stone to fold my legs under me and put my head down, breathing slow as I could manage. "I think you're right."

"Help me," Tamuril said, trying her hardest to stay awake. "At least to dress the poor girl."

I didn't know what order all those layers needed to be put on, and Verina couldn't tell us. The best we could do was don the short shift along with the light blue outer layer, which at least covered her from neck to foot. The rest, we had only the strength to stuff in a sack.

Jael and I managed shrugging into our shirt and pants before my Sister sank down and flopped onto her back with a giggle, staring up at the ceiling. I peered balefully at my boots and stockings which suddenly seemed too complicated to manage.

"I apologize," Krithannia said softly. "An aftereffect of … It often costs something to …"

"No worries, Elf," Osgrid said, tired but resilient as she went to unhook the privacy screen she'd put up, after breaking what small spell she'd given to it. "Tha's why we chose our back-up."

I watched her stick her curly, black head out into the hallway.

"Hey," she said, quietly gathering their attention. "Hey, lads ... Need a li'l help."

The first bootsteps were Rithal's, then others followed. They were still there. Had they been waiting this whole time? I'd have to ask them how long.

The males were allowed to come in. Rithal and Kellan went immediately to their eve witch, preparing to help carry her gear, speaking softly in their native tongue. The redbeard was worried, for certain, but her cousin seemed less so; Kellan smiled with apparent pride.

Willven and his lieutenant stepped inside with care, their postures stating they were keenly aware of this "women's space" where they wouldn't normally be. While the Captain scanned the room and made his way to Tamuril, Sohl went to gather Lady Verina off the floor, acknowledging the extra bag of her clothing.

I kept a pleasant, tired face, sure to avoid looking the psion in the eyes in case he didn't know about his grandfather. I wouldn't feel well in spoiling the tone in which Tami and Willven spoke, the way she was smiling at him. Seeing her face, whether mindlinked or not, he knew something changed for the better.

Talov and the Sal-Zayrian approached Krithannia, the engagement an interesting mix of familiarity and formality. While the Dwarven voice rumbled with a low and easy excitement, Sha-rish remained quiet, offering her his arm to help her up.

Then, of course, there was Deshi and Tak, peering at Jael and I as if they'd never expected to see Red Sisters so weak and unfocused in our sense of glee. Would having Shyntre and Auslan here instead feel more balanced?

"Coming, coming," Jael groused, trying to gain her feet as Tak nervously pulled an arm across his shoulders.

"Are you *sure* you don't want your boots on?"

"No! Too hot."

"We carry them," Deshi said, helping me after checking to make sure nothing was left behind. By then, the Templars had left with the Druid and Lady Verina, while Osgrid, Rithal, and Kellan gave their farewells.

"Ya got 'em, men?" Talov asked, hovering near Krithannia as the darker man did the strong work.

"We do, *Oltere*," Tak said. "Count on us."

Neither of us didn't want to be picked up and carried, but I needed to pause twice before we made it out into the hall, nearly overtaken by the various forms of stomach rebellion.

Despite Jael's own lack of balance, she wasn't eager to talk to or fall over Tak. I imagined because he tried constantly to be friendly while she seemed distracted. She kept acting as if she heard or spotted something. Unfortunately, I wasn't in any state to say whether we should be concerned or not.

We made our way out barefoot, turning the second corner out of the showers. The others were far ahead of us by the time we found our rhythm as two pairs of fighters carrying two pairs of boots.

Suddenly, up ahead, I glimpsed something hop out of a black shadowed corner. *What ... ?*

Then I spotted the familiar, red beady eyes.

"Graul?"

The shadow drake peered at us, his small, bristled face unreadable at this distance. He turned his head down the nearest hall.

"Uh-oh," he said, stiff wings lifting up without expanding.

Uh-oh?

"Somethin' wrong?" I slurred. "Izit M — ?"

The drake vanished into his own shadow.

Well, fuck.

"Wait, was that ... ?" Tak began as Deshi murmured something in Yungian.

The silent threat which slipped around that corner choked Reprisal's words. He strode right for us, his aura striking us in our chests.

The Dragon's son was awake.

"*W-wen-yung*," Deshi greeted, bowing slightly while making sure I didn't fall over.

Suddenly, unnervingly, he loomed over us, his presence so overwhelming I couldn't speak, leaving me not at all certain the Baenar hum had risen to the surface yet. His eyes were gold, but I didn't recognize them.

"What in fuck?" Jael growled, irritated as she looked up at him. "Move. We tired."

His tail snapped behind him, lavender tongue flicking out to taste her breath as she spoke.

"Reprisal," he rumbled, speaking too slowly for his usual manner.

"Y-yeah, Shadow?" Tak answered.

"I will take them from here."

Deshi swallowed. "We promise *Oltere* to see them to his office, *Wen-yung*."

To'vah eyes shifted to him as if contemplating something unpleasant. "Go."

"Yes," I whispered. "It's alright, Deshi, we can manage — !"

I gasped as the half-blood darted in, his long reach snagging my Sister and me out of the holds of both men without colliding. He lifted us with one arm each, and we were thrown over one shoulder.

"HAI!" Jael bellowed.

At first, I was just trying not to go into heaves, bracing with the heels of my hands until I cried out at the sudden burn. Why were his scales *scalding?!*

The To'vah-krav spun around in the hallway, taking long strides in the opposite direction from our escorts and picking up speed. I didn't know where he was taking us, but I didn't have the strength to fight or escape him.

I hoped the Davrin son with whom I'd Bargained woke up as well.

CHAPTER 28

M︺ BODYGUARD MOVED TOO FAST THROUGH THE REDOUBT FOR ME TO TRACK where we were going. He changed direction twice to avoid clusters of bodies and supplies blocking the hall while seeming to have a goal in mind.

I didn't realize we'd hit the same chute ladder that Krithannia had led us to three days ago until, looking down Mourn's tail toward the floor, I spotted a familiar, sandy-bearded hatch watcher. He'd jumped into my field of vision, his mouth silent and agape, his eyes wide, as the hybrid scaled the ladder.

If I had any doubt the Dragonchild would be able to open the hatch in his furious state, that was dispelled with a clunk, whoosh, and the scent of a late-night forest pouring in. He threw it open on silent hinges. Moonlight struck, illuminating the entire chute, and turning the guard's skin silvery blue as he paled.

At least the Sun was down and the air cool.

Even with a hatch built wide enough for a Dwarf, Mourn still couldn't fit through with both Jael and I bent over his shoulders. He tossed my Sister up and out first; she grunted as she landed in the grass. I tried to go limp, expecting the same treatment, but then felt his hand grip my pants at the small of my back and tug me down.

Sliding along his front, I gripped him as we'd trained in Augran, leaping across the rooftops. My legs snapped around him and hands gripped behind his neck because he was missing his harness. He wore his loose pants, at least, though his penis was rigidly erect and prodding my ass and thighs as he climbed up and out of the hole in the ground.

He breathed harder than his movement suggested he should, huffing near my ear, his limbs quivering with a hinted, worrisome fatigue.

"Mourn?" I said in Davrin. "Can you — ?"

"Quiet," he whispered, part plea, part demand as he pulled my hands from behind his neck and broke my ankle-lock with his tail.

"Wh — !"

I returned over one shoulder, trying to make the ground stop spinning as he scurried forward and kneeled beside my kicking, bare-footed Sister. Hauling her by one arm onto her knees, he leaned in, the other shoulder nudging her gut. His hand released her long enough to push at her back. Mourn stood up, scooping her up before carrying us away from the open hatch.

Jael wasn't in top form either if she couldn't resist better than that.

Shit.

The guards had to handle the door and inform Talov where we'd gone. Graul, Deshi, and Tak must tell him what had happened.

At the same time, Krithannia had been in no better shape than either of us after the ritual, and Isboern was busy assuring Tamuril and Verina were safe. I didn't see Rithal or Osgrid following with any urgency, though her crow might be out here somewhere with the Druid's falcon.

And then what? Was this what Mourn's old partners had meant about Jael and me not staying in the same room when he woke up? Did any of them have the slightest idea how to handle a To'vah-krav in this state? Could they know if something was truly wrong, or had this happened before?

Goddess, I hoped we didn't run into someone uninvolved who was in the wrong place and instant.

"Put us down!" Jael growled as we sped through the trees. "Where the fuck are you — ?"

"Shh!" I hushed, reaching for one dangling wrist.

She turned her head to look at me. Just what I needed.

~*Noise will draw others, like in the tunnels. Dangerous, he could kill.*~

She blinked, brows furrowing. *What are we going to do?*

~*I'm going to try to remind him of his Bargain. I need eye contact. You stay behind me and don't attack him unless he does first. Keep an eye out for Graul. If anyone is going to follow and keep up, it's the shadow drake.*~

Wide, copper eyes stared at me despite the jostling. *What is wrong with him?*

That, I couldn't say. Talov and Krithannia's reluctance to explain when they moved the comatose half-blood elsewhere suggested his awakening would be far more than a stretch and yawn before asking our names.

I'd also seen him as a giant, winged drake in our dreams. The new, trembling limbs had possibly been triggered to grow by my Sister touching him in that same shared vision. Then there was whatever had happened after he'd flown off toward that snowstorm and whatever had caused his body to awaken just now.

That he'd grabbed both of us must have something to do with that dream, as I wagered Morixxyleth had been "awake" for quite some time after his body dropped to the ground.

Assuming there is any reason to be had.

I picked up the rush of a waterfall under Mourn's hard breath and recognized where we were going. Not sure of the time of night, I hoped none of the Gherudum healers were out picking their plants and mushrooms. Or, if they were, had the good sense to run. Even I struggled with the fear roused by his aura.

Splashing grew louder in my ears as we crested the hill. I labored to breathe, drawing wafts of chilled vapor down my throat as Mourn approached the pool. He wasn't stopping.

"No, no!" Jael griped. "Cold! Too cold!"

Compared to the heat coming off Mourn's back, the shock *would* be intense.

"Put us down!" I yelled.

This time, whether listening or timing, he obeyed. Dropping to one knee, Mourn leaned forward and dropped us a short distance to the ground and into a patch of tall, moist grass.

Either avoiding eye contact or hardly present with us, the hybrid waded into the pool without a word or a glance back. Pushing through the current to the other side, he sat on the rocks directly underneath the falls, water dumping onto his back and shoulders, streaming down his body.

Finally, Jael and I started to catch our breath. Fortunately, no one else was here at the pool.

Should we run? she signed.

Brief but urgent, I shook my head. *He'll chase.*

How do you know?

I quirked one brow. *Would you run from a hunter that has your scent and can take down prey on four legs? Besides, remember the Humans. Safer in the center of battle with him, wasn't it?*

She made a face but didn't argue. Though the intensity of our capture and relocation had caused a surge of energy which cleared our heads from the giddy aftereffects of the ritual, what borrowed strength this had given us was swiftly draining away.

I still wagered that Mourn's confusion was temporary. Better to keep my bodyguard close and save what strength I had than run from him and closer to refugee camps.

Jael glanced toward the half-blood sitting under the waterfall, and I followed her gaze. His head was down, shoulders slumped, tail slithering through the rushing current like a snake working its way upstream. The water had pasted his pants to his legs, and I could make out his erection from here, lying against his left thigh.

The cold water hadn't caused it to shrink much.

Not what I expected.

My heart pounded in my ears as some of the shock wore off, spurred faster when he lifted his head to look at us. I hadn't expected to be abducted the moment he woke up, and the way his eyes shifted between us did nothing to soothe that.

Hot, horny, and aware of us both, he extended his legs, sliding off the rock. Wading out from under the falls, he was coming toward us.

Jael's heart skipped up, and she nudged me.

Loath to take my eyes away, I asked, "What?"

"Is he *steaming*?"

She was right. He was. Goddess, once he was out of the stream, water evaporated from the scales on his back in faint, white plumes. He hadn't cooled down much.

When our eyes finally met, I sucked in my breath, struck by a spike of panic and excitement in one. He wanted to fuck, no doubt.

I reached to pull my shirt over my head, and Jael dragged her eyes from the massive, approaching male.

"What are you doing?" she demanded, watching with disbelief as I tossed my shirt behind us and tugged at my hip ties.

"You asked about the payment," I rushed to explain, pushing my leathers down my legs. "Uh, it's sex."

"*It's what?!*"

"It's fine! I agreed! Get behind me, stay out of arm's reach."

I tossed my pants atop my shirt and rolled forward to intercept the Dragonchild's course. Fortunately, he welcomed me, moving in a straight path for the grassy bank of the pool. I attempted the same mental connection as in my dream once our gazes held for longer than a moment.

~Morixxyleth.~

He blinked.

On one knee, I touched my chest, covering both my pendant and throbbing heart, focusing. *~Kiabil. Kiabil.~*

"We have a Bargain," I murmured as he got within hearing distance over the falls.

His ears lifted a bit; he turned his head.

"Bargain, *To'vah-krav*," I repeated, watching his tongue dart out, his eyes raking over me. I quashed the impulse to draw away, my blood coursing cold and hot through my limbs. "You protect me, my baby, and I pleasure you."

He bowed his head once; I nearly missed it as his tail swept the surface of the water. He was out of the water to his mid-thighs; his cock flexed against the sodden material of his pants. My heart was slamming into my sternum.

"Not too rough," I said, a request I'd *never* expected to slip out like this after living through my Sisterhood trials.

But, no Red Sister had his size or strength.

"*Kiabil*," he responded, reaching out to seize me, dragging me off the bank and into the pool with him.

"Shit!"

Grabbing the back of his neck, my legs scrambled to get around him, feet kicking the rippling surface as his hand grabbed my backside for support. I competed for space with his other hand, which intently reached underneath me to pull down his bottoms and free his erection, despite my squeezing thighs getting in his way.

Eventually, we each succeeded in our goal — mine to hold on and not to drop into the cold water, and his to spread my ass cheeks and aim his pointed glans right between my netherlips. Residual slickness remained from straddling Tamuril, but my cunt wasn't near wet enough to take his size in one plunge.

"Aw, Godd — !"

I jerked as the head speared in, and he pulled back, pushing in again, hot flesh sinking deeper. I stretched around him, felt my clitoris tingle, standing up along with my nipples, and attempted a wriggling bounce to further grease him up.

He rumbled with pleasure, caressing my calves and feet with the coils of his tail and, for a time, this shallow fucking in shallow water was enough as I bounced in his hands.

This *was* the first time without foreplay involving his tongue and its sticky, tingling spit, allowing me to notice how slowly my cunt loosened up. I hadn't overcome the resistance enough to take in the hard swoop of his undercurve before he came the first time, grunting rather than roaring.

His prick spilled some hot, welcome lubricant inside me as he kept thrusting, gliding more easily as he drew out his pleasure. The gap of time between his coasting down and my realizing that his humps had started another climb was shockingly brief.

He'd also closed his eyes. Whether intentional or not, we couldn't make eye contact and I was unable to form a connection without it. His pearl on my earlobe had been silent this entire time.

For the time being, he shafted me, in and out, heart pumping in time as he focused on that one motion. His tail hadn't even played with my netherhole before he peaked again. With a grunt following the hiss of air through sharp teeth, the hybrid splashed a second hot load inside.

Now I was goddess-damned slippery.

Alright, so be it. This wouldn't be the first time I was meant to hold steady while someone wore themselves out using my holes.

Fuck me till you can't move, To'vah-krav.

We'd see who held out longer.

Mourn shifted gradually into deeper water as he worked toward his third peak. I had enough time to adapt to cold water creeping up my legs, backside, and hips. The cool mist from the falls didn't quite reach me as it laid a moist blanket of droplets on the Dragonchild as he kept his back to it.

His continued thrusting underwater washed the excess slipperiness away, and we regained greater friction. He took full advantage, pumping me vigorously until he got off that cliff a third time. His aura flared hard enough to make me dizzy, and he moaned, his tail wrapping around my ankle to squeeze where no one could see.

Whoa …

I was gasping after that one. It had felt different, somehow.

His eyes were still closed, and my sex had yielded enough to take all but his knot, which he hadn't yet tried to cram in. Although he was catching his breath, not once did he give me the impression he meant to withdraw. My sex flexed around him. He was as hard as he'd been at the start, ready to rut again at any moment.

Fucking Goddess.

Was this something to worry about?

"Hai!" Jael called from the far bank, and I winced. "*Hai!*"

Don't, don't taunt him —

"Sirana hasn't come yet! She's last!"

What?

The hybrid had cracked an eye open, looking at her, his sharp pupils expanding some. He listened as she spoke.

"Make my Sister come, Mourn! She deserves it for helping you!"

I glanced backward. Jael had stripped down naked while watching us, sitting on her ass with legs wide, fingers dipping in and over her slit. Her body's modest trembling, deep breathing, and stiff nipples corroborated the claim that she'd peaked before me.

Well, at least she wasn't attempting to stop him.

When the breeze shifted, Mourn seemed able to smell her. His tongue extended out, drew in, then pressed against his teeth as he breathed in. His cock pulsed in eager response as he waded toward her.

Uh-oh.

"You've no Bargain with her, Dragon son," I said in Davrin as my ass rose above the surface of the pool.

At last, his gold eyes glanced at me. Out of the void, his voice came through the pearl. *Understood, Kiabil. But I also agreed to share you with her, if so desired after she was freed.*

~*What do you mean?*~

He smiled, slight but recognizable, and a hopeful pulse in my chest.

Relax. I will turn you around. I will not drop you.

Oh, shit.

Checking his two-handed grip on my ass, Mourn lifted my body high enough to unsheathe his slick, standing cock. Using his arms, hands, and tail to keep me balanced, he rolled me across his chest.

"What the fuck?" Jael said with a brief, baffled laugh.

My bodyguard adjusted his hold continually until my back was flat against him and my thighs open. Carefully, he lowered me down until his warm pole nuzzled between my swollen, ruffled folds.

Jael's eyes dropped right to that spot, and she stared.

Mourn's tail reached up to caress both sides of our union, stroking the crease between my thighs and netherlips, a rumbling purr in his throat. I moaned in response, my cunt nursing his glans, and he crooned in smooth pleasure.

He pushed up and in, and I gasped. "Oh, yes!"

The lips of my Sister's mouth parted slightly as she breathed, watching without complaint. Mourn responded by wrapping his tail around our waists, granting me more stability as he took several strokes, easing deeper with each one. Until, finally, his undercurve swept over that spot inside I liked, making my toes stretch and curl.

Jael grinned.

I whimpered, reaching to caress my nub where there hadn't been room before. Mourn's tail peeled from my waist far enough to wrap gently around my wrist, tugging my fingers away from my center of pleasure.

"Hey —" I protested.

"Would you rather she helps?" he murmured in my ear, his question and accent clear as the Moons to Jael.

I met her eager eyes and mine answered. *Ooo ...*

She didn't need the verbal permission; my Sister crept to the water's edge as Mourn brought me closer. Teasingly close. Dipping her toes in, Jael tested her footing before standing in the pool with us, the water reaching her knees. She waded deeper to reach me, her sticky, fragrant fingers sliding up my inner thighs as she stepped in between my open legs.

Copper eyes glanced up at me, her teeth bright in moonlight. "Wanted to do this after the bath ..." she whispered.

Her head dropped, ear tips pointed toward us, and my cunt clenched down hard on Mourn's cock as she cradled my clit between her lips, her tongue flicking it.

"*Oh!*"

My bodyguard hissed through his teeth, chest vibrating as he growled. His staff plunged in, linking the pleasure spot inside me with the one Jael teased and sucked with her mouth. I could neither speak nor stop writhing. The tension built as I'd lost hold of their pace and rhythm.

I lied back and gave into it instead.

"Jael, *yes!*" I reached up, gripping Mourn's hard shoulders; they didn't seem as hot."Oh, Goddess, close ... !"

She teased me, going slow or sliding to the side before diving in again. By a new but welcoming sound from Mourn, I guessed my Sister's tongue might have swiped at his erection a time or two, tasting me as he withdrew. This encouraged him to keep fucking full-length while her sneaky fingers slid across my ass cheek, dipping into the crevice to find my pucker obscured by a big male's cock.

Her touch was feather-light at first but forced a squeak out of me, drawing my attention at the right moment. The tip penetrated, a sudden spark of sensation which blurred the boundaries, rushing to mix every other source of pleasure.

I yelped and, at long last, climaxed. Squirming, grunting, and moaning, my body held open and above the water, I shivered and shook through one of the most intense releases I could recall. The Moons above vanished in a swirl of sightless confusion, and the roar in my ears like a stampede surrounding us.

I surfaced gasping, vaguely aware of Jael squealing softly, gesturing with familiar desperation for us to follow her to the grass.

Mourn carried me that way, staying close as she hopped onto the bank and crawled a slight distance away. He shared my favorite view of her ass before she fell onto her back and spread her legs, rubbing and parting her netherlips like the horny slit she was.

With another growl, Mourn pulled his cock out before lifting us out of the water to set me down gently on my hands and knees between Jael's legs.

My head swam but I needed only her anticipation and his palm caressing me from ass to neck drop to my elbows and wrap my arms around her thighs. Leaning in, I attached my mouth, hardly needing to think to service her.

"Yes!" Jael peeped, one hand holding my forearm, the other reaching for my hair and ears.

My bodyguard loomed large above me, rough hands massaging my ass before spreading them so he could mount me again. I grunted against Jael's hot, musky flesh, taking nearly the entire length of his unique prick that time. I parted my knees more, rolling my hips in welcome.

Once Mourn got himself better seated, his tail wrapped around my thigh to hold me in place. His deep, steady thrusts held no doubt he would spurt inside me yet again while Jael writhed, my nose buried in her fragrant bush. His thumb teased my pucker, rubbing in circles and causing my sex to clamp down. My hungry slit clutched his length each time he speared in between my folds.

~*Goddess, I'm coming again* — ~

"*Yes,*" Jael seconded, teeth gritted, nodding before her head fell to the ground, lolling side to side.

Next to me, her heels dug into the grass. Wet strokes and the slap of skin surrounded us as my gut tensed in rising anticipation.

~*Yes* ... ~

"Soon," Mourn said hoarsely, a warning of imminent pleasure for each of us.

~*Yes!*~

His knot pushed up against me as Jael's hips rolled and threatened to escape my control. I grappled her, holding her firmly in place so my tongue could finish her off. Braced wide on knees and elbows, my focus fully taken, the To'vah-krav would decide whether I'd accept his breeding lock this time.

When the time came, he chose that I would.

"*Mmauph!*" I garbled, my mouth pressed hard to flushed, swollen cunt as the hard base squeezed into my body in one long push then started to expand.

~*Relax* ... *don't fight it* ... ~

Mourn's roar of orgasm drowned out Jael's, and they both overwhelmed mine. A song rushed through our auras, making itself heard only after that first, raucous burst had passed.

~*Oh, Goddess* ... *! Goddess, yes* ... ~

Jael was trembling as I rested my spinning head, my damp cheek turned against her belly. Mourn's warm thighs pressed to mine, his hands holding my hips as he bent over my back, panting for breath. I could feel his racing heartbeat between my legs thanks to the knot.

Behind me, his tail slithered in grass as he turned his head to peer around us. His tongue flicked out several times to taste the breeze as it picked up.

"Stakeouts," he murmured.

I presumed that meant either the Guild was watching us or had set up a perimeter to keep others from this area.

"Are you ... fully awake now, Mourn?"

He took several breaths before answering. "I am."

"Do you know where we are?"

"Yes." He wetted his mouth. "The Kerut Mounds. Dwarven redoubt underneath. We ... just escaped Manalar."

I exhaled, daring to relax as I held still and did not squeeze him. His knot began to shrink soon after, quicker than the first time. Jael's eyes drooped as she rested, as if she knew the threat was over.

He's back.

Chapter 29

Finally, I spotted Graul outside the redoubt, keeping an eye on us while hiding from the moonlight. Only the one glimpse, however, because he wanted me to see him. The shadow drake vanished again, and I suspected I wouldn't see him until we'd gone inside.

Meanwhile, the Sun wasn't ready to rise. We'd emerged deep in the night, after the second sleep had begun for the Humans, thankfully. I did not want to imagine the panic we'd avoided.

Mourn had been right about the stakeouts. There were men in the woods, but they kept their distance from us and, in turn, dissuaded any sleepless others from climbing this hill.

The hatch guard looked rattled, for certain, but let us in to climb carefully down the ladder. All three of us were barefoot and dizzy, either from hunger, magic, or both.

"Ye alright?" the sandy beard asked us vaguely, not looking directly at the big hybrid.

I smiled broadly. "Of course. A sudden event, but worth doing."

Jael snorted before she continued chortling, as if the ritual in the bath hadn't fully worn off or its effects had been revived by our poolside excursions.

"We apologize for startling you," I added, resisting a tug at the crotch of my pants rubbing a sore cunt.

The Dwarves' shoulders relaxed slightly.

"*Oltere* is comin'," he replied. "He asked, please stay put."

Mourn said nothing but obeyed, leaning against the wall, the tip of his tail flicking as his arms crossed. His stomach growled louder than mine, his jaw flexing when it did. We all had the good sense not to poke his mood, even Jael.

Sure enough, within a few minutes, Talov hurried down the hall with the fire-hair healer, Ragura, and her black beard brother, Rodge, close behind. The greybeard was slightly out of breath once he arrived, but he walked right up to the Dragon son, almost twice as tall as he was, and held up his hand.

"How many fingers am I holdin' up?"

To my surprise, Mourn broke into a reluctant smile. "Three. And I am well, *Oltere*."

"Aye, aye, good." The rest of the Dwarf's questions hung in the air as pale, green eyes swept over Jael and me. "Lasschen? Any injury?"

I shook my head. "I'm fine. Hungry."

"Ah, we're workin' on that. No worries." He beckoned us to follow. "C'mon."

Jael and I finally got to see the space where they'd been keeping the sleeping Dragonchild. This required us to enter a hidden stairwell behind Talov's office, where Jael and I had stayed for a time, and take the stairs down another full level. I hadn't realized there *was* another level but should have known better.

Talov seemed to be watching my face as the sound-proof door closed behind us. He'd paused, turned on the steps, his hand firmly holding the rail. He smiled up at Mourn. "Yup. Loads o' fun gettin' you down the stairs this time."

Ragura and Rodge chuckled softly, leading the way down, while Mourn sighed, his slow coiling tail communicating his unease.

"I apologize, Talov."

"Bah. Tell ya every time, never a need." Talov continued down after his kin with care. "We know yer still figurin' this shit out, an' it's not all in yer control."

"The timing was extremely poor. I know I compromised several secrets of this redoubt."

Talov paused to wait for us at the bottom, shrugging in a warmly lit hallway. "Ye've never once woke up quiet, kid. We deal with what gets handed us. A lot coulda been worse, don't flog yerself. Just come get somethin' tah eat."

This deeper set of quarters and work areas wasn't as extensive as what lay above us but just as functional and probably more secure. A space like this was better for the Clans to oversee the redoubt while allowing in many other races and unknown residents at once. I imagined there was another exit or two out from here without crossing through the populated floor.

Until Jael and I arrived, this level had been Dwarves only, standing guard for Mourn and Graul. The specific room we were taken to, however, held a strong scent that was decidedly *not* Dwarf.

Jael noticed, too, and wrinkled her nose. "What — ?"

Talov chuckled at our expressions. "Tha's the scent ov a young, male Dragonblood sleepin' on some gold inna closed room fer five days straight. Had some really interestin' dreams, too, from what Graul was sayin'."

"Five days?" Mourn echoed, distracted by the huffing, churring drake waddling toward him. He squatted down to pick up Graul and cradle him.

"Yup, only five." Talov grinned. "Not bad, eh? Was worried it might be thirty-two."

With care, the half-blood massaged the muscle between Graul's wings, frowning in thought. "I ... something might have ... woken me."

"*Eh-eh.* Don' get into it yet, kid. Eat, first."

Ragura and Rodge had peeled off from us earlier but returned quickly, having retrieved two loaded trays of mostly meat — whole fowl and haunches — with a side of roasted, multi-color roots. Mourn's spines lifted partway off his back as he scented the air. Those trays had his full attention as he followed the siblings to the mat where they set them down. He settled immediately, set down his dark companion beside him, and dug in with his hands.

Jael and I stared as the sound of bones crunching accompanied the sight of teeth shredding meat. My empty stomach was quite envious.

"Don't suppose he'll share?" I asked the greybeard.

"*I* wouldn't try. Might pull back a stump." Talov chuckled and winked at me. "Separate trays comin', lasschen. Ya like th' bread an' soup, I notice, an' I think the mix does ya an' the li'l one good."

The 'li'l one.' Huh bua ...

Tamuril had been "looking forward" like this, expressing the private wish that she could hold my newborn, such a rarity among her people. And now Talov had shifted his wording to *little one*, probably based on our talk in his office. Jael had asked to "understand" my hesitation about one of the largest forks approaching on my path.

In truth, I couldn't decide how to feel about that, but once our trays arrived, I didn't have to.

Jael and I kneeled and ate as hungrily as Mourn — who *did* share with Graul, I noted. Ragura and Rodge didn't stay but would be nearby. The sparse room contained just us eating and the greybeard watching, oddly pleased about it all.

Eventually, Mourn had filled his stomach enough to sit on his backside with legs crossed and think of his first question.

"Where is Krithannia?"

"Ah." Talov relaxed in his chair. "She's not in shape tah be here right now. But, after a rest, she will be."

"What do you mean? Is she alright?"

"She is, kid. Don' fret."

"What happened?"

The greybeard pursed his lips, nodding deeply into his chest. "Ah, well. She finally made some progress with 'er sister." Talov tilted his head toward Jael and me. "Thanks tah them, actually. But 'tis a bit ovva story at the end ov the last few days. Sure ya want tah start there?"

Mourn had glanced at us when Talov complimented our contribution. His tail slithered behind him as Graul crawled into his lap. Jael frowned down at her food, and I lifted my shoulders as the whirl of emotions refused to be sorted, calling up half a smile.

"Wait." His eyes scanned me. "Where is Soul Drinker?"

I grimaced. "Oh, well —"

"Secure," Talov said firmly. "Muted magic lock box in my office, which Sirana hid somewhere." He winked with the last remark.

Mourn must know that box because his shoulders relaxed slightly. "Very well."

I stared at how he'd moved, for his shoulders struck me as ... thicker? Wider?

Wait a flick ... I appraised the rest of him. "Have you, um, grown? Or am I mistaken?"

The males in the room seemed surprised, even Graul.

"Hah, spot on, lasschen," Talov said first, nodding. "Kid usually gains some weight after th' Dragon sleep."

"Ever since I can remember," the half-blood muttered, putting more food into his mouth.

That helped explain the sheer quantity he had eaten, beyond what I'd imagine after fasting for five days. I didn't know how he held it.

"Though, that dagger is a good place tah start," Talov said, drawing Mourn's silent focus. "Nothin' really bad happened, lucky, but it caused enough disruption tah change our first sleepin' arrangements."

Each looked to me to explain, I supposed since the Guild Mistress wasn't here.

"Krithannia let us use her room after you were moved," I said. "Me, Jael, and Tamuril. I put the relic under the mattress, and we got the rest we needed. But ... the victims also pulled me into a dream, and I was sleeping in the same room with —"

I stopped when Mourn's eyes widened, and his body tensed.

"Blue sand dream?" Jael asked, making a face. "Was alone, just follow voices. Try to find them."

"And I was awake," I said, "talking with Tamuril. Then we saw Jael reaching under the mattress, still asleep, and I stopped her, though we wrestled, and the Druid fled." I swallowed. "The danger *was* close. Gavin and Krithannia arrived after Tamuril told them, and he confirmed Jael had no bond with it."

Mourn slowly released his breath, willing to accept that.

"Then a delayed Malok weapon required some emergency surgeries among Reprisal," Talov dipped his bearded chin to us, "which, good work all around, helpin' them keep watch as Gavin worked an' gettin' Isboern soon enough. We didn't lose any, though two aren't on their feet, yet."

I noted when Mourn evaluated us in silent observation.

"We struggled tah find safe space afterward," the Dwarf continued. "Too much goin' on an' Tamuril needed Krithy's space more."

"The Druid didn't feel safe with the Davrin," Mourn said, his tone flat.

"Uh, correct. Though neither did anything tangible against 'er."

A nod. "Acknowledged. What next?"

"Ah, well, soon after, 'twas time tah get all th' women bathed. Krithannia was keepin' an' eye on somma the newborn mages an' escorted the other three Elves as well."

Some silent exchange happened between them and Mourn looked at me. "What happened in the baths?"

Jael picked at some minor meat on a bird bone, and I took a breath to speak. "Well ... um, we discovered some ... marks placed by a Naulor priest on her breasts."

"Punish curse," Jael added brusquely, wrinkling her nose.

"What?"

Mourn's voice held surprise and a startling dread, his tail pulling in close behind him, curving on itself. His pupils thinned as his ears flattened closer to his skull in a way I hadn't seen yet.

Graul churred and placed his front foot on his friend's chest, drawing his attention as if to keep him grounded.

Finally, the half-blood asked, "To punish what?"

"Interfering with 'paths not of her own kind,' " I said, "and ... not remaining 'pure.' "

Mourn's face tensed further. "Punishing what the Red Sisters did to her."

"That and more." I shrugged when they all looked at me, confused. "The Davrin encounter wasn't her first time, fortunately. But Krithannia said her brother was jealous, and I think she's right."

"Her brother," Mourn growled as though he knew more than the glimpse of insight I'd received from the Guild Mistress.

"The priest, yes." I glanced between the males present, noting Talov staring into memory. "Do you know his name?"

"Not ours tah say," the greybeard said wryly. "But fair tah tell ya he was Krithannia's husband once. How she an' the Druid call each other sisters, through that brother, cuz they're not any closer blood than you an' Jael."

Husband.

The Naulor had husbands like Humans? And Krithannia had been living in exile for centuries, without ever returning to him.

Well, fuck.

We waited through a long pause while each contemplated their private thoughts on the matter. My pearl was certainly quiet.

"But ya said 'er priest punished her fer somethin' before the Davrin?" Talov asked.

I looked at his face but wasn't certain whether the Dwarf knew the answer to his inquiry. Mourn's stillness suggested they had a guess.

"Um, yes. Growing too close to Willven's clan. In the Western mountains. No longer an observer."

Their eyes flicked to each other. *Yep, they knew.*

Jael looked astonished at first, but it passed quickly. "Vine-grower enjoys Humans." She wrinkled her nose slightly. "Makes sense."

"There are a lot of them up here to choose from," I said dryly. "Do not tease her for being lonely. Enough decades alone, without me, and I think you would pick one of the darker-skinned ones, at least one night."

She smirked. "Like the sorcerer, Sal-Zayr?"

Telling that she didn't argue.

"Sha-rish Urudre," Talov said, nodding. "Part of the Guild faction down South but was nearby when th' call went out. We've worked with him before."

"And others like him?"

"Many others!" the Tundar laughed. "Yer just on th' wrong part ov th' continent tah see their cities. Most have kin that came outta the Red

Desert some time ago."

While the greybeard grinned at my Sister's open astonishment, I thought of the Zayrian dancers in Alran the night we left.

"Was this around the time the Davrin Queendom fell?"

Talov looked at me, amused by the challenge. "Tha' was one ov the bigger surges fer refugees, yes."

Refugees.

Like now, running North out of Manalar. How often did the Humans have to move whole settlements? More often than the Tundar Dwarves, it seemed.

"So, if I may ask," he continued, "did th' Deathless tell ya that, or th' rune blade?"

"Both. Though Cris-ri-phon said it first, when Brom Troshin remembered who he was after meeting me."

"Noted."

Jael was staring hard at me; I finally looked at her.

"Queendom?" she said tightly. "In Red Desert?"

I answered as a matter of hard-won fact. "Davrin lived in the Desert once. The Taiding Clans remember, as does the Deathless. But also, their last queen is inside the rune blade, and I've spoken with her. She died by it, but acknowledges I am the wielder."

My Sister's expression shifted subtly, from irritation and confusion to a broadening wonder to a slow-dawning dread. She could have been thinking about Cris-ri-phon beside the sacred pool or attacking us outside the Temple. Or she could have been thinking about her beleaguered House on the Fringe and the mystery of her sudden mage-hood.

Regardless, this was enough weight on her thoughts to suppress an immediate slew of questions. She dropped her eyes to search the tray for scraps to nibble.

With a subtle huff of amusement, Graul did the same. The drake was listening to and understanding absolutely everything.

"So, what happened after you discovered the marks?" Mourn asked.

Impressive to have so neatly stuck a pin in that one.

"Krithannia took us outside —" I began.

"No, no," Jael interrupted, pointing at me. "You got sick, lost your food to see them. Your promise."

Oh, right.

"Promise?" Mourn echoed, tilting his head with curious concern.

Talov was smiling at me with his lips closed, hands folded neatly on his belly. I exhaled thinking about how to phrase it.

"I … wished I could start over, when we met," I began. "Knowing all this. I wouldn't have caused *more* harm."

"Why not?" he asked.

I shook my head. "No purpose. No pleasure. Made my mission harder. Do I need better reasons?"

The Surface males shook their heads. *Good.*

"So, I promised her I would not cause her harm and would not stand by to watch someone else do it."

Mourn hummed, nodding in thought as he turned it over.

"'Tis good ya said that, lasschen," Talov said, his voice gravelly for a moment until he cleared it. "Once ya *did* go outside an' ran intah Osgrid, tha's when Krithy got her idea."

"Osgrid is here?" Mourn asked.

"Aye. And Rithal came with her. Basically stayin' as 'er guard."

"Interesting. I wasn't sure if he would ever return."

"With th' right persuasion, looks like."

"And no ill blood with Sirana?"

"Not that we can tell. Been keepin' eyes on 'im, since he's been away so long."

"Have you spoken with him yourself?" I asked the greybeard.

"Not in private. Why? Is there reason to?"

"I don't know. He seemed startled to hear that you were present as *Oltere*."

"Ah, aye." Talov lowered his chin further into his beard, pondering. "Rithal stayed wit' Clan Baradum fer a while after losin' his family an' home. We couldn't get 'im tah stay, wasn't interested in union, nor would we help him get th' revenge he wanted. We talked a lot through a winter or two, though."

"Perhaps some of it stuck with him," Mourn said, "if he's returned here with Osgrid."

"Perhaps." Talov smiled a bit. "Maybe another chat is warranted, jus' tah see where his head's at."

"He might appreciate seeing Gavin," I said. "To hear what happened with the soul shard he helped to create. The end result and goal of that entire trip with the Ma'ab, dragging along Gavin and me."

Mourn, Graul, and Talov stared at me.

"He ... Rithal asked about him," I added.

Reflecting on this, the greybeard nodded with caution. "I'll keep tha' in mind. Thank ya."

My bodyguard exhaled. "So, how close am I to waking up?"

"Within two days," Talov answered, waving his hand toward me. "Sirana introduced Krithannia tah Osgrid, an' the two put their heads together tah find a way tah heal Tamuril's marks. They weren't sure but wanted tah put Sirana in th' center."

Mourn tilted his head when I did. "Because she's a psion?"

"Part, fer sure. Also because ov her promise."

"And ... they came up with a healing ritual?"

"They did. One that included anchoring a young woman's aura. Two in one. I can't speak fer th' details, but 'tis clear it worked. Tamuril was smilin' when she lay down tah rest."

"And the marks are gone," I added. "For certain."

Mourn's face softened, looking between us. "I'm glad to hear it. When did this ritual happen?"

"Right before ya woke up," Talov answered, his amusement growing as he went on. "So soon after th' end, in fact, that Krithy's still mendin' and yer two *caits* here hadn't put their boots on when ya showed up tah nab 'em away from Tak an' Deshi after scarin' 'em half dead!"

Mourn groaned quietly as the elder Dwarf enjoyed a good laugh at his expense. "I do not look forward to explaining that to them."

"Well. Give it some thought," Talov chortled, glancing at Jael's and my bare feet.

"Where *are* our boots?" I asked.

"Deshi gave them tah Gavin, since he didn't know what else tah do at th' time. I haven't had a chance tah grab 'em fer my office."

"Because you had to scramble to place stakeouts outside?"

He pointed a thick finger. "Exactly."

Jael's mouth twisted before she snickered. "So they listen to us in pool all the time?"

"Nah, they were told tah keep clear if they didn't want tah feed a hungry Dragonblood. None ov Reprisal is stupid, lasschen, though they might've picked up on th' louder stuff."

Mourn rubbed his forehead, closing his eyes on another sigh the same moment I recalled my ears ringing once he'd pressed his knot in.

My face and chest flushed with heat, the soft throb of my crotch mildly complaining that full stretch. "Should we expect rumors about a demon or monster in the hills last night?"

"Definitely," Talov agreed, "but th' kid's good at startin' those. 'Tis nothing new, we can manage." He paused until Mourn lifted his eyes. "Wanted tah say, though, ya came back tah yerself pretty fast an' didn't run too far. Good fer all ov us."

My ears opened, and my eyes widened. *That was 'fast?' How far has he run in the past?*

Mourn tapped one of the thicker bones on his tray, stripped of meat; he seemed tempted to gnaw on it.

"Truthfully, Talov," he said, "when I've gone that deep, I've never had a *Kiabil* who could speak so I could hear her."

I swallowed, my cheeks warm as Jael looked at me.

"Yeah?" Talov looked immensely pleased but also curious. "Th' psionics?"

"Not alone, but with something else ..." He trailed off, eyes sliding as he thought how to describe it.

I played with the edge of my leathers near my ankle. "Have we reached the point we talk about *your* dreams, Mourn? Assuming the ritual itself woke you up?"

Recognizable golden eyes met mine. "I think you are right."

"About which?" Talov nudged, as if he wasn't going to let the "kid" get away with such vagueness.

"About both points. I should speak some on my Dream this time, and," his gaze shifted to Jael, "I think the healing ritual was what woke me. Several ... surges. They brought my body aware and caused my Dream to change, then fade."

My Sister's eyes blinked rapidly. "Um, well, er," she stuttered, rubbing her palms against her pants. "Why look at me like that?"

I thought I knew. "How much do you remember of the ritual, Jael?"

She shrugged. "Foggy. Heard voices, heard you. Couldn't catch words. But ..."

"But?"

She breathed through her nose. "Pleasure. Tease-pleasure. I reach out and grab it."

"True." I glanced at the males as her face warmed. "She added to the magic by chasing pleasure."

"Chasin' it, hah?" Talov echoed with a knowing smile, leaning on one elbow with two fingers against his temple.

"Yes, I felt these peaks," Mourn admitted, causing the old Dwarf to perk up. "Probably a holdover from our sharing magic during the battle."

"Oh," Jael breathed. "Hm."

She did *not* want to meet his eyes.

"I was ... caught underneath, but not deep. I ... had no Words." The half-blood looked to Talov to understand. "Until Sirana Spoke them to me."

I caught the emphasis and mostly knew what it meant. The Dwarf and drake did as well, but Jael's face scrunched in mild confusion or skepticism.

"What dream I make fade?" she asked, sounding wary.

Mourn exhaled, broad shoulders lowering. He let go of the bird bone and licked the grease from his fingers. "Much of it will not be clear for a while yet. Change has occurred quickly in both my Dream and Waking ... I need time to reconcile them."

A glance at Talov confirmed this was expected.

"Mourn doesn't have other Dragons' kids he can ask about his sleep cycles," the greybeard explained. "An' his Sire is ... well, close-mouthed.

Most times."

The hybrid grumbled something under his breath, which Graul answered by lifting his head and fluttering his throat pouch. Mourn rubbed his shoulders behind the wings in response.

"You've always been the better example of a sire, Talov," he said. "To'vah or not."

Talov's cheeks bunched up. "Glad tah hear it, kid. No one deserves tah be an orphan wit' no one tah learn from."

Mourn exhaled a sigh through his nostrils, gently massaging sore spots on his drake. I followed the greybeard's example to sit and wait. Eventually, the Dragonchild returned to the conversation.

"I was chasing Cris-ri-phon in my Dream," he said, keeping his eyes down, "and the master he serves. The Deathless had returned to the same place he'd begun and had once again found someone to help him."

"His master?" Talov asked quietly.

"It's never him." His tail flicked. "I've wondered how long he watches the sorcerer suffer each time, before something always sets his aura back to something living."

Goddess, Gavin should be here to listen to this.

From the way Mourn was speaking and the look on Talov's face, my mind insisted on something eerily tangible. Like discovering the Desert merchant in my dreams could be recognized in another form while awake.

Just chatting with former Deathwalkers beside the sacred pool.

"This time, he's found Baenar essence."

I blinked out of my thought, meeting Mourn's eyes. He was gazing at me. "What?"

"I wager he hasn't found Baenar essence since they vanished from the Surface," the Dragonchild continued, glancing at Talov. "But now ..."

"Uh-oh." Talov held on to the arms of his chair, straightening up. "The ... uh, sire Sirana has a connection to?"

"Correct."

"Shit. So he's back fer sure."

"He's never been gone for good, and I believe he will hold on to his original essence longer, having tasted Baenar essence twice and reminded of them."

"Wait, do … do you think Gavin should know about this?" I asked nervously. "He already knew about the Deathless after rising from his … transition."

They thought it over.

"Perhaps yer right," Talov said, caressing the beaded braids. "An' it's past time tah check on yer passenger in th' lock box. Gotta check in with Krithy, too."

"The three of us could wipe down," Mourn suggested, "then meet you and Gavin in your office."

"Sounds good. But before we do, one more question."

"Speak it."

"Ya said the Deathless got another taste ov Baenar. I just wanna know if he *ate* that essence?"

Mourn's eyes flicked to me though he shook his head to answer. "No. I got him out of there before it could happen."

"Wait, you what?" I blurted. "Do you mean Auslan? Or Shyntre? Did you see him, too?"

"Too?" Jael echoed, baffled.

"I did," he replied.

"Both of them?"

He hesitated a split instant. "No. Just the one."

"And you spoke?"

"Briefly. After our escape." Mourn smiled. "Do you still want Gavin present?"

Damnit.

I sat back, trying to slow my galloping heart. "Will we start at the beginning in the office?"

"We will."

"Very well. I can wait."

"Awright," Talov said, pushing himself up. "I'll send in the kids with some soap, water, an' rags, then bring th' Deathwalker tah my office. Come on up when yer ready."

On his way out, the Tundar winked. "We'll bring yer boots, too."

CHAPTER 30

On silent feet, we stepped into Talov's office with Graul perched on Mourn's shoulder. Gavin was already here, sitting in one of the wide, sturdy chairs. His tall frame filled it out better than ours had.

My death mage must have not been too skeptical of the old Dwarf's request, because his grimoire was open, and his writing supplies were ready. His seat had been turned toward Talov's heavy desk and drawn close enough so he could use one side of it. He'd brought his full pack and spade with him, set to one side, and two pairs of Red Sister boots plus stockings stood next to them.

Krithannia wasn't here.

Gavin looked up as Mourn closed and warded the door, his inverted eyes sweeping over us. "Your spiders are perched above you."

Graul twisted his head stiffly, spotting them at the same moment I did, although I'd heard their trilling as soon as I'd walked in.

"Thank you," I said, moving widely around Graul to coax my two remaining spiders closer to me. They crawled eagerly onto my gloves, and I gathered them close before tucking them underneath my better-groomed and plaited hair.

I had my pendant still, my spiders were back, and my boots were within sight. All I needed was to reclaim Soul Drinker, but that could wait.

"I understand you've had a full day in various pools," Gavin said, deadpan.

Talov laughed, and Jael gave the death mage such a squint-eye that I started chuckling.

"More than you know," Mourn remarked with a smirk.

"Mm-hm. And is it true that you encountered the Deathless while you were 'traveling?' "

"It is."

"I wouldn't drag ya here under false pretense, Deathwalker," Talov said, filling his water pitcher at the sink to place it on a tray with four cups. "Waste of both our time, an' ya got more ov it."

"Mm-hm. And you said Sirana requested my presence for this discussion."

"Yup. Dede's Truth." Talov took his seat, setting out the pitcher and cups. "Ask 'er."

I smiled. "Did you not believe I would make that request?"

The pale walker thought about it. "I presumed you had finished the discussion, and I was here for the recounting."

I shook my head. "Not this time. From what I've heard so far, you might know the questions to ask, and Mourn is willing."

"Hm. Very well." Icy pupils shifted to Mourn. "I may record it in my cypher?"

The Dragonblood bowed his head. "You may. I believe what I witnessed were direct consequences of what happened at the Temple, and we will need your insights to determine how long your Lady's emissaries are tasked with guarding the pool."

In some odd way, Gavin seemed excited to hear this. We took our seats, Jael and I sharing one this time, and my scholar dipped his stylus in the inkwell, scraping off the excess.

"Very well. I am ready."

Mourn started over as he'd agreed, although because Gavin was writing it down and asking clarifications, I heard far more details about the hunt leading up to the moment he'd found my Consort than we'd heard downstairs with him speaking familiarly with his sire-figure.

"It always takes time to become aware when I Sleep abruptly like I did," Mourn began. "But once I was, I headed to Manalar."

"Is the sacred pool able to be sensed in this state?"

"Yes. One of the strongest pulls for those attuned to its Ley."

"*Are* you attuned?"

"In a manner of speaking. I have visited the place many times, both Waking and Dreaming. It is familiar, let us say."

"Could you detect any Ma'ab in this state?"

"Unfortunately. I needed to avoid them so as not to be delayed."

"Even if you did not get close, can you describe them?"

Jael and I both made a face when he recounted a distant entity in constant motion and always wailing. Its essence had been torn to shreds and remade, attached, and twined with barbs around a dense stone with a black corona.

"Unsettling," Gavin remarked dryly, writing his inscription. "Probably an officer of the Third Ascended. Any others?"

"One other. An object, not a sentient."

Mourn's description followed, containing a lot of magical cues which he seemed to expect Gavin would understand, but that I couldn't quite grasp. My scholar nodded consistently with his notetaking, however, confirming comprehension at the same time.

"If there are more objects like that," Gavin said, "the Godblood might not have long to decide when to challenge the Ma'ab for the pool."

"Surely the Grey Maiden's guardians aren't pushovers," Talov prodded.

"They are not. But the rest of the city and all its resources are there to be spoiled. If the Ma'ab grow impatient, they might leave nothing but that pool out of spite."

The greybeard harrumphed, taking a sip of water before passing a cup to us.

"When I reached the Temple," Mourn continued, "or, as it appears in my Dreams, the Greylands guardians were still present. One aspect of this agreement I wanted to confirm."

"Ah, excellent," Talov breathed. "No back door fer th' right plane walker."

"Correct, though one of them was there scouting it out."

"The master of the Deathless?"

"Correct."

Gavin lifted a finger, scratching paper as quickly as he could. "This is the Elven ruler Sirana described?"

"Correct," Mourn said. "Although, worth noting, he bears a pair of red leather wings in his Dream form."

"Noted. His name?"

The half-blood pursed his lips. "For now, it's better if you use the name he has given."

The Deathwalker lifted his eyes briefly from the page, contemplating that strange suggestion but accepted. "I believe the only one I have is 'Toushek.' "

"From the Red Desert. Good enough."

"Very well."

"Wait!" Jael blurted, not about to let that slide past her. "How is it 'bad' if you use name he gave *you*? Just tell us name!"

Talov knew the answer to this but settled to listen. Gavin seemed unbothered, and I was curious to hear the response.

Mourn exhaled, pausing to consider. "With Elves in Reverie, some names draw attention you don't want. I know Sirana has dreamt of him, where he gave her a name. One lesser known. I also know that he's connected to the sire of her unborn somehow."

"What?" I sat up, fear rushing through me as golden eyes locked on mine. "How do you mean?"

"Dreaming in Yong-wen, you saw figures watching from a distance the last time you found him in the sand trap. Correct?"

"Uh … yes? Yes. I did."

"They aren't searching for you, Sirana. They're searching for *him*, every time you get close. I'd rather not give any new names that might draw greater danger to you both in Reverie."

I swallowed, nodding.

Jael looked reluctant to embrace this but eventually slumped in our seat with a scowl. "Thought dreams not real."

"It depends if you are aware and traveling," Gavin said, eyes focused on his cypher. "If you have entered the traveling state, you may encounter others in a similar one. There are many Human souls who never travel in such a way outside their bodies. They spend little enough time within the mortal coil as it is."

"But Elves do," Mourn added, "largely because they live so long with their bodies. Naulor and Baenar often will 'travel' at some point in their lives, assuming they aren't held down by another influence."

"Like the Abyss?" I asked.

"Yes."

I hadn't heard anyone but Auslan speak of such "travel," and those had been called "visions." Like the Valsharess. Either Sivaraus as a whole had few travelers through Reverie, or no one deemed it prudent to mention.

"You have begun traveling with some frequency since coming up here, Sirana," Mourn continued. "I've observed enough to know you must be careful whom you meet, or what names you call out in Reverie."

The image of a large, winged drake returned to me; one who looked only somewhat like my bodyguard, resting after long suffering on the bank of a Desert river. Perhaps I wouldn't have been so certain of *knowing* him if I hadn't known the name his Sire had given him.

"I understand."

"So, Toushek was present at the pool," Gavin prompted.

"He was. And speaking to someone through it."

"Huh," Talov grunted. "Like speaking through th' back ov a mirror?"

"In a sense. Again, no new names you don't already know, but I realized Toushek had found someone he'd been looking for, and Cris-ri-phon was on the other side." His tail slid along the stone floor. "Suspecting who, I could not allow either of them to trap him. I dove between him and the pool's guardians and leaped through to reach the other side."

"And my Lady's emissaries allowed it?" Gavin asked, merely curious.

"They did not try to stop me."

Some nuance, there.

"And it worked?"

"Covering a vast distance in a blink, yes. I came out of a large well in a ruined courtyard within the Red Desert. The Deathless was there, as was Sirana's Consort. I encouraged him onto my back so he could ride away from the ruins."

"And he accepted?" I asked.

"Yes."

I breathed with relief, about to ask if Mourn had dropped Auslan by that river where I'd found him. I bit my lip and let him continue, glad I did. Morixxyleth *hadn't* taken Auslan to the river at all. They'd stopped at an oasis — yet another pool, the second one involved — where a red and black stallion had been drinking.

"The horse could take him somewhere safe," Mourn said. "A sandstorm was following us, and the longer I remained near him, the greater the danger I drew. So, I left him at the oasis with the horse I've seen traveling those dunes many times before."

"No name at all?" Gavin asked.

"No. I've never been given a name."

The Deathwalker made a note.

"I don't know what happened to him after that. I came out the other side in a different land entirely, and the rest ... I ..."

Mourn stopped, not blinking but his pupils changing subtly.

"This where it gets really deep?" Talov asked.

The Dragonchild dipped his chin near his chest. "It is ... as far as I can describe for now."

"Sounds good enough, then."

Gavin didn't argue. The Deathwalker finished up his notes, while I wondered if Mourn consciously recalled meeting first Jael and then me on that Desert riverbank, while he sat in that chair.

That place had been a borderland, I was certain. Mourn said he'd left the Desert through that oasis but returned to that river somehow. In pain.

Then we saw the snow, and I watched him fly away toward it.

"Think it's mealtime again fer all ov ya," Talov said. "Let's head it off, an' I'll check on Krithy." He smiled at Mourn. "Hate tah push it right out th' door, but we're gonna hafta make a deal soon with th' Templars about visitin' their own people in th' camps. Been holdin' it long as we can."

My bodyguard sighed. "I know. I'm ready."

AFTER WE'D EATEN AND I'D RETRIEVED SOUL DRINKER, TALOV'S OFFICE GRADU-ally filled with bodies until it resembled a heartier reflection of how we had first arrived at the redoubt.

This time, Willven Isboern was upright and carrying his golden shield, his four officers standing alert. Tamuril and Pilla stayed closer to Krithannia, who was the visibly tired one between them. Ragura and Rodge joined us, along with Osgrid, Rithal, and Kellan. Arriving last were Brian Wolf, Tak, Hawk, Sha-rish, and the four Yungian brothers, Peng-lok using a cane.

The office was quite full though introductions were quick, and only those who required a seat sat in one: Talov, Krithannia, and Wolf. Gavin had put away his scribing supplies for now, and the rest of us were standing after we pushed the extra bulky chairs along the wall by the sink.

"Welcome back among us, legend," Captain Isboern said, his smile unweighted for the moment. "I take it your communion was enlightening. One reason we have been called here?"

An interesting thing to say in front of his men. Tak and Deshi looked elsewhere for the moment, as Mourn took the opening, his tail rolling calm.

"It was, *Capitan*, and yes. My final spell to move all of us off the mountain was successful, but *Pisc'sagrad* required a cost in return."

I wondered if that was true while Isboern's men responded with a curious mix of shock and excitement. They had experienced the magical jump off the mountainside and into the river below, and they had carried their Captain unconscious to the Dwarven gate, so at least they weren't questioning the results.

"You beseeched Musanlo on our behalf," pronounced the officer Robi.

439

"I have never communed so directly," Mourn replied. "But *Pisc'sagrad* bears her own way of listening when need is great."

"Her?" said the red-blonde, astonished. "The sacred pool ... ?"

The Dragonchild smiled without showing fang. "Correct, *Tetente* Erik."

"How do you know?"

"Given that *Pisc'sagrad* answered him to save us," Isboern said with a warm smile for his lieutenant, "after our Bishops compromised their role, I believe we may take the legend at his word."

Robi briefly patted Erik's shoulder, and the Templars accepted.

"At what cost?" asked the red blond instead.

Mourn's expression didn't waver. Not a hint of annoyance as Jael tried to hide hers.

"The cost was to show me something related to the mission to reclaim her from the Ma'ab. Something I believe will help but could not be understood while I was awake."

"Yes," the Godblood breathed reverently, placing a fist on his chest. "I understand this, legend. It is the same for me with Musanlo."

"*Ci*," the dark-haired Imran whispered. "We witness."

His brothers agreed, and Isboern had gently quashed any remaining doubts among the Manalari about Mourn, which gave me a chance to reflect.

Had those been stars I'd seen in his eyes as he prepared his spell, or something related to the Ley pool? I remembered a deep, thrumming sound as the magic built, but much had been happening at the time.

I couldn't tell how much Mourn might be changing because of the audience. He had yet to speak to me through the pearl.

"I believe, then," Isboern continued, "we are here to discuss how to reassure and move out the final camps?"

Talov and Krithannia together looked quite appreciative.

"Yes," said the Guild Mistress. "We do not want either Ma'ab scouts or surviving *Dyos Guerrimos* at the Kerut fort to discover them. But we also have concerns about your safety, Captain, as there likely will be spies among your own."

None of the four Templars denied this, but Sohl asked, "Are any identified? Or suspected?"

I thought about Mathias sprinting out of the crowd after Isboern had saved the Inquisitor from his fall. There had been no time to track him or discover why he was there, because Jael had needed me.

The skin hunter may be serving the Deathless like the Deathless is a servant to another.

The quiet pause drew me out of my thoughts. Several of my non-Human allies were looking at me. I unstuck my mouth. "A man named Mathias Briar may have come through the gate."

"Mathias," Rithal rumbled, making a face. "Didn't he run off from the warp rot with Brom's daughter?"

"We spotted him among the crowd demanding the shield," Mourn said. "When the Templars were trying to calm and the Witch Hunters riled them up." He addressed the Templars. "You remember."

"Inquisitor Kegyek fell from the tower," Imran said.

"Pushed," Erik corrected. "By Keros. I saw him."

"And our *Capitan* saved his life," Sohl reflected, looking at me and Mourn. "You ran past us, climbing the stone to give chase."

"To rescue my Sister," I replied.

"Keros was not difficult to scare off," Mourn said, amused and convincing.

"But you saw Mathias Briar bear witness," Isboern said. "How is he a concern if he made it through the gate?"

"He's an interrogator, fer one," Rithal said. "Enjoys torturin' people, favorin' men. Fer another, he sells secrets when he has 'em."

"Pertaining to most recent events," Mourn added, "the daughter of a powerful sorcerer and Ma'ab nobility, may have a hold on him, whether coerced or paid for."

But at least the sorcerer's body had gone elsewhere. We only had to worry about Amelda in the flesh.

"So, Ma'ab spy is a safe assumption," said Wolf.

"Agreed. And our most connected target."

"So, live capture?"

"Ideally."

The Guildsmen made a mental note.

"Sadly," Isboern said, "we cannot suggest any of our own to watch for, not having been outside to see who has not moved on to Augran."

"That's alright, Captain," Krithannia said. "Our goal was always to arrange the connection to make any address you need, but also have enough eyes watching and reinforcements to call upon."

"Aye," Talov agreed. "A reasonable number could be persuaded tah go over five days. Got just over a hundred who aren't soldiers, th' real staunch ones, an' five hundred who're yer hale fighters an' wall defenders who aren't leavin' without their Captain. Still a lotta people tah watch."

Isboern seemed neither surprised nor dismayed by these numbers; I imagined this was for everyone's benefit.

The *Oltere* next motioned to Mourn. "Shadow's got senses th' rest ov us don' have, an' if anyone breaks cover an' runs, he can catch 'em fastest. Drag 'em back. An' ya know this place has solid confinement."

Isboern bowed his head but frowned with caution. "I am aware Shadow is also the bodyguard for the Red Sisters when among Humans. Will they stay inside, especially if he must chase after someone?"

"They must," said Erik, the other Templars nodding. "They will only scare the people, start rumors their Godblood is dominated by devils."

Sigh.

Jael appeared as irritated as I felt.

"Well," Krithannia began, "if you are willing, Captain, we wanted to consider Sirana assisting us with information from you, to better coordinate our people with yours and receiving early warning of any trouble you or your men sense among your own. How close would she need to be? Do you need to be touching, as before?"

Isboern sighed and shook his head. "If only she and I, no. I can maintain a willing bond for about half a league. The voice is stronger if they can still see me, though I do not need to see them."

"Ah! So staying atop a hill will suit."

"Quite well, Stormseeker."

"That is impressive," Mourn said, sounding to mean it.

The Godblood smiled. "Not as impressive as your methods of communication. It works through closed walls and across dozens of city streets all at once. I have never seen anything like that among men or Dwarf."

"Thank you. Although before you ask, no, these methods do not come by a deal with a devil."

Talov chuckled as Krithannia smiled with grace, answering Willven's broader grin as he nudged his men to laugh at themselves. He had decent success. The Guildsmen in the room looked modestly pleased but all kept their mouths shut beyond a quiet snicker.

I could imagine Isboern himself had some insight into those methods from the bare minimum of watching me touch my earlobe, but his officers didn't seem to have this knowledge.

"So, willya talk tah us from a distance?" Talov asked, fingers interlaced on his desk. "Tell us whatcha see?"

Willven smiled slightly. "I will, if you will grant me the slightest hint how we may be assured of our goal *without* sacrificing another Elf to ignorance or chance in place of an actual demon."

His lieutenants glanced at him at the mention of our race but did not challenge his statement.

"I will be with them outside," Gavin said.

That was new to me, although Krithannia and Talov looked pleasantly surprised.

"You will," she said. "You've decided?"

"It seems necessary. I would like to summon Nightmare."

"Nightmare?" Rithal asked. "Yer mare from the inn?"

"The same." Gavin looked at Talov. "Do you have any spoiled meat or rat corpses I may feed her, so she appears less gaunt?"

"Uh, sure, we can scrounge up something."

I gaped along many others. *By the Abyss, she's been buried in these hills this entire time ...*

Talov had started laughing by then, followed by several of the Guildsmen who'd seen the horse, though the Manalari and the Dwarves seemed disconcerted.

Mourn chuckled, visibly pleased. "I accept the balance, Deathwalker.

If anyone is foolish enough to attack you and the Sisters beside a horse with teeth like that, they deserve the terror coming to them." He looked at us. "Just try not to kill them."

"Even if they do," Gavin said without a tick of a smile, "we can still ask them questions."

The Templars, even Isboern, made the sign of their Sun the moment they realized what that meant.

Meanwhile, Jael had moved from annoyed and bored to brightly anticipating. She smiled at me and signed, *Beast sounds interesting.*

I smirked. *Might want to hold your nose until she's eaten.*

CHAPTER 31

THE UNVEILING OF THE GODBLOOD AND HIS SUN SHIELD BEFORE THE MANALARI would happen the next morning. The planning for it went late into the night until the second sleep.

"We're used to it," Tak said, stifling a yawn.

First, Osgrid and Rithal scouted around the hills outside where Gavin had told them Nightmare was buried, confirming the signs he'd described. The horse's corpse rested a few hills down from the waterfall where the two Dwarves first camped together.

"I shall revive her before dawn," said the Deathwalker, having obtained a canvas sack of bone and gristle scraps from the kitchen with a few rodents thrown on top.

Meanwhile, the four Yungian brothers prowled around to locate and clear the best places for me to stand with my Sister while remaining within Isboern's stated psionic range. Once they were finished, Krithannia rolled out a map of the redoubt's exterior, which included colored lines to suggest the steepness and relative crests of each hill in the area.

"I like," Jael murmured, leaning over to study it.

She couldn't read the text any better than I could, but the map was designed well enough to gather the basics without it. Krithannia smiled at her before marking three spots facing the largest refugee camp, making sure we understood their location relative to where we stood belowground.

She began with one on the same side where Nightmare was buried. "Gavin, Sirana, Jael, and Deshi start here. Be as still as you can, do not draw attention."

Her fingers moved to a higher point across from us, the middle one. The view of each spot would be blocked with a hill between them. "Torch, Peng-lok, and Nianzu will guard Tamuril and me here. This is also your fallback position if you must move. Meet us here. Sirana, speak through the pearl and we will know you are coming. If you stay on the side facing Willven, you should not lose his connection. We can get inside quickly if necessary."

She paused so we could memorize both spots then continued. "This third point is the secondary fallback point and our backup. Wolf, Tak, and Hawk will be waiting near another hidden entrance. Talov's kin will be ready to let us in at the signal."

Talov and Rodge confirmed with a nod, but Deshi signaled a question. "Yes?"

"The Night-mare cannot climb down the hatch if needed, yes?"

Most of us grinned at that mental image; all but Gavin, who seriously considered the question.

"Not especially," he said. "She could *fall* down, I suppose, but first I would give her other commands based on our circumstances."

Several of our grins overflowed into chuckling.

"Very good," Krithannia said, her smile as broad as the rest. "Based on all scouting since we arrived, we do not anticipate trouble forcing us to move. Know that we'll be restricting movement during the Godblood's address, the usual rounds going through a checkpoint farther from the main entrance. Anyone who approaches a hatch with intent to enter should be treated with suspicion. Report them, and, if necessary, capture them alive."

We acknowledged and confirmed the plan. Isboern and his Templars could be among their camps for a while. If no threat truly impacted his plans, the Godblood wanted to spend the whole day with his people, from early morning to late afternoon. Those of us watching, signaling, and reporting would have food and skins of water while he did.

Although a select few of us in the planning room were also aware of the instant powershift that would occur down South if the Godblood were killed among his own tomorrow, we had not been asked either to be a visible deterrent before his people or to double-check his choices.

"The lad waited long enough at our askin' an' knows better than most what's at stake," Talov said. "He's got th' shield tah leap out o' trouble. Not like he an' his men aren't a force of reckonin' on their own."

Indeed, the Templari could set the Kerut Hills on fire with that collective sunburst spell.

Afterward, before the dawn could be hinted at, Mourn chose to alter his appearance once more — and rather painfully from the lingering sense I had through the pearl when he showed himself. The half-blood had shifted into a tanned, brown-haired man with a face I hadn't seen before, one easily nondescript to any who glanced at him by lantern or glowstone.

"While you raise Nightmare," he said, "I will walk around the camps and sniff a few tents. Perhaps I can determine whether Mathias is here at all."

"And if he is?" I asked.

Mourn smiled with thin Human lips. "I shall bring him to you. Stay at your first observation point. I will find you there."

Good that he didn't see it necessary for us to stay inside and wait. I wanted to witness what Deshi had described about the mare going into the earth, if in reverse.

We exited quietly out of the higher-hill hatch point — the same one Jael and I had been through twice before — but instead of climbing higher toward the waterfall, we traveled down and vaguely in the direction of an eventual sunrise.

Deshi clearly knew where to go but followed behind Jael and me while Gavin led the way. We reached a brief arrest in the decline, one which dipped down and up before the hillside continued toward the open meadows below. I imagined this spot would collect a lot of water whenever it rained, so the ground would be soft and difficult to see from a lower elevation.

Good choice.

Though she'd been told what to expect and we gave the two death mages plenty of space, Jael seemed apprehensive as Gavin withdrew his scalpel and rolled back his sleeve.

"The beast is really dead?" she asked me.

Before I could respond, she sucked in a breath of shock and disgust as the death mage cut his pale forearm quite deeply, letting his black blood flow. We watched it drip thickly onto the soil, each of us shivering as he spoke in the dead tongue.

"Sounds like ... Malok?" she whispered again, cringing.

"Same language," I agreed, *"but also a focus for a death mage."*

She cocked a white eyebrow, noting that I wasn't even queasy. Her nostril curled as Gavin continued his ritual with Deshi praying behind him with his head bowed, hands clasping his Nyx-blessed dagger in its sheath.

"Both a language and a focus," she repeated, eyes narrowing.

I tilted my head and waited as Gavin kneeled to push some pieces of bone from his pouch into the darkened spots of the soil.

"Like To'vah?" my Sister asked.

Both my eyebrows lifted. *"Well ... yes."*

"When we were joined," she whispered, adding the hand sign for combat, *"speaking those words made my mouth and throat burn. Made all of me burn when the magic manifested."*

"Oh." I pressed my lips tight. *"I don't know. I think you must ask him."*

"You can tell me, though. Am I a ... a Dragonblood focus because of that fight with the eyeless warriors? Like the Human woman becoming a healer during a healing, and this cat-eyed bua muttering about death behind this walker?"

I swallowed as Gavin extended his long, stained fingers, pushing them deeper into the earth in one stroke than should have been possible. Jael watched him, her question hovering behind us as the Deathwalker grunted, pushing his hands into the ground up to his wrists.

Whispering something sibilant and final, he pulled straight up.

Nightmare's eyeless, flesh-torn skull popped out of the dirt, resting in Gavin's hands with the spine connected. Jael covered her mouth before a squeak could escape. I could make out the blackened, filthy mane and count the vertebrae along the neck, though the desiccated hide and flesh still clung to her bones.

The Deathwalker tugged again, a subtle, icy glow entering his eyes. His black teeth showed as he gritted them, but all his focus was on his long-time mount. A hoof drove its way out of the ground next, the earth turned oddly liquid while the corpse shifted and struggled as though trying to escape a swamp.

"A rat, please," Gavin said, reaching his hand out, never taking his eyes from Nightmare.

Deshi hopped down to seize the bag of animal scraps, passing him a stiff, whole rodent. The Deathwalker pressed it up against the horse's sharp, exposed teeth, which opened at once. She bit into it, shredding off pieces and grinding them to mush. I never saw her swallow; the crushed rat seemed to soak into her.

Gavin extended his hand. "Another."

Deshi obeyed. Soon after this second rat disappeared down the long gullet, Nightmare regained the strength to lift herself fully out of the ground and stand on cracked hooves.

Jael shifted in front of me, fists tight inside her gloves, and I touched her shoulder. *"Calm. I have a magic object that tells her not to attack me."*

She exhaled slowly, nose and lips conveying her aversion to the scent and appearance of the animal. I couldn't blame her; nothing about Nightmare was pleasant in this state. She really did look like she should be put back in the ground, as not even carrion birds might eat her.

"She looks much better after she's eaten," I said with a grin. *"Sort of like me."*

Jael cocked a brow over her shoulder but smirked and shook her head at the comparison. *"I'll wait and see before I agree."*

"Come," Gavin said, cleaning his scalpel before putting it away. "Let us take position for Mourn to find us and let her eat the rest of the bag there."

My Sister sighed, holding her peace until we'd reached our stakeout place overlooking the refugees of Manalar. By then, the long cut along Gavin's arm had closed, confirmed when he checked it and finally rolled his sleeve down.

"*Can he even be hurt?*" she asked. "*Or could you keep stabbing him and he just looks at you?*"

"*Let's talk about that later,*" I said with discomfort. "*Though my under-standing is he would be highly aware of someone stabbing him. He's not numb.*"

"*Hmph. If you say.*"

"Quite a bit of commentary," Gavin remarked as we got settled on the shaded lookout, upending the bag to let the rest of the rats and bones fall out. "May we assist?"

With hooves clomping, bones crunching and odd, squelching pops and snaps coming from within the horse, all at once, Jael shelved her idle curiosities about his anatomy. Instead, she asked a question which surprised me.

"Can you see what mage I am?"

My ally's face was rather ghastly under the trees dappled by moonlight, and he never stopped frowning as he looked her over. His irises winked out briefly before returning.

"You bear a familiar trifecta of gold, purple, and black winding thro-ugh your life aura, though it is underdeveloped," he said, knowing full well what had happened in the crypt. "I see the same in Mourn, though his is vivid and his life aura significantly different from yours. I imagine you bear a potential affinity for Draconic magic."

Jael let that sink in, although I wagered that she'd long since begun to suspect; Gavin just confirmed it for her. She swallowed, troubled as she looked at me.

"Keros told me I was 'clean,' and would claim my magic, make me serve Manalar." Her breath picked up with her heart, white teeth flashing. "I ... not clean anymore. Mourn ... felt me. While he sleep. He ... claim my magic instead?"

I drew in my breath slowly, shaking my head. "No. He saved you *and* your magic. He helped anchor your damaged aura because I asked him to."

"What you mean? Why? What happen?"

"Let me show you," Gavin interjected, digging into his pack.

We paused to watch him withdraw a dagger wrapped in cloth. Once the death mage unfolded it and held it out balanced on his palm, I recognized that pure silver shining under the Sister Moons.

"Do you remember this knife, Jael?"

She blinked at him. "Huh?" After another moment, she gasped and recoiled. "Yes! K-Keros ..."

"The Inquisitor was a death mage," Gavin said to her. "And he used this on you, attempting to somehow make you vulnerable to Keros without cutting flesh."

Jael snarled, appearing like she wanted to punch either him or the dagger he displayed but couldn't decide which. I took her shoulders, wrapping my arms around her from behind when she started quivering.

"When Mourn and Sirana brought you to us, hiding in the crypt," the Deathwalker continued, "you were comatose and would stay that way or go mad if you ever became aware. I listened to them talk about what could be done to revive you."

"Could be ... d-done?"

He kept his unsettling gaze on her. "Very little, as I understand it. Only another Elf-blood mage could merge with your aura and heal it, but because you had not discovered your own affinity, you would adopt theirs to gain that necessary anchor to continue living. Otherwise, you would never have awakened in the crypt. This is not a 'claiming,' as I understand it, but there certainly shall be echoes between you from sharing magical patterns."

"Wh ..." Shivering, she twisted her neck to look at me. "Why his ... patterns?"

I licked my lips, speaking gently. "Our choices were Krithannia or Mourn. That was all. I'm sorry ... they asked me to decide for you. And I did. I thought a Davrin blood who'd never given up fighting suited you better than a scholar bearing the secrets of a priesthood I knew nothing about. I think there was a reason Krithannia brought in Osgrid for Verina's anchoring. She dissuaded me from considering the added weight of what she carries."

Jael stood, shivering less as she thought it over. Deshi waited in respctful silence, keeping watch around us.

I added, "You did so well at the Temple city, Sister. You paid back the cost and never gave in. Mourn can teach you to fight even better, please remember that."

To my cautious relief, I spotted half a smile before she spoke.

"Mm. Better choice, yes. Only … do not want …" She made a motion, like pulling against something attached to her wrists. "Chains. From him."

Chains.

The metal bracers permanently bonded to Mourn's wrists came to mind.

"Nor does he have any he'd force on you."

"Does not?"

"No," I said. "I am certain."

Jael looked at Nightmare searching with newly flexible lips for bone fragments in the dirt, gathering, snapping, and grinding each with thoughtless, methodical motions of her jaw. The mare had eyes again, moist and dark with a glassy stare. She'd filled out enough to pass as living from a distance at night but had some way to go before she'd fool anyone in the day.

"Hope you correct," she said, claiming a nearby boulder to sit and think about what we'd said.

I let her be while we waited for Mourn to join us.

ONCE NIGHTMARE LOOKED AND SMELLED FAR BETTER THAN SHE HAD COMING out of the ground, Gavin made sure my knucklebone talisman was properly attuned and that the mount still obeyed my psionic directions.

"Excellent," he murmured, satisfied. "I'd not recommend jumping onto her back and racing on these slopes, but she can and will defend you with her teeth and hooves."

Interesting. I hadn't thought about directing her to chomp someone's arm, but if she got a good hold, the injury would be crippling.

Before much time passed, someone approached. We stood up and hid behind tree trunks, peering down the refugee side of the mounds. Gavin and Deshi went still, listening until they also heard someone stumbling toward us.

Finally, I reached to touch my earlobe. ~*Mourn? I hear someone coming. Is it you?*~

Me, and another. He just woke up and is unsteady.

I knew exactly who to expect.

"He found him," I whispered, looking at the others. "Mathias."

Soon enough, heavy breath and muffled grunting grew audible for each of us as a man was force-marched up the steep slope. When Mathias came into view, his racing heart reached my ears as he tried to climb with his wrists bound tightly in front of him. He was blindfolded and gagged, stumbling frequently.

Mourn had returned to his birth form to remind and intimidate him once the eyes were uncovered. He also pushed the skin hunter square on his back at irregular intervals, keeping him off balance until Mathias collapsed on the lookout, puffing for air not far from my boots.

"*Tonash hetha*," the Dragonchild rumbled, waving his arm before dragging his claws down through the air.

The appearance of a sheer rock wall overtook the trees around us, cutting off our view of the refugee camp. That one change created a space unrecognizable as the front of the redoubt, even if one became familiar with it over the last few days.

Have no worry, Mourn said to me as he signed to Jael. *The illusion is also a ward against approach until we get this sorted. Talov and Krithannia have been informed.*

He repeated that information in Guild sign for Deshi, who bowed at his waist in response and, finally, took Gavin farther to the side to explain.

Meanwhile, I peered down at Mathias in the dark. He *had* made it through the gate with the rest of those fleeing, the same man I had traveled with for weeks, talking about Red Sister interrogations. I'd even sucked him to climax in the bushes, getting caught by Witch Hunters, and triggering the uproar that resulted in Gavin's death.

And I'd watched the man toy with and torment Jacob in the shed behind Brom's Inn, for only a fragment of his total time, until the man-hunter was satiated and agreed to pass his victim over to the Deathwalker for one final ritual.

Cunning, dangerous, I signed to Jael. *Tortures for entertainment. Will kill to escape.*

She confirmed, obviously curious but stubbornly unimpressed.

Mourn signed the suggestion that she move out of sight while Gavin stepped closer to me. Jael accepted, and the half-blood approached to remove the Human's blindfold but not the gag.

I could tell Mathias couldn't see us well at first, but enough moonlight filtered down to highlight my hair and Gavin's ghoulish face. After enough blinking and opportunity to catch his breath, recognition touched the man's face.

He smiled through his gag as he huffed, a bound-up laugh seeping through the tight wad of cloth shoved into his mouth. Moans and vibrations entered his throat, which didn't translate to actual words but conveyed his desire to speak as he climbed to his knees.

~Has he said anything to you?~ I asked Mathias's abductor, who hadn't stepped into his line of sight yet.

No. Once I found his scent, I went for silence. He was sharing a tent with four other men, all asleep.

I smirked. ~Do you want to know what he's trying to say?~

If you are in the mood to listen. If not, I can put him to sleep again and secure him underground for later.

If I truly hadn't cared what the skin hunter had been up to with the Deathless and his daughter, that would have been easy to do. As things were ...

~I want to hear the first words out of his mouth, yes.~

Very well.

Mourn crouched and crept up behind the man, a small knife appearing in his right hand, and swiftly, startlingly cut the gag at the base of Mathias's neck, pulling the cloth away and swatting the back of his head.

"*Blaugh!*" the man blurted, spitting out the wad. "Argh … fuck, what … ?"

Mathias turned his head to see who had hit him but Mourn had practically disappeared within the deep shadow. None of us were foolish enough to give him away. The man checked around him twice more, noting Deshi nearer to Gavin though he seemed to gloss over my Sister hiding behind me.

Finally, the man said what he'd been so eager to say.

"Sirana, you made it. Shit, Gavin, you both made it out!" He laughed, not caring about the noise, though it didn't seem to carry. "Divine fuck me … That was wild. Okay, *before* you do anything to me, I just have one question."

He paused with bated breath, his eyes inviting us to play.

So be it.

"One question," I said.

His shoulders lifted with his next breath. "*Please*, tell me you have the dagger with red markings on it. The one you stole from Brom."

As though I could forget. *And that wasn't a question.*

I weighed my answer before opening one side of my cloak to show him the weapon on my belt, my spiders and I prepared if he lunged. He didn't.

The skin hunter appeared to melt from sheer relief. "Yes … Good. Oh, fuck, I can't believe you still have it."

Mathias was rambling, but no one interrupted. Even Gavin seemed content to wait and watch while the group let me handle this opening tease. I couldn't think what to say that wasn't him leading me, so I let the void fill the air instead, testing how much he could stand before talking.

"Okay, so," Mathias said, "you probably didn't know Amelda and her father can track that dagger, at least to get in the general area."

My stomach threatened to chill down, but I stood how Elder D'Shea might when she was quiet: placid and unsettling at once.

He went on.

"Amelda is with the Ma'ab army at the walls right now, telling them everything about you." The corner of his mouth quirked as he tried to get a response out of me. "It might take some time, but they'll come after you as long as you carry that dagger. They'd love to take you both. Or … wait, the Ascended love to have all *three* of you."

He looked pointedly at Gavin and paused again. My scholar glanced at me, but the silence was working well enough that I just exhaled slowly through my nose. If Jael felt agitated, she kept it hidden.

Mathias shook his head and rolled his eyes. "Alright. So you'll lead them right to the 'Godblood' and this squat hiding hole unless you're planning to sprint out. I don't care if you do, but if you have any plans for that thing other than keeping it, I can help you."

Finally, I smiled. "I wish that were true."

He blinked, huffed another small laugh, and added to the pile. "I saw Kreshel Divigna watching us all leaving, you know, Kurn's father that he never shut up about? The Hellhound was just standing there on the bank as the last streams of people ran for the cave. He and his dogs could have destroyed the Templars, their Captain, everyone, right there at the end. But he didn't because he was looking for *you*."

Though I resisted reacting to this, he must have spotted something because he chuckled. "Luck must have been riding piggyback if he fucking missed you."

Divigna hadn't missed me.

He saw me. We met eyes.

And I didn't understand what I'd felt.

"So, I was going to recommend," Mathias took a breath, "find some way to return it to Amelda. If you take it home, they'll *find* your home."

I didn't know if this was true or a bluff, but the confirmation of where and when he'd seen the Eternal Hellhound was the most convincing of the many threats he'd suggested so far.

Had Divigna really been looking for me? If so, why hadn't the Hellhound charged into the river to scoop up both me and the dagger?

Because of Mourn? Or dissuaded by something else?

"Sirana," Mathias said with a hint of annoyance. "I know Gavin doesn't give a fuck what happens to him. He's already declared war on Ennikar. But I'm pretty sure you have a lot of good centuries left in you that you'd like to live instead of winding up on a cutting table dissected by the Physician."

Damnit. Sick again.

And he could see it.

"Amelda said she heard about long-lived creatures the Ascended kept at the capital, to study them. They're still looking for ways to make others like Divigna, who has for a hundred years now made babies and killed whole villages for them."

A hundred years. As long as they'd held Vesram.

"You want to be fodder for something like that? End up like whoever they caught before?"

I knew who they'd caught.

The Eternal Hellhound ... watching me.

Yet doing nothing. That strange moment couldn't be related to Vesram's mother, could it? The Sathoet wouldn't tell us what happened to her before he left the crypt.

My sleeping geas stirred, squeezing my chest as Mathias's voice grew louder, making my ears ache.

"Do you *hear* me, Sirana? You. Are. In. *Danger.*"

I blinked down at him. He met my eyes, smiling like he had when we'd traveled across the grasslands together.

"I can help you. I swear."

Mourn stepped out of the shadows, planting his palm on Mathias's brow to speak a Word, as he once had for a small boy in a stable's hayloft in Yong-wen.

"V'dri."

The skin hunter's eyes rolled up in his head, and his body slumped down, falling unconscious to the side. My heart throbbed in my chest as I struggled to speak. Though my eyes met those of my bodyguard, I didn't know what to say. Jael squeezed my shoulder, and when I looked at her, I'd never seen her so scared. She was biting her lip to stay silent.

"It's nearing sunrise," Mourn said. "Let us secure him before taking our places for the day. I don't expect further trouble, though we should be prepared."

I watched in silence as he picked up our prisoner, throwing him over his shoulder.

"Deshi and I shall stay here and wait for you," Gavin said.

"As you wish," said the half-blood.

Jael and I were about to follow him to the nearest hatch when Mourn paused and turned around.

"The Guild leaders were talking," he said, "and we want to see this four-century era of the Bishops end without their death mage equivalents filling the same role. We're siding with Captain Isboern to prevent it."

Gavin grunted. "As am I."

They were going back to Manalar.

"Good." Mourn glanced at me. "After Isboern has done what he can to boost his people's morale tomorrow and send those who will leave to Augran, we are in agreement. He shouldn't wait too long to lead them where they want to go."

We're going back.

For certain.

"We are considering all ideas on how to disrupt the Ma'ab leadership in the field," Mourn continued. "To *encourage* them to break camp and return North. Perhaps you can give it some thought, Deathwalker?"

Deshi blinked with astonishment to watch Gavin smile, though he did not show his teeth. "I have already given it some thought."

"Oh?"

My scholar turned his head South. His blue irises flickered as they had during the storm surge on the Great Lake, yet the night was still.

"In the company of my Lady," said the Herald of Nyx, "I've weighed an option which might interest the Guild. Only a matter if the cost can be met and is deemed worth it."

Mourn smirked, his tail curving with interest from root to tip. "We will consider *all* options, Herald. Thank you."

My bodyguard glanced at my Sister and me, bowing his head and signaling that we follow him as he took Mathias inside. I drew in a long, slow breath and stepped with him through the trees.

While the Dragonblood had Slept, I hadn't been sure what he would want to do about Manalar, given his past with that Temple and his Bargain with me. Now, I did. Resolving the two were intertwined and, as before, Gavin's purpose led us in the same direction.

Even though men no longer had my Sister in their clutches, the tapestry hadn't changed enough to know if my Queen's vision had been thwarted. The same as it had been a few days ago, the safest place on the web might be at the center of it.

We'll go back and end the war they started.

The Deepearth must remain closed, Sivaraus undiscovered.

Time grows short as I search for the path on the Surface to take me home.

Shadows of the past and hounds of the present snap at my heels while I carry the one weapon which would lead all our enemies back with me.

Unless I stop them first.

Coming next: *Shadows & Hounds: Sister Seekers Book 10*!

Thank you for reading about Sirana and the Davrin Elves of the deep! Please support the author and help readers to find the dark fantasy they'll love by leaving a review for Sister Seekers on Goodreads, Bookbub, or your favorite retail site!

Curious how **Lethrix** first got involved with the **Davrin Elves**? Want to snatch some added insight about the magic and bloodlines of D'Shea and Rausery being uncovered?

Pick up the first Tales of Miurag anthology: The Deepearth, and read about secrets lost and entangled between the Valsharess and the Black Dragon.

I also have fantasy maps, timelines, and a glossary! Read extra tidbits about the characters and places in the story.

Visit Etaski's series lore at World Anvil!

Sister Seekers is an adult epic fantasy with an ever-broadening scope.

Found family is a core theme throughout. Perfect for fans of entwined plots, challenging themes, immersive worldbuilding, and elements of erotic horror. Sexuality and inner conflict play into character growth with nuance, intrigue, action, and magic.

Follow Etaski and Subscribe to her newsletter at her website.

ACKNOWLEDGMENTS

Immeasurable thanks to my friends holding on and helping to prop me up while I worked through a challenging time.

Eris Adderly, Ile Depak, Axelotl, Leonard, Dark Pulse, NecrosisBob, & Pastor of Muppets.

Love and gratitude to my Hubs as we grow together through the decades.

Special appreciation to Doc Kangey, the anchoring presence working behind the scenes. Check out our hard work and lore yet to come at Etaski.com & Miurag.Etaski.com

THANK YOU, my Top Patrons who support all my efforts and keep those signed paperbacks comin'!

Sir Cumference, Baelus, Jesse C., Does, John K., Julie S., Paul B., Carla H., Briana R., Josanna, RainbowNight, Lesley PLAY, Kalculyszero, NotSoWeird, Zenor , Kelly D., Lady Dia Meter, Raymond T., Zeroharas, Johnathon Matlock, Chris R., Daolord, Melwinne, Bradley L., and Roy Meyer, and in loving memory, Stacy Meyer.

ABOUT THE AUTHOR

Etaski has entertained herself with fantasy stories since the first day she sat on a school bus looking out the window. When hand-written letters were disappearing, she scribbled no less than five pages to be worth the postage. Her early stories were written by hand, and she had a writer's callus and three embarrassing novels before graduating high school.

She studied science, archaeology, history, and theater. Frank discussions of sexuality or death were rare growing up, so she wrote fantasies, theories, and observations within stories for deeper contemplation or just to be entertained.

History speaks little on sexuality, yet biology demonstrates how it sways basic choices. Drama reveals our strongest bonds but may fade to black at its most intimate. In the Sister Seekers, the sex and the story are inseparable, and their discoveries will change the journey of Miurag without cutting away.

Etaski's Website: etaski.com
Etaski's Book Page: etaski.com/sister-seekers
Etaski's Series Lore: miurag.etaski.com
Etaski on Patreon: www.patreon.com/etaski
Etaski on GoodReads: www.goodreads.com/etaski
Etaski on BookBub: www.bookbub.com/authors/a-s-etaski
Etaski on Facebook: www.facebook.com/asetaski
Etaski on Mastodon: mastodon.online/@etaski